"TWENT
TILL LIG

"Brace yourself, Wilf," said Ursis. "One can never accurately predict the results of a lab experiment." Simultaneously, the pod's strobe beacons began to flash more rapidly.

While the Bear at the test console increased the flow of energy to the pod, *Ivanov*'s Helmsman was compelled to send more and more power to the Drives on the lab ship—enough so that the whole bridge began shuddering uncomfortably.

The Helmsman suddenly bellowed over his shoulder to the Pod Operator, who was peering into his consoles with apparent consternation. Something was clearly out of control. "Sweet mother of Voot," he muttered suddenly. "If she broaches at this speed, we'll all be killed—especially with that brute ready to swing us around."

While Brim watched in horror, the whole network of girders outside ruptured in a churning cloud of hullmetal shards. The bridge abruptly went dark...

THE TROPHY

Also by Bill Baldwin

THE HELMSMAN
GALACTIC CONVOY

Published by
POPULAR LIBRARY

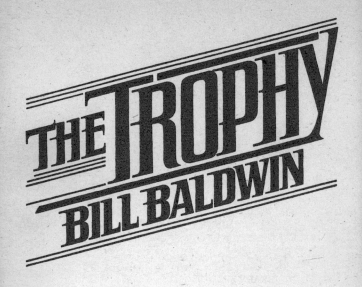

THE TROPHY

BILL BALDWIN

POPULAR LIBRARY

An Imprint of Warner Books, Inc.

A Warner Communications Company

Popular Library books are published by
Warner Books, Inc.
666 Fifth Avenue
New York, N.Y. 10103

W A Warner Communications Company

Printed in the United States of America

First Printing: January, 1990

10 9 8 7 6 5 4 3 2 1

The Mitchell Trophy

Following the Treaty of Garak in 52000, intragalactic commerce began to expand at breakneck speed. The Great War had introduced literally millions of people on both sides to space flight and forced loosely linked dominions all over the galaxy into new dependence upon one another. A burgeoning transportation industry found itself pressured for more and more speed as frontiers rapidly expanded to the most remote parts of the galactic spiral, and beyond.

To conquer distance, to couple new power generators with the subtle properties of HyperSpeed Drives and hull configurations, then spur all three to the limit of their potential—that was the challenge. The urge to produce the fastest starship in the known Universe became an obsession that captivated the best technical minds everywhere.

Among the major galactic dominions, this burning quest for speed was eventually subsidized by government treasuries and entrusted to special government employees who contended as much for national honor as for personal glory. The starships they flew evolved rapidly from reconditioned war machines that coursed through space at perhaps forty thousand times the speed of light to such engineering masterpieces as Sherrington's M-6B in which (then) Lt. Commander Tobias Moulding, I.F. achieved an absolute velocity of nearly 112M Light-Speed late in 52009.

A major part of this battle was fought in the laboratories of great commercial enterprises by designers who repeatedly pushed themselves to create faster and more powerful systems. But the final proof was in absolute performance, and prodigious races became the battlegrounds where these creations were actually put to the test.

The most distinctive of the competitions—for the Mitchell Trophy—offered little in the way of a stipend to the victor; moreover, its rules seriously restricted the nature of vessels that could enter. Yet those same starships are largely credited with extending the boundaries of civilization beyond the galaxy and into the Universe itself.

Mitchell, son of a Rhodorian industrialist, believed that practical starships were the key to intragalactic commerce, and therefore to the survival of civilization itself. He concluded that true starship utility depended not only upon raw HyperLight velocity through deep space but, in equal measure, upon the ability to land and take off readily from the surfaces of planets anywhere. Accordingly, he began a speed competition for private starflight societies and personally donated its unique trophy to be awarded at yearly races until one society won three times in a row, thereby gaining permanent possession. Each year's race was to be hosted by the previous year's winning society. But despite Mitchell's hopes to keep the race out of state arenas, military and government-employed Helmsmen competed regularly.

From *The Galactic Almanac*
(And Handy Encyclopedia), 52015

CHAPTER 1

End of the Line

"Thraggling Universe, Peretti—the gravs have tripped out. I can't keep her on course. Crank 'em up—*now!*"

"Power's *gone*, Mr. Brim. Readouts say she's blown the feed tube."

"Better send out an alert then, Sparks. Looks like we're going in. Pam, get everybody down in the cabin."

While Hamlish frantically broadcast the timeworn litany of trouble in deep space, Wilf Ansor Brim struggled alone with the old starship's controls. Beside him Jana Torgeson slumped over her co-Helmsman's console, reeking of cheap meem. "Morris," he yelled into a flickering display, "see about jettisoning some of the cargo back there!"

"Ain't enough of us here ta do much good this trip, Mr. Brim," Morris responded with a smug look on his face. "Warned ya before we left, we did. . . ."

Brim ground his teeth. At the beginning of the trip, there had been hardly enough hands to staff *Jamestown*'s bridge, much less handle a cargo bay. "I understand," he growled. "But you'd better do all you can. The more you get rid of, the more chance we *all* have of surviving the crash."

"*That* puts things in a whole new light, Mr. Brim," Morris responded. His thin visage disappeared from the screen like a gray wraith.

Dressed in a tan civilian Captain's uniform—a threadbare remnant from some long-defunct spaceline—the thirty-seven-

3

year-old Brim shook his head. No wonder Morris had never been in the Fleet. He'd have spent his whole life in the brig. Through the ship's forward Hyperscreens—normally transparent crystalline windshields that simulated conventional vision when traveling faster than LightSpeed—he watched the first tongues of flame begin streaming aft from protrusions on the hull. Reentry time and no gravs! He shook his head in disgust. All he had to work with now was the steering engine. The little gravity kicker wasn't much, but it gave him a chance—one of the few he could presently think of. Like any good Helmsman, he always tried to have a trick or two up his sleeve, just in case Voot decided to strike—which, in this case, he surely had. Suddenly, the ship jolted.

"There goes the pallet of hullmetal rolling machines," Morris reported from a display. He was now dressed in a bright orange space suit and helmet.

"Good work," Brim acknowledged through clenched teeth. Those big machines were worth a whole lot more than old *City of Jamestown* herself. Luckily, they'd been insured by their wary owners before takeoff. Little StarFleet Enterprises could never have raised that kind of ante in a million Standard years. Without them, however, there would now be no hauling fee, and Universe knew the company needed every thraggling credit it could earn. He shook his head in frustration and peered down at the solid undercast, still c'lenyts below. At least the ship didn't seem to be falling so fast now. . . .

"That's the last of the mobile crawlers," Morris reported momentarily. "Cargo deck's empty, all right?"

Brim nodded. "Very good, Morris," he said. But it wasn't very good at all. Even if he managed to bring the old starship in without killing anybody—which was still quite problematical —things looked bleak for StarFleet Enterprises. *Jamestown* was the only ship left in the fleet.

"Port Authority's dispatched a rescue tug," Hamlish reported presently. His beige-colored uniform was a lot newer than Brim's, even though it did start life in a different spaceline. "I've given 'em our predicted landing coordinates, just in case we get there."

Brim laughed grimly to himself. They'd get there, all right. No way to go anywhere else with only a steering engine. "I'll have the space radiators out, Jana," he ordered absently, preoccupied with his own readouts. Moments later, he shook his head in disgust, then reached over the gray-haired woman's rumpled form to activate her controls himself. Almost immediately, old *Jamestown* began to shudder and rumble while long, tapered panels deployed from either side of her torpedo-shaped hull. In the presence of any atmosphere at all, they had a startling effect.

Peretti chuckled contemptuously. "Not much left to cool with those old radiators, is there, Brim?" He was the only one in the crew with a new, made-to-order StarFleet Enterprises uniform. Clearly, he had access to funds above and beyond anything the faltering spaceline could disburse.

"Not radiators—wings," Brim snapped through his teeth as he concentrated on flying. One mistake now and they were all dead.

"Wings?"

"Yeah, wings," Brim answered instinctively. In the Fleet, it had once been his duty as Principal Helmsman to help train junior officers. "You haven't logged much time in these old kites, have you?"

"What's that got to do with the price of cawdor nails?" Peretti asked defensively, attempting to pull his coat over a sizable paunch.

"Not much anymore," Brim grunted while stratoturbulence rattled the old hullmetal plating, "but if you'd spent any time at all with these old ships, you'd know that their radiators are shaped like wings—as a safety feature. Probably for situations just like this."

"Passengers are down," a woman's voice interrupted from the alternate console—his main-cabin display had been out for the last month.

"Very well," Brim answered, conjuring her face in his mind's eye: Pamela Hale, the Chief Stewardess. During the war years, she'd been executive officer of a battlecruiser. Pam was at least ten years older than himself and still stunningly beautiful. "Better get *yourself* down while you're at it," he added, "and strapped tight, somewhere against the aft side of a bulkhead. Local gravity won't hold long after we hit."

"I *thought* I heard the gravs go," she said from the intercom. "Can't Peretti get them going?"

"They're dead," Peretti interjected apathetically. "Like us, probably."

"No problem," she quipped easily. "A lot of people I run into these days died years ago."

Brim smiled. Hale was a brave one, all right. He guessed that she'd probably seen enough wartime action that nothing in the Universe could much faze her. "As long as those steering engines hold out," he said—hoping he sounded a lot more assured than he felt—"I'll bring us in." He glanced out the Hyperscreens again and shook his head. He couldn't even see where they were going to make landfall.

"Well, don't let me keep you, then," Hale said in the same bantering voice. "I wouldn't want anybody to think I was interfering with operations or anything."

"Go strap yourself down," Brim teased. People like that could calm a thraggling thunderstorm if they wanted to. He wondered how she'd ever wound up in an end-of-the-line outfit like StarFleet. He guessed it would be quite a story.

Outside, reentry flames were now flooding along the decks, and *Jamestown*'s great, tapered radiators looked like dazzling sails spun of light itself. In the raging slipstream, their thunder raged through the old starship like a disruptor barrage.

"Going through about fifteen thousand irals," Hamlish reported, peering over Torgeson's still-inert form.

"Thanks, Sparks," Brim acknowledged. "I can use that kind of help a lot more than communications now."

"I'll switch consoles then," Hamlish grunted, and dragged Torgeson to a nearby jump seat. She wore a nondescript green jumpsuit and Brim noticed she had worn holes in both her boots. Afterward, the little COMM Operator slid behind the co-Helmsman's readouts and adjusted his glasses while he grinned awkwardly. "You'll have to tell me what you want to see."

"Start by calling out the altitude every couple thousand irals or so," Brim said grimly. "My altimeter conked out this morning."

"Twelve thousand irals," Hamlish announced presently. "I guess we've slowed some, haven't we?"

"Yeah," Brim agreed, "the rate indicator shows that." It was better, but still awfully fast. "Button up the cargo holds, Mr. Morris," he warned, speaking into the display.

"Cargo holds are secure, Mr. Brim," Morris replied calmly.

Brim envied him his space suit; it would be a big help in a crash landfall. Since passengers didn't wear them, however, bridge crews couldn't either.

"Ten thousand irals, and the checkout panel's lit, Mr. Brim," Hamlish reported.

"Got you—read the checklist to me as it displays."

"Aye, Mr. Brim. Shoulder harnesses?"

"Check," Brim answered, struggling into a network of faded webbing. He wondered how strong it actually was after all these years.

"Buoyancy chambers?"

Brim checked an emergency area beside the altimeter read-out. Three green lights—the old rustbucket *thought* she could float, anyway. "Ready," he said hopefully.

"Eight thousand irals."

"Check." The undercast seemed to be coming up at them faster as the distance narrowed. He shuddered.

"Steering engine on continuous power?"

"Continuous power—check."

"Autoflight panels?"

"Off," Brim said emphatically. Under these circumstances, he wasn't about to trust anybody's hundred-year-old autohelm.

"Emergency beacon?"

"It'll be on soon as you hit the green panel under your forward Hyperscreen."

"It's on."

"Check."

"Six thousand irals. That's the last item from the panel checklist, Mr. Brim."

"Very well," Brim acknowledged. "Just stay where you are. I'll call out a few more items myself in a moment."

Suddenly, they plunged into the clouds. At once, torrents of rain began to thunder against the fiery Hyperscreens, transformed instantly to steam while the old starship bounced and groaned in the darkening gloom. They were soon in such dense vapor that their forward position light bathed the outside world in a ghostly white glow, while the rotating beacon blinked dazzling green across it like disruptor fire.

"Speed brakes?" Brim asked. "Five lights over there on panel two."

"Five lights . . . on."

"Good work, Hamlish," Brim said. Then, "Pam, are you strapped in down there?"

"With my back against a bulkhead, Wilf."

"What about the passengers?"

"Safe as I can make 'em."

"Wish me luck, then."

"You bet—*real* good luck, sweetie."

"Three thousand irals . . ."

A heartbeat later, they broke out into driving snow over a seascape of whitecapped swells. Brim glanced at the leaden gray combers below while ice suddenly frosted the fast-cooling Hyperscreens. He switched on the heat and melted it, but he didn't need ice to tell him that it was *cold* down there.

An altitude warning horn sounded. "One thousand irals," Hamlish reported.

"Thanks," Brim acknowledged, almost wholly consumed in setting up his landing. "What's our airspeed?" Now, he was clumsily turning upwind across the troughs of the swells. They suddenly looked bigger than battleships.

"Airspeed one sixty-three." Hamlish's voice was getting tight and squeaky.

Brim chuckled to himself. He wasn't the only one terrified by the view through the forward Hyperscreens. Only a few hundred irals separated them from the rolling violence of those swells. "Brace yourself," he warned. "Here we go."

"Pull up! *Pull up!*" cautioned the ship's altitude alert.

He punched the alarm into silence as he rolled the port radiator into a rogue gust, then dropped the nose slightly. Speed meant lift, and he'd soon need all of the latter he could get. Somehow, he had to set her down on the relative calm of an upward slope while traveling in the opposite direction. Long patterns of lacy spume marked the troughs parallel to his flight path. A sudden gust threw *Jamestown*'s nose to starboard again; this time, she began to crab sideways. Grinding his teeth, Brim rolled the port radiator lower. After what seemed like an eon, she began to line up again—but now, no more than thirty irals separated her belly from the crest of an oncoming swell. Time to get her down. Brim carefully raised her nose till she slowed, barely maintaining lift. Timing was everything now; a false move and they were all dead. The old starship trembled violently as the radiators began to stall, but Brim deftly willed her airborne with the steering engine at full forward until—moments before the next crest passed beneath the hull—he brought the nose up sharply, then plunged behind the mountainous wavetop as it surged astern, dousing the Hyperscreens with foam and spume.

A split click later, old *Jamestown* smashed onto the back of the wave, launching two massive cascades of green water high overhead and shuddering back in the air while Brim struggled to raise her nose from the next impact. Suddenly he stiffened. In the corner of his eye he caught a large inspection hatch hanging from the leading edge of the port radiator. It had clearly torn open at the first violent impingement, and was now scuffing the surface in short bursts of mist. Before he could react, it caught the roiled surface, then separated in an explosive cloud of spray, dropping the wingtip precipitously. In desperation, he put the helm hard to starboard, but it was too late. The radiator's tip dug into the water and the starship cartwheeled. With the steering engine at full detent, he struggled to whipsaw back on course, and *almost* made it—but not quite. When the ship slammed into the next wave, her nose was still down. The concussion knocked out the local gravity and pushed the *City of Jamestown* violently back to starboard. Loose equipment cascaded wildly along the bridge floor while the air filled with screams from the lower decks and Brim's face smashed into the readout panel. The starboard Hyperscreens gave way to a tempest of dazzling high-voltage sparks. Before Brim could move, green water erupted onto the flight bridge like an explosion.

Spluttering and coughing, Brim fought against the shoulder straps in a desperate effort to keep his head above the flood. Whining emergency pumps began to labor in the background as waves surged in all directions through the flight bridge. Then the water stopped pouring in as the old starship reared her nose skyward, hung for awful clicks, and plunged back in a great welter of spray. Moments later, she careened to a stop, rolling wildly, parallel to the endless ranks of swells. Somehow, she was down.

With Hamlish back at his station anxiously contacting various manned compartments to see who might have survived, Brim secured the few controls that yet needed attention, then leaned out the side window and looked sadly back along *James-*

town's listing hull. Here and there, her plates were wrinkled like cheap tissue paper. The spaceframe had clearly given way in a number of locations. He'd done his best for the old girl. It simply hadn't been good enough.

He shook his head as he watched a tug materialize out of the driving snow overhead and begin setting up a landfall. Clearly, this was the end of the line for old *City of Jamestown*—and probably StarFleet Enterprises as well. Then he took a deep breath and pursed his lips grimly. For all practical purposes, he supposed, it was also the end of the line for Wilf Ansor Brim, at least economically.

Later, Brim balanced himself precariously atop *Jamestown*'s shattered bridge as the tug pulled them slowly into harbor. Two bright green hawser beams crackled from optical bollards on the stubby, hunchbacked rescue ship to the nose of the ED-4, but for the last hundred c'lenyts or so, those beams had disappeared ahead into heavy fog that set in as the storm subsided. There was no sky and no horizon, only the mist, cold and wet on his face. The sea's leaden swell was long and slow, littered with ice fragments. Listing heavily to port, *Jamestown* sloughed unwillingly through the sluggish water, shouldering aside half-frozen mush that streamed past her ruined flanks and tumbled in her wake with a distant, whisperlike chuckle. Aft, he could see the misshapen curve of the hull, the dull, corrugated segment outside the failed generator chamber, a number of open hatches, the stubby KA'PPA tower, and farther on, white arcs of foamy water jetting from the pump outlets.

Then it started to snow again. Small white flakes whirled past his face like moths near a Karlsson lamp. He shivered. His old tan uniform didn't heat well anymore, and a tear below the collar let a lot of frigid dampness in. But it felt better trembling out there in the cold than sitting uselessly below. With the Hyperscreen frames empty and open to the weather. *Jamestown*'s bridge was, for all practical purposes, just as cold and wet as the outdoors. Besides, the wrecked, waterlogged consoles tended to remind him of his own fortunes during the last two years. Somehow, none of it seemed credible—not even now.

Less than two months after he (then Lieutenant Wilf Brim, Imperial Star Fleet) reported to a new assignment aboard I.F.S.

Thunderbolt, Emperor Nergol Triannic and his League of Dark Stars had unexpectedly sued for an armistice. The war had ended precisely three standard weeks later, with Triannic sent into exile on remote little Portoferria, orbiting a huge gas giant in the sparsely populated ninety-first region of the galaxy. During the peace euphoria that followed, the *Thunderbolt* was expeditiously paid off, declared surplus, then towed to the breakers—early victim of the Congress for Intragalactic Accord, or CIGA. This burgeoning new organization had quickly infected the Imperial Government as well as the Admiralty when the war's patriotic fervor began to wane.

Brim's own career had followed the same path a short time later. After six weeks of inactivity at the great Fleet base on frozen Gimmas-Haefdon, he had been summoned to a large auditorium at one of the headquarters buildings, packed in with other recently orphaned Fleet officers, and indifferently discharged with a month's credits in his pocket, a one-way ticket to anywhere in the Empire, and a printed citation ("suitable for framing") from Greyffin IV, Grand Galactic Emperor, Prince of the Reggio Star Cluster, and Rightful Protector of the Heavens. "We wish to personally thank you," the citation began, "for your tireless devotion to the cause of..." Heartsick, Brim had thrown it away—the signature was clearly a fake. He'd seen the real thing the day he'd been awarded the Emperor's Cross, and that citation was actually signed. He'd even met the Emperor in person. During another life, it seemed now. . . .

Afterward, with throngs of other displaced Blue Capes, he'd made his way back to Avalon, the Imperial capital. Even if he had wished to return to his native Carescria—which he did not—nothing remained of his earlier life there. After the Helmsmen's Academy and the life of an Imperial officer, there was no returning to that poverty-blighted desert, not even with the specter of approaching destitution. And his meager savings had dwindled predictably in the fast-paced, explosive life of Avalon City—capital of nearly half the galaxy.

Brim shook his head as the fog thickened again, making him blink. There would certainly be no income from *this* trip—not with a jettisoned cargo and a wrecked starship. He shrugged as the mist isolated him completely for a moment. It was some satisfaction to have spared everyone on board, especially the passengers, unfortunate wretches that they were. Most of them were clearly on the bottom rungs of the Empire's economic ladder. They were the only kind of fares little StarFleet Enterprises could attract: people who could pay so little they'd take passage on a clapped-out antique like *Jamestown*.

Just to get to Avalon. . . .

He laughed with half-cynical compassion. All too soon, they'd find out—as he had—that they'd only gone from some distant frying pan into a brand-new fire. . . .

The fog cleared again for a moment, revealing a bleak forest of gantry cranes, most of them inactive. When the huge port reverted to a peacetime economy, many of the great commercial terminals had been forced to close their piers from lack of traffic. Brim shook his head; it certainly wasn't the kind of postwar paradise he'd once imagined. But then, he'd been a bit more idealistic in those days, expecting people to feel some appreciation—perhaps even a little obligation—for returning veterans and the wartime sacrifices they'd made. He snorted. The CIGAs took care of that with their ceaseless attacks on everything even remotely connected with the military. Instead of making him feel as if he had finally earned some worth in the Empire, he'd gotten the idea early on that he was actually part of a national embarrassment. The war was over, and the sooner people could forget about every part of it, the better.

He shrugged, then started momentarily as Pam Hale materialized out of the fog, expertly negotiating the wet hullmetal on spike-heeled boots as she took her place beside him. A full-length cloak and hood covered everything but her face with woolly tan. She had soft, mist-covered features: a dimpled chin with generous lips and high cheeks, a pug nose, and enormous blue eyes whose corners were developing a network of tiny wrinkles. "Not a pretty sight," she observed, nodding toward the empty docks and boarded-up cranes. "A lot of folks are out of work now that peace has come to the Empire."

"Yeah," Brim muttered. "Unless someone's actually aiming a disruptor at them, most people these days don't seem to attach much importance to Fleets *or* Blue Capes."

She met his eyes. "You're right," she agreed, "they don't." The she shrugged wistfully. "Though the Admiralty does seem to maintain adequate ships in commission for people with the proper pedigree—'political interest,' I think is the term they use."

Brim nodded. So far he could see, that was the normal way of the Universe. In the end, all privilege was skewed toward wealth. Every Carescrian knew it, fatalistically expected it, even. That didn't mean he particularly liked being treated the way he'd been treated. At one time, he'd hoped that things would change. But those hopes had been short-lived indeed. And, he supposed, it was easier for him to return to being nothing than to experience it for the first time, as were many of his presently out-of-work ex-Fleet colleagues. Only Margot made things *really* difficult for him. He felt for the ring she had given him, hanging from a chain around his neck. He hated being nobody, because of her.

"What'll you do now?" Hale asked, interrupting his musing. "I doubt if Iverson can keep StarFleet running with no starships to fly."

Brim snorted grimly and nodded. "I doubt it, too," he said. There was no use pretending otherwise. The little company had been in a precarious financial position for a long time. It was the only reason they'd hired him in the first place—he was willing to fly for almost no pay at all. He shrugged. "Maybe I'll go into another line of work," he said lamely.

"Oh?" Hale looked at him with an expression of concern. "What else do you know how to do?"

"Well," Brim said, struggling to maintain his facade of confidence, "this isn't the only flying job in the Universe. Who knows, I might just get myself a job jockeying one of those hot starships they're getting ready for the Mitchell Trophy Race."

"*Really?*" Hale asked with an exaggerated look of awe. "I thought the Imperial Starflight Society was only for the rich and famous. Or is there something I should know about you, Wilf?"

Brim grinned in spite of himself. "No," he answered, "I've got no secrets—nor fame nor money. So I guess I won't show up in A'zurn for the races next year." He shrugged. "I suppose I don't know precisely what I'll do next, but I'm bound to find *something*." Deep down, the thought cut him like a knife. How could he carry on a romance with a Royal Princess like Margot Effer'wyck if he had to live in a slum and work as a common laborer, with calloused hands? He ground his teeth. That part of his rapid economic descent frightened him more than anything else. But then, maybe it didn't matter much anyway. After all, her duties left her little time to spend with him these days. He forced the dismal thought from his mind. "How about you, Pam?" he asked. "What kind of plans do you have?"

"Like everybody else, Wilf," she said, "I'll find *something*. I always have before." She looked away into the fog. "Something . . ."

Brim knew she wasn't any more sure of herself than he was.

At length, the tug dragged *City of Jamestown* into a filthy basin adjacent to a salvage yard. While Brim sat disconsolately at the Helmsman's console, blowing on his hands to keep them warm, she was floated over submerged gravity pontoons that eventually restored her to the standard twenty-five irals altitude that starships maintain while at rest. After this, heavy cranes nudged her broken hull over a dilapidated stone gravity pool where she connected with a rusty brow indifferently smeared with bright patches of orange anticorrosion compounds.

"Not exactly the royal landing pier on Lake Mersin," Peretti observed gloomily.

"It's a lot better than the bottom of Prendergast Bight," Hamlish countered.

"I guess," Brim allowed, but his sentiments were closer to Peretti's. In the Fleet he'd always landed on the lake, close in to the city instead of the drab, sprawling commercial port hundreds of c'lenyts to the austral pole. He looked down at the brow, just concluding its efforts to attach itself with *Jamestown*'s sprung main hatch. The first person across was J. Throckmorton P. Iverson, owner and Chief Executive of Star-Fleet Enterprises, pushing upstream against a stampeding throng of passengers who wanted to be rid of starships forever. When finally he stepped onto the bridge, wearing a food-spotted gray business suit, scuffed shoes, and threadbare cuffs, he had the dazed look of someone who had been recently smashed between the eyes by a meteor. With his fat pink cheeks and narrow, near-sighted eyes, he looked more like a bookkeeper than an entrepreneur. "I, ah, hear nobody got killed," he said, glancing around hesitantly.

"*Nobody*," Brim assured him quietly. "Three or four were a little shaken when their seats tore loose, but nobody was seriously hurt, except old *Jamestown* herself." He peered down at his boots. "I guess she's gone for good."

"Yeah," Iverson said, clearing his throat nervously and looking across the old ship's twisted decks. "Looks like she's gone, all right, the way the hullmetal's wrinkled."

"Sorry," Brim said lamely. Nothing else seemed appropriate.

Iverson dropped his eyes and rubbed the back of his neck. "Wasn't your fault, Brim," he admitted quietly. "Everybody more or less expected the generators to go pretty soon. We just thought that, well, you know, maybe she'd last one more trip and pay for the repairs she needed so badly. I guess we should have told you."

Brim felt his gorge rise, along with a nearly uncontrollable rage. "You mean you *knew* about that power supply tube?" he snorted, taking an angry step forward, "And you let me take all those people into *Hyperspace* anyway?"

"Well," Iverson said, shrinking back and wringing his hands. "We didn't exactly *know*, you understand . . ."

Brim took a deep breath and, shutting his eyes, let out a long sigh. What use was it? Everything was all over anyway, with no one badly hurt, at least in a physical sense. And Iverson never would understand. Bean counters didn't see things the way Helmsmen did—they weren't *supposed* to. After a long silence, he unclenched his fists. "It doesn't matter, Mr. Iverson," he said. "Just pay us off and we'll be on our way."

Iverson nervously pinched the fleshy part of his hand. "Y-yeah," he stuttered, "T-that's what I came to talk about, Brim."

"You *do* have the credits to pay us, don't you?" Brim demanded, narrowing his eyes.

"Um," Iverson stammered, "I d-don't exactly have that much *now*, but . . ."

"But," interjected a deeper voice from the aft companionway, "Mr. Iverson is counting on that many extra credits once he's sold this twisted wreck for scrap—and paid *me* for the services of my tug." Centered in the hatch was a squat, muscular man dressed in white satin coveralls and a gray ebony cloak. Wearing a black velvet cap gathered and puffed over the crown with elaborate ribbon lacings, he had a massive frowning brow, sharp nose, pointed moustache, and the cold gray eyes of a professional assassin. Brim recognized him in a moment: one of the most influential—and reputedly dangerous—men in Avalon's dockyard milieu.

"Zolton Jaiswal!" Iverson grumbled, a disagreeable look forming on his face. "I, um, was just coming to see you."

"Ah, I am comforted to know that, friend Iverson," Jaiswal pronounced without changing his own brooding demeanor. "We of the salvage brotherhood have been expecting the arrival of your ship for quite a while, now. Old *Jamestown* has functioned without repairs much longer than many of my colleagues expected." He laughed sardonically and stepped into the bridge. "They clearly reckoned without placing Mr. Brim in their equations—as I did *not*. That is the reason my tug arrived alone." He chuckled quietly. "Everyone else assumed that you must have taken the old ship to another port for repairs. They stopped anticipating your call for assistance. On the other hand," he said, placing a hand over his heart, "I continued to monitor the distress channels, certain that you—with neither assets nor credit for such costly work—would count on Mr. Brim here to keep your rickety equipment in operation until the last possible moment. And of course," he added, "I was right."

Iverson's face twisted with resentment. "So you waited," he continued in a bitter voice, "like the rest of the carrion-eaters who have feasted on the Fleet since Triannic's xaxtdamned Treaty of Garak."

"Think what you will, Iverson," the little man said with a grim scowl. "But were it not *me* here, someone else would be scrapping those ships." He touched the neck clasp of his cloak. "Like others, you mistake good business practices for traitorous double-dealing. But I am just as patriotic as the next man on Avalon, perhaps a little more, were the truth known."

"More like a thraggling CIGA, from where I stand," Iverson sulked.

Jaiswal's lip curled with ill-concealed rage. "Fortunately," he said, drawing a saffron plastic envelope from his cloak, "I am under no obligation to endure your petty insults. But you *are* under obligation to pay *this*."

"Yeah," Iverson groaned, with a look of utter defeat. "I know—let me have the invoice."

With a grim little smile, Jaiswal handed it over.

Iverson glanced at the scrap of plastic, then set his jaw and took a deep breath. "Pretty xaxtdamn sure of yourself, weren't you," he snorted. "You've already included the tow to the breaker's yard."

Jaiswal shrugged indifferently. "I can make you a separate invoice, should that be necessary."

"Maybe I'll get some other estimates," Iverson spat back petulantly.

"Suit yourself, Iverson," Jaiswal sighed with a detached shrug, "but your rent on *my* gravity pool is high, as are the fees for my tug that even now waits—with its meters running—to tow this ship to the breakers."

Iverson clenched his fists and looked down at his worn boots. "I suppose you already know how much old *Jamestown*'s worth as scrap."

"To the very credit," Jaiswal said, inspecting his fingernails. "I had an estimate made from my tug. The amount you receive will precisely cover the credits owed to your crew plus my towing invoice, with a modicum extra that will pay Mr. Brim, here, for making the trip. Imperial law requires a certified Helmsman aboard all commercial tows, as you know."

"You bastard," Iverson groaned lifelessly. "I'm almost sorry Brim didn't let her sink."

"She would have sunk, Iverson," Jaiswal reminded him, hands at his chest, palms up, "without Brim at the controls. And you would now be up to your reddish neck in murder charges for every passenger lost in the crash."

Iverson shook his head and looked at his feet again. "You don't have to remind me," he said.

"I assume it is settled then?" Jaiswal asked. "Shall we tow this wreck to the breakers before you owe me more credits than she is worth?"

Iverson peered around the cabin for a moment, fastening his gaze finally on Brim. Peretti and Hamlish were already packing their gear. "You'll ride her?" he asked.

"Yeah," Brim agreed, "I guess I might as well. Looks as if that's the last I'll ever get from StarFleet Enterprises."

"You're right there, Brim," Iverson assured him. "Poor old *Jamestown* was the last card I had to play." Then he laughed cynically. "Nergol Triannic and all his StarFleets never even touched me during the war. It took the CIGAs and their xaxt-damned *peace* efforts to *really* mess up my life."

"And shatter the Fleet," Hale added from the companionway. A small traveling case hovered at her heels, and she was dressed for the outdoors.

Brim stepped to the hatchway, frowning. "I guess you heard you'll get paid," he said, a discreet specter of perfume tempting his nostrils.

"Yes, thank the Universe," she said quietly, "Hamlish left the COMM channel open."

"I guessed that Jaiswal might do something like that," Brim said. Then, on an impulse, he took her hand—surprisingly soft and warm in his. "What can I do to help you?" he asked.

"You're helping right now," she said softly, smiling down at her hand. "And, of course, I *am* still alive."

Brim frowned and shook his head. "No," he protested. "I mean—"

"I know what you mean," she stated quietly. "And I appreciate it. But there's nothing much anybody can do about me—except myself. Besides, Mr. Brim," she said with a wink, "you'll be tied up for at least two days with the tow, and by that time, I intend to be well on my way—wherever that way turns out to be."

Brim nodded and released her hand. He expected that she'd waste no time. Unless he missed his guess, there was considerable resilience under all her feminine sleekness. "I hope our paths cross again, Pam," he said. "You're pretty special."

"You're pretty special yourself, Mr. Wilf Ansor Brim," she chuckled grimly. "Maybe we can get together the next time." Then she peered past him into the bridge. "Don't take any wooden credits, gang," she laughed. "Especially you, Jaiswal —I'd hate to hear that there was anybody around slick enough to take *you* for a ride."

"Even wooden credits from such a sweet hand as yours would seem precious to me, splendid lady," he said, bowing elaborately and fixing her with a penetrating stare. "Perhaps I can drop you off somewhere in my limousine."

Hale raised her eyebrows, and she considered the dark little man for a moment with new interest. "All right," she said at length, "perhaps you can." She turned for a moment to wink at a surprised Brim, then started back down the companionway, her traveling case bobbing along the treads after her. "I'll be outside the brow, Jaiswal," she called over her shoulder. "Don't be long." Then, except for the exquisite afterglow of her perfume, she was gone.

The scrapyard of Z. Jaiswal & Co., Shipbreakers, at the dismal seaside town of Keith'Inver was ugly—extravagantly so. Located on Inver Bight, a bend of the Imperial continent's bleak and nearly treeless boreal coast, the mean little village incorporated cheap wooden housing, bad sewers, and worse pavement. During winter, which was both heavy and long, the air was chilly, and the dampness penetrated to the marrow of one's bones. Local dwellers coughed and sneezed and watched advertisements for useless patent remedies, in an age that had all but forgotten disease. It was a grim annex of the Imperial capital that never appear in tourist ads. Due to a perverse ocean current, its sky was gloomy most of the year, as were its gray, squalid landscape and most of the structures that interrupted its cheerless uniformity.

Defunct and empty, *City of Jamestown* listed silently in thick quayside scum, moored alongside the unkempt corpses of I.F.S. *Treacherous*, a relatively late-mark T-Class destroyer, and the battle-worn I.F.S. *Adamant*, an ancient frigate. Behind these luckless starships, busy cutting torches were already throwing showers of sparks over the grimy, opened hull of I.F.S. *Conqueror*, once-mighty flagship of Vice Admiral (the Hon.) Jacob Sturdee during the historic battle for Atalanta. Busy, weatherblackened derricks hoisted massive plates of dulled hullmetal from the great starship's savaged cadaver and dropped them unceremoniously into waiting scrap barges bound for collapsium forges elsewhere in the galaxy.

Halfway across the bay, a cloaked, one-eyed hunchback with a crooked mouth and twisted hands bent over the controls of an open ferry taking Brim to Keith'Inver's public dock and the single daily train to Avalon City. The Carescrian shivered in biting, wind-driven dampness, hardly able to gaze back at the old warships. But no matter where he cast his eyes, some gallant vessel was being dismantled. Z. Jaiswal & Co., had ample jobs, all right—for people with no regard for what they were doing. He ground his teeth at the appalling irony going on before his eyes. In six years of bloody, pitiless warfare, the enormous battlefleets of Nergol Triannic had been unable to achieve what the Imperial Admiralty was doing to itself of its own volition. With a bit of assistance, of course, from Nergol Triannic's Treaty of Garak, as well as patriotic organizations like the Congress for Intragalactic Accord.

Brim shook his head sadly as the unkempt ferry ground alongside the terminal wharf. The Treaty of Garak: CIGAs stalwartly claimed it had ended a war—but had it actually? Were Nergol Triannic's minions *really* sending ships to the breakers as they claimed? He'd called Leaguers a lot of vile names in his day, but "quitter" wasn't one of them so far as he could remember.

He carefully counted out his fare to the hunchback, then climbed to the grimy surface of the wharf and made his way to the train platform. A lot of other people claimed that the treaty was only a ruse. And if they were correct, then the only benefit would accrue to the League, buying them time to recover from the unsuccessful attack on Atalanta at Hador-Haelic. And while powerful CIGA peacemongers—many within the Admiralty itself—busily demonstrated their willingness to banish war by calling for more cuts in the size of the Imperial Fleet, the League of Dark Stars was probably rebuilding theirs in secret, biding time until they were handed their goal of galactic domination on a silver platter.

After a chilly wait, Brim watched his train snake out of its tunnel like a long segmented needle, then sigh into the station, radiating heat as it slowed to a hover over its single glowing track. A door hissed open and Brim, alone on the dingy platform, stepped inside, taking a cramped seat at the rear of the windowless third-class compartment. He looked at his timepiece and nodded to himself. With a little luck at the Avalon end, he'd be back in his flat just in time for the message Margot promised to send when she returned.

That thought produced visions of loose golden curls framing a glamorous oval face, languid blue eyes, generous lips, and a brow that frowned in the most lovely way possible every time she smiled. Her Serene Majesty, Princess Margot of the Effer'wyck Dominions and Baroness of the Torond was not only Brim's one true love—as well as extravagant lover—she was also intelligent, courageous, and deliciously heretical. At the time she and Brim met aboard I.F.S. *Defiant*, she specialized in perilous covert missions to League planets that produced some of the war's most valuable intelligence information. However, once Emperor Greyffin IV, her uncle, caught wind of these dangerous activities, he forbade them to continue. A politically dictated marriage (to Baron Rogan LaKarn, first in succession for the throne of the Torond) was simply too valuable an asset to risk. Temporarily stymied in her efforts at direct action, she continued her military career by directing an important intelligence organization in Avalon, and even found time to secretly participate in the defense of Atalanta, during which she was severely wounded.

Wryly, Brim considered her coming visit. He'd seen so very little of her since his return to Avalon. Not that he could blame her for it. She was, after all, obligated to accompany her husband wherever he went. And LaKarn was a devoted traveler. Until he was someday crowned Grand Duke—upon the eventual death of his mother—he ostensibly served as Ambassador to the Empire, with residence in Avalon. But the "residence" part was little more than a joke, as was his post at the embassy. Like many other superwealthy young men of the postwar civilization, LaKarn was on a pleasure spree, traveling regularly among the great cities of the galaxy, visiting celebrated spas and casinos, and hobnobbing with other members of a new, fast-moving, freewheeling leisure class.

During the rare times Brim and Margo had been able to steal a moment together, she often decried the meaningless life she was forced to live. But during her long absences, Brim found himself struggling bitterly against resentment for the vast difference between his own deepening poverty and the lavish lifestyle she followed.

Little more than a metacycle later, he was back in Avalon, hurrying through the wintry streets on foot. With the job market as unpromising as it was, he needed to save every credit, especially if he expected to eat with any regularity. As he crossed over a busy thoroughfare, speeding limousines below reminded him of the days past when he traveled these same boulevards in similar transportation—once in one of the Emperor's own. And even though he'd been poor most of his existence, the taste of the good life he'd received in the Fleet was not easily forgotten, nor relinquished.

A large and colorful holoboard farther along the street touted someone's news service. Brim stopped to look. What caught his eye was a sleek starship in the background of the ad. Lean and powerful-looking, it was one of the three modified attack ships the Imperial Starflight Society planned to enter in the Mitchell Trophy Race, scheduled to take place in less than a year as he remembered. By the Universe, he thought to himself, *there* was a ship he'd like to fly! He grinned and thought of Pam Hale's words about being "rich and famous." Well, he might be broke and obscure, but he'd once rubbed elbows with a few of the swells that belonged to that exclusive club, although he suspected they'd be ashamed to admit they knew him these days.

He sighed as he made his way up a narrow staircase to his apartment. Cooking odors from neighboring flats reminded him that the last morsel he'd eaten was a cold box lunch provided by the tugboat captain almost a day ago. Tonight, he would skip supper as well. He wanted to toast Margot's visit with good Logish Meem, and that meant he must economize.

He keyed the lock on a peeling, age-stained door, then entered his chilly one-room flat, nearly devoid of furniture, or much of anything else for that matter. As his funds had dwindled, he had sold off most of his meager possessions—even his prized wartime medals and a rare old Sodeskayan blaster— always optimistic that new employment was around the corner. But it never was. So many jobless Helmsmen were idle on the streets of Avalon, and so few ships were still in commission, that only the well connected found jobs; skills were secondary attributes in that cutthroat market. Unfortunately for Brim, "connecting" with the influence he unquestionably possessed meant accepting help. And that was something quite beyond his experience.

Seating himself on a carton before a battered public correspondence socket, he called up his mail. Immediately, messages appeared from Nikolai Yanuarievich Ursis and Anastas Alexyi Borodov, wealthy Sodeskayan Bears and comrades from a thousand days of desperate warfare. They were again solicitously offering employment on freighters of G.F.S.S. (Great Federation of Sodeskayan States) registry.

Concluding one more time that the Bears' proposals were made more from compassion than from actual need, he turned them down by return mail, writing of fictitious opportunities that would keep him lucratively busy for a year or more. When he finished, his face burned with embarrassment; he had an almost morbid fear of receiving charity. Carescrians might collectively be the poorest people in the Empire, but they were also proud, and fiercely independent.

Another message was from Lieutenant Commander Regula Collingswood, now married to Erat Plutron, one of the surviving old-line Admirals in the Imperial Fleet. She was also an officer of the Imperial Starflight Society, if he remembered correctly. Her note was one more invitation to Bemus Hall, their ancient manor house near the boreal shore of Lake Mersin. Brim shook his head sadly; Collingswood too was concerned for his situation. With deep appreciation and considerable regret, he sent a polite message of refusal. Facing that magnificent person from his present poverty was simply unthinkable, as was accepting help from flighted A'zurnian embassy officials who, in still another message, were making their regular check of his situation on behalf of a nation whose everlasting gratitude he had earned in a bygone land campaign. He politely refused this as well. If a person couldn't make his own way in the galaxy, then he didn't deserve to live, and that was that.

As usual, he saved Margot's correspondence for last. Hearing from her was almost an obsession with him, but lately, he had begun to view her messages in a new and altogether unsettling manner.

During his tenure in the Fleet, the tremendous disparity in their economic circumstances had never seemed very significant. Then he had been an officer, and surely on his way up. These days, however, while she was still a Royal Princess, he was now a nobody, with few prospects of any kind. It bothered him that poverty seemed to distort his point of view, especially because he was reasonably sure that she remained constant in their star-crossed love affair. If anything, the messages she sent were now even more loving and erotic than they ever were before her marriage.

Within the metacycle, he discovered that her latest posting was no exception. "Wilf, dearest love," she whispered as her flushed countenance faded for the last time from the display, "soon, we will be together, and I shall no longer have to do this for myself." After a few moments, he wiped his brow, then checked his face in the mirror for the thousandth time. Her "soon" was less than two days hence. He hoped to Voot that the swelling in his bruised nose would subside by then.

Brim's run-down bed creaked as Margot drowsily rolled a leg over his hips and covered his face with wet, perfumed kisses. "I love you, Wilf," she sighed drowsily,—"more than the Universe itself. . . ."

Strangely wide awake after a long evening of unrestrained lovemaking, he gently caressed her silky hair with his free hand until her breathing evened out and she lay still in his arms. In the late-night silence, his mind's eye retraced their surreptitious meeting that evening in the romantic shadows of a snug, out-of-the-way bistro. Somehow, his cheap clothes didn't seem so noticeable there, and from the time he kissed her long, tapering fingers, all the hopelessness of his current life healed in the warm glow of her soul. Later, she had even made his shabby walk-up seem like a suite in some grand hotel as, garment by garment, she slowly bared her glorious body, then drew his face into a glorious tangle of moist golden curls.

In the stillness of the night he let the warm perfume of her breath restore his shattered spirit. Clearly, she cared for him as much today as she had on that glorious evening years ago when they first made love in her private suite at the Effer'ian embassy.

Then—infernally—a wave of despair swept all the warmth away. In those days, he had been Wilf Brim the Helmsman, a proud man with a mission and a future who could damn well contend for the most desirable woman in the Empire. What mattered most in that wild tumult of battle were skills, guts, and confidence. He had them all—in great quantities. Lately, however, it seemed that skill and guts counted for very little in the peacetime Empire of CIGA politics. And to his everlasting shame, he deathly feared that he was now losing his confidence. It was a long time before he finally drifted off into a confused state that only vaguely resembled sleep.

He awoke with a start to quiet weeping from the pillow next to him. "Margot," he whispered with anxious concern, "what is it? What's wrong?" By the glow of his wall heater, he could see her cheeks were streaked with eye makeup.

She only buried her head in her hands and began to cry aloud until her body was wracked with violent sobs. Truly distressed by this time, Brim held her close in his arms, caressing the back of her neck and her shoulders until she seemed to regain some control and the fitful wrenching subsided. When her breathing returned to something like normal, he put his lips to her ear. "Want to tell me about it?" he asked in a whisper.

With her face still buried in the crook of his arm she shook her head. "No, Wilf, I don't," she murmured bitterly, "but I must." Without another word, she slipped from the bed and stepped to his sink where she turned up the lights and began to wash her face.

Even in Brim's anxiety, the sight of her ample buttocks and long, shapely legs were enough to cause a familiar excitement in his loins. Margot Effer'wyck was absolutely the most desirable woman he had encountered anywhere in the galaxy. What could have happened to her? He bit his lip. All he could do was wait patiently until she decided to share her troubles.

Inspecting her face in his tiny mirror, she at last turned and made her way back to the bed where she settled cross-legged beside him and took his hand in hers. "At first," she began, peering at him with a grave look, "I thought I ought to keep this from you for a while." She sighed quietly as light from the heater turned her hair into a golden halo. "But tonight," she continued presently, "I suddenly awoke with the fear that if I did, I might lose your trust. And without that, I would lose *you*, Wilf Brim."

Her red-rimmed eyes gazed at him with such fierce emotion that Brim raised himself to a sitting position. "You can tell me, Margot," he said gently.

Almost as if she were at prayer—he'd actually seen people doing that—she bowed her head and closed her eyes for a moment. Then she looked him directly in the eye. "I'm pregnant, Wilf," she whispered quickly, as though the words themselves were bitter in her mouth. "I'm going to bear Rogan's son in a little less than eight months."

From a thousand c'lenyts distance, Brim heard his breath catch and he felt the sharp knife of dismay turn in his gut. "His son?" he asked weakly.

"His son," Margot repeated with the same intense look. "I'd managed to prevent that from happening for a long time, but

... well ..." She shrugged. "We were in Tarrott after touring the League a few weeks back. Rogan was dickering with Gorn-Hoff for three of their attack ships he wants to modify for the Mitchell Trophy Race, and, well, you can imagine how a big consortium like Gorn-Hoff entertains. . . ." She raised her open hands guilelessly. "At any rate, after a huge banquet and a *lot* of Logish Meem, I simply *needed* company, and for once Rogan didn't let me down." She took a deep breath. "If it's any recompense, I was thinking about you most of the time—especially when ..." She paused and smiled ruefully. "Anyway," she continued, "it wasn't until morning that I remembered I'd taken no precautions—and I was too embarrassed to ask for *that* kind of medical help in a foreign domain. Besides," she added, "Rogan would have killed me—he's been trying for a long time." She looked into his eyes again. "There," she said grimly. "Now you know everything about it."

Brim fought his emotions to a draw and gently lifted her chin until she was looking into his eyes. "It's all right," he said gently. "It was bound to happen someday. . . ." But somehow, inside it *wasn't* all right. He gazed at her small breasts and the sensual curve of her stomach and suddenly things were different. Instead of his usual stirrings, the sight of her golden pubic thatch sent a wave of regret coursing through his spirit like a gust of icy air. It was as if LaKarn had been there all night with them, watching.

"Are you all right, Wilf?" Margot asked with a sudden look of concern.

Brim took a deep breath. "Yeah," he said presently, "I'm all right. I guess I just wasn't ready for that kind of news. . . ."

Margot gently bent to kiss his fingers. "Neither was I about a week ago," she said with a shake of her head. Then, a shadow of concern passed across her eyes and she threw her arms around his neck. "Hold me for a moment, Wilf," she begged anxiously. "I don't want to let this thing come between us!"

Brim eased her head back to the pillow. "The Universe knows I love you, Margot," he whispered ardently, "—better than life itself. And tomorrow I shall love you even more—for every tomorrow I live to see." It was no meaningless platitude: he meant every word. Then, he brushed her damp eyelashes with his lips and began to gently kiss her on the the mouth.

After some time, she began to clamp his shoulders more

tightly and her breathing became labored. Suddenly, her mouth opened and her tongue darted between his lips while she rolled onto her side and rhythmically crushed her groin into his hip. "Wilf," she moaned in a low voice, "I need you again. . . ."

At that moment, panic struck Wilf Brim with the force of a runaway starship. He wasn't ready. He ground his teeth and concentrated.

"Wilf," she urged breathlessly, throwing her leg over his waist, "hurry! I have to leave in less than a metacycle." *She* was ready, no doubt about that.

Totally incredulous, he squeezed his hand between them to make certain. It was true. "I-I'm not ready," he confessed with a groan. "I can't."

"You what?"

"I can't," he croaked, rolling over on his back.

"Oh, Wilf, my poor darling," she whispered in dismay. Suddenly she covered him with her body, placed her hands on his cheeks, and smothered his face in gentle kisses. "It's all right," she whispered in a voice filled with compassion. "You don't have to prove anything to me—ever. I *love* you. That's all that counts."

In spite of her tender words, Brim couldn't relax. "Oh great Universe," he moaned between clenched teeth, "now I've failed you in *this* too." He rolled from under her and swung his legs onto the floor, sitting with the sheet gripped in both hands as if it were his only anchor to sanity.

Margot quickly knelt beside him with her arms around his neck. "Wilf, Wilf," she sobbed. "What have I done to you?"

"Nothing," he answered, his voice cracking with emotion. "It's just that . . . well, I can't seem to win for losing, these days." He put his face in his hands, feeling the emotions welling within him.

Suddenly, he felt her hand at his groin. "Dearest Wilf," she whispered, urging him onto the bed again.

She never got to finish. Discreet rapping at the door preceded the unmistakable voice of Ambridge, her chauffeur. "Madam, we must make haste. The household plans to awaken much earlier than usual today."

Brim felt her whole body go rigid beside him. "I hear you, Ambridge," she called presently. "I shall be there in a moment." She hesitated for no more than a click longer, then placed her hands on his cheeks and kissed him full on the mouth. "Wilf," she said as she sprang from the bed and began to pull on her clothes, "you must *not* let this affect you in any way." She frowned as she struggled with the buttons on her ornate blouse, then turned to look at him full in the face. "You are no less a man this morning," she said, her hands on her hips, "than you were last night when you caused me to wake everyone in this building with my happy moaning."

Still in a state of shock, Brim could only sit numbly while she stepped into her shoes. After a long moment, he got to his feet and held her cloak. "I don't know what to say, Margot," was all he could mumble.

"Wilf," she said with a look of deepening concern on her face. "Wilf, *look* at me. You certainly aren't the only man this has happened to. I mean—"

Quiet but insistent rapping commenced at the door again. "Madame," Ambridge whispered.

"I'm on my way," she answered over her shoulder. "Wilf, are you going to be all right?"

Brim gathered the remaining shreds of his ego and pulled himself erect, feeling more than a little foolish standing naked in front of this very thoroughly dressed woman. "I'm all right now," he lied, nervously fingering her ring as it dangled from the chain around his neck. Somehow the metal felt unnaturally cold. "Don't worry about me."

"You're sure, Wilf?"

"You can count on it." He took her in his arms and kissed her on the mouth while Ambridge continued to knock at short intervals. "You'd better go now," he said after a moment.

She nodded. "Don't *ever* forget that I love you, dearest," she said. "'For thee, my own sweet lover, in thy heart, I know myself secure, as thou in mine: We were and are—I am, even as thou art—Beings who ne'er each other can resign; It is the same, together or apart. . . .'" The she opened the door and was gone in the blink of an eye.

During all those dreary years that followed Admiral Kabul Anak's first great attack on Carescria—the raid wiped out every member of his family—Wilf Brim had become convinced that he could never again find the necessary tears to cry.

He was wrong.

CHAPTER 2

Claudia

In that last half-metacycle before dawn, Brim managed to throw on his clothes and stumble blindly out into the cold, sleety streets. Anything was better than the solitude of his dingy room, and the raw memories of his latest and most painful failure. It was too awful to contemplate.

Considerably later, after losing all track of time, he found himself shivering on the waterfront of Lake Mersin beneath the landward end of the causeway leading to Avalon's Grand Terminal Island. He was tired and hungry, but no force in the Universe could make him return to the place of his shame. He was also cold—the heating elements in his clothes hadn't worked for months now, nor was his lightweight jacket much good at stopping the raw wind that swept in off the lake. Had *City of Jamestown* held together for one last trip, he had planned to buy his heated suit back from the used-garments dealer. He shrugged. The way things were going in his life, he would soon be lucky to have any clothes at all.

He looked around at the mean streets leading to the dilapidated waterfront. He'd not been in this part of town since his cadet days when he'd come to the section looking for . . . entertainment. He shook his head determinedly—after last night, *those* thoughts were strictly off-limits. Ahead, he noticed a queue of ragged-looking people waiting patiently in the driving sleet, hands in their pockets, arms tight against their bodies to conserve heat. Those at the head of the line were singly entering one of the grime-blackened storefronts in a shabby row facing the wharfs. From time to time, others exited from another door, some to stand in a small crowd at the end of a short jetty, others to disappear with a dejected shuffle along the littered waterfront streets.

Something about those figures moving out onto the jetty set them apart. Brim frowned—what was it? Suddenly, he knew: they walked with the rolling gate of space sailors, professionals who understood how to carry themselves in any kind of gravity gradient.

He stopped behind the last person in line, a thin and angular woman with a sharply hooked nose, prominent chin, and pock-marked cheeks. Her eyes, however, were a dead giveaway for a starsailor—they had the permanent narrowing people got after spending a lifetime staring out into the void. She wore a stocking cap over her stringy gray hair, a faded Imperial battle jacket from which the insignia had been removed, and heavy woolen slacks with worn Fleet-issue boots. "What're they giving away up there?" he asked, nodding toward the storefront.

The woman laughed scornfully. "These days, nobody's givin' out anythin' to anybody," she said, "especially ex-Blue Capes. Where have *you* been since the Treaty of Garak, mister? Ain't you heard about the CIGAs?"

Brim looked her in the eye. "Same place you've been, I'd guess," he answered emotionlessly. "And I've heard the CIGAs, all right. Too much."

The woman stomped her boots in the wet slush and returned her attention to the storefront. "Thought so," she said. Then she fell silent.

"You still didn't tell me what the line's for," Brim prompted after a while.

"You never asked."

"Yeah. You're right; I guess I didn't. Why's everybody in line?" For better or worse, he seemed to be in it, too. At least ten other ragged figures had queued up behind him while he talked.

She laughed derisively. "I guess you haven't been down this way very often—*Mister* ex-officer," she hissed. "But we're seein' more and more of your kind every day."

"You still didn't tell me why you're in—"

"Jobs," the woman said, "IGL Spacelines. They recruit people for the lower decks in places like this. You know—menials."

Brim nodded. He'd heard; he'd simply never before had a reason to ... Suddenly he frowned. There was ample reason now. His funds were almost gone after his meal with Margot and their bottle of Logish Meem. He'd had to hassle with her for the right to pay for everything, but she'd finally given in, clearly to save what little pride he retained. Soon, however, that pride would cost him dearly. His rent was due in exactly one week, to a landlady totally devoid of compassion. At that juncture, he would have to either find *some* employment or accept help from someone. Otherwise, he would become one of the city's growing cadre of homeless veterans who slept in doorways or under bridges. Even that was almost better than accepting help.

He stayed where he was, shuffling along in the line. Just about everything he owned of any value was on his back, and he couldn't bring himself to return home. Presently, he found himself through the door and into the relative warmth of a shabby room whose peeling walls were covered by holoposters advertising IGL's great starliners. One, nearest the bare light pictured a city of canals, proclaiming:

Royal
A'zurnian Getaway
Odyssey

Lifting on a biweekly schedule.

Book Early
for the

Mitchell Trophy Race

at

Magalla'ana,
A'zurn

Brim ground his teeth. The Mitchell Trophy Race. Margot's naked body suddenly replaced the holoposter in his mind's eye —only she was rutting with LaKarn and making a baby after dickering with Gorn-Hoff for starships to compete in *that* race!

"Well, c'mon, mister," a man demanded behind a scarred desk, "none of us have all day. How many years in space you got?" He had a fat, greasy face and wore the quasi-military uniform of Intragalactic Spacelines, whose winter tunic was clearly too warm for the room. He was sweating profusely as he peered nearsightedly into a battered display.

"Twenty-two years in space; almost five of them in the Fleet," Brim answered, trying to keep his eyes from the poster. Even for a Carescrian, he'd started flying early.

The fat man made a face and looked up. "Just in case I might believe that kind of corgwash, mister," he growled, "what kind of work you lookin' for?"

Brim forced his mind to concentrate. What kind of experience did he have? Clearly, they weren't looking for Helmsmen in a place like this.

"Come on, mister," the fat man chided again. "Either pay attention or let somebody else in." He wiped his nose with a pudgy finger.

"Um . . . I guess I can do b-baggage handling," Brim stammered. Before he learned to fly the dangerous ore barges that earned him his berth in the Helmsmen's Academy, he'd worked at a lot of menial jobs.

"Baggage handlin'," the man repeated, his pudgy fingers thrumming a filthy console while he squinted into the display. "Yeah, good choice," he said presently, "we got a couple of round-trip berths on S.S. *Prosperous*—big 'un, departin' tonight for Hador-Haelic and the city of Atalanta." He looked up at Brim. "You look like you're pretty strong, all right. They'll like that. But you got no seniority with IGL, either—leastwise, you don't show up on the company's books under Brim. So they'll expect you for extra duty in the galley if you want the job."

Brim considered a moment. If nothing else, it would mean a warm, dry place to sleep for a while. And at the rate things were going, that might be a definite improvement in his lifestyle.

"Get a move on, Brim. There's lots of people outside that'll take the job with no thinkin'."

"I'll take it," Brim said.

"Where's your stuff?" the IGL man asked. "You'll have t' get the next launch t' catch 'er."

"Everything I own is on my back," Brim asked.

"All right," the man said, bending to his console again, "that's it. Remember, it's a *round*-trip job and there's laws against jumpin' ship in the middle. This ain't no free trip to Atalanta, no matter how many jobs they've got there during their reconstruction. Unnerstand?"

"I understand," Brim said, eager to be on the way to *anything*.

He spent most of the next metacycle on one of ICL's shabby, fly-spotted work stations, trying to ignore the holoposter and keep his mind from the open wound that Margot had become while he completed the million and one legal forms required by the Empire for intragalactic employment. Then, having been issued a temporary scrap of a badge reading, NEW MENIAL, he made his way onto the cold quayside. One more job remained before reporting to the pier.

Transferring his last credits to a public correspondence system, he sent a brief message (via text, the least expensive delivery method available) to a confidential destination Margot maintained for just such circumstances:

Dearest Margot:

Last night proved how much I need to put together
some sort of new life for myself: one in which I can look
you in the face once more. Please trust that I am safe,
that I remain unchanged in my love for you, and that I
shall someday return. Care for yourself in the way I
would care for you, were I able.

All my love,
Wilf

Within two metacycles, he was balancing himself on the icy open deck of a labor-pool launch as it skidded around the edge of a colossal gravity pool supporting IGL's premiere starliner, the S.S. *Prosperous*. Far overhead, he could see the big ship's conoid bow and farther back, her high, rakish superstructure, completely distorted by the extreme perspective. After a complete postwar refitting, she was resplendent in dazzling white with the vivid IGL logo blazing forth from the center of her bridge. The last time he'd seen her this close, she was finished in wartime ebony hullmetal and he was on his way to A'zurn for the first land campaign of his experience.

As the launch drew to a halt at the lowest embarkation platform, he looked up to see passengers gliding into the big ship on moving walkways through lofty, gold-tinted glass brows. He shook his head as he dodged a sheet of icy spray, wondering what sort of skills one needed to obtain such luxury in peacetime. Then he shrugged sadly. Whatever they were, all seemed far beyond his own wretched understanding.

"All right, bums," a tough-looking IGL officer barked from a freight elevator, "in here on the double. We've work aplenty for the likes of you."

Before he swung himself to the wave-slick platform, Brim craned his neck for a last look at the ship's brooding control bridge, nearly one hundred fifty irals overhead. While he stood there, transfixed, he felt a sharp jab in the ribs. He looked down to see a pair of young IGL surface officers: slim, perfectly uniformed, and effete, as nonflying officers often seemed to be. One was brandishing a baton.

"On your way, Menial," he said contemptuously. "The only way you'll see the bridge of *that* ship is with a mop in your hand." He laughed at his own joke.

"That's right," the other sniggered. "What do y' think y' are, a Helmsman or something?"

Whines and rumbles of imminent landfall cascaded on Brim's ears as he desperately sprinted toward the menials' compartment. He'd been the last hand to leave the galley because it was his responsibility to make a final cleaning pass over the slops compartments and the garbage crusher. Now, with the ship's mammoth gravity generators droning at idle—about to be reversed at any moment—he knew he had only cycles to strap himself in before Pandemonium broke loose along the big starship's keel. He could almost feel it.

"Hands to landing stations! Hands to landing stations!" a clamorous voice brayed over the blower. "All hands to landing stations!"

Brim glimpsed an unmistakable cityscape as he raced past a viewport. At the same moment a Helmsman ten decks overhead activated the big ship's lift modifiers and skewed her gravity gradient forward. Brim understood all too well what was about to result, but there was nothing he could do save brace for the inevitable, which followed immediately. A mighty gravitron flux, racing like an invisible piston through the corridor, sent him sprawling along the metal deck, then dashing his head into a bulkhead in a sudden storm of swirling lights. Abruptly, everything went black.

He awoke to someone tugging painfully on his arm—an IGL officer? His eyes were too blurred to be sure.

"Wake up, you xaxtdamned lazy beggar," the wobbly apparition demanded in a deep voice. "Thank your lucky stars that little evening nap of yours didn't get you killed when we made landfall! Now off to your duty post on the double—understand?"

Still bewildered from the terrific blow, Brim dumbly struggled to his feet and floundered along the hallway, holding his aching head with both hands. It felt as if his brains had been pounded by a meteor.

"And Menial," the man called after him, "try to be a little cleaner about yourself in the future. You smell like a sack of garbage!"

Brim clamped his mouth shut and stumbled along the hall. He had, he reminded himself for the ten thousandth time, signed up for the job of his own free will. And in truth, the constant baggage organizing that occupied much of his first two days out was good, honest work. In fact, he found it almost enjoyable. But when all the million and one traveling cases were at last sorted and properly stowed, the officers wasted little time in appointing him to the ship's monster galley as a Slops Mate. After that, he spent nearly every waking metacycle contemplating garbage of every species, vintage, and stench— often while he was knee deep in it. The word *intolerable* couldn't even half describe the remainder of his passage.

And now, it was reasonably clear why there was always a shortage of Slops Mates. The poor devils either slipped on the rancid grease that perpetually coated the slops ramp, thereby joining the very garbage they were processing, or they were simply dashed to flinderation when they couldn't reach safety during takeoffs or landings.

He frowned as he passed another viewport. Outside, past the colossal overhang of *Prosperous*'s hull, he could see the winking early-evening lights of Atalanta—a city he had once helped save. His eyes followed the great upsweep of City Mount Hill as it became one with the darkening sky. And even in the failing light, after a lapse of more than two years, scars from the great battle waged above the city were easily visible, as were countless construction sites. Everywhere he looked, builders' derricks intruded on the skyline.

Brim nodded to himself. There was no putting it off any longer. With all that construction, there simply *had* to be job openings. A lot of them. And no matter what sort of work they called for, the worst would—by definition—be a lot more desirable than cleaning garbage chutes. He shrugged. There was really no decision. He'd made up his mind the first day he pulled slops duty.

Glancing over his shoulder, he checked to make certain the corridor was empty, then turned and continued on his original course to the menials' compartment. A plan was already beginning to form in his mind—one that had served him well in the Great War when he was trapped aboard a Leaguer ship.

The grimy chamber where Brim slept was nearly empty when he arrived, but even though most of the hard-used menials who bunked there were now at their stations, it still reeked of overworked, underwashed bodies. Quickly stripping to the skin, he donned the shabby clothing he'd worn the day of his departure. Over this, he pulled the only clean set of IGL work togs he possessed. Then, rumpling his privacy blanket as if he had merely relinquished the recliner to report for duty, he hurried off toward the baggage holds.

On his way, he made one hasty stop, in a compartment marked BAGGAGE SUPERVISORS ONLY. Boldly entering the restricted office unit, he strode past four IGL officers—three women and a man—seated in front of a situation terminal that was clearly tuned to one of Atalanta's seamier broadcast stations. None so much as bothered to look up as he made his way across the room to a rack of logic scribers: the same kind of portable writing board carried by everyone in the Universe who ever took an inventory or made a survey. Selecting a battered-looking veteran of what must have been hundreds of transgalactic journeys, he quickly erased its contents, then exited the room—again without eliciting any reaction from its "legal" occupants—and continued along the corridor at a trot.

When he arrived at the hatch to baggage hold number four, his assigned duty station, Brim carefully peered around the coaming, waited until the deck was clear of IGL supervisors, then stole into the maze of lofty chutes that held traveling cases to be unloaded. Selecting a large, expensive-looking grip at random, he hefted it to the floor and activated its "follower" unit, recording the registration number on a "Personal Delivery" form that he'd called up from his scriber's memory. Then, with the grip bobbing along at his heels, he signed the scriber with a flourish—*Peter Mason*, a name he'd drawn from some distant recess of his mind—and strode out across the main floor of the baggage room as if the orders he'd just drawn up and authenticated were real.

Before he arrived at the heavily guarded personnel exit, Brim was interrogated by no less than five suspicious IGL officials. Presentation of the scriber alone was enough to get him past the first four—none of them even bothered to read it.

The fifth, however—a two-striper—was a different matter entirely. He not only took the scriber from Brim's hands, he read it carefully, frowning when he came to the signature section, clearly trying to remember someone on the IGL staff with the name of Mason. "Who is this Peter Mason, Menial?" he demanded, his narrow face wearing a look of haughty suspicion. He was a well-cared-for-man in his sixties, but his red hair was dark as any twenty-year-old's. He also wore a large CIGA ring encrusted with gaudy stones.

Brim felt his brow break out in perspiration while the officer studied his forged scriber. Could it be that Peter Mason was a real name? "I don't rightly know, sir," he said, deciding hastily to play on IGL's predilection for rank consciousness. "When I saw the four stripes on his cuff, I thought I'd better do what he said. He wanted this grip delivered in person to the terminal, an' I wasn't about to ask any questions. . . ."

"*Four* stripes, you say?"

"Aye, sir," Brim affirmed, "I don't rightly know much about IGL ranks, but I sure didn't want to fool with the likes of him, if you get my drift, sir. He looked like a tough one, he did. . . ."

"I see," the man said while a frown formed on his face. He considered for a moment more—in which Brim sternly reminded himself to breathe—then handed over the scriber. "Well, er, off you go, then, Menial," he ordered reluctantly, "and don't let me catch you loitering on your way back."

"Aye, sir," Brim said, knuckling his forehead and starting down the corridor at a run, the grip careening after him at full clip. "You won't find me wastin' time on *this* ship, ever—an' you can believe it, sir," he called over his shoulder. Then he scampered down a companionway taking the treads two at a time.

Within cycles, Brim found himself approaching a crew exit hatch. Beyond, the yellowish brilliance of Karlsson lamps streamed from the end of a long, covered brow. Freedom was less than a hundred irals distant; however, one last obstruction remained: a crystal guard column. And there was no way he could enter the brow without passing it. Gathering all the courage and brashness he could muster, he marched toward the opening as if he expected the guard to let him past on sight.

Inside his transparent enclosure, the man was tall and raw boned with unintelligent eyes, a lumpy nose, and a great lantern jaw that fairly begged to be punched. He appeared to be in vigorous conversation through his terminal with a sultry-looking woman whose lavishly made-up face and fantastic green eyelids suggested a well-established profession. Without interrupting his dialogue, the man thrust an officious hand out a small window to block Brim's path.

"I've gotta hurry, Officer," Brim protested in an exaggerated whisper through the window, "this traveling bag was promised at hatch fifty-one more'n five clicks ago. Somethin' about a lady gettin' caught with the wrong guy in her bed last night . . ." He flashed the scriber. "See?" he said, pointing first to the display, then to the flashing ID tag on the traveling case. "They match."

His heart skipped a long beat when the terminal prattled angrily and the guard's eyes opened wide with rage.

"Nobody," he growled resentfully at the display, "says anything like that to *me*—'specially the likes of *you*, ya slut!"

The terminal responded noisily with something unintelligible, whereupon the man looked blindly at Brim with a frenzied expression on his face, as if he were trying to put words to his rage.

Heart in his mouth, Brim could only flash the scriber again. "Got to hurry," he mouthed theatrically.

Without another glance, the guard waved him through while he shouted a great torrent of invective at the display. Brim heard little of it, nearly outrunning the traveling case again in his haste to clear the IGL crew area, which he did before the next five cycles had passed.

Much later, hurrying inland on foot, he hoped guiltily that someone would restore the purloined traveling case to its rightful owners. He'd abandoned it with his IGL work togs behind a gigantic potted o'gett fern in the crowded terminal. Presently, he was climbing City Mount Hill, following one of the stone tram alleys that crisscrossed Atalanta, dodging huge top-hampered interurban cars that thundered by from both directions at perilously high speeds. When he'd put at least five c'lenyts between himself and the IGL, he veered into one of the older parts of the city to shelter for the remainder of the chilly spring evening in a dark storefront. And even though his teeth chattered from time to time, he couldn't remember when he'd last felt so much at ease and at home, anywhere.

He awoke when the great star Hador was just beginning to tint Haelic's broad horizon with tenuous shades of red and mauve. In the dusky half-light, he watched a little native Zuzzous crackling down from the nightward sky toward a waterfront landing, its beacon flashing like a firefly. Atalanta! He was hungry again, dying for a hot cup of cvceese'. But he was also free. And that alone seemed worth the trip.

From his vantage point on City Mount Hill, he could see all the way to the civilian districts of the harbor and the colossal form of *Prosperous* brooding on an immense canal-side gravity pool amid IGL's sprawling complex of warehouses and terminals. The big ship's myriad position lights and scuttles glittered like stars from a private galaxy. He shook his head. *Magnificent* was the word she brought to mind. He'd loved the big ship when he'd first laid eyes on her years ago, and his sour experience as a menial had changed nothing. People who loved starships—and the stars—as much as Brim did were a tough lot to discourage.

He shrugged, surmising the harbor authorities would have given up searching for him by now. His name would soon be posted as a "jumper" in waterfront police departments of a dozen ports of call throughout the Empire. But aside from the postings themselves, he was fairly certain that nothing further would result from his jumping ship. The loss of one Slops Mate more or less could have little real significance. Besides, he chuckled to himself, IGL had actually gained in the transaction —menials weren't paid off until the ship returned home; therefore, he'd worked the outbound leg free. A fair trade, he calculated. And with his pay, they could keep the remainder of their garbage, as well.

While one of the city's million-odd sable rothcats brushed against his legs, he contemplated his first real view of the city in slightly more than two years. Atalanta's administrators had clearly accomplished much in the way of rebuilding since the League's last great attack was rebuffed. Everywhere he looked he could see new tile roofs in a million reds, browns, oranges, and greens, along with walls that didn't quite match their neighbors and domes whose surfaces were patched with varying degrees of metallic luster. But, as he had noted the previous evening, unrestored vestiges of destruction were equally evident—to his Helmsman's eye, perhaps more so. The whole cityscape was pockmarked with empty lots, tumbled masonry, yawning windows, and skeletal remains of burned-out structures. Perhaps the most poignant reminder of that ferocious battle was the empty crag that once cradled the Gradgroat-Norchelite's now-vaporized monastery. He stared in awe, remembering its colossal, flame-shaped spire and the curious motto that appeared over its massive doorway.

In Destruction Is Resurrection;
The Path of Power Leads Through Truth

While Hador's first rays painted the great melted pinnacle with subtle traces of crimson and coral, he glimpsed elaborate scaffolding and the beginnings of a huge circular wall. Smiling to himself, Brim nodded his head in approval. The Gradygroats were already at work rebuilding their once-famous edifice. Norchelite friars were never ones to let a little destruction stand in their way. Brim knew that from experience.

He frowned. How his life had changed! Once, long ago in his days as a Fleet officer, Gradygroats and their monastery had seemed interesting to him—important even, in a strange sort of way. Now, his whole existence seemed to be taken up with things like occasionally filling his empty stomach or finding shelter for the night. He shook his head and glanced across the harbor to the Fleet base where a light cruiser soared effortlessly up from the bay. Even at a distance he could pick out the lines of a Vengeance-class starship. As it thundered out toward space, a charge of emotion surged along his spine. In spite of everything, it was hard to disregard the memories he'd accumulated at the sprawling military complex. Especially memories of Claudia Valemont, the beautiful, long-haired Division Manager who had been his friend and occasional paramour while I.F.S. *Defiant* called Atalanta its home port. He smiled wryly, watching Hador's brilliance at last reach down to sparkle on Grand Harbor itself. Even now, it was hard to decide if Claudia had been more lover than friend, or the other way around, during those frantic months after Margot's wedding. One thing for certain, however: she'd been absolutely the number one cook in *his* known Universe. Memories of her kitchen still made his mouth water.

Claudia, too, was gone from Brim's life—by his own choice. He had gradually stopped answering her messages when his fortunes began to sour in Avalon. Loss of her sparkling correspondence had been a high price to pay for his pride, but it seemed a lot better than letting her discover what a failure he'd become in civilian life.

He squandered a few moments more in reflection before he put his hands in his pockets and started off downhill, this time toward Atalanta's ancient waterfront district to look for work. Perhaps, he considered, some day he *might* still attempt to get in touch with her. But it wouldn't be until he had made a lot more of himself in this new, postwar environment than he'd been able to do so far.

In less than a metacycle of brisk walking, he found himself caught up in a half-familiar maze of shadowed streets and murky canals fronted by dilapidated warehouses built of age-darkened brick and stone. The still air was filled with arcane and familiar scents from a whole galaxy of commerce. Across a short expanse of cobblestones and glowing tram tubes stood the decrepit warehouse he'd formerly known by the fictitious name of Payless Starmotive Salvage. Now cold and tenantless, it had once been secret headquarters for one of the war's most brilliant intelligence coups against the League. Brim had obtained his Emperor's Cross on that mission. Now, the defunct old building somehow reminded him of himself.

He looked around him. If he were going to find work, he reasoned, this district seemed to be a perfect place to start. Even at an early metacycle, the byways were crowded with busy people who hurried along with purpose in their steps. Brim wondered what they all did. Most were dressed in what he remembered to be Atalantan working clothes: for the most part, loose, baggy trousers or full skirts with brightly tinted shirts and vests. Coats were either loose sack or sleeveless with high necks and narrow turnover collars, many paired with bright, multi-hued hats and vividly decorated guild aprons. A colorful, cheerful people, Atalantans, Brim remembered. He meant to become one of them as soon as possible. If nothing else, the CIGAs hadn't really taken hold of this war-torn town. People here understood the need for strength.

Clearly, he considered, scanning a new building that was going up a few blocks away, a lot of construction jobs went begging in Atalanta. They'd have to, even if the city's reconstruction were only proceeding half as fast as it appeared to be. But where to find one? *That* was the question. His travels had already taken him into three storefronts that looked for all the world as if they contained labor offices. Businesses like that tended to have the same look everywhere; in Avalon, Atalanta, or even Carescria. The trouble was, he could barely speak, much less read or write, the Halacian dialect natives used. And that had proved to be a tough obstacle indeed. Job interviews, he found, simply didn't work in sign language; he'd eventually discontinued each one, having accomplished nothing. He shook his head. If only he could bring himself to contact Claudia. She would help; he knew she would. But all he had left now was his pride, and he wasn't about to give that up, too.

During the next metacycles, he entered two more of the placement offices, with no better luck in them than he'd experienced in the others. Both times, he ended up back on the sidewalk feeling thoroughly frustrated—and even more hungry as morning wore into afternoon. Stopping beside a sidewalk shop to get his bearings, he sniffed the delicious aroma of freshly brewed cvceese' while his mouth began to water. It had been a long time since he'd put anything in his stomach.

Suddenly, he frowned and peered across the street. Directly opposite the shop was one of Atalanta's ubiquitous Gradygroat missions. Why hadn't he thought of them before? During the war, he'd had dealings with friars from all parts of the order, and he'd never met one of them who didn't speak at least some Avalonian. At the time, he'd given it little thought. As an officer in the Imperial Fleet, one made certain assumptions about language. He laughed at himself. He'd been getting just a bit too big for his breeches in that Fleet cloak, he mused, and filed the little revelation away for future reference. Such a small dose of comeuppance might prove valuable someday, if he ever managed to dig his way out of the hole in which his life had apparently come to rest.

Dodging across the busy street, he pushed open the door to the mission and stepped into what appeared to be a huge, round chamber. He smiled. Everything bore an uncanny resemblance to the colossal room in the Gradygroat's now-destroyed monastery, as well as to the orbiting space forts that had played such an important mission in the salvation of Atalanta.

In this little canal-side mission, however, it was all illusion, effected by clever use of holopanels. The floor appeared to contain the monastery's shining rings of "destruction," "resurrection," and "truth." A shaft of light from a lenslike "power" aperture beamed from the center of the ceiling to the center ring where a circular desk replaced the jeweled cone of the original. However, all but the latter—and its occupant—were holographic shams.

Inside the desk sat a rotund friar whose curly black beard covered most of his face. He had a great fleshy beak of a nose, somber, inquisitive eyes, and the look of a man who had experienced a great deal of the galaxy—good and bad. He was dressed in the long, crimson gown of a Gradgroat-Norchelite friar and clutched a steaming mug of cvceese', whose aroma nearly drove Brim up a wall. The man gave a genial nod and said something Brim could not understand at all.

"Does, ah . . . anybody here speak Avalonian, Father?" Brim asked hesitantly.

"I speak many languages, young man," the Friar answered this time in flawless Avalonian, the kind Brim had encountered only at the Imperial Court. "Welcome to the Juniper Street Mission. Father Amps at your service."

"Th-thank you, Father," Brim stumbled dumbly. He found it was difficult to stop staring at the mug.

"Ah, can I help you in any way," Amps asked after a few moments of silence. He smiled understandingly. "Perhaps a cup of cvceese?"

Brim swallowed hard. "I'd *love* one," he said, half embarrassed at how anxious his voice sounded. Presently, he was sipping a scalding hot mug of sticky-sweet cvceese'. Somehow, it brought back his days on the bridge of a warship, when he fairly lived on the stuff during his long metacycles at action stations. "Thanks, Father," he said quietly. "You can't know how good this tastes."

"Hmm. Perhaps I can," Amps said, his eyes peering momentarily into a distant time. "Once, in another life, I knew a great deal of hunger. How can I help you. Mister, ah . . . ?"

"My name's Brim, Father," the Carescrian answered. "Wilf Brim. And I'm trying to find work." He blurted out the words as though they'd been poisoning his system. "I need a job so I can eat—but I don't know enough Halacian to apply anywhere."

"I won't ask how you got to Atalanta," Amps said gently. "But I assume you haven't been here very long."

"A valid assumption," Brim admitted.

"When was the last time you ate?" Amps probed abruptly.

Brim shook his head. "I'm not looking for handouts, Father," he said quietly. "I'd rather earn my credits. The sooner I can do that, I'll be able to take care of the food situation myself."

"You didn't answer my question, young man. When was the last time you ate?"

"It's been a while," Brim admitted, "but that's not important. What I need is—"

"I understand," Amps interrupted firmly, "but you'll have an even harder time finding what you're looking for if you're thinking about food." He reached into the desk and came out with a carton of energy bars. "Eat a few of these, Wilf," he said. "After that, we'll see what we can do about finding a job agent who speaks Avalonian."

Brim started to protest, but the little man held up his hand.

"You can owe the order for whatever you eat," he chuckled. "I doubt if it will threaten the budget for this year—even with our new construction." Then his face took on a serious countenance. "It's all part of being a Norchelite friar," he said. "Some of us tend orbital forts, others preach, and still others, like me, assist their fellow creatures. All serve the order, each in his own way."

"But I'm not a Gradygr—" Brim protested, catching himself a little too late.

"I didn't for a moment think you *were* a Gradygroat," Amps said with a grin, imperturbably using Brim's slang for the Gradgroat-Norchelite Order. "Offhand, I'd guess you were once an officer of the Imperial Fleet and are presently out of work." He grinned. "Were I to speculate further, I'd also probably guess that you jumped ship after S.S. *Prosperous* made landfall yesterday evening."

Brim felt a wave of apprehension grip his chest. Had he just walked into an IGL trap? He tensed and his eyes darted toward the exit.

"Calm yourself, m'boy," Amps said with a chuckle. "If I were in cahoots with IGL, you'd *already* be on your way back to the ship. Now sit yourself on the counter here and put away a couple of those energy bars. While you're doing that, I'll see if I can't find someone who can get you a job. If you don't mind construction, you'll have no trouble finding a job in *this* city."

Brim looked the friar in the eye and decided he might as well trust him. "I'll work at damned near any kind of construction job, Father," he said, meaning every word.

When Brim was most of the way through his third energy bar, Amps looked up and chuckled. "You *were* hungry, weren't you, Wilf?"

"Not anymore, Father," Brim answered, grinning with his mouth still half full.

"Good," Amps laughed. "Put several more of those bars in your pocket and then look at this," he directed, tilting his display to face outward. "The agent you want to see has a storefront about ten c'lenyts from here, on the other side of City Mount Hill. I'll lend you fare for the interurban. You can return it at any alms box—when you're feeling a little more flush than today." Then he chuckled. "We'll just call ourselves even on the energy bars, though," he added. "It gets pretty hot around here in the summer, and you can imagine what *they'd* be like, melted in an alms box."

Within two metacycles, Brim was talking to a burly clerk dressed in a green checked shirt and light tan trousers made of something that looked a lot like canvas. His reddish hair was long and tied at the nape of his neck by a small black ribbon. He had a strong chin, a short, bulbous nose, bushy ginger eyebrows, and intense, watery green eyes that didn't let go once they fastened onto you. A sign on his desk announced, ARGYLE G. BEAVERTON, FACTOR.

"What sort of work do you do, Brim—normally, I mean?" Beaverton asked in a gruff voice.

Brim shrugged hopelessly. "I'm a Helmsman," he said.

"Hmm," Beaverton quipped with mock deliberation, "we haven't *quite* finished our entry for the Mitchell Trophy Race yet, but when we do, we'll be sure to look you up."

"Couldn't ask for more than that," Brim returned wryly. It was clear that there was no escaping Mitchell's xaxtdamned race or its awful reminder of Margot's pregnancy and his failure as a man. Grimly he forced himself back to the present. "Do you suppose somebody out there might have something *else* for me to do?" he asked, managing a smile of sorts.

The man consulted his terminal. "Well," he declared with a chuckle, "we've got more construction jobs than we can fill in a million years. Ever drive a grav loader, for instance? I could place a hundred loader jockeys this morning."

Brim felt his spirits soar. "You bet," he said "I put in a couple of years driving those things when I was a kid. Where do I sign up?"

Beaverton bit his lip. "I may have put that the wrong way," he admitted with a frown. "What I meant to ask was, do you have a *license* to operate a grav loader?"

"A license?" Brim asked. "We never needed a license back home."

"Unfortunately," the man said, "you need one *here*. It's all part of the guild system, and rigidly enforced."

"A guild system," Brim mused. "Well, I guess grav loaders are out, then."

"Plenty more jobs where that one came from," Beaverton assured him. "Ever do any work with synthetic roof tiles?"

"No. Afraid not."

"Surveying?"

"Um, no."

"Woodworking? Cabinetry?"

"A little, but . . ."

"Glazing?"

"No."

"Hmm. How about gardening?"

"Well . . ."

"Yeah, I understand. You *are* a little shy on experience, I guess."

"I can drive just about any kind of rig."

"Not without a guild license, you can't. And guilds take a residency of at least a year. When I talked to Friar Amps, I sort of got the idea you hadn't been here too long."

"I haven't," Brim admitted.

"Hmm . . ." Suddenly, Beaverton snapped his fingers. "I'll just bet you'd be good with one of those particle beam axes," he exclaimed. "You know, the open grid cages about the size of an oil drum with handles on the side and top—got a big cathode injector filament inside, firing through a tube of focusing coils. They use 'em to cut foundations out of rock where there isn't a lot of working room—instead of blasting."

Brim frowned. He wasn't very familiar with heavy construction equipment, but every little boy who had grown up anywhere near an excavation knew that particle beam axes could make more noise than a supernova at a hundred irals. "Yeah," he said, searching his memory. "I think they're powered from some sort of portable beatron—on a gravity sled, aren't they?"

"You've got it—that thick connecting hose is really the power transmission line." Beaverton looked up from the display. "Dirtiest, hardest, noisiest job you can get. Guilds won't have anything to do with them—too damned dangerous. But the pay's right, if you can stand the dust and the noise—*and* you don't kill yourself."

"The pay's good?"

"It's gotta be," Beaverton said. "Otherwise, they couldn't get anybody to run one. Not with all the other jobs around."

"I'll take it," Brim said on a sudden hunch. "Sounds like just what I'm looking for."

* * *

Brim stood shirtless beneath the late afternoon sun, mopping sweat from his brow with a great red handkerchief. (He now carried one wherever he went.) Overhead, cries from angry seabirds interspersed with the din of heavy construction machinery. His present building site was close by Grand Harbor, not far from the big Imperial Fleet base. He could often smell the clean odor of the sea, along with a lot of construction dust. On the job, his teeth always felt gritty.

Nearby, surveyors dressed in the bright green and yellow colors of their guild were busily verifying the corner he had just melted in solid rock for the foundation of a government office building. Not a bad job of it, he judged, in spite of the cramped space. Corners were tough; they took a delicate touch—and this one especially, because of the irregular shape the building would take when it went up.

Brim smiled to himself as he rested, just a little smugly perhaps. The construction company had called him specially for the job. Operating the bulky machine turned out to be elementary for someone accustomed to aiming objects the size of a starship, and he'd quickly established himself as the best beam axe operator in the area. In nearly five months of arduous work, he'd found a permanent place to live, was making good credits —for a sweat laborer—and was back to the superb physical shape he'd maintained while he was an officer in the Fleet. He even managed a small weekly offering in one of the the ten-million-odd alms boxes the Gradygroats maintained throughout the city.

Abruptly he turned his eyes skyward to watch an ebony destroyer thunder up from the bay and bank steeply over the construction site, its many turrets and antennas silhouetted against the bright blue sky. The ship was still low enough when it passed overhead that he could see its Helmsman through the bridge Hyperscreens. His breath caught while the ground shook to the beat of its mighty gravs, and he watched with enchantment until it had flown out of sight. Clearly, he might be out of the starship business, but the business was far from being out of him.

Above him, at the edge of the excavation, a colorfully dressed lunchtime crowd had gathered to watch. From the nearby Fleet base, he guessed. He'd gotten used to audiences; construction seemed to naturally draw people's attention.

"Corner seems perfect, as usual," the Lead Surveyor announced presently, looking up from his instrument. "You can start the next one anytime you want."

Brim nodded and hoisted the beam axe to his shoulder. "Thanks," he acknowledged with a wink. "See you back here in about a metacycle," he said. He had just started to guide the beatron's gravity sled to his next marked corner, across the excavation site, when he thought he heard someone calling his name.

"Wilf! Wilf Brim!"

Startled, he turned and peered up into the crowd. Hardly anyone knew him in Atalanta, except for Claudia Valemont.

He bit his lip. There she was—in a short, yellow pelisse that accentuated her upthrust breasts, tiny waist, and elegant legs. She was waving to him from behind a dusty crystal viewers' railing, a small figure with long brown hair that flowed almost to her waist. For a split click, it was almost as if she were there beside him. A rush of emotions gripped his chest like a great fist.

"Wilf? Is that you?" she called, breaking into a smile.

Suddenly angry with himself, he stiffened. He'd been careless. Working this close to the huge Fleet base, he was bound to run into her. Ears burning with shame, he quickly turned away, as if he'd encountered a stranger. Then he hoisted the axe so it hid his face and slinked off across the excavation, tugging the beatron by its cable. That magnificent woman, a prominent civilian manager at the Fleet base, had loved him when he was Principal Helmsman of a light cruiser in the Imperial Fleet. What would she think of him now?

As soon as he reached the site of his next corner, he cranked up the beatron until its shrieking howl insured that he'd hear no more of Claudia's voice. Then he lost himself in the strenuous act of carving rock. He operated the heavy machine without a break, working until he was exhausted. But when he released the trigger, she had gone.

He nearly killed himself to complete the remainder of the foundation by day's end, vowing that he would accept no more assignments this near to the base. So far as he was concerned,

Wilf Brim was dead—temporarily, perhaps, but dead all the same. He was determined to avoid everyone from his former life until he'd restored at least some of his lost prestige.

With the final corner inspected and approved, Brim powered off the beatron, coiled its transmission cable, then secured the axe to brackets on the gravity sled and pushed everything to the lorry exit for transportation to his next contract.

He nodded to himself. *Contracting* for jobs—that was by far the best part of his new existence. He'd never before worked as an independent, without an immediate boss. Now, people sought him out, and he made job arrangements according to his own best advantage, not his employer's. It was a good existence, and with bonuses he actually earned a bit more than he had as a Helmsman.

After a last check of the rented axe and beatron, he pulled on his work shirt, then strode across the dusty excavation toward a personnel gate and the ancient gravcycle he'd purchased earlier that month. It was the first vehicle he'd personally owned in his thirty-eight years, and he found he was quite proud of it—especially the oversized, twin-beam generator that one of its many former owners had installed. He took a deep breath of sea air, anxious to be home. He was bone-tired this afternoon. A shower would feel wonderful.

As he walked, he couldn't drive Claudia's face from his thoughts. Over the years, he'd forgotten how beautiful she really was—a wartime mistake he made nearly every time they were separated a week or more. It seemed that he simply wasn't willing to believe his own memory. He laughed. Someday, he promised himself, once he'd managed to recoup some of his fortune, he was going to get in touch with her again.

He was hardly out of the gate when Claudia appeared from between two equipment buildings, threw her arms around his neck, and planted a long, hard kiss directly on his mouth. "A lot of people have been looking for you, Wilf Brim," she said breathlessly when they both came up for air.

Caught completely by surprise, Brim could only stammer. "I-I d-didn't know anybody would—"

"Gorksroar," she said with a cross look in her brown eyes, then immediately smothered his lips again.

This time, Brim folded her in his arms and kissed back until they were both a little breathless.

When they were finished, she gently pulled away and looked at him for a long time in silence. "Wilf," she whispered at last, a worried look on her face, "why didn't you?..." Then she stopped in midsentence and shook her head. "I already know," she sighed in resignation, "because you're Wilf Brim, that's why." Presently, she placed her hands on his cheeks, drew him to her lips, and they kissed again for a long time. "Wilf Brim," she said after a time as she gently extracted herself from his embrace, "I am beginning to have some very familiar stirrings, where I shouldn't."

For a moment, Brim thought he might be having some too. And he'd managed to purge any vestige of those thoughts from his mind since his last night with Margot. Panic beset him for a moment when he began speculating what Claudia would do if she discovered that he couldn't. He shuddered. He'd rather die than have that happen again. He began to recklessly conjure some justification for not going home with her when her words started to penetrate his panic.

"... I'm married now, and I don't think I ought to ..."

"You're *what*?" he interrupted.

"Wilf, listen to me. I really *would* invite you home so we could talk, but I'm *married* now. And those few kisses are all I need to know that, well, things clearly haven't changed with the way I feel about you, and..." She shrugged, and raised her hands palms up. "It just wouldn't be fair to him—or you." Then she frowned and looked down at her tiny feet. "—or *me*," she added in a low voice.

Brim's face burned with embarrassment. He was both relieved and hurt by the news, although he had to admit it to himself that he was a lot more hurt than anything else. Not that he'd ever had her all to himself, or anything even approaching that. She'd maintained her considerable male following throughout their brief relationship, but at least he'd always considered himself one of the *special* ones. He took a deep breath. "Well, ah, congratulations, Claudia," he said, hoping against hope the only emotion on his face was one of delight. "Do I know him?"

"You met him one night," she said softly. "Remember Nesterio's Racotzian Cabaret?" she asked. "We went there the first evening we spent together—and talked almost the whole night."

Brim nodded. "Of course I remember," he said, harking back to the war years. "It was after a wardroom party aboard a heavy cruiser. . . ." He closed his eyes. "I.F.S. *Intransigent*," he said, snapping his fingers. "And it was one of the most unforgettable evenings I have ever spent." It was no exaggeration.

She lowered her eyes and made a peculiar, almost sad, little smile. "Me too," she whispered.

"Your husband," Brim reminded her, "—he was there?"

"Who?" Claudia asked, pulling herself back from somewhere a long distance away.

"The guy you married," Brim prompted gently, taking her hand in spite of himself. "You said I'd met him at Nesterio's."

Claudia gave him a little laugh. "Oh, yes," she answered, allowing her hand to remain for a moment before she withdrew it, "you did. I married Nesterio."

Brim nodded, somehow not surprised. "Quite a guy," he said equivocally. "He saved your life, or something, didn't he? After a raid, I think."

"That's right," Claudia replied, dropping her eyes. "He saved my life. . . ."

And then, suddenly, there was nothing more that seemed safe to talk about.

Following a long, embarrassed interval, Claudia looked into Brim's face again. "I must be going, Wilf," she said. "But, well, we've got to stay friends. Give me your address. After I get my head in order again, I'll be in touch."

Brim suddenly froze. How to say he couldn't bear to see her again, that he was ashamed he was no longer a Helmsman? In a flash, it came to him. It wasn't necessary! She didn't seem to *care* what he did. The subject had never even come up; he himself had been too busy to think about it. Before he quite knew what he was doing, he'd blabbed out his address. Then, in clicks she was on her way. This time, however, he got no kiss.

He watched her skimmer careen around a corner, and she was gone. Clearly she was still operating the same decrepit little vehicle she'd used all through the war. He wondered how either of them had survived her driving. Savoring the fresh memory of that stunning face, he stood for a moment in silence, wondering . . . What if he'd persisted in his original resolve to give up Margot shortly after she married? Would he and Claudia be together now?

He stopped pursuing that train of thought immediately. One chooses one's path he affirmed, climbing into the gravcycle's worn saddle, then one follows that path and never looks back.

Little more than a week later, Brim strode from his tiny apartment and picked his way through Atalanta's fragrant pre-dawn darkness to his gravcycle. It was soaked with a dull glaze of dew, and he carefully wiped its seat with his huge red handkerchief. In doing so, he accidentally swiped loose a folded sheet of plastic that someone had wedged between the machine's tiller and readout panel. He shook his head. Another advertisement. Hardly a morning went by that there weren't a few stuck somewhere on the powerful little machine. Imagine how many he'd accumulate if he were driving something the size of a limousine!

As usual, the gravity mechanism was difficult to start, and when finally it did catch, refused to maintain any kind of steady output, although it did manage to startle a large rothcat that was stalking a moth nearby. The little machine grumbled and hiccuped uncomfortably while Brim dismounted and hunkered down to peer through a tiny porthole in the ion chamber. The two plasma beams were completely out of sync, as usual. He chuckled and shook his head wryly. The weather must have changed again; it didn't take much to throw the whole thing out of kilter. He reached inside his saddlebags, retrieved a pair of torquing tools, and, inserting them almost by feel, delicately twisted first the left, then the right until . . . *there*, the beams matched perfectly. But he didn't really need to see them at that point; he could hear the results. The dyspeptic belching had already tapered off into a silken growl that would have pleased even a Sodeskayan Drive engineer. Damned fine little machine, he thought happily—and fast as it was sweet.

As he drew the torquers from their sockets, his left hand brushed a heated cooling fin. Swearing, he dropped the tool. It landed squarely on the advertisement, which, close up, didn't look like an advertisement at all. No pictures, no headlines, simply a small folded sheet of plastic with . . . He switched on the cycle's headlamp. There were initials on the outside: CVN. CVN? Quizzically breaking the seal, he unfolded the sheet:

Wilf:

We have an opening here at the Fleet base that seems more suited to your talents than "axe operator," even *though you do* seem to have gained quite a reputation lately in the construction trades—I've checked. The job title is "Diagnostic Helmsman," and it calls for someone who can fly nearly anything that comes in for repairs. It's not a high position, but the work's steady. And it's a start.

If you think you might be interested, come to the main entrance tunnel of our new Headquarters building tomorrow at the beginning of Morning watch. Before you reach the leftmost turnstile, you'll see a door marked "Duty Crews, Base Operations." Use the "Visitors" button and give your name. Someone will be expecting you.

Claudia Valemont-Nesterio

Brim felt a surge of mortification crimp his gut. Just as he'd suspected! He was now an object of her pity. He squeezed his eyes shut in humiliation. Why in all the Universe had he given out his xaxtdamned address? Crumpling the note into a ball, he tossed it into one of his faded saddlebags and gunned the grav, opening its verniers before he even mounted. Then, bitterly forcing all thoughts of Claudia and her note from his mind, he thundered off at high speed toward the day's construction site. Better to find any kind of work than accept charity. Especially from a former lover.

Early on, however, he discovered that the possibility of a flying job wasn't something he could brush aside so easily, even when his mind ought to have been elsewhere. Nearly half a Standard year had passed since he'd laid hands on a starship's controls, and almost four times that since he'd flown anything that was in any decent state of repair. If only he'd been able to locate Claudia's worse-than-damned offer for himself. . . .

"Watch it, Brim!" someone bellowed in a panicky voice.

"You're cuttin' too far off the base line, for xax' sake. *Look out!*"

Blasted from his reverie, Brim released the trigger just before his bucking machine mowed down a whole set of foundation girders. "G-got away from me for a click," he said, his face burning with shame. He'd *never* done that before.

"Hey, Brim," a lanky, rumpled supervisor in scarlet shirt and blue overalls called from a nearby platform, "you all right?" The man's baggy eyes were mournful, he had a fat, bulbous nose, and one upper tooth was missing, square in the center of his mouth.

"Yeah," Brim assured him, "I'm all right. I just, uh, turned my ankle on a rock. See?" He kicked a small rock close to his foot.

"All right," the supervisor allowed, dubiously. He didn't buy the rock pretext any more than Brim expected. "You be damned careful from now on," he added. "That axe of yours coulda' took down the whole framework—and you'd have worked the rest of your life to pay us back for all that col-steel. Unnerstand?"

"Understand," Brim said penitently, "—it won't happen again, believe me."

Throughout the remainder of the morning, Brim concentrated on the axe as if existence itself depended on it. But even that didn't prevent him from dreaming about the Helmsman's job all during his lunch break and every click in which he wasn't actually using the axe to cut. The more he thought about the job, the more he wanted it, especially since the sky seemed to be perfectly saturated that day with every kind of flying vehicle known to intragalactic civilization.

His resolve crumpled before he even finished the day's work. Midway through the afternoon, he mopped his brow with the red handkerchief and ambled over to the supervisor's platform. "I won't be able to make it tomorrow," he called through the open door.

"Whadda' you mean you won't make it tomorrow?" the supervisor demanded angrily.

"Just what I said," Brim stated evenly. "I've got personal business."

"Who the xaxt's going to finish this hole here? There's a lot more work to go—and none of it's spec'ed for anybody that qualifies at less than Master Axeman. How'm I gonna get somebody like that on *this* kind of notice?"

Brim nodded. The man was right—contracting came with certain obligations. He took a deep breath. "You won't have to get somebody," he promised. "I'll knock it off myself—tonight —before I go home."

"Voot's beard, Brim, you'll xaxtdamn well knock *yourself* off, too. Those axes are tough! I've seen 'em wipe out bigger men than you in just a morning."

"I'll live," Brim returned quietly.

"Maybe," the supervisor said. "But who's gonna inspect your work?"

"Who needs to?" Brim asked. "You ever see me fail a cut?"

"Well you sure as Zorkt weren't all that grand-lookin' when you damn near took down the framework a while back," the supervisor retorted. "Besides, rules is rules, ya know—and *my* rules calls for inspections."

"Hey, it's all the same to me," Brim answered. "If you'd rather inspect than have me finish this foundation, suit yourself. I doubt if I'll have a hard time finding other places looking for a good axeman."

"Yeah, well . . ." The man frowned and scratched his head through gray, stringy hair. Clearly, Brim had scored a point. He turned to a weather-beaten construction manager bent over a nearby console, clearly deep in concentration. "Whadda you think?" he demanded.

"Let him finish," the old man replied without looking up. "He'll be all right, believe me."

The supervisor's eyebrows raised for a moment, and he waited for a justification—which he didn't get. "All right," he conceded after an embarrassing pause, "—ah, go ahead and finish the job. But just you keep in mind that if the work ain't perfect I won't pay. Got that?"

Brim laughed. "I got that," he said evenly. Striding back to his station in Hador's pitiless afternoon brilliance, he hoisted the big machine to his shoulder, braced himself, and squeezed the triggers. It was going to be a long, hot work day.

CHAPTER 3

Old Friends

The following morning, Brim parked his gravcycle in the visitors' lot outside Base Headquarters, and grimaced. The monstrous new building was four times the size of its predecessor and incalculably more elaborate. For a moment, he wondered how many fine warships had been scrapped to pay for the colossal glass structure. Unfortunately, Gradygroats alone seemed to know how to make buildings into weapons, and even they'd managed that only once.

Then he shook his head. Military matters were no concern of his. In Avalon's new CIGA-riddled Admiralty, it seemed that the perception of strength was far more important than the real thing. Every day, the Fleet got weaker while the League got more bold. Only the week before, Zoguard Grobermann, the League's Minister of State, had issued a trumped-up warning to Fluvanna, a tiny but strategically critical domain astride the Straits of Remik. Along with Rogan LaKarn's Torond, Fluvanna provided most of the Empire's supply of celecoid quartz kernels from which Drive crystals were grown.

Taking a deep breath, he joined a colorful, noisy throng of Halacian civilians streaming through the main entrance tunnel. Just before he reached the guards at their turnstiles, he jostled his way left and stopped at a door marked with a small plaque that read, DUTY CREWS, BASE OPERATIONS.

Except for the plaque, the door's surface was otherwise featureless. However, a button marked VISITORS and a scanner lens were set into the right-hand frame at about eye level. Brim reached out to press the button, the scanner lens was clearly for flight crew members only. But before he could do it, he found himself stepping aside, deeply affected by a sudden onslaught of anxiety.

Or was it embarrassment?

His head was in turmoil; it *couldn't* be anxiety. He still considered himself to be as good a Helmsman as any: better than most, truth to tell. It had to be embarrassment, pure and simple. He didn't belong in flight crews any more. He might have made himself into one of the city's best beam axe operators, a considerable accomplishment in construction circles. But on the other side of that door, his axemanship wouldn't even rate a cup of cvceese'. Biting his lip, he tried to get a grip on himself while he stared at the entry button.

"I say—were you going in?" a cultured, masculine voice asked. At the same time, a long index finger touched the glowing scanner window and the door started to swing on silent hinges.

Brim jumped, startled from his reverie. "Er, y-yes I was," he stammered, abruptly focusing on a pair of blue eyes that sparkled with good-natured humor, a grand promontory for a nose, and the droll, confident sort of smile that fairly shouted wealth. The man was tall, blond, and, Brim judged, about the same age as himself. He was wearing the distinctive blue cape of an Imperial Fleet officer with the device of a Lieutenant Commander on its left collar just above his Helmsman's insignia. He also wore the discreet red-on-green insignia of the Imperial High-Speed Starflight Team, quite a distinction in anybody's book. The uniform sent a twinge of emotion through Brim's gut. He'd forgotten how much he missed his own uniform and the feeling of belonging it provided.

"Right ho," the Commander returned with a grin. "Then I have just done both of us a favor." He motioned Brim through the door and followed him inside. "I say," he drawled presently, "I don't believe I've seen you around the ready room before. Was there someone you were meeting here perhaps?"

"That's what I'm led to understand," Brim replied. "But I don't know who it is—someone here was supposed to be looking for *me*." He peered around the crowded room. It looked like any of the thousand-odd ready rooms he'd encountered during his wartime travels: a little on the dingy side already and cluttered with awkward furniture. Here and there, knots of people were drinking mugs of cvceese' or viewing newsframes; many were playing cre'el, a game of chance that Brim never had found time to master. Situation boards covered one whole wall, updating their brilliant colors in what appeared to be real time.

"Oh, I see," the Commander said doubtfully, turning to hang his Fleet cloak on a nearby rack. Beneath, his uniform was clearly custom made. "Ah, on business, perhaps?" he asked with a frown.

Brim felt his face flush. "I'm sorry," he said. "I suppose you *are* wondering what I'm doing here." He laughed in spite of his embarrassment. "My name's Wilf Brim. I'm applying for a civilian Helmsman's position I understand is open at the base here."

"Ah, so you're a Helmsman, too," the Commander exclaimed, extending his hand. "Well, I'm glad to meet you. Tobias Moulding's my name—and no tired jokes, please. Call me Toby for short." He frowned. "You were with the Fleet yourself at one time, I expect?"

"A thousand years ago," Brim said, gripping the other's hand.

"It's a bad thing the CIGAs have done at the Admiralty," Moulding said with a frown. "But then I'm sure nobody has to tell you about *that*." He took a deep breath. "Certainly Minister Grobermann had the situation firmly in mind when he sent his threatening message to Fluvanna. Not much we could do without Drive crystals."

Brim only shrugged. "I don't keep up with the League much anymore," he said. "I'm simply anxious to get behind a helm again."

"Well, I hope you will," Moulding said. "But first, we'll need to find out who it is you should report to." He looked around the room. "I say, chaps," he called out. "This man's name is Brim and he's here to see somebody about one of the civilian Helmsman's positions. Who's doing the checks this morning?"

Presently, one of the cre'el players—this one also a Lieutenant Commander—looked up from his game. "Tell him I'll be with him when I finish this tomer, and not before," he said, clearly resenting the disturbance.

Moulding looked at Brim and raised an eyebrow. "That's Cravinn Townsend," he observed with a look of embarrassment. "Friendly sort, isn't he?"

Brim shrugged wryly. "I guess I can't blame him—I never had much truck with civilian fluff merchants either," he said, remembering only too well his attitude toward nonmilitary workers when *he* was a member of the Fleet. Things that went around had a way of coming around, he filed that away for a better future, too.

"Big of you," Moulding said, looking at him quizzically. "I'm not sure I'd have reacted in the same way."

"You're not looking for a job, either," Brim chuckled. Then he spied the ubiquitous cvceese' brewer, steaming away in a corner. "Come on," he said, "If you've time, I'll buy us both a mug." Inside he laughed—he'd become a big spender again! It hadn't been so long ago that he'd had to beg for one at a Norchelite mission.

"Seems fair," Moulding said, striding to the great brass machine that was leaking steam at any number of complex pipe joints. "I open the door; you buy cvceese'."

Brim threw a credit in a battered tin, then poured a mugful and stood in silence for a moment, sipping the sticky-sweet liquid that threatened to permanently scald his throat. No Logish Meem ever tasted so good as cvceese' first thing in the morning. Somehow it went together with ready rooms as naturally as clear sky goes with clean, fresh air. He smiled to himself. Even if he didn't have a uniform, by Universe, he *did* belong here.

Abruptly, Townsend let out an oath, pushed himself back from the table, and sauntered across to Moulding with a sour look on his face. He was tall and loose-fitted in a sloppy way with a round, flat countenance, sneering eyes, and a manner that suggested arrogance in ample quantities—the way of a small-minded person who had managed to far outstrip his own competence. Significantly, not a single battle star adorned his cuff. The man had never seen combat, but he did wear a showy gold CIGA ring on his finger. "This is Brim?" he demanded with a disparaging thumb and a sneer of disdain.

"That's who he says he is," Moulding answered with a frown. "But I suppose you might just check with him personally, what?" He made a little bow. "Mr. Brim, may I present Lieutenant Commander Cravinn Townsend, Imperial Fleet?"

"Glad to meet you," Brim offered evenly, extending his hand.

Townsend never acknowledged Brim's gesture. "I don't suppose you have anything like a space suit, do you?" he asked. It was more of a statement than a question.

"No," Brim admitted. "I'm afraid I'll have to check one out." He'd left all his belongings behind in Avalon.

"Wonderful," Townsend spat. "You must really know somebody important around here." He glanced at Moulding. "We'll probably have to furnish his underwear as well. Did you know that this clod is also a Carescrian?"

Moulding's straw-colored eyebrows rose slightly and he turned to look at Brim with curiosity. "I say," he remarked, "a *Carescrian*." Then he nodded. "I think I may have even heard of you, Wilf. Had quite a lot to do with the battle for Atalanta, didn't you?"

"A little," Brim said, "but then, so did a lot of people."

"Yes, I thought so," Moulding said, a little smile of interest forming on his lips. He turned to Townsend. "I shall take it upon myself to show him where one gets a temporary issue of space togs," he said. "What are you two scheduled to fly this morning?"

"A T-twenty-nine."

Moulding nodded. "Figured," he said. "Hot little beast, what?"

"Yeah," Townsend laughed, turning his face from Brim. He whispered something behind his hand that ended with, "and I'm *just* the one to do it."

"I see," Moulding said skeptically. "Well, I shall bring the fellow to the ready line in about . . ." he checked his timepiece, "say three-quarters of a metacycle. All right?"

"Make it a metacycle," Townsend said, starting for the cre'el table he had abandoned. "I've got some unfinished business over here." Then he laughed suggestively over his shoulder. "You'll want to be at the ready line to watch," he said to Moulding.

"Oh, I will indeed be there to watch," Moulding assured him in a droll voice. "In fact," he added quietly, almost to himself, "I don't think I'd miss it for half of Avalon."

Brim took everything in. Except for Moulding, it sounded like the Helmsmen's Academy all over again. His wealthy classmates as well as his instructors had done everything in their power to make his life difficult, to make him quit. And they had failed. Townsend was no different; he would fail too.

"Well, Wilf?" Moulding asked, looking Brim in the face. "I can't imagine you missed his bloody intentions, so you know full well what to expect. Shall we still go check out some flying togs?"

Brim nodded grimly. "I don't think I'd miss it for half of Avalon either," he replied. "Too xaxtdamned many CIGAs there for my liking."

Little less than a metacycle later, the two men stood at the ready line beside a stubby little T-29G, two-seat advanced trainer of the Imperial Fleet for more than fifteen Standard years. Barely sixty-four irals in length, it was equipped with a powerful R-1820-86 spin-gravitron generator that provided astonishing acceleration. But with no Drive-crystal system, it was limited to HypoSpeed velocities. Brim had just finished an external walkaround; as he expected, it was in excellent repair as it bobbed in the light breeze above a portable gravity pad. A small puddle of coolant had dripped from the spin grav overnight, but as Brim well knew, when no coolant was leaking from an R-1820, there was probably none in the cooling chambers and some had better be added immediately. He stood in his borrowed space suit and felt a warm breeze from the bay on his face. He could hear the rumble of gravs bellowing from the run-up area and the other noises that came from a busy spaceport. A thrill teased his spine—nothing else in the Universe could match this. Spaceflight—the stars! He took a deep breath. It didn't matter who owned the space suit—he *belonged* here.

"Professional preflight job," Moulding observed, breaking into Brim's daydream. "The ship meets your approval, does she?" he added, while he brushed a stray wisp of yellow hair from his eyes.

Brim laughed. "Yeah," he said, unable to stifle a grin of pleasure. "I wish brother Townsend would hurry. It's been a while since I had my hands on a set of controls where everything works."

"Hmm," Moulding mused. "Yes, well, look here. That chap's been known to be *quite* late at times." He rubbed his chin, then thumped the little spacecraft's hull affectionately with his fist. "Tell you what," he said. "I can certainly take responsibility for letting you into the cockpit. Why don't you just pull the boarding ladder up and get started." Then he grinned roguishly. "Perhaps," he added, "if Townsend doesn't show up, I'll throw on some space togs, and you can take me up for a spin."

Brim made a mock salute. "Sounds like a plan to me," he said, extending the little ship's boarding ladder. In short order he unlocked the front canopy, pushed it aside, then settled into the snug front cockpit, virtually surrounded on three sides by an array of readouts and controls that had been familiar since his days in The Academy. He shut his eyes while the odors of the ship transported him to another life. Plastic, lubricating oils, logics and sealants—all intermixed with the spicy odors of organic insulating compounds. And *polish*: military vehicles always reeked of polish, no matter what their function. This T-29 was no exception.

For the next few cycles, Brim busied himself checking circuit breakers, valves, and switches. Then he preset the readout panels and peered out into the parking area—still no Townsend. He checked the energy choke: fully closed. Inverters: off. Next he punched all the circuit breakers in. Finally, he stood on the seat and again peered off toward the locker room, shading his eyes from Hador's glare. Townsend was still nowhere in sight. Shrugging, he slid into the seat again, and held his hand in the air. "Spinning up," he called down to Moulding.

Moulding quickly stepped back from the gravity pad. "Right ho, old chap!" he exclaimed. "Go to it!"

Brim switched on the spin-grav master, slid the power switch forward to ACTIVATE while he counted three clicks, then returned it to ENERGY ON and watched the grav panel display ENERGIZED. With the plasma thus set, he advanced the thrust control halfway off between OFF and MINIMUM, then hit both RUN and ENERGY BOOST in unison; the R-1820 whined and began to spin. He glanced at the interruptor. It began strobing almost immediately—an excellent ship, he considered, while a mindless grin of delight spread across his face.

Eight strobes...nine strobes...ten. Brim mashed START

and the spin grav fired thunderously, shaking the little ship's spaceframe with a jarring rhythm while he fed in delicate thrust-control and plasma-form motions to take the machine from a few random zaps to a point where all eighteen ion chambers were sparking on cue. Moments later, the interruptor steadied and the noise and throbbing died to a velvety purr. "Look's like she wants to fly," he shouted.

"I do, too!" Moulding shouted back. "I shall be back before you finish your preflight checklist." He started for the center at a run, but never got much past the gravity pad before Townsend pulled up in an open skimmer, his flabby face red with anger.

"Who said you could start that ship?" he shouted at Brim. "Who even gave you permission to board? Xaxtdamned Carescrian imbecile—I'll teach you to—"

Moulding grabbed the man's arm before he could reach the boarding ladder. He was smaller than Townsend, but the look in his eyes brooked no nonsense. "*I* gave him permission," he growled.

Townsend stopped abruptly, then took a step back. "Oh," he said, looking down at Moulding's hand. "I see."

"That's a good chap," Moulding said, releasing his grip with deliberate slowness. But the steely look in his eyes remained. "I'm counting on you to provide Mr. Brim with an impartial check ride, old boy. Don't let me down."

Townsend rubbed his forearm and scowled. "Oh, he'll get a ride, Moulding. One he won't forget."

"That may well be so," Moulding agreed, then glanced up and met Brim's eyes for a moment. He winked, then looked back at Townsend with a little smile on his face. "But then," he added, "unless I miss my guess, Townsend, so will you."

Within fifteen cycles, Brim had completed the ship's preflight checks, while Townsend silently haunted the rear cockpit like a wraith. As whining electric motors drew the canopy shut, he could see that Moulding had taken up a position off the starboard forequarter, and was standing with his hands behind his back, cape blowing in the breeze. "Ship's ready for internal gravity, Commander," he reported on the intercom.

"Well, switch it, then. Don't tell me about it," Townsend sniffed. "After that, you may taxi out to the takeoff area. I've filed a flight plan. And be careful, mind you. These are touchy ships."

"Aye, Commander," Brim said between clenched teeth. He pulled on his helmet, then called the tower for clearance and switched to internal gravity. While the little ship lifted from the gravity pad and hovered on its own, he endured a brief moment of nausea that tied his stomach in knots. Finally, he got his clearance, locked the steering engine into taxi mode, and slid the thrust control into run-up position. At his wave, a Crew Chief dressed in bright yellow coveralls shut off the optical moorings, and the T-29 moved off the gravity pad. Moulding grinned as they taxied past and held his thumb up in the universal sign of good luck.

"You'll need it, Carescrian," Townsend laughed archly over the intercom.

Brim kept his silence. While the spacecraft rolled out, he made a final panel check and selected the Stability Augmentation function on the navigation board. Within a few clicks, a white star illuminated on the mode selector, indicating that the ship had located and was tracking at least three stars in its pre-programmed catalog. If Townsend were as sloppy a Helmsman as promised to be, the system might save both their lives. At the run-up area beside the bay, he waited for takeoff clearance while he spun the R-1820 through military power and completed his takeoff checkout list. Then he taxied out over the water to the departure vector. Ahead, a solid ruby light flashed out of the bright distance. "Your ship," he announced to Townsend. Somehow, in the last few cycles, the morning had become a lot better, in spite of the blockhead riding aft.

Townsend advanced the energy choke to military power but held in place for a few moments to let the plasma build. Then he released the gravity brakes and the T-29 began to dash across the water, gaining speed with each moment.

After about fourteen clicks, Brim began to frown. They had plenty of takeoff velocity now—why weren't they lifting? He checked the readouts as their speed increased. Everything looked normal. Glancing at the flight systems panel, he started to scan for a malfunction when suddenly Townsend pitched the nose up violently and the little ship began to climb like the old-fashioned chemical rockets he'd seen in school. A split click later, the T-29 started to roll around its forward axis as if it were drilling a hole in the sky. Biting his lip, Brim grabbed the seat on either side of him to keep his hands from the controls.

Soon they were nearly fifty thousand irals up, but the rolling climb continued unabated. Was the ship malfunctioning or was Townsend merely showing off? Brim decided to wait things out for another few clicks and braced himself for anything that might transpire.

An instant later, the T-29 whipped around in a wild yaw and headed back toward the surface. But an abrupt decrease in power told Brim all he needed to know about their wild maneuvering. Townsend was still in control, and whatever game the arrogant numskull was trying to play, it was clear he actually thought that he could frighten a combat Helmsman by a little stunt flying. Taking a deep breath, Brim settled back in his recliner, relaxing while the little ship's spaceframe creaked and groaned under the violent maneuvers. With the Stability Augmentation system in backup control, there wasn't much even a total incompetent could do to get them into trouble. But truth to tell, Brim had endured enough Townsends to fill a cesspool. Now he was simply waiting. This match had two periods, and the second was his.

His turn came after a purposely crabbed landing that almost cost them a surface loop; Brim could feel Townsend desperately fighting the controls for half the landing vector. When presently they coasted to a hovering stop just off the surface of the water, Brim almost felt honored. The simpleton had tried so hard to frighten him that he'd almost caused a crash.

"Your ship," Townsend announced disdainfully. But his voice had a slight edge. He knew how close he'd come.

"Very well," Brim acknowledged in a calm voice. He took his time running a number of checkout routines, then accelerated into a normal takeoff run and gently lifted ship, climbing slowly while he tested himself. It was, after all, months since he'd been at any controls. By the time they'd climbed through thirty thousand irals, however, he knew all he needed about himself and the ship. He was satisfied. Then he began to wait. What would happen next was entirely up to Townsend.

"Well, come on, Brim," the man taunted presently. "Anybody can take off and climb." He laughed cynically. "You must have convinced somebody you know how to fly. But so far, all you've shown me is that you're a typical Carescrian phony. Let's see something exciting if you fancy a job flying for the Fleet again."

"You're sure that's what you want?" Brim asked.

"I am not in the habit of wasting words on lowlife trash like you," Townsend growled. "Now either show me some flying, or I shall take us back to the base immediately. Unlike you, I have important things in my life."

"I see," Brim said through clenched teeth. "As you wish." Quietly, he shut off all external COMM, then punched four circuit breakers controlling the little ship's Stability Augmentation system. For the maneuvers he had planned, it would just be in the way.

"Hey, jerk," Townsend complained promptly, "you just shut down the SAS—you want to get us both killed?"

"Perhaps I do," Brim said quietly into the intercom. "Are you ready to die?" At that, he rolled the ship inverted and shut off the spin grav. The T-29 began to fall like a rock.

"Xorked Universe!" Townsend swore in a panicked voice. "What are you doing, zukeed?"

"Locking you out of the control system, for one thing," Brim answered, punching more circuit breakers. "—and your escape mechanism," he added. "You said you wanted some excitement —well, by Voot's beard, that is precisely what you are about to get." While he spoke, the still-inverted ship was dropping like a meteor, with less than a thousand irals to go.

Townsend had begun to scream incoherently and pound on the canopy with his fists when Brim at last fired off the spin grav at no more than thirty irals altitude and then began to streak along the surface toward the Fleet base, still upside down. In moments, he sped over the breakers (coating his windshield with spray!), cleared the run-up area at no more than twenty irals, then zoomed through an outside loop that ended, inverted again, at precisely the same twenty irals of altitude. Clicks later, Brim rolled the ship rightside up and continued inland at high speed toward Atalanta's City Mount Hill, dodging hangars and trees with the fluid control inputs he'd used as a youth, racing ore barges through the perilous ore shoals off Carescria. After a few moments' play, however, he cranked the ship into a tight turn, then laid it on its side while he flew through one of the narrow stone arches supporting Harbor Causeway, this time to the sounds of Townsend vomiting in his helmet. It hadn't taken long at all. Too bad, he thought. Already, it was time to go home.

Soaring out over the base again in a gentle turn, he activated the external COMM and called for landing clearance. As he expected, he got it quickly; he'd just broken every rule in the book! He laughed. This would certainly be his last time piloting any kind of a government spacecraft. For just a moment, he felt a pang of regret for the trouble he knew he had just caused Claudia. Then he put her out of his mind. It wasn't he who had asked for today's little jaunt around the base; therefore, she would just have to understand.

Finally, with Townsend still spluttering in the backseat, Brim caught the winking ruby flash of a landing vector, cut power to his spin grav once more, and made landfall dead-stick, bringing the ship to an effortless hover on its own gravity in a few easy hull lengths. "Your ship," he said, as they bobbed gently above the swells.

Silence.

"Well?"

After a long while, Townsend's voice came weakly over the intercom. "I can't d-do it, you bastard," he groaned weakly, "too s-sick."

The words were accompanied by more feeble spitting noises, so Brim switched off the intercom and taxied along the maze of canals that lead to the ready line. He smiled wryly. If nothing else, it had been fun getting back at the controls again. He hoped he wouldn't have to pay for his pleasure by doing time in the brig, but the kind of lesson he'd just been handed regarding government employment was worth at least that. After today, he would never again waste his life mooning after another government flying job. From now on, it was civilian employment *exclusively* for Wilf Brim. And if that meant that he wouldn't fly for a while, then so be it. He was making a good enough living with his axes.

He had just turned onto a ramp leading back to the ready line when a Base Operations skimmer bobbed in front of him with flags flying officiously. A flashing sign across its stern commanded, FOLLOW ME. Shrugging, he pulled in behind the little vehicle and trailed it all the way to the main concrete apron of gravity pads that separated the headquarters building from five square c'lenyts of gravity pools and canals it commanded. Most of the pads were in use by other utility craft of various shapes and sizes; however, one—located in the first row nearest the

glass walls of the Administration section—was unoccupied.
And it was to this pad that the Security skimmer directed him.
He frowned in the bright sunlight as he swung the nose of the
ship. Three people were standing on the far side, and the one
dressed in a close-fitting yellow jumpsuit was certainly Claudia
—he could pick her out anywhere. He grimaced and swallowed
a lump in his throat. Her much-deserved anger would be difficult to endure.

The man to the right of her was . . . Moulding, of course! He,
too, had every right to be angry—furious, even. A pity, Brim
considered with a grimace; the blond officer seemed to be a
decent sort of person, even if he was wealthy.

But who was the other man? Dressed in a severe civilian
business suit, he had a familiar look about him. Suddenly,
Brim's heart jumped as the distance narrowed. No one else in
the Universe had *that* combination of features: the dark complexion, thin, dry lips, pockmarked jowls, short-cropped hair,
and eyes that could drill holes in hullmetal. They could belong
to no one but Bosporus P. Gallsworthy, formerly Principal
Helmsman of I.F.S. *Truculent*—and one of the finest Helmsmen
in the Fleet. Brim hadn't seen him for seven years or so, but
clearly the man had retired into civilian life. And whatever he
was doing there, it didn't bode well for someone who had just
broken nearly every flight regulation on—or above—the base.

With a shrug, Brim concluded that their anger could wait
until he properly shut down the T-29; it made little sense to take
his troubles out on the ship. Then, driving the little trainer onto
the ample gravity pad, he carefully set both gravity brakes,
stopcocked the energy choke, and powered off the spin grav. As
soon as the boarding ladder deployed, he heard the rear canopy
rumble open. Presently, in the corner of his eye, he watched
Townsend stumble to the pavement, then bolt headlong toward
the Headquarters locker room, looking neither left nor right as
he ran.

Cycles later, when he finished inerting the ship's systems, he
once again focused his eyes and his attention on the trio waiting
to vent their ire on him. Strange though, he ruminated as he slid
the canopy back: each of them now seemed to be grinning at
him.

* . * . *

At the foot of the boarding ladder, Brim loosened his helmet, then carefully rotated it forward and off, squinting at the three silhouettes walking toward him in the sudden, unfiltered brightness. Folding his arms on his chest, he stood his ground, feet apart, chin thrust out in the fresh sea breeze. If retribution was indeed his lot, then it might xaxtdamned well come to him. He braced himself.

Gallsworthy broke the silence in his distinctively hushed voice. "Humph," he began, gripping the Carescrian's hand in a rare show of feeling. "It's been a long time, you young pup." Then, with no warning whatsoever, he began to speak in a boisterous voice that was entirely out of character with anything Brim could recall. "Perfectly *dreadful* series of malfunctions you had out there, Brim." he bellowed. "Ah yes—it's certainly clear you've lost none of your extraordinary flying skills. Humph."

"Malfunctions?" Brim stammered in bewilderment. He glanced at Claudia for some explanation, only to encounter a perfectly spiritual countenance, brown eyes turned reverently toward the heavens.

"All three of us watched from the control tower, m'boy," Gallsworthy affirmed boisterously before Brim could even open his mouth again. "I was *especially* impressed when your ship rolled itself on its side and you still managed to safely steer it under the stone bridge. Splendid Helmsmanship! Splendid."

"Yes, right ho," Moulding added, even more stridently, slapping Brim on the shoulder and nodding in an eloquent manner toward a pair of scowling Safety Officers in blue and gold uniforms who were charging around the corner of the gravity pad, clearly intent on grabbing someone. They stopped just short of Brim, puffing officiously. One was a mousy, nervous woman with the mean, narrow eyes of a martinet; her partner was a nondescript and rather stupid-looking man of about twenty who badly needed a shave. Both wore boots with the gleaming, patent-glass finish favored by security guards everywhere in the galaxy. "A *great* show of Helmsmanship," Moulding continued to Brim without stopping for breath, "carried out under the *most* difficult of circumstances. It is certain that *you saved Lieutenant Commander Townsend's life.* Few men in the Empire could have pulled it off the way you did."

At that, both security officers turned to Gallsworthy with a look of consternation.

"S'at what happened, Commissioner?" the woman asked deferentially. "A malfunction, like? We thought that . . ."

"Humph. Just what *did* you think, madam?" Gallsworthy demanded loftily.

"Um, we thought that, um . . . the dark 'aired one 'ere was out joy ridin', Commissioner," the woman explained, pointing at Brim. "We're gettin' *awful* complaints from when 'e flew under the bridge, we are. Scared the bevoots out of a whole tramload o' tourists. Couple o' 'em even jumped in the canal."

"Certainly preferable to his crashing *into* the bridge," Claudia asserted. "Better to soak a few tourists than dump a whole tramload into the canal—along with the tram—I should think."

"No question, Madam Claudia," the other officer agreed, knuckling his forehead. "We 'adn't no idea 'e was in trouble."

His partner kept a grudging silence, but her eyes showed little accord with his words.

"Of course you had no idea," Gallsworthy conceded grandly. "Humph. You were only doing your jobs—and doing them splendidly, I might add." He inspected his fingernails for a moment. "In fact," he went on presently, turning to address the woman exclusively, "I might even cause a personal memorandum of commendation to be placed in your Headquarters files extolling—humph—the great intelligence that you and your partner have shown in the handling of this potentially awkward situation. Do I make myself clear?" he demanded, fixing the woman with a cold stare.

"A . . . a *commendation*?" the woman asked in sudden astonishment.

"My own personal commendation, Officer," Gallsworthy said. "Now do I make myself clear?"

"*M-most* clear, Commissioner," she stammered with a deep bow. "My partner and I are honored, indeed," she added, this time almost reverently.

"Very well," Gallsworthy said, even more imperiously than before. "On your way, then. The letters will be sent with today's dispatches."

"Thank you, Commissioner," the officers recited in almost perfect unison. Then they saluted and quickstepped the way they had come, shoes glistening in the sunlight.

Clearly, Brim thought, Commissioner Bosporus Gallsworthy had garnered considerable power and authority since his days nearly six years ago aboard old I.F.S. *Truculent*. Brim kept his silence and waited for someone else to continue.

Gallsworthy broke the silence again, but only after the Security skimmer had started up and was actually gliding along the apron toward the run-up area. "Claudia," he ordered quietly, pointing to the T-29, "have this little beauty towed to Repair and completely dismantled by technicians you can trust to discover something appropriately wrong. Humph. After our friend Brim's display of aerobatics this morning, everyone's going to have questions—from Atalanta's city fathers to the head of my own Security Department."

"At once, Commissioner," Claudia replied, drawing a communicator from her purse. She turned toward the little trainer and began whispering instructions.

Glancing wryly at Moulding, Gallsworthy shook his head and indicated Brim with a casual toss of his thumb. "As I said when you burst into my office grumbling about Townsend," he chuckled, "that idiot wasn't about to make serious trouble for ol' Wilf, here. This madman is trouble—always has been, always will be, so far as I can see. We've needed someone around here like him for a long time—to keep things stirred up, a little. Humph."

"I think I understand," Moulding agreed with a twinkle of humor in his eye. "Wilf," he said, extending his hand. "I look forward to working with you—not only for your renowned Helmsmanship, but because I think we are probably going to be good friends."

"Not so fast, you two," Claudia broke in, replacing the transmitter in her purse. "Wilf hasn't accepted the job yet. He doesn't even know what it pays. Perhaps after his morning with Townsend he won't want to work here." She placed her hands on her hips and looked Brim in the eye. "How about it, Wilf?" she asked. "I think these gentlemen are taking quite a lot for granted; don't you?"

Brim felt his head spin. So far, this hadn't turned out to be the most entertaining morning of his recollection. "Well . . ." he started gallantly.

Gallsworthy frowned and nodded. "Humph. I suppose she's right, Brim," he interrupted. "I apologize for that. The position's at a Lead Helmsman's level—roughly First Lieutenant's pay. And—humph—yes, I did put you through a bit of difficulty this morning—but then I had to."

"Oh?" Brim demanded with a raised eyebrow.

Gallsworthy nodded. "Brim," he said with a serious face, "from what I could discover after some—humph—discreet inquiries, you were—in *my* mind—showing signs of what the veterans' organizations euphemistically call 'adversarial hostility.' Without the sugarcoated words, it sounded very possible that you'd built up so much anger you weren't fit to be a military Helmsman anymore—and you'd have had damned good reason, young man. You faced more than your share of rotten luck." He grimaced, then shrugged. "So I made you fly with the greatest simpleton on the base. The way I looked at it, if you could still pilot a ship after taking the garbage I knew he would dish out, then you were all right." He nodded toward Claudia with a wry look. "Humph. I could have saved us both the trouble, had I listened to this one—or a *number* of other people whose help you'd spurned over the last couple of years. They never lost faith in *you*, Brim—but I don't think the inverse is necessarily manifest, is it?"

Brim shook his head. The anger was there, all right. It was all his; he'd placed it between himself and the Empire he'd once served. Never again could he blindly love authority as he once had; there were too many scars, now. But for the first time he was beginning to realize that he had also somehow managed to extend that same animosity to his more fortunate friends as well. And as a result, he had doubly suffered when he failed to accept the help they offered. "I-I should have done some listening, too, I'm afraid," he admitted in a low voice.

Claudia touched his forearm. "That part of your life is over now if you choose, Wilf," she said. "Will you join us?"

Blinking back tears that threatened to burst from his eyes, Brim nodded and turned to Gallsworthy. There were no questions or conditions. "I'll take the job, Commissioner," he said quietly, covering Claudia's hand with his for a moment before he released it, "gladly." Then he shook his head ironically. "And I was so xaxtdamned proud of the way I could handle an axe . . ."

Gallsworthy chuckled quietly. "If I ever catch you flying like that again around my base," he said, "I may take one of those axes to you."

Brim looked up with a little grin. *That* was more like the Gallsworthy he'd once known! Glancing at the man sideways, he frowned. "Surely not if I am victim of still another malfunction, Commissioner," he replied, fluttering a hand over his heart with a look of righteous bewilderment. "You wouldn't ask me to risk my life, would you?"

Gallsworthy shook his head as they started for the Headquarters building. "Xaxtdamned Carescrians," he chuckled to no one in particular. "Humph. There's no living with them at all . . ."

During the weeks that followed, Haelic passed from summer into the clear, crisp days of autumn while Brim saw the return of his old confidence. In deep space, he quickly established himself as one of the base's premiere Diagnostic Helmsmen, although he often found his piloting talents (as well as his courage) stretched as much by untried starships as they had been by Leaguers during the war years. And much closer to the ground, after a frosty evening's ride on his gravcycle, a honey-blond flight dispatcher wasted no time proving that his troubles with Margot had been only transient—beyond the shadow of a doubt. Even Townsend checked out of his life by accepting a permanent change of station to Avalon where his CIGA contacts would be more politically valuable.

And during rare moments of relaxation, he resumed correspondence with a number of the old friends he had once forsaken—except for Margot Effer'wyck-LaKarn. On his first attempt to contact their confidential maildrop, he had been advised by old Ambridge, her chauffeur, that less than a week following their last stolen evening together, she had been sequestered at her husband's palace in Rudolpho, capital of the Torond, *incommunicado*.

He was, however, able to keep abreast of LaKarn himself, try as he might to avoid even the mention of the man's name. As the Mitchell Trophy Race approached, the public media had little else to report about. In fact, for an entire week preceding the event, the Baron became positively loquacious in his role as sponsor of two Gorn-Hoff 380B-5 fast attack craft entered by his Royal Starflight Society. Brim wondered if he planned for

Margot to accompany him to Magalla'ana for the races and how such a journey would affect her child who must certainly reach term during that time.

When recordings of the first race day reached Atalanta on speedy packet ships, Brim spent most of his time in deep space, flying at least twice as many missions as he normally scheduled. Most of the other Helmsmen either stayed home or concocted some excuse to watch broadcasts on one of the base's huge, three-dimensional monitors. That night, he returned to his apartment so fatigued that he took to his bunk immediately and fell into a deep sleep without even consulting the news service to which he indifferently subscribed.

During the remaining race days, he continued filling in for absent colleagues from early morning until everyone but night-shift Helmsmen had departed for home. Only late in the evening of the final race did he find time to catch up on the galaxy's happenings. And thus it was that he became one of the last people in Atalanta—or anywhere else, for that matter—to discover that LaKarn's race-modified Gorn-Hoffs had been able to garner only a third-place win.

Second place had been won by an old friend, actually one of Brim's apprentices aboard I.F.S. *Defiant*, Aram of Nahshon. The young flighted native of A'zurn had piloted a R3C-1 prototype from the new A'zurnian starship plant at R'autor, established soon after his domain was liberated from the yoke of League occupation. Brim was so elated about the young A'zurnian's achievement, he almost missed the name of the winning Helmsman. In fact, it was the man's face and blond hair, recorded beside the sleek, brooding form of a new Gorn-Hoff model—the TA 153-V32—that initially caught his attention. Only after he stared at the monitor for a long time did he cue an information channel to assure himself that the handsome, black-uniformed Controller, an OverPraefect, was indeed the Leaguer whom he suspected. He was not mistaken.

The name was *Kirsh Valentin*.

For years, memories alone had been quite sufficient to send Brim into wild spasms of anger whenever he thought of Valentin. The sight of his face was even worse. Those cruel blue eyes had once callously looked down at him as he lay in the cold deck of a Leaguer starship waiting for death to deliver him from the agony of his torture. Only lady Fortune—in the person of

Lieutenant Commander Regula Collingswood—had saved his life that day, and he had sworn that he would someday revenge himself against the Leaguer. He'd had only one chance at it, so far—and had utterly failed.

In fact, the picture of Valentin so upset Brim that he nearly passed up an ancillary announcement used as filler in the special race supplement:

> Born: Rodyard Greyffin A'zurn LaKarn to fashionable Princess Margot Effer'wyck-LaKarn and Rogan LaKarn, Baron of the Torond. The trendsetting royal couple's first child was delivered in Magalla'ana, A'zurn, during a final heat of the Mitchell Trophy Race. Dowager Princess Honorotha LaKarn, current monarch of the Torond, attended the birthing. She reports that mother and son are both doing splendidly. At the time, Baron LaKarn was occupied with the race committee and could not be reached for comment. The royal family plans to return to the Torond within the next few Standard days.

Brim had little time to reflect upon either event. He was simply too busy keeping up with his own career to worry about things he was powerless to change. He was also a somewhat different man from the Wilf Brim who had fled Avalon nine Standard months in the past.

One frosty evening, shortly after Brim returned to his apartment from the base, his correspondence was interrupted by an unexpected knock at the door. Frowning—he permitted himself few friends and expected even fewer visitors—he got to his feet and opened the door, then staggered back into his living room, grinning in happy consternation. "Nik Ursis!" he blurted out. "Dr. Borodov! By the very hair of Voot's tangled beard, where in the Universe did you two come from?" With that, he fairly leaped through the door in a vain attempt to embrace the two elegant Sodeskayan Bears, both dressed in civilian clothes.

Ursis, the younger of the two and Dean of the famous Dityasburg Academy on the G.F.S.S. planet of Zhiv'ot, stood a quarter again as tall as Brim. He had small, gray eyes of enormous intensity, dark reddish brown fur, a long, urbane muzzle that terminated in a huge, wet nose, and a grin so wide that fang jewels on either side of his mouth blazed in the light of the doorway. On his head he wore a colossal egg-shaped hat of curly wool that covered his ears and added at least an iral to his already formidable height. His black, knee-length greatcoat—embellished by two rows of huge gold buttons and jasmine waist sash—was cut in the military style with a stiff collar, embroidered cuffs, and a wide skirt. Crimson trousers bagged stylishly over his thick calf-length boots, the latter of black leather so soft that it bunched at the ankles. On his left hand he wore a delicately embroidered, six-fingered glove of ophet leather. The other hand held a prodigious bottle of Logish Meem.

The other Bear—Grand Duke (Doctor) Anastas Alexyi Borodov and master of vast baronial estates in the deeply wooded lake country outside Gromcow on the G.F.S.S. mother planet of Sodeskaya—was chestnut in color, much older, somewhat bowed by his years, and stood only a little taller than Brim. His eyes, however, sparkled with youthful humor and prodigious intellect behind a pair of old-fashioned horn-rim spectacles. And, although his graying muzzle was not nearly so intimidating as that of his companion, enormous sideburns provided him with a most profoundly intellectual countenance. He also was splendidly dressed in a handsome, ankle-length greatcoat of thick gray felt that was closed at the waist with a narrow leather belt. From the open collar emerged a heavy vest of darker felt with high, embroidered collars fastened by a delicate necktie of golden rope. Unlike Ursis's soft walking boots, Borodov's were clearly made for riding, cobbled of far stiffer, shiny leather and equipped with unobtrusive spurs secured at the ankle by delicate belts. And, although he also wore a massive hat of curly wool, it was much wider at the top than it was at the headband and gave his head the look of a wooly funnel. "Perhaps, young Brim," he suggested peering over his glasses at the open door, "we should go inside to drink the meem and catch up on old times. It has been much too long since we sat together discussing troubles of the galaxy."

"Is true, Wilf Ansor," Ursis admonished. "During your months of disappearance, you troubled many of your friends—Anastas Alexyi and myself not least among them. Am I correct, Doctor?"

"Most correct, Nikolai Yanuarievich," Borodov replied with

a pointed glance at Brim. "'Old snow and wooden floors turn skies blue in the autumn,' as they say."

Brim shook his head in mock concession. Sodeskayan homilies made little sense to human ears. "If you say so," he chuckled while he guided his friends through the door, eagerly looking forward to a rare evening of companionship.

And indeed, the Bears' visit *did* begin the way he anticipated. Borodov opened Ursis's huge bottle, then poured a magnificent vintage of Logish Meem into Brim's humble collection of cvceese' mugs. And only when these had become empty were they held upside down in the air while the three comrades toasted in the Sodeskayan style: "To ice, to snow, to Sodeskaya we go!" The friendship they shared was a special closeness forged in the hellish disruptor fire of countless, desperately fought battles against the League of Dark Stars.

Afterward, there should have been a thousand old stories to retell . . . jokes not always funny at the time they happened, but now hilarious almost beyond belief . . . valiant Blue Capes and starships, gone forever except in the memories of those who still honored them . . . a whole wealth of general catching up for Bears and Carescrians both. But somehow, none of these conversations even got started. The Sodeskayans were already consumed by their current mission and could talk of little else.

"You came halfway across the galaxy for a meeting of the Imperial Starflight Society?" Brim asked in amazement as Borodov refilled their cups. "What sort of interest could either of you have in an amateur outfit like the ISS? Did you see the antique they entered in the trophy race? It *looked* great, but it flew like it had an asteroid in tow—forty-nine point seven eight M LightSpeed, full bore! Valentin won at better than sixty-two."

"We saw both ships, and how they performed," Borodov said soberly, tamping a charge of Hogge'Poa into his Zempa pipe. "That is *precisely* why we have come—the Great Federation of Sodeskayan States is, after all, a part of the Empire."

"I understand that," Brim replied, struggling to stifle a gasp as aromatic 'Poa smoke filled his small apartment. Sodeskayans loved the odor, that to Brim smelled like something between smoldering yaggloz wool and fumes from a radiation fire. "But I didn't know the ISS *had* any Sodeskayan members. From what I understood, it was never much more than a swank social club for wealthy Avalonians."

Borodov nodded. "Your understanding is essentially correct, my friend," he said, frowning thoughtfully at his pipe, which appeared to have extinguished itself in spite of his efforts. "Until the war, those societies conducted starship racing in a *very* amateurish fashion indeed. The powerful socialites who formed their race committees wished only to bask in the dangerous glamour of starship racing, without necessarily participating in person. By unwritten fiat, they purchased their racers at military storage and reclamation facilities and left the flying side of things to contractors. It was all a big, infatuating game," he snorted, "right up until this year." With that, he took out a pocket laser and began a new attempt to relight his recalcitrant pipe.

"When the League of Dark Stars broke all the old unwritten rules," Ursis continued in place of his companion, "they also twisted the whole concept from a grand, pangalactic celebration of affluence into a downright arrant display of military prowess. Instead of bumbling through as had all the prewar winners, these Leaguers tailored every detail for one particular task— winning. Which, of course, they did. Handily. If it hadn't been for young Aram and his new starship factory on A'zurn, your friend Valentin would have won first and second places! And do you know why the Leaguers did it?"

Brim pursed his lips and shook his head. "I guess I hadn't been paying that much attention to the whys, Nik," he explained.

"Think of it this way, Wilf," Ursis explained. "Except for those obscenities who call themselves CIGA, anybody with even half a brain understands that Triannic will resume his war just as soon as he thinks he can win it. He's already taking his first steps with threats against Fluvanna, and competitions like the Mitchell Trophy Race are perfect places to show off military hardware, as well as attract new allies." He looked Brim directly in the eye. "Allies like your friend and mine, Rogan LaKarn," he added pointedly.

"That's my take of the thing, too," Borodov growled with a nod. "But just try to explain that to any of the CIGAs in Avalon," he said, "especially those blasted zukeeds in the Admiralty. They not only lack interest in the truth, but have sufficient power to avoid hearing it very often."

"CIGA scum will not always be in the ascendancy," Borodov predicted darkly. "But until that time comes, we must have ways to counter them." He looked at Brim. "And now, friend Wilf, you begin to understand why Nikolai Yanuarievich and I have come halfway across a galaxy to attend a Royal Starflight Society meeting. Certain patriotic forces in the Empire are quietly reacting to the League's unusual win at A'zurn with their own meticulous preparations for the next race—preparations made with quiet, but almost limitless, government assistance."

"And believe me, Wilf," Ursis added, "we are not unique. Similar arrangements are going on all over the galaxy, even as we speak. This year's competition was also the unofficial prelude to the war's next phase." He laughed darkly, indicating the handsome lavender vest he wore over a richly embroidered white shirt and golden rope necktie. "We no longer wear our blue Fleet Capes, my friend, but we still fight for the same cause, eh?"

Brim nodded uncertainly. "If you say so, Nik," he equivocated. Sodeskayan Bears were known all over the Empire as rather parochial patriots.

The Bear shook his head soberly. "I do say so, Wilf Ansor, and proudly, I might add. Moreover, because of this, I am certain of where I stand in relation to the future—as is my friend and mentor Dr. Borodov." Then he rose. "But do you know where you stand?"

Brim felt his eyebrows rise as he looked from one Great Sodeskayan Bear to the other. "I don't think I know what you mean," he started. Then, abruptly it all came home to him. "You mean," he gasped, rising to his feet in astonishment, "that I—a Carescrian—ought to join the ISS with you?"

"In spirit, that is *precisely* what we mean, Wilf Ansor," Borodov said, taking the pipe from his mouth and looking over his glasses.

For a moment, Brim nearly succumbed to a wild, cynical urge to laugh in the old Bear's face. Ultimately, however, he managed to choke everything back in consideration of their long-established friendship. Both Sodeskayans were clearly serious. He shook his head. "Nik, Dr. Borodov," he said earnestly, shrugging his shoulders, "I have no place in this crazy mission of yours—whatever it is. I don't particularly like aristocrats—present company excepted, of course. And besides all that, I'm not even so sure how much I love the xaxtdamned Empire. I got pretty hungry there for a while after the war—and I wasn't alone. A lot of us Fleet types got dumped like so much trash when we weren't needed any more."

"That you were, Wilf Ansor," Ursis answered quietly. "But you, at least, did not have to be hungry. Only your own anger prevented friends from helping you."

"But I didn't want charity," Brim snapped defensively, in spite of himself. "I couldn't stand xaxtdamned charity—from anybody."

"As I recall," Borodov interjected gently, "no one offered charity: not Nikolai, nor Commander Collingswood, nor Crown Prince Onrad, nor any of the half-dozen others who badly needed your services and had credits to pay."

"*You*, Wilf Brim, turned *us* down with cock-and-bull stories about phantom 'business deals' that were supposed to keep you too busy to accept our offers," Ursis inserted firmly. "Remember?"

Brim felt his face burn. That part of it was certainly true. "Yeah, Nik," he admitted, looking down at his boots. "You two did try to come through for me, a lot of times. And there were others. I haven't forgotten that. But my friends and what they tried to do for me doesn't excuse a whole Empire for the heedless way they treated other veterans who fought and sacrificed. I know what those poor people went through. I talked to them when they were hungry. I saw the hurt in their eyes—while rich bastards like these ISS dudes went on a spending spree all over the galaxy."

Ursis quietly ambled across the room and placed his hand on Brim's shoulder. "Wilf," he said emotionally, "there is no way I can refute your complaints. They are true. But, as you know so well, there are no guarantees concerning this life—only that it goes on toward eventual dissolution, carrying with it most of the inequalities that have existed since the dawn of history. What remains important, then, is that we get on with what we do, all of us. Old comrades once more need your help. And this time let me assure you beyond all shadow of a doubt that *you*, as well as your talent as a Helmsman, are *absolutely* necessary."

Brim shook his head and closed his eyes for a moment. "I don't doubt you, Nik," he muttered. "It's just that I don't think that this bitterness will go away that easily. I'm doing all right working as a civilian here on Haelic. Sometimes, I even feel as if I belong among the people at work, no matter where I come from." He shook his head and frowned. "But what kind of future could I, a relatively shabby Carescrian, possibly have among people whose chief talent seems to be giving expensive parties?"

Borodov laughed. "About the same sort of future Nikolai Yanuarievich and I plan to have with these persons. You see, we are only consultants to the Society, not members. Of their new Racing Committee, only Regula Collingswood and Prince Onrad are actual members. The rest of the "Special Operations Staff," as we are called, are all hirelings—mere employees, and only temporary at that. If you sign on, the Society will simply 'borrow' you once in a while from the base here, and then friend Gallsworthy will bill the Society. You won't have to give up your new job—or even lose your seniority."

Brim felt himself involuntarily smile, in spite of his churning emotions. "Well," he admitted bleakly, "even a hard-core cynic like me can't complain much about a deal like that. What is it you want me to do?"

"Why don't we come by for you first thing in the morning and take you to the meeting?" Ursis suggested, retrieving his greatcoat from a chair. "That way, you can talk directly to the people who are actually setting things up."

"Somehow," Brim said with a frown, "I have this uncomfortable feeling that the next part of my life has already been planned by someone else—behind my back."

"Someone else plan your life?" Borodov asked in mock astonishment while Brim held his greatcoat. "Who would do a thing like that?"

"Hmm," Brim mumbled, following the two Sodeskayans outside as they strode toward a huge, chauffeur-driven Rill-21 limousine skimmer hovering discreetly at the curbside.

"See you soon, Wilf Ansor," Ursis called over his shoulder. "We'll be here for you at Morning: one-thirty."

"I'll be ready," Brim answered, sounding a lot more confident than he felt. Ready for what? Then he grinned. His life was clearly about to destabilize all over again, in rapid order. This time, however, the whole process might just prove to be entertaining.

CHAPTER 4

Grand Admiral
Kabul Anak

The ISS held its conference at the sumptuous Grand Koun-dourities Hotel in the heart of the Atalantan business ring. An imposing structure of great apparent age, Brim had been past it countless times, but never inside. Strangely enough, it was old Borodov who seemed to be most familiar with the magnificent hotel. "The Grand Koundourities," he commented as the limousine skimmer approached through heavy, early-morning traffic, "is the largest and oldest civilian structure on all of Haelic, as I recall. It was completed for the fifty-first millennium celebration here in the Standard year 49999." Elegantly dressed as he was the previous evening, the Bear pointed toward the massive stone building's domed central tower. "During the early five tens," he continued, "it held one of the earliest KA'PPA beacons in existence, and for decades was recognized throughout all known space as the 'Haelic Light.' You can still see the KA'PPA's twelve supports—they look like ornate minarets. Emperor Vargold Narrish IV took his course bearings from that beacon during his early explorations of the Korrellean Sector. And speaking of famous historical figures, it was in 51489 I believe, that Professor David Lu appeared in the main lobby to present Atalanta's City Directorship with his latest Hypercrystal, the basis for all of today's Hyperscreens. Not only that, but here's still *another* interesting fact," he added as the chauffeur brought them to a halt under the grand portico. "Did you know that the Grand Koundourities was once used as a giant brothel?"

"A brothel?" Brim asked, getting out and peering around with a grin on his face. "Sure doesn't look like one now."

"Nevertheless," Borodov went on with a grin, "it *was* at one time. Seems that the Garomptar of Pathipett once found himself stranded in Atalanta with his huge star yacht disabled and scarcely an Imperial credit to pay for repairs. Luckily, some three hundred of his most seductive wives were also aboard for his pleasure. So, before word of his financial straits became generally known, he hastily moved his harem into the Koundourities here, took out numerous ads in the local pleasure media, and within three months he'd earned enough to cover the girls' rooms *and* his starship repairs, with a handsome profit left over for his own private coffers." He laughed. "It's said that the girls loved it. They were normally required to remain faithful, and one imagines that even a very strong man could have made the rounds no more than five or six times a year."

"Universe," Ursis whispered reverently.

"How does he know all that?" Brim asked Ursis as they made their way past a veritable army of colorfully uniformed doormen, through a set of gigantic beveled glass doors, and into a bustling indoor court with marvelously high, arched ceilings that reminded him more of a nicely finished starship hangar than a hotel lobby.

"Baxter Calhoun owns it," the younger Bear explained as if it were common knowledge throughout the Universe. "He wanted Anastas Alexyi and me to stay here, as his guests."

Brim stopped in his tracks, stunned by the Bear's words. "Baxter Calhoun owns *this*?" he asked in astonishment. "You mean our *Commander* Baxter Oglethorp Calhoun? Of I.F.S. *Defiant*?"

"The same," Borodov assured him. "I thought you of all people would know, especially since he's a fellow Carescrian."

Brim shook his head. "He never let me in on much of anything but a lot of good advice," he answered. "But how come you two didn't take him up on his offer to stay here?" he asked.

"If anyone around this hotel knew I was Calhoun's guest," Borodov laughed, "I wouldn't be able to endure the fuss they'd make. Besides," he laughed, "my gamekeeper tells me the beds here are much too soft for old Bears like me."

"And I," Ursis laughed, "simply followed suit. It was easier."

"I see," Brim chuckled absently, stopping to peruse the window of a media shop while Borodov and Ursis checked at the information desk. He shook his head. During his year aboard I.F.S. *Defiant*, he'd certainly guessed that Calhoun was a wealthy man. But he'd had no idea how wealthy.

"Wilf—you're here! The Bears got in touch with you," a familiar voice called from nearby. Brim whirled around just in time to be captured in a wild embrace by Regula Collingswood, his onetime commanding officer on two fine warships.

"Captain Collingswood," he exclaimed, wrapping the woman in his own arms. "How wonderful to see you again!"

"The name's Regula, Wilf," she admonished, smooching him on the cheek, then stepping back for a better look, "or hadn't you noticed that I'm no longer wearing a Fleet cloak."

Brim grinned. "I noticed, all right," he said. In civilian clothes, it was plain to see why she had so completely captured the heart of her husband—and whispered long-time lover—Admiral Erat Plutron. She was a statuesque woman, tall and ageless with a long, patrician nose, piercing hazel eyes, and soft, graying chestnut hair that she wore in natural curls. She was dressed in a lavender business suit fronted with a great cascade of white ruffles. "You look *wonderful*," he added—as indeed she did. An extraordinary starship commander during the war, Regula Collingswood had never, even for a moment, let the power of her station interfere with the basic femininity that shaped everything about her personality.

"That's better," she said in mock severity, then took the elbow of a slender, attractive young woman standing beside her, holding a briefcase. Brim felt a momentary excitement when the woman's enormous brown eyes met his and paused with fleeting interest before she turned toward his old commander.

"Wilf," Collingswood said, "You must meet Anna Romanoff—quite an extraordinary person—who has taken on the position of Secretary for the Imperial Starflight Society. Anna, this is the man I have been talking about for weeks."

The woman extended a warm, manicured hand, and again momentarily captured his eyes before she spoke. "I am pleased to meet you, Wilf," she said formally, in a soft voice that had just the slightest trace of some regional accent he couldn't identify. "Regula has said some rather wonderful things about you." Her satiny, reddish brown hair was parted in the middle, then gathered into a loose braid at the back of her head. She was small, Brim noted—very attractive, with a distinguished nose and slightly pouted lips. Clearly a businesswoman in every respect, she was outfitted in a light tan dress with a scooped bodice beneath which she wore a white sweater that hinted of an ample bust. Her modest skirt revealed very little of what Brim suspected were shapely legs, and she wore low-heeled business shoes. A sexy woman by nature, he conjectured, who was determined to do business in spite of that. He found himself holding the softness of her hand somewhat longer than he'd planned, and smiled in spite of himself when he let go. "The Captain—er, Regula—tends to embellish the truth about her former crews," he said.

"Somehow, I doubt that," she answered softly. "Regula also warned me that you are modest to a fault." Then, before he could react, she turned to Collingswood. "I shall meet you after lunch at . . . Brightness: one-thirty. That way, we shall have time to go over your numbers again before the General Assembly. Delighted to have met you, Wilf," she added, nodding toward Brim at the last moment. Then she hurried off across the lobby with a peculiar little prance that Brim found most attractive—and feminine.

"Quite a lady, there," Brim said, impressed, for some reason, out of all proportion to their brief introduction.

"Yes," Collingswood said. "We were lucky to find that one. With her reputation for no-nonsense business management, she's in demand all over the Empire. I think she took the job out of pure patriotism. Voot knows she works every moment of her life." Then she peered at him oddly. "She's pretty, isn't she?"

Brim nodded and grinned at his old commander. "She is that," he agreed, "and she has a cute way of walking, too."

Collingswood frowned for a moment, then smiled in an odd way. "I suppose that's true," she said, as if she had just made some sort of decision, "Anna does have a cute way of walking." She had an almost motherly look on her face as she spoke, if indeed anything about the former starship captain could be construed as motherly. To Brim's recollection, he had heard her mention childbearing only once—as being the best advertisement for birth control she could think of.

"Ah, Regula—here you are!" Borodov exclaimed as he pushed his way through the throng. "Nikolai Yanuarievich," he called over his shoulder. "We no longer have to find them; they have found us!"

Soon, all thoughts about Romanoff were swept away by a second joyous reunion in the lobby, with Collingswood hugging and being hugged by the two magnificently costumed Sodeskayans in a manner that badly disrupted cross-lobby traffic with onlookers.

And what little traffic movement that remained was promptly shut off completely by the appearance of Crown Prince Onrad, heir to the Imperial Throne at Avalon and present Chairman of the Society. Even had he not joined an already noisy reunion, his magnificent blue Fleet cloak—that of a Vice Admiral—would have stopped traffic anywhere. He was slightly taller than Brim, and considerably heavier: a comfortable looking man of obvious royalty. His hair was dark brown and he wore a short, pointed beard with a moustache. In Brim's way of thinking, however, it was the man's eyes that set him apart. He had a way of looking at people that bespoke genuine honesty. The Carescrian had grown far too skeptical to believe that any monarch anywhere could afford to make totally equitable decisions much of the time. Politics simply got in the way of such things. But he nevertheless trusted that the Empire would be in capable hands when one day Onrad ascended to the High Throne in Avalon.

"Aha!" the prince said with a wide grin. "I might have known the four of you would find each other." He too got a long hug from Collingswood while the Bears bowed respectfully at either side. "Now *this* is what I call a welcoming committee," he whooped over his shoulder to a stiff-looking General dressed in the tan and red uniform of Greyffin IV's Imperial Army. The imposing officer had stopped with his gray briefcase a regulation eight paces to the rear. "Next time, Zapt, see if you can't set up something more along *these* lines."

Lieutenant General Zapt, who clearly had no sense of the moment whatsoever, bowed and clicked his heels. "I shall see what can be arranged, Your Majesty," he said, his voice just audible over the bustle of the crowd.

With one arm still around Collingswood's waist, Onrad extended his hand to Brim. "Good to have you back among us,

Brim," he said, with his usual firm grip. "You worried quite a few people when you disappeared a while back."

"I'm sorry, Your Royal Highness," Brim said, feeling his face flush with embarrassment. "I'd reached a difficult time in my life about then."

"I take it everything's all right now?" the Prince asked pointedly.

"Everything is now excellent," Brim answered.

Onrad pursed his lips impassively and nodded. "General," he commanded, "will you deliver that letter for Mr. Brim?"

A moment later, General Zapt stepped forward and delivered a gray plastic envelope to Brim's hand, then quickly returned to the background. His face was an expressionless mask, but alert, gray eyes betrayed the soul of a battle-hardened trooper.

"From an old friend of yours—my cousin Margot," Onrad explained impassively. "I visited her last week in Rudolpho."

Brim's heart leaped nearly from his chest. "H-how gratifying that she should remember me," he said, struggling to contain himself from ripping the envelope open there in the lobby.

"That *is* nice, Wilf" Collingswood said with a sudden look of concern in her eyes. "You two certainly became fast friends when we were stationed on Gimmas-Haefdon years ago. I understand she and Baron LaKarn have a son now." She shook her head. "Never *could* understand what she saw in that stuffed shirt."

Onrad laughed wryly. "She didn't have much choice in the matter, Regula. Father dictated the whole thing to keep Mama LaKarn's Torond and its celecoid quartz Drive crystal kernels more closely bound to the Empire. They control half our supply, you know."

"That's what I'd heard," Collingswood said with a grimace. "Poor Margot."

"We all have *some* burden to bear," Onrad said, glancing perceptively at Brim for a fleeting instant. "Margot's tends to be heavier than most." Then he took a deep breath. "Enough of that sort of thing. Regula, Borodov, Ursis—have you three talked Brim into joining us yet?"

"We only just found him last night," Ursis said with a grin.

"That hasn't allowed much time to talk about anything yet," Borodov added, peering over his glasses.

"And I *just* ran into him a few moments before you did," Collingswood put in.

"I see," Onrad replied. For a moment, he smiled at some private thought, then he nodded. "Tell you what," he said, looking at Collingswood and the two Bears, "I need to see the three of you for a few moments concerning the membership committee rules. Wilf, why don't you take one of these comfortable lobby chairs for a few cycles, then join us in the grand ballroom for the opening ceremonies?" He consulted his timepiece. "At Morning: two forty-five. That will give us an opportunity to conduct our business—and you can amuse yourself with that letter."

Brim bowed. "Very well, Your Highness," he agreed. "I shall plan to join you in the grand ballroom at Morning: two forty-five sharp."

"General Zapt, a badge for Mr. Brim, if you please." Onrad commanded. Instantly, the wraithlike General handed Brim a holobadge containing the latest three-dimensional representation of his head and shoulders that had been recorded in base security. With that, the Prince and Collingswood swept grandly past, the two Bears and General Zapt hurrying along in their wake.

Brim watched the little convoy maneuvering through the throng. Try as he might, it was difficult to feel any great indignation toward Onrad for having taken his decision for granted. In truth, he doubted if princes could operate *without* making a lot of assumptions. They simply wouldn't have enough time. Besides, he was under no obligation to anyone. If he decided against employment with the ISS for any reason, he could always turn in his badge, leave the hotel, and that would be that. He hurried to one of the lobby's great wing-backed easy chairs where he impulsively ripped open the envelope, extracted two sheets of pale coralline manuscript plastic, and began to read:

Dearest Wilf,

In the long months since we last met in Avalon, you have seldom been far from my mind. In that way, you have sustained me through what you must by now have discovered has been a virtual captivity. Until this day,

Rogan has successfully blocked all of my many attempts to communicate. Cousin Onrad, however, is far beyond my husband's reach.

I trust that by now you also know that I have finally delivered my son, Rodyard. Not only has he introduced a whole new love into my life, he has also brought a fresh set of responsibilities. And in no way would I even attempt to claim that I remain unchanged because of him. The truth is that I am totally changed. Only in my love for you do I remain constant, even though I know that our relationship must now endure its second drastic permutation. That change is something that we must someday work out, my dearest, but only when our eyes can meet as well as our minds. For now, Wilf, be certain of my love, but be forewarned that I no longer exist as the Margot Effer'wyck you once knew.

Now, time grows short, and I must complete this message. Onrad confesses to me that he will soon offer you the position of Principal Helmsman for the Imperial Starflight Society, but he is not at all certain you will accept. He refuses to discuss the basis for his doubts, but I suspect that I know. I spent the last night of my own freedom looking helplessly at your despair. After the reward you received for your wartime sacrifices, you could retain very little love for our ungrateful Empire or its people.

Nevertheless, I pray to the very Universe that you will somehow find it in yourself to overlook these all-too-obvious transgressions. One glimpse into Kirsh Valentin's eyes and you would know why you must. Wilf, these competitions have suddenly become much more than quests for pride or even an outlandish token like the Mitchell Cup. The real trophy is now the crass promotion of industrial and scientific capabilities—factors that attract allies whose added might can insure achievement of more fundamental goals: conquest and power. Believe me, I know. My own husband is already strongly attracted to the tyrant's cause.

Onrad has returned now, so I must end. The Universe speed your flight, my darling, until we touch again.

> Love thou the land, with love far-brought
> From out the storied Past, and used
> Within the present, but transfused
> Thro' future time by power of thought.

> —Cennone

I love you,
Margot

Brim devoured Margot's letter, reading it over and over again, examining each elegantly handwritten word for all possible meanings while he desperately attempted to create her face in his mind's eye. He was so preoccupied that he nearly missed the opening ceremonies. When he finally consulted his timepiece, only moments remained in which to hurry across the crowded floor, catch a jammed lift to the fifth level, and sprint to the grand ballroom, where he arrived, rather out of breath, with less than a cycle to spare.

An imposing doorman in a purple uniform trimmed with gold glared at Brim. He was backed up by ten government types with short haircuts and massive chins who looked totally out of place in evening clothes. "The employment office," he proclaimed regally, "is two flights below, at the *other* end of the hall."

Brim peered up at the man and flashed his badge. "Glad to know that, friend," he said impassively. "Let me know if you find work." Then he opened the door for himself and strode through as if he had been a member of the ISS for the last thousand years.

Inside, under a colonnade that ringed the perimeter of the great, circular room, it was instantly clear to Brim—who was wearing a plain blue tunic over white civilian trousers and walking shoes, the best clothes he owned—why the doorman had tried to prevent him from entering. Beneath a high, magnificently-colored *trompe l'oeil* ceiling of mythological space creatures in flight, a glittering assemblage of perhaps two hundred unquestionably affluent people had assembled, dressed for the clear and singular purpose of impressing each other. They were seated at ten large, circular tables, noisily laughing and talking, while artfully ignoring the extravagant ministrations of at least a hundred servants in ill-fitting evening clothes who scurried here and there, lugging huge trays of goblets and bottles. The air was heavy with odors of fine wines, liquors, cigarettes of every scent, perfume, and the delicate scent of glowing panthion blossoms that were placed everywhere in great baskets and sprays. Music from a small orchestra wove through the conversation and muted clatter of tableware.

At the far end of the room on a raised dais, a long, straight table had been set for twelve. In the center, Prince Onrad presided over the whole assemblage, flanked by Regula Collingswood and a brooding aristocrat whom Brim immediately recognized as Onrad's longtime confidant and trusted friend, the Duke of Washburn. At Collingswood's left sat Anna Romanoff, unobtrusively staring into a portable information terminal. And beside Romanoff posed a svelte woman with captivating gray eyes whom Brim recognized as Veronica Pike, Director of the Sherrington Hyperspace Works, a small but highly reputed starship manufacturer. Poised and enigmatic as a gryphon, she was dressed in severe light gray business apparel that accentuated long, sable hair and a flawless, tawny complexion.

Grinding his teeth in embarrassment, the Carescrian speedily concluded that there was no place in the room for a credit-strapped Helmsman named Wilf Brim. Turning abruptly to avoid a large, bovine maitre'd whose obeisant professional gaze had just trapped his glance, he reached for the door handle at precisely the same time that Toby Moulding rose from a nearby table occupied mostly by people in Fleet uniforms. "Wilf!" he called, "Here, sit with us. I've been saving you a place."

Brim shuddered, attempting to conjure some excuse that would allow him to escape. But he was too late. In a moment, Moulding had ushered him to a chair between his own and a comfortable-looking, middle-aged man dressed in a brown herringbone tweed jacket with dark flannel trousers and pointed Rhodorian boots. "Mark," Moulding said, putting his hand on the man's shoulder, "I want you to meet Wilf Brim—a person you'd want to know even if he weren't about to do some flying for you."

The man had a sizable nose, damp, humorous eyes, and a drooping black moustache of truly prodigious size. His woolen coat and trousers hinted of a cool home climate, and he wore an old-fashioned white shirt and necktie. "Glad to meet you, Wilf," he said, extending his hand. "Mark Valerian's my name."

"Glad to meet you," Brim said, gripping Valerian's hand in his own. The man's name rang a bell somehow, but he couldn't quite place it. "I'm at the Fleet base here in Atalanta," he added, slipping into his chair.

"I work for Veronica Pike over at Sherrington's," Valerian returned.

"Sweet Universe," Brim swore, suddenly recalling where he'd heard Valerian's name before. "You're the designer who engineered the attack launch for I.F.S. *Intractable*, aren't you? —the one built to Abner Klisnikov's specifications."

Valerian's bushy eyebrows arched with sudden amazement. "Where in the galaxy did you hear about that overpowered beast?" he exclaimed. "I thought that little kite was blown to atoms when *Intractable* hit a space mine back during the war."

"Not quite," Brim replied with a growing sense of excitement. "She *was* eventually destroyed in the war, along with a grand old starship named *Prize*. But she lasted long enough that I got to put in quite a few metacycles at her controls. I even took her on a mission—and, yeah, she *was* a bit overpowered with those two big spin gravs, but all in all . . ."

Moulding laughed as he took his seat. "Somehow," he said, "I thought you two might have a lot to talk over, but I didn't know about Abner Klisnikov's starship. Universe."

"What's this about Klisnikov's starship?" a handsome woman in an exquisite uniform broke in. "Abner was the greatest Helmsman of all time, I understand."

"Yeah," another interjected. "Let's hear . . ."

At that point, the harried waiters arrived to serve luncheon. In addition to goblets of vintage Logish Meem, they brought rich soups, delicate luncheon *saucisson* from rare game meats, cheese of every flavor and persuasion, yeasty breads fresh from the oven, fruits from all over the galaxy, *glacés* and desserts of every conceivable description. It slowed, but never completely defeated, the eager conversations that ebbed and flowed among the very serious deep-space advocates at the table. The banquet took fully two standard metacycles to consume, but by the end of it, Brim had come to understand that not *all* of the ISS members were wealthy fops, although it was reasonably clear that most were wealthy beyond his own wildest dreams. To his surprise, he was sitting with the elite Imperial Fleet's High-Speed Starflight Team.

Following a second dessert course, the Duke of Washburn brought the meeting to order, or at least to a semblance of order. At most of the other tables, conversations went on unabated, albeit in a quieter tone. Many of the socialites were nodding in their chairs while Romanoff recited the minutes of the last meeting, and some actually fell asleep while Collingswood went through the motions of introducing the Society's reorganized racing plan.

Brim's eyes met Valerian's for a moment. "Are they like this all the time?" he whispered.

"I don't know," Valerian confided quietly beneath a glowering frown. "But if wealthy people *have* to act this discourteously, I think I'd just as soon stay indigent, thank you."

Brim was about to comment further when Onrad rose to speak. That served to quiet the irritating hum of conversation that pervaded the room.

"Today," the Prince announced in his most monarchical rhetoric, "the Imperial Starship Society begins an altogether new racing curriculum—one that will forever change the way we conduct our competitive activities." With that, he explained at length that Sherrington Hyperspace Works had already been retained to design and construct a special racing hull under Chief Designer Mark J. Valerian. Furthermore, the Sodeskayan firm of Krasni-Peych, whose galaxy-famous research center was located only a short drive outside Gromcow, would supply both a gravity propulsion system and Hyperspace Drive.

Brim grinned to himself. That explained a few things, including the presence in Atalanta of his two Sodeskayan friends. Then his heart stood still when he heard his own name.

"Additionally," Onrad proclaimed, "not only has the Admiralty directed the Fleet's renowned High-Speed Starflight team to act as our consultants, we have ourselves engaged the services of Mr. Wilf Brim, an extraordinary Fleet veteran and

Diagnostic Helmsman from the base here at Atalanta, to serve as Principal Racing Helmsman for the Society. . . . "

Brim felt his face flush as polite applause rippled through the room. He glanced at Moulding and Valerian, then shrugged. "First I heard about any of this," he whispered.

"You mean he didn't *ask* you beforehand?" Moulding queried in astonishment.

Brim chuckled. "Why bother?" he asked. "There isn't a Helmsman alive who'd turn down a berth in the Mitchell and he knows it." Then he turned to Valerian and grinned. "Especially if that Helmsman flew one of Mark Valerian's ships before."

"Well, I thank you kindly," the designer said with a pleased look of surprise on his face. Frowning mightily, he seemed to deliberate for a moment, then after some sort of conclusion reached inside his coat and withdrew a folded scrap of cheap, yellow note plastic. "Tell me what you think of this," he said, handing it to Brim.

The Carescrian felt his eyes widen with genuine awe as he unfolded the scrap of plastic on the tablecloth between himself and Moulding. On it, Valerian had sketched three views of a starship that could only be described as an aerodynamic master-piece—a graceful collection of fluid, elliptical curves that represented a total departure from the last two centuries of angular, wedge-shaped design. Brim turned the elegant little starship in his imagination: a truly handsome conformation of second-degree conics that managed to integrate hull and superstructure into one perfectly aesthetic whole. After what he realized must have been considerable time, he looked up from the drawing and peered into Valerian's eyes. "Universe," he whispered almost reverently, "I'd probably *kill* for a chance to fly something like this."

"Do you suppose you could use an accessory to that killing?" Moulding asked. "I'm sure any of us on the Team will be glad to help."

Brim grabbed Moulding's hand. "You're on, Toby," he said, "but I have a feeling that we'll need *everyone's* help before this thing is over."

A ripple of quiet cheering went 'round the table as the others raised a toast with their goblets.

"In that case," Valerian said, looking around the room with a frown, "I suppose His Bloody Cocksure Highness over yonder is going to have his way *again*—despite this gaggle of high-brow society blockheads at the other tables." He swiveled his chair to face the two Helmsmen and tapped the yellow scrap of plastic with a long, slim finger. "The problem is," he drawled, "this time, things aren't going to turn out entirely the way Onrad wants them."

Brim raised an eyebrow while the remainder of their table-mates leaned forward in expectation, hanging on Valerian's words.

"Complex systems like starships don't just come together instantly," the designer explained, "especially new ones that have to be faster than anything else in the galaxy." He took the drawing from the table and tucked it back into his coat. "It takes time to produce this kind of a design, even when we hurry. And," he continued, nodding toward the two Bears at the other end of the table, "I can't believe that our Sodeskayan friends are going to come up with their new drive much faster."

Brim nodded understandingly. His experience getting I.F.S. *Defiant* ready for action had been an excellent lesson in the difficulties of new starships. And *Defiant* hadn't been even half as radical as what appeared to be on Valerian's mind.

"What happens if you aren't ready for next year?" a Lieutenant on the far side of the table asked.

"Onrad will simply have to wait," Valerian said with a shrug.

"Think he will?" another queried.

"If he wants to race this beauty, he will," Valerian stated, patting his coat pocket. "But then, he'll be pretty sure Sherrington can make it worth his while," he added, "especially now that these two have agreed to fly."

Brim grinned. "In that case, brother Valerian, keep in touch. I don't plan to be anywhere else for the next year or so."

"Nor do I," Moulding echoed.

"Oh, I shall *assuredly* keep in touch, my friends," Valerian warranted with a grin. "We've got a trophy to win."

True to Valerian's prediction, neither the radical Sherrington hull nor its new Krasni-Peych Drive was ready in time for the race at the League capital of Tarrott; therefore, no Imperial entry appeared in the Mitchell lineup of 52004. Onrad blustered, but in the end conceded that some things, like the creation of new starships, were beyond even his most heavy-handed cajoling. Eventually, he even decreed that certain of the Society's operational consultants should attend the contest as guest observers. And so it was that Wilf Brim and Toby Moulding found themselves disembarking from a passenger liner into a city whose citizens, only a few years before, would gladly have blasted either of them into subatomic particles on sight.

For Brim, whose most memorable face-to-face encounter with Leaguers had been punctuated by excruciating pain and brutal torture, the visit produced strange emotions, indeed. They were no stranger, of course, than the journey itself, his first as a paying customer on a starliner rigged out for peacetime service. S.S. *Montcalm*, a twin-Drive fast packet, launched the previous year by A. G. Vuklin in the domain of Peret'nium, was totally unlike the occasional converted transports on which he had normally traveled during the war. Unfortunately, his intimate knowledge of the menials who labored below decks to insure his comfort took the edge off what might have been an expansive feeling, even riding in the tourist section.

Now, standing in the pompous, oppressively columned terminus of a city whose very name embodied death and destruction, a sense of oppression enveloped him like a heavy, wet canvas. Little wonder Sodeskayans refused to attend the race, even though Leaguers were now forbidden by treaty from the Bearskin coats they fancied. Everywhere he looked, people strutted along the concourses wearing colorful military uniforms with holstered blasters and decorative daggers dangling from their belts. There were the League's "normal" military Legionnaires dressed in coarse gray uniforms; sinister Controllers in jet black finery; Labor Corps Associates outfitted in ochre; ONL (National Transport Workers) officers in vivid red; the Youth Corps in umber coveralls with wide yellow sashes; girls of the XLD (Alliance of Cloud League Maidens) in severe green jumpers; even six-year-old *Gru'mphe*, or Child Troopers of the Leaguer confederation, dressed in black like mini-Controllers. All moved with some terrible inner zeal, barking orders at one another as though they were still at war. And everywhere was the sick-sweet foulness of TimeWeed, the mysterious narcotic all Controllers were known to smoke.

Brim became so absorbed in the arrogant spectacle that he was quite startled when a smiling, well-dressed little man in the dark gray livery of the Imperial Foreign Service tapped Moulding on the shoulder. He had a long, narrow face, a prominent nose, and laughing eyes whose humor even a permanent glower could ill suppress.

"I say," he drawled, peering discreetly at a microdisplay on his left wrist, "you two must be Moulding and Brim."

"That's us," Moulding answered with a frown. "And . . . ?"

"'Arry Drummond from the Imperial Embassy," the little man explained. He deftly extended the tiny holobadge of an Imperial Attache in the palm of his hand. "'Is 'Ighness Prince Onrad sent me out to fetch th' two uv you to the embassy. 'E figured it'd be easier wiv' me drivin' since you'd both probably feel uncomfortable wiv'out a couple of disruptors between yourselves and the bloody Leaguers 'ere."

"He had *that* right," Brim chuckled. "I've never seen so many of their uniforms all in one place."

"Makes you wonder what it's like when they actually give a war," Drummond said, leading the way toward a huge, over-burdened archway marked DIPLOMATIC ONLY in Vertrucht, the League's language.

"I think I'd just as soon not find out," Brim quipped. He meant it. If this one terminal were any indication, every man, woman, and child in the whole League was ready to resume fighting at a moment's notice.

Outside under the massive portico, Brim and Moulding climbed into the rear compartment of an imperious Majestat-Baron limousine skimmer. Moments later, Drummond deftly set course into one of a wide band of cableways, the League's version of normal highways. Near these cables, automatic devices in Leaguer vehicles could take over and "follow the wire," as the expression went. The driver then had only to effect cable switches at the proper times to reach any destination, steering with rudder-pedals for short distances off the ends. "All hands to action stations," he joked as they meshed with the bustling, mostly military traffic. "This is going to be more like an invasion than a visit."

Tarrott was located near the center of a large, temperate continent in the boreal hemisphere of Dahlem, a small planet orbiting a bright trinary known collectively as Uadn'aps. The city was roughly triangular in shape and divided by both the meandering river Eer'pz and a brutally linear canal known as the Conquest Waterway. On the nightward side of the city, the river was dammed into a sizable body of water, Lake Tegeler, that served as a landing area for the vast intergalactic starship terminal and also as the site of the race.

The centerpiece of historic Tarrott, however, was its Avenue of the Conquerors, a wide band of cables and pavement that traditionally formed the city's lightward-nightward axis. From time immemorial, it had served as the main political artery of an entire domain, scene of countless military pageants and parade ground of League power, a most imposing and famous byway. At its nightward end rose the galaxy-famous Martial Gate, striking symbol of its government's philosophy. Located precisely five c'lenyts nightward from the great spaceport, it was a majestic series of arches resting on twelve splendid riotinic columns. Its perfect proportions were based on those of the Propylaea, an enigmatic artifact in the Twelfth Realm, apparently abandoned by a race of sentients that had disappeared without a trace from the Universe long before the contemporary system of domains achieved interstellar flight. At the top of the gate was a gigantic statue depicting the allegorical Goddess of Victory (or Peace, depending on which period of League history one chose), her chariot drawn by four leonine gryphons, whose great wings were caught forever in gleaming metallic flight.

Settled in the comfortable seat of Drummond's skimmer, Brim could only stare in awe as they pulled into the main stream of traffic and threaded their way through one of its central arches. The monument had been created centuries ago by one of the greatest of Leaguer Romantic artists, sculptor-architect Gotfried Bernard Buss, and even today, its flowing beauty seemed to embody all that was good about the League. But its arrogant theme stood for all that was hateful as well. Brim looked out the window at twin rows of huge, amber trees lining the roadway, bracing himself in the seat as Drummond bounced back and forth among the cables, dodging other black Majestat-Baron limousines speeding importantly by with sirens blasting the afternoon air. There were few people to be seen on the sidewalks for such a large city. And those who were afoot appeared to be driven by some compulsion. Outdoors, Tarrott seemed to be more conducive to machines than to flesh and blood; it was not a comfortable, or comforting, place.

"Busy place, ain't it?" Drummond commented as he swerved into a faster traffic cable.

"Glad you're driving instead of me," Moulding answered with a grin.

Presently, he recognized the templelike Royal Cultural Center, built for feebleminded Emperor Renzo the Magnificent in the 48000's. It now served as home of the State Enrichment Directorship, whatever that was. Small by other galactic standards, the overblown-rococo structure made up for in glitter what it lacked in size. Beside it stood a building Brim recognized from his Arnholtt Guidebook as Schlegel University: a restored palace originally built for Prince Gonlow'e, Renzo's half brother. Walkways and small parks around the building were filled with students, as purposeful and uniformly clothed as if they were marching in a parade. The Carescrian shuddered. What kind of peace could the future bring if whole generations were being raised as warriors? His answer seemed all too clear. Farther along the great avenue, he recognized five clustered, interlocking domes of gleaming gold, surmounted by a great KA'PPA antenna. It was there Neuffman Van Zeicht had perfected the Raddiman-Gebritz generators that once powered nearly a thousand years of starships. After five millennia, the complex structures showed no sign of age and were still in constant, active use. "Factory zone, Toby," he joked.

"Right ho," Moulding commented wryly. "Couldn't miss the local Gorn-Hoff branch office."

Brim laughed. Nearly everyone knew for a fact that Valentin's speedy Gorn-Hoff TA 153-V32 had been modified for racing in those very labs. And the League's powerful new racer for this year's contest, the Gantheisser GA 209V-1, had also been developed there—although the Leaguers were attempting to convince the galaxy that the unique starship was little more than a "normal" Gantheisser production machine.

Not far past the laboratory domes was a huge and totally new statue honoring Leaguers who had fallen in the "War of Heroes," as the just-ended conflict was known throughout the League. The massive statue of a Controller was erected on a plot of land that once boasted a royal palace which in its day dominated the whole center of the city. A few blocks beyond on the left, an immense brick-shaped structure with black glass sides disrupted the whole skyline. The League Chancellery. Everyone on both sides of the war knew its grim, unrelieved lines. It contained the Congress of the League, a number of reception halls for state occasions, and an auditorium that seated five thousand people. In addition, the guidebook made reference to "several highly rated gastronomic establishments." Brim snorted to himself. The Chancellery might rate highly in a Leaguer gastronomic guide, but it was doubtful to even his untrained eye that it would ever win a prize for architectural merit. It stood, pompous and contemporary, in contradiction to the other neoclassical (albeit haughty) buildings that populated the avenue. He settled back and considered that his first views of the great stone and metal city had done nothing to soften his feelings about these once-mortal enemies. He nevertheless resolved to keep an open mind as long as he could.

At last, Drummond slowed for a great intersection, eased into a curb cable, and swung their big skimmer onto a tree-lined avenue of the diplomatic quarter. "Next stop, th' Imperial Embassy," he announced. Here were block after block of embassies from every domain wealthy enough to maintain intragalactic trade. Some of the largest were those of the League's wartime partners: pompous mansions built in the prevailing Leaguer style with colonnades and balconies from which visiting dignitaries could greet Leaguer crowds. One of the newest and most garish was decorated with the Torond's coat of arms. Frowning, Brim wondered if Margot might be in the city for the races. The mere thought of such a possibility was enough to start his heart pounding, and he shook his head in negation. He took a deep breath and forced the thought from his mind. Business first.

Moments later, they braked onto a wide driveway that skirted a triad of shimmering flame fountains, then stopped beneath a tasteful metal portico at the entrance to the Imperial Embassy. "Won't keep you gentlemen 'ere more 'an a couple of metacycles at the most," he explained. "But we've found it's good to understand a little about 'ow the Leaguers operate on their 'ome turf. Those bully boys paradin' all over can get a little rough if you don't know about their rules."

Brim nodded as painful memories flashed past his mind's eye. "I've noticed," he growled under his breath. Then he frowned. The embassy faced a small park across the avenue that seemed to exist for the sole purpose of containing a large and uncanny likeness of Nergol Triannic, the League's exiled emperor. But no nameplate had been affixed to the heroic statue's base.

"What d'you think of the statue?" Drummond asked while he hoisted their traveling cases from the luggage compartment and activated their ground repulsion units. "It 'asn't got an official name, but everybody around 'ere calls it 'Cousin Nergol.'" He laughed. "*Almost* ugly enough, ain't it?"

"It'll do by half," Moulding declared, staring at the menacing shape as if it were some sort of monstrous viper poised for an attack.

Brim kept his silence. In spite of the CIGA's vehement protestations to the contrary, no governing body with peaceful intentions could have purposely erected anything like that across the street from an old adversary. Chilling waves of apprehension passed over him. As he suspected, the war—*his* war—had merely evolved into another stage. And before it was over, this one promised to be a great deal more sinister and dangerous than the period of open conflict that had preceded it.

Taking momentary leave of Drummond, the two Helmsmen stepped inside the embassy's elegant, marble foyer, then followed signs to a small auditorium where they joined three other civilians for a short, informal briefing in which Imperials were urged to conduct themselves, at least publicly, in the most conservative manner possible. No surprises expected, nor received.

The briefer, a middle-aged Public Relations Analyst with a bald head, a large paunch, and the air of one who was quite accustomed to teaching, described "normal" Leaguers as talkative, full of abrasive good humor, and even reasonably friendly, despite their penchant for uniforms. Except for some peculiar beliefs, they posed no particular threat to anyone going about his normal, daily routines. It was the Controllers one had to watch at all times. And they were everywhere, enforcing every law to the very letter, with no room for interpretation. It seemed that the TimeWeed they smoked destroyed their reasoning process and made them bullies. *They* were the ones to watch. But Brim already knew that. Far too well.

Afterward, Drummond stopped them on their way from the auditorium. "Before we continue on to your room, Mr. Brim," he said quietly, "they tell me there's somebody 'ere who would like to spend a few moments talking wiv you."

Brim raised an eyebrow. "I don't know anybody in Tarrott," he protested, "at least anybody who might want to talk to me."

Drummond shrugged. " 'Is 'Ighness Prince Onrad's the one who sent me," he said in a confiding tone. "An' it probably won't take too much time. You know 'ow these diplomatic things go." He smiled. "I'll show Lieutenant Moulding an excellent bar we 'ave for *special* guests. Prince Onrad's waitin' for 'im there right now."

Brim shook his head in mock defeat. "Anything for the Prince," he said. "He's about the embassy, I take it then."

" 'E is," Drummond said. " 'E said to tell you that 'e'd probably see *you* in the evenin'—when you 'ad more time to spend with 'im."

"More time?" Brim asked. "What else have I got to do this afternoon?"

"Beats me, Mr. Brim," Drummond said, leading the way along a side corridor, "but 'Is 'Ighness evidently thinks you'll be busy with someone. 'E 'as me standin' by for as long as it takes."

"I'll try not to keep either of you too long," Brim said to Moulding.

Drummond stopped by a door at the end of a hall and put his hand on the latch. "Lieutenant Moulding and I have got all the time in the Universe this afternoon, Brim," he said with an abrupt change of character. "I wouldn't want to think you'd wasted even a click of it worrying about either of us—or anything else for that matter." With that, he opened the door and swept Brim inside with a firm hand in the small of his back. "You can ring when you need me—the bell's on a chord in the bar."

As the door clicked shut, Brim found himself in a darkened, paneled lounge off a side corridor. Except for a tiny, well-stocked bar, the room was small and intimate. The kind of room, he guessed, where *real* diplomacy was carried out, not the opulent ballrooms where phony conferences were posed around ornate tables for public consumption.

Squinting while his eyes accustomed themselves to the dimness, he jumped when a woman's figure rose from a shadowed chair on the opposite side of the room and started toward him.

"Margot!" he gasped, his heart suddenly pounding as if it would burst from his chest. "Margot!"

Then his arms were abruptly filled with perfumed softness, her lips smothering his with warm, wet kisses, and for a long time, his mind went whirling aimlessly. When at last he opened his eyes, hers were still closed. He paused while her breathing steadied, then gently kissed her eyes, salty and wet with tears. "Margot," he whispered. "Sometimes I thought I'd never see you again."

She nodded silently, then opened her eyes and seemed to peer directly into his very spirit. "And I was so afraid for you —every waking moment. It seemed like a million years."

Brim pressed her cheek to his. "I survived—for this day," he said gently.

She hugged him tighter. "Oh, Universe," she whispered, "I've missed you so much, Wilf." After that, she became silent for a long time, as if fighting some terrific force within herself. Finally, she bit her lip "Can you still love me now that things have changed so . . . ?" she asked. Then her voice trailed off into silence again as if she were afraid to finish.

"You mean now that you have a child?" Brim asked, puzzled.

"Something like that, Wilf," she said vaguely, moving her head back slightly so she could focus into his eyes again. "There is now another part of me—an important part, and one that most likely will last as long as I exist. Can you accept that?"

Brim unexpectedly felt something seize inside himself. Here, in this room, he found he couldn't answer the question as he'd expected he might. He'd certainly thought enough about her motherhood over the last year or so. He knew he could accept it. But this child? Involuntarily, he raised his hands in supplication. "I-I don't know, Margot," he stammered in a sudden agony of emotion. "I never took him into consideration that way."

"You've got to, Wilf," she said, pushing herself gently from his embrace. "I tried to tell you about me in the letter Onrad smuggled out. I guess I didn't do a very good job."

In the light, Brim could see that she was dressed in a white silk blouse and black velvet skirt with high-heeled boots. Her blond hair was piled loosely on her head, and she wore a single strand of pearls around her neck. As usual, she looked stunning. He shook his head, "I simply read into your words what I wanted to hear," he heard himself admit, "not what you were trying to say." He led her to a small sofa and they sat in silence for what seemed to be ages. Finally, his mind formed the one simple question at the root of his problem. "I wonder," he said, "do I really know you anymore, Margot?"

She nodded sadly. "A fair question, Wilf," she answered, again looking deeply into his eyes. "And the answer is partially yes. But only partially."

"Do you still love me?" he asked.

"More than ever, I think," she answered. She smiled and frowned in her own unique way. "Yet I love Rodyard, too. Differently, of course. The important part is that I find my affection for him doesn't subtract from some finite 'love pool' within me. It's an *extension*—an increase, if you will." She looked at him beseechingly. "Does that make any sense at all?"

Brim thought a moment. It seemed to make sense; but then, he wanted it to. What he failed to understand was how he felt about the child. He shuddered when he remembered how he had been affected by Rogan LaKarn's child long before he had even been born. After a long moment of silence, he took her hand. "How do we get things started again?" he asked. "I mean . . ." He shook his head. He couldn't put his thoughts into words.

She laughed ruefully and nodded her head. "I don't know," she said. "I'm not even sure what 'getting started' means." She turned to him with a sad little look in her eyes. "Perhaps if I were to take off my clothes here?" she asked.

Brim took a deep breath. "Well," he admitted, feeling a familiar stirring in his loins, "I suppose that's *part* of it. At least it always *was*—before I . . . I couldn't that night."

Margot laughed quietly. "Wilf," she said, turning to place the softness of her hand against his cheek, "forget about that night back on Avalon. It wasn't your fault—the whole Universe had ganged up on you. Besides," she added with a look of distress, "this time, it has nothing to do with you. It's *me*." She shook her head. "Do you think for a moment that I'd be sitting here like this if I were my normal self? You know me better than that. We'd be noisily rutting on this couch right now—and I wouldn't even care who watched us through the spy peepers."

"You mean you don't *want* to anymore?" Brim asked.

Margot frowned and shifted in her seat. "I'm not sure that's a proper way to put it, Wilf," she answered with a serious little smile. "It's almost as if we'd just *finished* doing it—and I was at the relaxed end of some great, protracted orgasm. I guess my body's still all taken up with, well, other things right now. It's simply not very conducive to . . . well . . . to having the kind of affair we'd been having—like sneaking halfway across a galaxy for one night in bed." She looked at him imploringly. "Do you have any idea what I'm trying to say to you Wilf?" she asked.

Brim tenderly put his arm around her shoulder. "No," he said, "I don't suppose I do."

"Can you live with that?" she asked.

He frowned. "I'm not really sure," he admitted, astonished by his own words. Something very basic had changed since that night in his shabby apartment, but as yet he couldn't completely define what it was, or perhaps didn't *want* to.

Margot suddenly looked frightened. "Th-then what's to become of us?" she asked.

"Eventually," Brim said, again utterly surprised by his own lack of emotion, "everything we ever wanted in life." He folded her hand in his. "So long as I *really* love you and you *really* love me, Margot, it seems to me that all we have to do is wait. Eventually, we'll be together again."

Margot suddenly threw her arms around his shoulders. "Do you mean that, Wilf?" she asked. "Really?"

"I can only prove it to you some time in the future, Margot," Brim answered. "And," he added, probing deeply into her eyes, "*you* will have to tell me when that time has come—for it will be *you* who determines it."

After that, they stood silently, wrapped in each other's embrace until the tiny chime of Margot's timepiece sounded from her purse.

"I've got to go," she said.

Brim nodded. "Until then," he said with a strange, empty feeling in his stomach. "You'll let me know."

"Yes, my dearest," Margot whispered, opening a panel in the wall, "until then." Beyond, in a dim passage, stood two chauffeurs dressed in the green, white, and red colors of the Torond. "We shall see each other more often now that my captivity has ended," she said. "And I *shall* let you know. I shall shout it to the very Universe." Then she squeezed his hand and was gone, hurrying down the passageway as the panel slid noiselessly shut.

During the next few days, Brim and Moulding spent most of their waking metacycles poking around the race district, making the most of the HELMSMAN: ALL ZONES guest passes they had been issued as members of the Imperial Starflight Society's racing committee. At first, they were hesitant to enter the shed area where the starships were being groomed for the race. Then, utterly amazed at how much leeway the passes actually permitted, they began to barge through every hangar—Moulding in full uniform, Brim in casual civilian clothes—studying whatever they could lay their eyes on.

The racers themselves were tiny in comparison to normal starships; even the largest carried a crew of two or three at maximum. Floating on custom gravity pads, these special machines came in every conceivable shape and style. Some were slim and graceful, optimized for efficient operation within the race's dictated atmospheric takeoff and landing areas; others were squat and clearly shaped to enclose the maximum propulsion apparatus possible within an envelope of minimum mass-to-drag ratio. Still others disregarded atmospherics almost completely, relying on brute power to achieve speed objectives in the void of space where a preponderance of the racing would be done. All, however, shared one characteristic in common: they were colorful. R'autor RC3-5s from A'zurn raced in gleaming silver with red and white stripes curving gracefully from diminutive Hyperscreens to Drive outlets; Dampier DA.39s, first native entries from LaKarn's Torond, were colored a stunning orange-green with national colors vertically striped on their huge gravity-generator outriggers; businesslike Gantheisser GA 209V-1s from the League were purest white with gleaming red sponsons and bridge highlights; Velone-451s from Beta Jagow raced in bright green with jasmine racing bands and black accents. Brim, who had spent most of his flying years on clapped-out ore barges or uniformly obsidian-colored Fleet warships, found himself fascinated by the colorful spectacle.

Out on breezy Lake Tegeler, speeding pleasure craft and tour boats roiled the waters all day, trailing endless wakes that gleamed against the deep blue like white ribbons of foam among the endless march of waves. In the starship lanes, great liners came and went, their rumbling thunder linking the great capital city to the distant ends of the galaxy. Now and then, one of the racers would crackle out to a takeoff vector, freezing every form of movement on the sparkling surface until it had completed its tests, whatever they happened to be.

And in the background, forbidding ranks of gray warships hovered at their moorings, tier upon tier of grim superfiring disruptors parked fore and aft. Brim shuddered; these huge Leaguer ships clearly didn't exist in the filtered vision of the CIGAs. But when it came time to fight—and that time *would* come—what Imperial ships would remain to face them?

The race pavilion itself encompassed a broad, paved apron on the austral banks of the lake. Facing the inland perimeter of the apron was an imposing grandstand with a colossal crystal bubble that could be moved into place during inclement weather. Shed areas where the starships were prepared by their various crews were sited at either side of the grandstand. The "sheds" themselves, were identical cylindroid hangars, individually fitted out and equipped by the racing teams that inhabited them. Fronting each of these was a fixed, "standard" gravity pool whose dimensions and parameters had been agreed upon among representatives of the contestants months prior to the race. It was from these that the racers would depart and return, like the commercial starships of Mitchell's dream.

Each shed took on the personality of the domain to which it had been assigned. The Leaguer shed, for example, had four of the gleaming new Gantheisser racing machines parked out back, as backups. Inside, the walls were lined with precisely ordered rows of accessories for use by veritable armies of technicians in white laboratory coats who swarmed over the two racers that were being readied for the actual contest. Brim shook his head as teams of meticulous Leaguers carried out complete practice shop drills timed by a Controller with a huge chronometer. These people were out to win their second race in a row—no ifs or buts about it. He wondered when he would encounter his old adversary Kirsh Valentin.

In contrast to the machinelike organization in the Leaguer's shed, an absolute confusion of activity seemed to spin around the Torond's two graceful Dampier starships. Mechanics and technicians were everywhere, swarming over the two DA.39s like a plague of insects. Brim needed no coaching to take *that* team's efforts seriously, in spite of his personal attitude toward Baron Rogan LaKarn. Mario Marino built first-rate starships.

Brim had special friends in the A'zurnian shed, and had purposefully saved that visit for last. Otherwise, he'd strongly suspected that he might see little else on the lakefront. And he was substantially correct. As soon as he and Moulding arrived, they were treated as if they had personally signed on as members of the A'zurnian racing team. Brim's special friend Aram of Nahshon was off planet for the day, but others had been alerted for the arrival of two Imperials, and they were afforded hospitality that was clearly reserved for visiting dignitaries.

Metacycles later—after much fine Logish Meem and a most detailed inspection of the A'zurnian's chunky little R'autor RC3 racer—the two Imperials had just climbed into their skimmer when Moulding pointed at a long, pretentious Majestat-Baron limousine coming off the cable toward the Leaguer's shed. "Important bus if I ever saw one," he observed. "Suppose we ought to drive over for a closer look?"

"Sounds like a plan to me," Brim chuckled. "After all, these guest passes make us all bosom buddies. Right?"

"Right *ho*," Moulding agreed sarcastically. "Brothers all under the skin—or something like that."

Without even linking their car onto a cable, Brim steered a direct course (more or less) across three parking lots with the rudder pedals alone. "Never did believe in their damned guide wires," he joked as they jolted at right angles across a number of cableways.

Moulding shook his head sagely. "Brother Brim," he answered, "if you keep this up, you're going to make things very difficult when you apply for League citizenship."

"Ah . . . *yeah*," Brim agreed, with his index finger raised cheerfully. "That's precisely what I had in mind." Moments later, they whirred through a huge ornamental garden, careened around a fountain in a cloud of tumbling flowers, and drew to a halt in a parking stall near the front of the Leaguer's shed. The big skimmer was just coming to a stop under the portico, where an honor guard of gray-uniformed Legionnaires braced at stiff attention. As the two Imperials debarked and strolled to the front of their car, the alert Commander met Brim's eye. His hostile glare made it amply clear that the Legionnaires behind him were in place for more than the ceremony.

Grinning, Brim shot a rakish salute to the man, then settled back to watch as the hulking Majestat-Baron began to disgorge its passengers—all Controllers.

First out was a brutish Galite'er, Leaguer equivalent of an Imperial Commodore. Heavyset and totally bald around his high-peaked cap, the man had vast shoulders and a massive frame that seemed to threaten his tight black tunic with every movement he made. After him came a dwarfish, middle-aged woman—an OverGalite'er—who walked with a distinct limp, as if her right foot were damaged in some way. She was followed by another woman, a buxom, athletic-looking Praefect who was much younger than the other two.

"Hmm," Moulding observed, raising his eyebrows in approval. "Now *there's* an improvement if I ever saw one."

"Maybe," Brim answered, "but I'll bet she wears her blaster to bed."

"Uncomfortable, that," Moulding conceded, wrinkling his nose.

"More than one would imagine," Brim quipped from the side of his mouth.

Last out of the Majestat-Baron was a tall, well-built figure of a Provost who, even from behind, made Brim's scalp bristle. Instantly, the Commander of the honor guard stepped from his position and took the man by his elbow, nodding toward the two Imperials in the parking lot as he spoke.

"Looks as if you're being tattled upon," Moulding quipped. "Perhaps this will teach you to not to drive through Leaguer flower beds so indifferently. . . ."

Still with his back to the parking lot, the tall Provost haughtily dismissed the Legionnaire, then called something to his companions. Only the Praefect responded, turning for a moment and nodding before she followed her two superiors through the door. This accomplished, the man spun on his heel and peered out into the evening darkness, his aristocratic features highlighted by the overhead lights.

Brim inadvertently caught his breath.

"Friend of yours?" Moulding asked.

"An acquaintance," Brim growled through clenched teeth.

"We got together a couple of times during the war. His name is Kirsh Valentin."

"Somehow, I thought I recognized him," Moulding said grimly, watching the Provost start across the parking lot toward them, his boots clicking smartly on the pavement.

As Valentin approached, Brim leaned casually against the cable car, his head spinning with loathsome memories; the man represented everything he detested. Suddenly, his churning emotions turned to icy calm, almost as if he were on the bridge of a starship preparing for battle. He took two steps forward, then settled calmly with his hands on his hips, legs apart, waiting. It was Valentin's territory. He could make the next move.

The Leaguer stopped a short distance from Brim, smiled, and clicked his heels. "Well, my once and future antagonist," he said, peeling off a white glove and extending his hand. "It has been a long time, hasn't it?" He smelled both of cologne and TimeWeed.

Brim gripped the proffered hand. It was cool and dry. "Probably not long enough, Valentin," he said, meeting the man's gaze with a sardonic grin. "—for either of us."

Valentin laughed. "Ah, Brim. You Imperials take life too seriously. The war is over, my friend. And forgotten. We are no longer enemies: merely competitors. Spend some time considering what your one-time shipmate Puvis Amherst has to say. That organization of his, the Congress for..." He pinched the bridge of his nose.

"Intragalactic Accord," Brim prompted as if he had just pronounced a truly evil malediction. He'd heard that the cowardly Amherst—once a shipmate aboard I.F.S. *Truculent*—had become a major force in the CIGA, but he had no idea how famous the man had become.

"*Yes*," Valentin remarked, "the Congress for Galactic Accord—'CIGAs' you call them. Well, you should listen to what they have to say. That movement represents the future—a truly nonaggressive society whose time has come." Then he snickered. "But of course," he added, opening his arms in a magnanimous gesture that wounded Brim to his soul, "you don't even wear a uniform anymore, do you?"

"In spite of the thraggling CIGA traitors at home, some of my friends still do," Brim replied through clenched teeth. "Commander Toby Moulding, meet Kirsh Valentin."

Valentin clicked his heels and bowed slightly without offering his hand. "I am honored to make your acquaintance, Commander," he said.

Moulding smiled at the obvious snub. "Yes," he agreed quietly, "you are."

Contemptuous anger blazed momentarily in Valentin's eyes. "Your score, Commander," he acknowledged. For a moment, he inspected his perfectly manicured fingernails, unconsciously grinding his teeth. "How regrettable," he observed at length, "that you Imperials have been unable to ready a starship for the races this year. But I am told that you both inspected our Gantheisser GA 209V-1s today, so you will already know that the race would have been ours in any case. That must be *some* recompense."

"Races are never won until the finish line is crossed," Moulding reciprocated. "I wasn't aware that any official heats were run today."

"Ah, my dear Moulding," Valentin chuckled, raising his hands palm up to his waist, "of course the race must be *actually* run, but can there be any question about its resolution?"

Moulding stuck to his ground. "I'm dashed if I'll concede you the race, Valentin," he said hotly. "No matter how good that new Gantheisser looks, it won't be the winner until it is actually fastest over the race course. And quite a lot can happen between now and then, you know."

"True," Valentin allowed, "but it won't. We have left nothing to chance. You will see this is true when I personally pilot the winning starship." Then his eyes narrowed. "And for next year's race," he added, this time looking directly at Brim, "there is nothing your poor Sherrington Works can produce that will compare to the Gantheissers we have under development. Believe me. I have already seen the mock-ups."

"Next year at this time," Brim said, "I shall be quite glad— and ready—to discuss next year's racers. Right now, this year's is quite enough for me to digest."

"True," Valentin said. "I trust you will be present at the finish line?"

"Count on it," Brim said. "I wouldn't miss a moment of it."

"Good," Valentin said, pulling on his white gloves. "Then you will watch me win." He chuckled cynically. "It will prepare you for next year—if Valerian and your silly Bears can actually cobble a new ship together by that time."

"We'll see next year, won't we?" Brim answered.

"Indeed we shall," Valentin relented with a smirk. "But I really did not come to argue racing tonight," he said. "Actually, I came to personally extend *you*, Commander Moulding, and your civilian friend, an invitation to a Chancellery reception tomorrow night before the race. Kabul Anak is in the capital for the races and is interested in meeting you both. Formal attire, of course."

Brim met his partner's eyes. "How about it, Toby?" he asked. "I can't imagine you traveling without a formal uniform, and I'll bet the embassy can throw together something appropriately civilian for me."

Moulding grinned. "I'm sure they can," he said. "Provost Valentin, I accept your kind offer. I have always hoped I should one day meet the famous Admiral Kabul Anak."

"And I," Brim added. "Perhaps one day we shall even have the honor of meeting Nergol Triannic himself."

Valentin's eyes narrowed. "The Emperor's exile will come to an end in good time, Imperials. You may count on it. Then..." His voice trailed off and he nodded to himself as if rehearsing some secret thought. He took a deep breath. "I shall look forward to the honor of meeting you again tomorrow evening," he said, dropping the subject of the exiled Nergol Triannic like a hot coal. Abruptly, he came to attention, clicked his heels, and started off toward the shed. As he cleared the entrance, six armed guards took their places on either side of the portico, and a sign lighted on the door itself: NO ADMITTANCE.

Clearly, the League's peaceful countenance existed only during daylight metacycles. Brim and Moulding left immediately for their hotel, each deep in his own thoughts.

The special reception was officially in honor of the race crews, but its published guest list made it clear that the event was really given to impress influential hangers-on who attended the race more as a social event.

Brim spent part of the morning studying a protocol manual supplied by the mysterious Drummond, who also volunteered to locate a suit of formal civilian evening clothes—no easy task, considering that most of the civilians who owned such outfits were also planning to wear them to the same event.

In fact, however, Drummond did show up with a black cutaway coat, trousers, and a ruffled shirt, along with two harried tailors. Their task of fitting Brim into clothes cut for someone considerably larger would surely have been easier had they started with a week in which to make their alterations. As it was, the bustling women effected excellent modifications to both the coat and the trousers in miraculously little time. Brim and Moulding arrived at the reception in an embassy limousine only a few cycles after the appointed time.

At night, the grim Chancellery was even more forbidding than in the daylight—an effect heightened by great searchlights that illuminated its vast flanks of black glass. As Drummond carefully threaded his embassy car into the wide driveway, the streets were packed with thousands of curious onlookers who pressed noisily against glowing guide ropes patrolled by legions of gray-uniformed guards carrying blast pikes.

Outside the cavernous portico, a great arc of flags on lofty flagpoles flowed and snapped in the night breeze creating a spectacle of color against the unrelieved blackness of the naked glass walls. Elsewhere, bunting decorated—or did it *hide*?—every surface from which it could be hung, and the broad Chancellery lawn fairly bristled with formations of battle-suited Legionnaires, their stiff-jointed commanders fiercely holding Leaguer standards: long poles, each topped by a gilded krieges'bat gripping two wreathed daggers in its claws.

"I don't know why they call it the League," Moulding commented quietly, returning the formal salute of at least a hundred Controllers as he alighted from the car. "With all the armed Legionnaires around here, most of those poor chaps on the street must feel like prisoners."

Inside, the Chancellery's cavernous entrance hall had its calculated effect: Brim was duly impressed. Only it reminded him of an overdone trade hall he'd once entered on some cheap little planet determined to impress its neighboring domains at any cost. The Leaguer architects had used polished white granite everywhere, on the walls and the ceiling—even the floor, where most of it was covered by thick, ebony carpeting. Fantastic chandeliers glowed and sparkled form hidden light sources like miniature galaxies. And above the hubbub, sinuous music from a large orchestra in a free-floating crystal globe interposed itself through an atmosphere that was already tinged with the sick-sweet odor of TimeWeed.

Brim and Moulding gave their names to a tall, blond, and blue-eyed protocol officer in a light blue uniform, then joined the long reception line. Out on the main floor, hundreds of uniformed supernumeraries darted among the elegant revelers, carrying trays of drinks and edibles and smiling so zealously that they seemed—at least to Brim—as if they might be candidates for the Gradgroat-Norchelite priesthood. A whole legion of others along the wall, however, stood rock still, their menacing eyes constantly in motion and their hands close to the huge holstered blasters that so cleverly blended into their uniforms.

"I say," Moulding whispered facetiously under his breath, "you don't suppose those bloody blasters are loaded, do you?"

Brim raised his eyebrows. "How could you even suggest such a thing?" he asked. "I thought *everybody* knew they carry meem in those holsters."

"Probably explodes when you drink it," Moulding grumped.

After nearly a metacycle, they neared the head of the line and Brim got his first good view of Grand Admiral Kabul Anak —the man who had assumed the reins of government in his Emperor's absence. Much smaller than Brim expected, he had usually been pictured in Imperial propaganda during the war as a huge, menacing giant. In real life, he appeared to be much less frightening—almost mundane. Brim was certain he would have walked past the little man on the street without particularly noticing him. He had long, gray hair to match a short beard and dense sidewhiskers that completely covered his ears. His exquisite Admiral's uniform—with all its decorations, campaign ribbons, and badges of rank—failed to conceal a late-middle-age paunch, and a certain drooping of the shoulders that was clearly the result of grievous war wounds sustained at the decisive Battle of Atalanta. It was said that nearly two-thirds of the man's body had been replaced in a healing machine after his super battleship *Rengas* had been reduced to tangled wreckage in a ship-to-ship contest with Erat Plutron's dauntless old *Queen Elidian*. Nevertheless, although clearly fatigued, he was quite gallantly clasping his guests' hands, exchanging a few words, then smiling as he passed them along, nodding to an aide for the next introduction. It almost seemed as if the man truly *wanted* to be liked, although Brim had grown far too cyncial about politicians in general to credit that with much thought.

Anak was also amazingly adept at all the handshakes that had developed throughout the domains of the galaxy. He gripped hands, elbows, and forearms; kissed fingers; bowed; and even bussed cheeks. And sometimes when attractive women were involved, he held on to these salutes for an extended time, especially if the salute involved a hug or a facial kiss. Brim smiled as he watched. The old space fox might well have boring moments in his job, but he clearly made the most of good ones when they came along!

He chatted briefly with the handsome A'zurnian couple ahead of the two Imperial Helmsmen, made his little gestures, then nodded to an aide in a snow white uniform trimmed by gold cord.

"Helmsman to the Imperial Starflight Society, Commander Tobias Moulding," echoed straightaway through the hall.

The Admiral's tired face slipped into boredom as he gripped Moulding's hand, and his eyes wandered momentarily onto the reception floor. The two exchanged a few perfunctory words that Brim couldn't hear, then Anak nodded once more to the aide.

"Principal Helmsman to the Imperial Starflight Society, Private Citizen Wilf Ansor Brim!"

Brim stepped before the Leaguer Admiral and extended his hand. For some reason, he felt no nervousness in the presence of this infamous personage and arch enemy of almost everything he held decent. "Your Excellency," he said, as directed by the protocol book he had studied in the afternoon—only he said it in perfect Vertrucht, the native language of the League.

"Ah, you *do* speak our language, don't you, Brim?" Anak said, smiling slightly and looking intensely into Brim's eyes. "I had almost forgotten." His handshake was cold and dry, but firm. Up close, his countenance regained all the legendary greatness that, over the years, Brim had bestowed on him in his imagination. Kabul Anak seemed every iral an Admiral.

"I learned your language in my youth," Brim answered, "aboard Carescrian ore barges."

"Yes, I know," Anak answered, looking Brim in the face. For a moment, he stood in silence, his blue eyes burning into the Carescrian's very soul. Abruptly, he shook his head. "How you must hate me," he said with an expression of genuine pain.

Brim could hardly credit his ears. "A-admiral?" he stammered in astonishment.

"I am aware," Anak continued quietly, "that during my first raid on Carescria, your young sister was killed. She died in your arms, if I am not mistaken."

Brim stood for a moment in silence, terribly aware that he was delaying a line of influential and important dignitaries, yet unwilling to break the awful conversation. "That is correct, Admiral," he heard himself say.

"Perhaps, then," Anak answered, "you will feel that the score is somewhat evened between us when I tell you that my only son died while attacking an Imperial convoy just prior to the battle for Atalanta." He took a deep breath, as if fighting some deep emotion. "His Gorn-Hoff 380A-8 was destroyed during a stern attack by the light cruiser I.F.S. *Defiant*," he continued quietly.

Anak's words hit Brim like a meteorite. "I don't know what to say, Admiral," he muttered.

"There are no adequate words, Mr. Brim," Anak said, nodding to his aide for the next guest, "only the understanding that *two* sides exist in every war."

Stunned, Brim moved on to the next dignitary in the line, but he never even heard the woman's name, nor, for that matter, the names of the other Leaguers he met that evening. Except for Valentin, of course, who never had time for him anyway. In fact, the appearance of Margot in a magnificent white gown was one of the few events that registered as the revelry continued. LaKarn himself was in an expansive mood, and stopped to greet the Carescrian as if he were some long-lost friend. Brim shook the man's hand, then bent to kiss Margot's beautiful tapered fingers. But when he peered into her eyes, he could see how much pain and embarrassment the exchange was actually causing her. After listening to the Baron boast pointedly about his new son for a few moments, he made a mindless excuse and joined Moulding, who was talking to a group of fashionable young Imperials—patriotic members of the Imperial High-Speed Starflight Team on temporary duty to study the race firsthand.

Subsequently, Anna Romanoff's appearance might well have

been the best part of Brim's evening. She looked the very picture of high fashion in a soft reddish brown knit coat that reached to her knees, a matching skirt, and an onyx turtleneck sweater. She was also, however, under close escort by a handsome Commander in the uniform of the Lombardian Fleet. Brim chanced to meet them a number of times during the next metacycle, but after their first encounter, the Commander made it quite clear he had little interest in furthering relationships with mere "private citizens," even though Romanoff herself appeared as if she might harbor ideas to the contrary.

Neither Brim nor Moulding stayed late at the reception. The first heats of the race were scheduled in the morning, and both wanted to be fresh for the occasion. Even so, Anak preceded them out of the reception hall by thirty cycles. On the way home, Moulding asked him what he and the Admiral had discussed during their rather extraordinary conversation in the reception line.

Brim shook his head. "Let's just say that I learned something important about warfare from the Admiral, Toby," he said.

"And *that* was?" Moulding asked.

Brim thought a moment, then looked his friend directly in the eye. "I learned that the other side could bleed, too," he answered. "For some reason, that had never occurred to me."

CHAPTER 5

Lys

Next morning, Brim and Moulding arrived at the Imperial box in the grandstand area just after dawn transformed the morning skies from lavender to pink and then to gold. Colossal outlines of two Leaguer battleships dominated the far shore of Lake Tegeler, their massive disruptors somehow at odds with the peaceful sunrise. One, the extensively rebuilt *Lias Mondor*, had been badly damaged at the Battle of Atalanta; its adjunct, a new super-Rengas-class ship named *Burok* was still another of the advanced warships Anak was building in flagrant violation of the Treaty of Garak. Leaguer bureaucrats simply claimed she was half her actual mass, and nobody questioned their words—at least nobody with any authority.

At the race complex itself, black and crimson Leaguer flags fluttered in the central grandstand and shed areas. From the pavilion area, one could view only takeoffs and landings—and, of course, the start/finish line. The race circuit itself, however, was far out in space along a triangular route with legs of 494.8, 228, and 277.2 Standard light-years, each turning angle marked by a huge type-19 beacon star. To complete the contest, crews had to make ten laps (negotiating two sharp angles and one easy curve each time), then return. They flew the course against the clock: fastest computed speed took the trophy—for one Standard year. According to the rules, any competitor who managed to win the trophy three times gained permanent possession.

Uadn'aps was halfway toward its midday zenith when Rogan

120

LaKarn ostentatiously lead Margot to a seat in the Torond's royal box, thereby affording Brim—only a few irals distant in the Imperial section—his first close look at Rodyard. Wearing a miniature Grenzen's uniform, complete with peaked cap, jodhpurs, and high boots, the child was carried in the arms of a squat, masculine-looking attendant who seemed more like a bodyguard than a nurse. And prepared as Brim might have *thought* he was to meet Margot's child, the strange, melancholic sensation of loss he got from the encounter was far out of proportion to anything he'd imagined. Once—a million years ago, it now seemed—he had dared hope to father his own child with the beautiful Margot Effer'wyck. Now, that vision seemed dead and cold as space itself.

Moments later, for some reason known only to himself, the child turned to fasten his steel blue eyes on Brim, staring intently with a kind of insight that bordered on recognition. And in that brief interval, a new and more sinister shadow added its own unique darkness to the Carescrian's already gloomy mood —a distinct and menacing impression of presentiment.

Brim recognized the sensation immediately; there was certainly nothing unfamiliar or mysterious about it. He'd often experienced similar awareness in combat when he spied a League warship closing in at a distance: an unavoidable menace to be dealt with at some future juncture, but not right away.

A time would come—unquestionably—when he must likewise deal with young LaKarn. He knew it in his bones. Now, however, more pressing matters demanded his immediate consideration, and he turned his attention to the race.

Precisely at Morning:2:0, stirring, martial strains of "The Conqueror," the League's national anthem, split Lake Tegeler's cool morning air, while a prototype Renkers attack ship dived steeply over the grandstand, then executed a shrieking pull-up and thundered out toward space, spinning vigorously around its central axis. As the sound of the Renkers faded into the sky, loudspeakers announced the arrival of Kabul Anak, personally representing the exiled Nergol Triannic. Brim watched the little man take his seat with mixed emotions, then shrugged off the previous evening as a temporary aberration, nothing more. Precisely ten cycles following Anak's arrival, a traditional trumpet fanfare yerked out the official opening of the contest and the Starter, a grizzled veteran Controller, gave a little speech about sportsmanship from his platform directly in front of the grandstand. He spoke in Vertrucht. Brim wondered how many of the actual contestants could understand it.

Individual heats were flown in reverse sequence from the previous year's finish order. Therefore, the actual race began when doors to the Ripernian shed slid open; that small dominion had managed to finish dead last. While a huge brass orchestra yerked out the Ripernian national anthem ("There Is No Star Like Ripern"), a powerful crawler tugged their wedge-shaped star racer outside on a portable gravity pad, its support machinery thundering. Nearly thirty assorted mechanics and technicians in matching lavender coveralls marched on either side of the little vessel, then assisted in transferring it to the gravity pool.

Following this, the technicians swarmed up ladders and spread out over the hull for a final inspection, the colorfully dressed crew climbed aboard amid sporadic cheering from the grandstand, and the gravity generators fired off in a great rush of noise and distorted light. Moments later, the Helmsman waved from his little flight bridge, an army of Legionnaires cleared a path from the gravity pool to the water, and the little starship trundled off toward the water amid rolling thunder from its twin generators. Just short of the shore—and a safe distance from the grandstand in case of malfunction—it stopped in a circle of N-ray hydrants while special teams of experts hurried to enable its Drive. Then it moved out over the water and headed for the takeoff vector.

Each starting gate consisted of two pylons accurately positioned in the water and equipped with three sets of lights: ruby for "nonready," amber for "start signal pending," and green for "race." When a ship was properly positioned just short of the pylons, its Helmsman signaled that he (or she) was ready by the simple expedient of standing on the brakes while directing full power to the gravs. This sent a great cloud of spray sweeping aft from the racer that quickly built hundreds of irals into the air. In acknowledgment, the Starter switched on the amber pylon lamps, then took his flag from a rack, held it dramatically over his head, and snapped it smartly down between two light-sensitive poles that activated the green takeoff lamps on the pylons. The actual race clock was started by the ship's passage between the pylons—and subsequently stopped when the ship returned between the same gates at the end of its run.

In no time at all, the Ripernian entry was bellowing along the lake, remaining just above the surface for nearly two c'lenyts before it lifted in a near-vertical climb and disappeared into the cloudless blue sky, although its deep thunder persisted nearly a cycle before fading below the clamor of the spectators.

Moments later, a second Ripernian ship was manhandled onto the gravity pool. . . .

For the remainder of the day, and well into the long spring evening, each racing team took its turns at the starting pylons. Spectators followed the race on miniature scoreboards at their seats that showed the elapsed time at which each contestant snapped around one of the turning points. During much of the contest, it appeared as if LaKarn's Dampier DA.39 might take first place, with A'zurn's stubby little R'autor in a solid second. But as the last heats approached, Brim got a distinct feeling that the competition was far from over until the League had run its heats.

In a blaze of searchlights, the Leaguer crews—identically dressed in spotless white coveralls—manhandled Valentin's sinister-looking Gantheisser GA 209V-1 onto the gravity pool, and within thirty cycles, Brim's old nemesis was turning in times that shaved whole clicks from the day's fastest runs. By the time he landed, it was clear that the next race would again be held in Tarrott.

As Valentin climbed from his Gantheisser amid a blaze of searchlights and thunderous applause, the League was now within a single race of capturing the Mitchell Trophy permanently. Brim sat silently, grinding his teeth. Had he fostered any questions about his commitment to the race, they were now totally gone. Only Valerian's voice rang in his ears, obscuring the thunderous cheers of the crowd: *"We've got a trophy to win."* Brim meant to do everything in his power to make sure that happened.

Less than a metacycle later, as if to add insult to injury, the number two Gantheisser ran a close second—piloted by the shapely and long-legged Praefect who had preceded Valentin into the League shed while Brim watched from the parking lot.

Both Brim and Moulding quietly departed Tarrott early the next morning, but soon after their return to Atalanta, the Carescrian embarked alone for Sodeskaya. He intended to learn everything he could about Krasni-Peych's new Drive, as well as the starship for which it was intended. One thing was now clear in his mind: he did not intend to watch Kirsh Valentin win anything again—ever.

Only a month later, the League began a second warlike confrontation, this time issuing trumped-up charges against its neighboring dominion of Beta Jagow. During the Great War, forces from this diminutive ally of the Empire had seized a thirty-planet area claimed by the League; now Zoguard Grobermann, the League's Minister of State, complained that ex-Leaguers on five habitable planets were being held in unwilling subjugation. This time, he openly threatened to send "forces" that would rectify the situation. He made no mention of *what* forces he might send, but the message was nonetheless clear: the League could back up its threats with warships.

The immense Sodeskayan passenger liner with its sleek lines and spacious accommodations seemed nothing less than incredible from Brim's delighted point of view. Clearly an engineer's ship from bow to stern, *Ra'dio Kruznyetski Kondrashin* was not only fast and economical, she was also luxurious beyond Brim's wildest dreams. If the recently launched vessel were any indication of what he might encounter at Krasni-Peych's research complex outside Gromcow, his visit to the planet of Sodeskaya promised to be an interesting one indeed.

He had also discovered shortly after his arrival in the ornate boarding salon that he had somehow been assigned to first-class accommodations. Surprised and apprehensive that he might have to pay for the upgrade—which he doubted he could— he'd inquired immediately about the situation and was informed by a Purser that nothing concerning his passage could be altered. Apparently, the upgrade of his original "tourist"-class reservations had been arranged for, as well as prepaid, in Gromcow, by order of Imperial Authority.

Now, as a guest on the spacious flight bridge of the big starship, Brim relaxed in the deep cushions of a luxurious jump seat and watched the crew set up for landfall on wintry Sodeskaya. The curve of the big planet had long since become a level, albeit cloudy, horizon in the forward Hyperscreens, and the Helmsman—one Ivanovich Kapustan Bokh—was setting up for his final approach into Gromcow's Tomoshenko Memorial Starport. Bokh flew smoothly and without effort, hunched attentively over the instrument panel while he scanned the readouts and peered now and then through the Hyperscreens, his great furry head and powder blue AkroKahn Captain's cap protruding above the seat back. "We Helmsmen of excellence must hang together," the smiling Bear had said, shaking Brim's hand on the latter's first visit to the flight bridge, "—there are so few of us in the first place."

After that, Brim spent much of his time with the crew—all Sodeskayans—realizing that here was an opportunity to rub elbows with some of the best starsailors in the Universe. Cursed with relatively poor eyesight in comparison to other spacefaring races, few Bears cared for the actual business of starflight, preferring instead to employ their vast intellectual energies by engineering vessels for others to operate.

Gromcow Tower was reporting low IFR with dense clouds right down to minimums. Forward, there was only gray to be seen; *Kondrashin* had been within the clouds since the fifteen-thousand-iral mark, descending slowly in a precisely timed holding pattern. There were light bumps, but Bokh clearly had the touch. He was handling the forty-five-thousand-milston starship as if she were a small trainer.

Moments after the Gromcow tower issued permission to land, Bokh smoothly banked the big starship into a descending turn and captured the ILS beam within the first few clicks, almost as if he were a Leaguer following some sort of bizarre cable system. At the middle marker, they picked up the ruby landing vector only just above minimum altitude, but once the starship was configured and the power was set, there were no perceptible changes in altitude whatsoever until the final flare-out. Absolutely no sensation in pitch, roll, or power—Brim's kind of Helmsmanship. And the landing that followed was equally good. Bokh flew through the driving snow with that special consideration for machinery that marked a true professional. He put *Kondrashin* onto her gravity foot with the feather-light touch most good Helmsmen got one time in twenty.

Once they were moored on one of Tomoshenko's massive gravity pools, Brim thanked the Sodeskayan Helmsman and his assistant for the masterful ride, but since both were filling out reports, they didn't get much of a chance to talk. Afterward, he hurried to his stateroom to collect the few valuables that weren't in his luggage, planning to make directly for the main boarding hatch to meet Ursis and Borodov. But he never made it.

Dressed in even heavier greatcoats than they had worn on Atalanta and laden with a number of large boxes, the two Sodeskayans stopped him at the door to his stateroom. Their choice of clothing gave Brim pause to wonder if his old heated raincoat was indeed going to keep him from freezing to death in the winter hemisphere. After all, both Bears also wore *natural* fur coats under their clothing.

"Aha, Wilf Ansor," Borodov exclaimed, beaming from ear to ear. "It is high time you visited the G.F.S.S. I have been looking forward to this for many years now!" With that, he dumped his armload of packages on a nearby settee and hugged Brim until the Carescrian nearly feared for his life.

The other Bear laughed, taking Brim's hand and pumping it vigorously in the Imperial manner. "Anastas Alexyi is not the only one who has anticipated your visit with great expectations. We have *much* to show you."

"About Holy Gromcow as well as our new StarDrive," Borodov interjected with a smile, releasing Brim so he could breathe again. "Both are magnificent," he added, "but only Gromcow is *glorious* as well."

"And cold enough at this time of year to turn you into furless icicle," Ursis said, picking up Brim's worn raincoat. He scratched his head for a moment, checking the coat's environmental controls. "This is what you brought?" he asked.

"It's all I've got," Brim replied.

"Well, it would serve," Ursis judged, nodding his head professorially, "—but when in the G.F.S.S., one should wear what Sodeskayans wear, to coin a phrase. Is that not correct, Dr. Borodov?"

"Indeed," Borodov agreed. "And it is to that end that we have brought these," he stated, indicating the packages on the settee. "We have a chilly excursion to make presently. It will be well if you are dressed warmly for it."

Frowning, Brim began to explore the boxes. They contained a slate-colored greatcoat with huge silver buttons and high, soft boots much like Ursis's; a huge, egg-shaped hat to match the one on Borodov's head; heavy gloves; and a long, woolen scarf of bright crimson. "How in the Universe am I going to pay for all of this?" he asked, turning to his two friends. "In fact, how am I going to pay for that first-class upgrade to my ticket?"

"You *aren't*," Borodov declared, as if the answer were so obvious that it hardly rated consideration.

"Well, somebody's got to pay for gear like this," Brim protested hotly. "Remember, I took thermodynamics in school, too, and there is *no free lunch*. Anywhere in the Universe."

"True," Ursis agreed. "But nothing in the laws of thermodynamics forbids the giving of gifts in a spirit of true friendship."

"But . . ." Brim countered.

"No buts about it," Ursis said, scowling suddenly. "I thought we had discussed such nonsense in Atalanta." He shook his head. "That xaxtdamned pride of yours, Wilf Brim, will someday yet overwhelm my good humor."

Brim turned to Borodov, but the old Bear only nodded his head sagely. "One can give without loving, Wilf Ansor," he said, "but it is impossible to love without giving." Then he smiled. "Nikolai Yanuarievich and I simply had no choice."

Brim took a deep breath, and clasped their six-fingered hands in his. "I am probably hopeless, my friends," he said, looking from one to the other, "but I am also *surely* grateful. This outfit is magnificent."

"Plus," Ursis said with his usual grin, "it is also *warm*. Your furless self will most likely appreciate that even more than the friendship before this visit is over."

Gromcow, itself—Holy Gromcow—had existed in one form or another since the beginnings of recorded Sodeskayan history. And indeed, the modern city grew like a tree in concentric rings from its ancient core: the Great Winter Palace, now home of Nicholas the August, present Knez of the G.F.S.S. and arguably the mightiest noble in the Empire of Greyffin IV. Not that the outward growth had been smooth or even steady. Great fires, wars, and occasional revolutions constantly stirred the skyline, so that in any district one might encounter a mix of modern, ancient, and nearly anything in between. The miracle of the city was that it all fit as aesthetically as it did.

Tomoshenko Memorial Starport was located on a huge, artificially heated lake outside the city. This was fed by the wide

Gromcow River that bisected, a considerable distance upstream, the austral quarter of the Old City Center and ran through the grounds of the Great Winter Palace.

The terminal itself could only be described as cavernous, with brilliant lighting, rich decoration, and an extravagant use of marble with mosaics that set a standard of opulence seldom approached in the galaxy. Brim walked in awe through the gleaming and spacious edifice, wondering why he perceived no arrogance in the design of *this* grossly overdone station, as compared to the one in Tarrott. Smiling foolishly at his own parochial outlook, he followed his two Sodeskayan friends outside to a huge limousine skimmer emblazoned with the Great Imperial Seal, where two massive, smiling chauffeurs waited to take them to the research center on the far side of the city.

Brim found that approaching Gromcow was a series of pleasant surprises: one moment the big limousine was in gently rolling countryside, spinning past snow-covered fields and wintry, bare woods populated by cozy log cottages trimmed with elaborate fretwork; the next moment, thick clusters of elegant apartment houses loomed beside the right-of-way, their grounds filled with young Bears playing happily in the driving snow. The transition from country to city was abrupt indeed.

After a few blocks, the right-of-way evolved to paved streets, jammed with steady streams of pedestrians as well as all manner of vehicles. The buildings in this section were contemporary, constructed of gleaming metal and glass in angular shapes of towers and columns, all connected by fantastic networks of graceful crystal bridges. Interspersed with the buildings were parks, filled with statuary and Bears, as well as people from every race in the galaxy; this was also the embassy ring. Here and there, the crowds parted to make way for groups of young Bears of both sexes marching raggedly behind banners and singing boisterously. Colorful trams of two and sometimes three streamlined cars glided through the snow-covered squares, bells clanging as pedestrians darted across the roadway in front of them. Even archaic wheeled carriages drawn by huge Sodeskayan droshkats—an unusual breed of nonflighted gryphons— rumbled over the cobbles, easily keeping time with the superbly congested traffic.

By the time their limousine reached the inner ring of the city, the throngs had become a bobbing sea of kerchiefs, caps, and wooly monstrosities like those that Ursis and Borodov habitually wore. Everything here spoke of the many golden ages of Sodeskayan art, music, and literature. Within its historic streets were Gromcow's lavish art galleries, most of its famous Bearish theaters, the galaxy-famous Conservatory of Music, and countless monuments to the titans of Bearish literature. Wherever the pavement narrowed, as it did often in this oldest section of town, the imperturbable pedestrians spilled onto the streets. Fascinated, Brim spotted villagers shuffling along in belted smocks among splendidly dressed executives swinging briefcases. Between breaks in the crowds, he glimpsed shop windows, filled with commodities from all over the galaxy. Colorful posters hung from every lamp post, portraying Bearish servicemen dressed in greatcoats and battlesuits There were no CIGAs in Sodeskaya—the G.F.S.S. was one of the few Imperial dominions that had ignored Triannic's Treaty of Garak, in spite of heated orders from the Imperial Admiralty. The Sodeskayan high command merely changed the device everyone wore on his headgear, renamed all services as numbered divisions of a nebulous "Home Guard," then continued to reinforce their defenses as before. It was another example of the *very* loose ties between Knez Nicholas and his so-called dominant government in Avalon—although many believed that Greyffin IV himself privately applauded the Bears' independent action.

Not until he arrived in the old city did Brim begin to understand why he could settle back comfortably in the midst of this milling confusion when he'd felt so restive in the ordered calm of Tarrott. It was because vibrant Gromcow, in all its disordered hubbub, was a city of warm, living *individuals*, whereas Tarrott, in the final analysis, was a city optimized for machines— and sentient beings who behaved more like components of a system than flesh-and-blood people.

Abruptly, just as it had earlier changed from country to urban congestion, the surroundings once more underwent a transformation. Teeming streets gave way to apartments, then to light industry, and then once more to sparsely populated fields and woodlands. Centuries before, a smog-and-haze-clogged Gromcow had decreed that all heavy industry would move to satellite towns, thus at least diluting (if offering no further improvement of) the atmospheric pollution that seemed to go inexorably hand in hand with efficient industrialization.

It was still snowing heavily, but the busy lanes of the right-of-way were clearly marked by hovering globes that kept traffic flowing as smoothly as if it were a midsummer day. In no time, a vast complex of factories emerged through the driving snow, and the chauffeur exited along a broad thoroughfare leading through towering stands of evergreens. On the far side of the trees, they drew to a halt on a wide courtyard just short of three massive gates that were clearly a main plant entrance. Above the center portal, huge Sodeskayan characters spelled out КРОСНЫ-ПЕЧТУ—Krasni-Peych. The courtyard was patrolled by what looked like a full brigade of soldiers with formidable Khalodni N-37 blast pikes slung over their shoulders. Immediately, two Lieutenants in high, black boots, olive green greatcoats with royal blue epaulettes, and billed military caps, also trimmed in royal blue, strode purposefully to the car while subordinates looked on attentively, their six-fingered hands slipping nearer to their weapons. Ursis opened his window and exchanged words in Sodeskayan with one of the officers, then handed him a large envelope closed with the Great Cachet of the Knez. Gesturing respectfully, the Lieutenant unsealed the envelope and withdrew six holobadges, two of which he handed to his partner for the drivers. After peering assiduously at each of the backseat's occupants, the Lieutenant suddenly grinned, bowed deferentially, and, handing back the badges, waved them toward the gates with a smart salute. A few moments later, the big limousine was on its way through the huge complex between high buildings with massive doors; great, circular gravitron towers hundreds of irals in height, topped by multifaceted crystal globes, and connected at various levels by intricate bridges; numerous funnel-shaped structures that appeared to be wrapped by a layer of thick crystal tubing that glowed and pulsed in varying colors; as well as ordinary office buildings whose warmly lighted windows gave glimpses of laboratories, libraries, and offices. Presently, they drew to a hover above another snow-covered apron, this at the end of a long Becton-type gravity-cushion tube, commonly used by starships in place of water for hard-surface landfalls. Above the cooling fins of its power terminus hovered a sleek NJH-26 star launch—a Sodeskayan executive transport renowned throughout the galaxy for its elegance and speed. Moments later, the three were walking through the blizzard, snow crunching under their boots as they made their way toward the little ship's glassed-in brow. On either side of the tube right-of-way, evergreens stood out in dark emerald against the snow and clumps of tall birchlike trees formed tangles of long, white fingers against the cloud-darkened sky. With his new badge bobbing from the collar of his greatcoat, Brim found himself walking as all Gromkovites walked in winter, hardly lifting his feet, almost sliding them over the surface, balancing at every step, and treading solidly without slackening his pace. In the muffled silence of the snowfall, he wondered idly if so much ice and snow ultimately affected the posture of everyone in the city.

Inside, the cabin was comfortably warm and paneled in dark wood. Deep-cushioned sofas lined the walls with four Bearsized easy chairs at each corner. Soft, indirect lighting illuminated a sumptuous lunch set out on a low table equipped with an expressing apparatus that filled the air with delicious aromas from freshly brewed cvceese'.

"Help yourselves, gentlemen," the blue-clad AkroKahn Helmsman called through a forward hatch that opened onto the ship's flight bridge. "It's a short enough trip out to the *Ivan Ivanov* that you'll have to do some serious eating."

"Thanks, Kovonchino," Ursis answered. "We shall do our best." Then he turned to Brim with an embarrassed smile on his face. "We laid on a few snacks," he said.

"Yes," Borodov seconded. "In case you might be hungry after your travels."

"Or *us*," Ursis added with a sly grin.

Brim was about to answer when the entrance hatch whined shut and the Helmsman warned, "Switching to internal gravity!"

In panic, Brim tried to forget the nearby food as his stomach turned upside down and he clamped his teeth together and held his breath. No matter how many thousands of times he'd gone through switches to or from internal gravity, he'd never overcome his tendency toward a weak stomach at the transition point, even though weightlessness bothered him not at all. Forcing back his gorge, he swallowed mightily, then gasped in a great draft of air. "Ah," he stammered, sinking queasily into one of the aft easy chairs, "you two go ahead and start. I'll just sit here for a few moments while I get back my space legs . . ."

Scant cycles later, they were hurdling along the Becton tube—while Borodov wolfed down his second Kagle sausage.

The *Ivan Ivanov* was not at all what Brim had expected—in actuality, it was *two* starships, the old Sodeskayan merchantmen *Sovaka Doynetz* and *Nadya Gordovsky*, joined amidships by a network of great hullmetal girders. On the port-bridge wing of *Gordovsky*, Borodov pointed through a Hyperscreen to a large pod mounted in the center of this network, braced by additional beams and spars like some sort of monster insect caught in the center of a web. "There it is, Wilf," he said, "—the new PV/12 starship Drive. K-P has toiled over the design theory for nearly ten Standard years now; it took the Mitchell Trophy Race to put the project on a front burner."

"They've started calling it the 'Wizard,'" Ursis added with a grin. "Everyone expects great things."

Brim nodded thoughtfully. "We may need some magic to keep up with next year's Gantheisser," he said, "at least if what that bastard Valentin says has any truth to it."

Ursis frowned and peered through the Hyperscreens. "I suppose we shall have part of that answer in a few moments," he said with a sage nod.

Outside, clamshell doors swung slowly open in the forward end of the pod, exposing hefty focusing rings. Behind them was a typical HyperDrive blast tube. Space radiators mounted along the finned side of the pod were beginning to glow reddish orange as super-Tesla coils pumped enormous power to the new Drive crystal. *Ivan Ivanov* was traveling at a fast cruise; when the K-P engineers fired off their new Drive, it would thrust *forward*, against the mass and momentum of the two old merchantmen. To Brim, the whole thing served to drive home the terrific force and power that would be at his command on the bridge of Valerian's new starship. He shook his head. "Awesome," he muttered to himself. He meant it.

Presently, a pattern of twelve powerful strobe beacons began to flash at the same time a klaxon horn clattered on the bridge. "The count has begun," Borodov warned, looking up from a situation display at his elbow.

As he spoke, the deck trembled beneath Brim's boots while muted thunder from the old merchantman's Drive increased significantly from below decks. Aft, the ship's twin Drive plumes flared up dramatically as she swung off toward open space. Clearly, the single Helmsman piloting both old hulls was preparing to combat some *tremendous* counterforce.

An urgent voice announced something in Sodeskayan over the blower.

"Twenty clicks till light-off!" Ursis translated. "Brace yourself, Wilf Ansor. One can never accurately predict the results of a lab experiment." Simultaneously, the pod's strobe beacons began to flash more rapidly.

Brim took a grip on the Hyperscreen coaming as the blower announced. "Five . . ." He had heard enough Sodeskayan to at least count to ten. "Four . . . three . . . two . . . one . . . *zotrob!*"

The next instant, a shimmering cobalt glow exploded around the forward end of the pod, followed by an eerie, sapphire Drive plume that was more of a Drive *beacon* in Brim's reckoning. Unlike "normal" plumes from standard Sheldon-type Drive crystals that appeared to flow aft until they faded into the blackness of space, the Wizard's exhaust wake extended out like a beacon of pure blue light that enclosed a gleaming necklace of saffron-hued refraction bodies marching slowly in the opposite direction of thrust. The effect was absolutely unlike anything he had ever experienced.

And clearly, the Wizard Drive produced thrust in prodigious amplitude. While the Bear at the test console increased the flow of energy to the pod, old *Ivanov*'s Helmsman was compelled to send more and more power to the Drives on the lab ship—enough so that the whole bridge began shuddering uncomfortably.

The Helmsman suddenly bellowed over his shoulder to the Pod Operator, who was peering into his consoles with apparent consternation. Something was clearly 'way out of control; Brim could tell from the way the hull was working and grinding. Outside, the pod had visibly bent the great hullmetal girders and was now swinging its great blue beam in a vast cone like some Brobdingnagian child playing with an equally colossal handlight. "Sweet mother of Voot," Brim muttered suddenly. "If she broaches at this speed, we'll all be killed—especially with that brute ready to swing us around." Involuntarily, he grabbed at a nearby console, but he knew it wouldn't help.

Ursis bellowed something that sounded like a warning, but

he was quickly drowned out by a mounting rumble that shook the framework of the hull.

While Brim watched in horror, the whole network of girders outside ruptured in a churning cloud of hullmetal shards. Instantly, Wizard Prototype Number One disappeared aft, headed up-galaxy for the center of the Universe in a blaze of turquoise light. Brim was thrown to the deck as the starboard half of *Ivanov* lurched savagely off course and slewed wildly, its massive hull struggling with its own powerful steering engines. The bridge abruptly went dark while Bears roared in alarm and loose debris from a hundred consoles cascaded through the air, smashing to rubbish on the bulkheads or the ceiling.

Abruptly, Borodov's happy voice soared over the confusion. "*Wonderful!*" he roared. "I say that it's *wonderful!*" Then he, too, was drowned out—this time by the *Ivanov*'s Drive, which thundered up wildly for a moment as the Helmsman struggled to regain control of the runaway starship. When it finally abated, the wild surges of gravity also ceased and Pandemonium on the bridge died down to a stony silence.

Power was finally restored while Brim dragged himself painfully to his feet. He checked to see how old Dr. Borodov had fared—Ursis was helping him up from the deck. "Are you all right, old friend?" the younger Bear asked with a great deal of concern in his voice.

Borodov shook his furry head and blinked a few times. "Am I all right?" he asked in a voice delirious with elation. "But how could I be *anything else*? Such power! Such performance! Ah, friend Nikolai Yanuarievich," he said, "it is for our human compatriot that I am *now* concerned." He looked at Brim. "We Bears have only to perfect controls for this *wonderful* monster called Wizard. Wilf Ansor, here, has to *fly* with one!"

"He's all right," Ursis answered with a wink. "How about you, Wilf Ansor?"

Brim grinned. "I *think* I'm all in one piece," he chuckled. "Besides, like Dr. Borodov, I'm sort of caught up with thoughts of flying with one of the beasts."

With that, all three turned to peer through the Hyperscreens that were just then beginning to translate again after the power failure.

"Voof," Ursis said reverently.

"Double voof," Brim answered. Outside, the *Sovaka Doyn-*

etz was just limping back on station, steered by someone in an emergency helm. Something—possibly the runaway test pod itself—had dealt the old merchantman a tremendous blow that staved her hull from the midships radiator section to a few irals from her stern. The starship was rolling wildly, her bow hunting up and down as if she were confused.

"I'd say she's taken some damage to her steering engine," Borodov observed dourly.

"At least her hull appears to be sound," Ursis said, "which is as lucky for us as it is for her crew. Presently, Krasni-Peych will begin development of the Wizard/R. Then, we shall *assuredly* need strength."

"The Wizard/R?" Brim asked.

Borodov nodded. "R stands for *reflecting*."

"I still don't understand," Brim admitted.

The Bear laughed. "At present, only a few individuals in the whole Universe *do*," he explained. "But reflecting Drives represent the true future of starflight, at least in the eyes of Krasni-Peych. The prototype Wizard you saw today is only a first, brief step in development of this new technology. In spite of its novel engineering, it still operates on the long-established single-crystal/single-pass principal, where energy passes once through the crystal, exciting its lattice structure and providing HyperSpeed thrust." He stopped, glanced at Ursis, and smiled. "Perhaps you will be so kind as to carry on for me, Nikolai Yanuarievich?" he asked.

The younger Bear nodded. "Reflecting Drives," he proceeded, as if he were lecturing at the Dityasburg Institute, "are composed of one or more crystal *shells* grown around a central core in layers. The most simple example is a core surrounded by a single, thin shell. During normal operation, both fire aft as a unit, with the shell contributing as much as twenty-five percent of the total thrust. However, when short bursts of speed are necessary, the outer shell's thrust can be *reversed*, directing its output energy forward into a ring-shaped, focusing reflector that feeds back directly into the core. This, we calculate, will increase the unit's thrust aft by as much as forty percent—but only for brief periods of time."

Brim glanced through the Hyperscreens at the limping *Doynetz*. "You'll need a hefty pod structure to test *that* beast," he said with awe.

Ursis nodded his huge, shaggy head. "Those words may have just won you a most prestigious Sodeskayan award, Wilf Ansor," he said gravely.

"An *award*?" Brim asked with interest. "What for?"

"Understatement of the year," the Bear answered with a grin, "—and in this case perhaps understatement of the *century*."

Sodeskayan Rescue Service vessels were standing off the damaged laboratory vessels less than a metacycle afterward. . . .

Later, having returned to the surface much earlier than they had expected, the three friends killed time in a Krasni-Peych recreation complex before Brim's departure to the planet of Rhodor. The large, ornately panelled dining room in the complex was lighted by crystal chandeliers and a huge, blazing fireplace at one end. Waiters dressed in formal uniforms with white aprons darted here and there serving tables of Krasni-Peych clients and employees from all over the Empire—and beyond. In the background, a strolling peasant orchestra played melancholy Sodeskayan music on enormous stringed instruments. "Valerian seemed to take the whole thing pretty well when I messaged," Borodov was commenting. "But then, it did relieve the pressure on Sherrington to finish their M-five for next year's Tarrott race. It's clear to me that we can never complete our Wizard in their promised time frame."

"I understand," Brim said. "But you say Valerian still claimed he could produce a competitive racer in time for the next race."

"I read his words with my own eyes only cycles ago," the old Bear declared, lighting his Zempa pipe again.

"He might just be able to do such a thing," Ursis declared. "A number of improved Drives were developed during the war. Perhaps with one of them in place of the Wizard, he can at least make the new ship competitive."

"Sounds like the best shot we have at the race right now," Brim admitted, "and we've *got* to enter some sort of competitive ship, or we'll simply give the trophy away." He shrugged. "I suppose I'll find out everything when I get to Rhodor." Just then, he looked up to see Anna Romanoff follow a majordomo into the big room, leading a group of human administrators. Brim recognized a few from the ISS meeting in Atalanta. His eyes met Romanoff's almost immediately—in a room full of Bears, furless beings like humans tended to stand out conspicuously. Slim and almost fragile looking as usual, she was dressed in a simple, dark blue business suit that, for all its professionalism, did little to conceal what was clearly a most alluring figure. She smiled and made a little wave as she sat; then a portly, red-faced man in executive pinstripes began speaking to her from the corner of his mouth while pointing assertively at a portable display.

"One can only pity poor Romanoff at this moment," Ursis observed with a wise nod of his head and a chuckle. "I have had encounters with that man myself: Sforzo Granada, self-appointed protector of the Society treasury."

Brim shrugged. "Probably comes with the job," he observed. "She looks like she can take care of herself."

"True," Ursis said, taking a sip of meem. "But one gets the distinct impression that she might prefer to be spending her time with *you*, Wilf Ansor."

"Nice thought," Brim said, feeling his face color in spite of himself. As he had observed in Atalanta, Anna Romanoff was just plain sexy.

"I should imagine so," Ursis observed. "Were I drawn in such a way to human beings, I might say that she appears to be a genuinely attractive woman."

At that moment, they were joined by a group of bantering propulsion engineers from the Experimental Section, and the conversation became *very* technical.

On a whim, Brim excused himself from the ad-hoc academic caucus, got to his feet, and made his way among the tables toward Romanoff. Sforzo Granada was still prattling on, every now and then punctuating his remarks by poking a pudgy finger at the display. "Pardon me, Miss Romanoff," the Carescrian interrupted with a smile he was hard-pressed to conceal, "do you suppose you might spare a few moments to discuss, ah . . . er . . . Drive financing?"

Romanoff looked up, frowned for a moment, then returned his smile with a little one of her own—mostly with her brown eyes. "Drive underwriting," she corrected demurely, toying with the huge lace ruffle she wore at her neck, "—and yes, we *should* spend some time discussing the subject." She glanced at Granada who was peering disapprovingly at Brim as if he were some sort of panhandler. "I shall be finished here in just a few cycles," she said. "Shall I meet you at the table with your friends?"

Brim nodded, and grinned again in spite of himself. "Thank you, Miss Romanoff," he said. "I shall attempt to have all the facts together by that time."

True to her word, Romanoff appeared only a few cycles later. Immediately, the Bears stood and cleared a place, old Borodov introducing her around and ordering a goblet of Logish Meem as if she were an honored guest. The delicate business-woman seemed oddly surprised at the attention. When the Bears eased themselves back to their technical conversations, Brim looked at her and grinned with embarrassment. "Hmm," he said. "I'm afraid I've already run out of things to say—at least anything that might interest a real financier."

Romanoff took a deep breath. "I shouldn't be too sure of that, Mr. Brim," she said. "You can't imagine how much I long to hear someone talk of *anything* but finance once in a while." Then her eyes grew as large as saucers. "Like what happened to the *Ivan Ivanov*. It's all over Krasni-Peych that the Wizard got out of control this morning. And I understand you were aboard. Was it awful?"

"Oh, I was aboard," Brim said with a chuckle, "and it could have been awful. But it wasn't. The test pod ripped away and banged up one of *Ivanov*'s hulls, that's all. Nobody even got hurt—more to the credit of Lady Fortune than good management, according to the Bears." Then he stopped and wrinkled his nose. "You called me *Mister* Brim, didn't you?"

"I did," Romanoff said with an arched eyebrow. "You called me Miss Romanoff, you know."

Brim thought for a moment. "That's a fact—I did," he admitted. "I guess I just thought that's the way businesspeople talk to one another."

"I don't know you well enough to repeat the kind of names we really use," Romanoff said with a laugh. "We're a pretty contentious bunch when it comes right down to things."

"Tell you what," Brim suggested. "How about calling me Wilf from now on? That way, I can go ahead and call you Anna. It'll be simpler for both of us."

"Wilf," Romanoff said with a relieved look on her face, "you've got a deal. But we won't have much time to practice this trip. I've got to make a business call to another client here on Sodeskaya before long." In spite of her words, however, she did appear to relax for a moment—the first time that Brim could remember seeing her that way. She sipped her meem carefully for a moment, then looked him squarely in the eye. "How does it feel to pilot a starship?" she asked suddenly, almost as if she were embarrassed by the question. "What's it like to command all that power—have it at your very fingertips?"

This time, it was Brim who raised an eyebrow. He grimaced. "Why..." he started. "I never really thought about it." He shrugged. "It's just something I do, I suppose."

"Can you tell me?" she persisted.

"I don't know," Brim answered truthfully. He thought a moment. "I think I could show you a lot easier," he said, glancing through the window. Outside, near the end of the Becton tube, a little Sherrington Type 224 hovered on a gravity pad. "If you had a couple of cycles, I could probably take you aboard that little executive ship out there." Then he shrugged. "Maybe some other time, when you don't have so much else to do."

Romanoff frowned for a moment. "You could actually take me on the bridge of *that* starship?" she asked with an excited look in her eyes. "Right now?"

Brim pursed his lips. "Well," he said, "I'd have to ask my friend Ursis about it first."

"Would you?" Romanoff asked. "I suppose I could make my call later."

Elated by the opportunity to accommodate this most attractive woman, Brim tapped Ursis on the arm. "Do you think there's any possibility of Anna and I going aboard the little 224 out there?" he asked, nodding toward the window.

Ursis peered out at the flight apron, turned to glance for a moment at Romanoff, then smiled. "Hmm," he mused. "It seems to me that the Principal Helmsman for the ISS certainly ought to be able to check out a Sherrington—for instructional purposes, if nothing else." He nodded his head, as if testing out his reasoning. "A moment," he said, raising a long index finger, "I shall see what I can do." With that, he excused himself from his colleagues and ambled over to a house phone, where he carried on a short conversation with someone Brim couldn't see. He was back at the table in a matter of moments. "It is taken care of, Wilf," he declared. "By the time the two of you have reached the boarding tube, the ship will be powered up. I am informed that it is ready to fly." He looked at Brim. "We should leave for the terminal within three metacycles at the latest, Wilf, if you are to catch the AkroKahn liner for Rhodor."

"Maybe we ought to skip it," Romanoff said hesitantly. "I'd feel terrible if I made you miss your ship. Everyone in the Society knows how important it is that you visit Sherrington."

The look on her face made it abundantly clear to Brim that she was seriously concerned. He grinned. "It's all right, Anna," he assured her. "Really. We don't have to fly it, you know."

Romanoff smiled. "Well," she said, taking a deep breath. "I really would love to see the bridge—if you're sure this isn't going to be too much of an inconvenience to anyone."

Brim chuckled. "I can assure you that one Wilf Ansor Brim will feel no inconvenience—and," he continued, indicating the table of chattering Bears. "I'll bet these research types won't even notice that we're gone."

"All right," she said almost shyly, "let's do it."

Ursis winked surreptitiously as they excused themselves from the table. *He* knew. . . .

The flight bridge of the Sherrington starship *Alesander Neyvsky* was exquisitely laid out. It should have been, Brim mused as he settled into the Helmsman's recliner. It was clearly brand-new—and also one of Knez Nicholas's *personal* transports. Beside Brim, Romanoff had seated herself in the right-hand seat, gazing with fascination at the control panels. As he switched power to the console, and color patterns began to cascade over the panels, she started a little in alarm. Then she blushed and put her hand to her lips, watching him from the corner of her eye. "Well, what did you expect?" she laughed in feigned defensiveness, brushing a stray wisp of hair from her forehead. "After all, it is my first time on a flight bridge."

Brim grinned as he glanced across at her. Anna Romanoff *was* a good-looking woman, no doubt about it. And one of the things that made her so attractive was that she seemed to have no idea how really lovely she was.

"That's a curious look you're giving me, Wilf Brim," she said presently. "Did I say something wrong?"

Brim shook his head. "No," he said, a little embarrassed at being caught in his daydream. "I don't think you could say anything wrong, Anna," he added in a mumble, then turned to the instrument panel. "Ah . . . this cluster of green indicators," he began, suddenly feeling as bashful as a teenager, "is the set of gravity controls . . ."

It took nearly a half-metacycle to complete his description of the little starship's myriad controls and indicators—interspersed with the businesswoman's frequent questions, many of which required thoughtful answers. When they'd finished, Brim sat back in the seat and grinned in honest admiration. "I doubt if many instructors at the Helmsmen's Academy ever get so thoroughly interrogated," he said, indicating the fully energized panel with a sweep of his hand. "We've actually got this little ship ready to fly." Then he frowned and looked at her conspiratorially. "You sure you couldn't put that client off for another metacycle or so? I mean, there's still plenty of time for me to get to the terminal, and we wouldn't have to go for a long flight."

Romanoff's eyes glanced around the little flight bridge, then focused through the Hyperscreens toward the end of the Becton tube. She took a deep breath and half stifled a grin. "I really shouldn't . . ." she began hesitantly, "but . . ." She shook her head while a delighted expression filled her eyes. "Oh, Wilf, I'd *love* to." Then she frowned. "But what about your friends Nikolai and Dr. Borodov? Are you sure they're not going to mind?"

Brim shook his head. "I've touched elbows with the two of them for years," he said. "If they weren't enjoying their colleagues, they'd have let me know. Sodeskayans may be polite, but they're also anything but bashful." He looked into her eyes. "How long can we stay out?"

Romanoff glanced at her timepiece—a handsome, sparkling bauble that suggested quality. It fit, Brim thought. "Well," she said hesitantly, "I suppose I could make my call later in the evening." She suddenly looked him in the eye. "I'll take as much time as you can give me, Wilf," she declared.

"In that case," Brim said with a grin that defied all control, "what do you say we get this little beauty up in the sky where it belongs?"

"What do you say we do?" she asked softly. Within fifteen cycles, they were on their way into deep space.

While Brim put the 224 through its paces, he and Romanoff

found more than enough to talk about: starships, the ISS, even the League's latest threats against Beta Jagow. But somehow, he felt an unstated constraint that limited their conversation to "safe" subjects, nothing especially personal, even though he found himself increasingly drawn to this alluring woman. She was obviously a private person, even though her expressive brown eyes made it quite clear that she was anything but bored with his company.

The Carescrian found himself suddenly quiet as he prepared for a sunset landfall on the Becton tube, pulsing steadily in its still-distant forest clearing ahead. Unexpectedly, what had started as a casual lark appeared to be ending not at all the way it had started. There was clearly something about Anna Romanoff that attracted him; he'd felt it the first time they'd met. And now that he was beginning to know her, that attraction was turning to downright fascination. He shook his head and quashed the little fantasy before it developed any further.

As the tops of the giant conifers blurred past, he rolled the 224 slightly—filling the flight bridge for a moment with reddish light from the setting sun—then coasted in over the fence toward the end of the Becton tube. At the last instant, he lifted the nose and settled gently onto the gravity gradient. As the little starship glided to a halt, he stole a glance at Romanoff, relaxed in the recliner beside him with an absolutely enthralled expression on her face. At that moment, he felt like a little boy who has just scored a SyncBall goal in front of the parish heartthrob.

Later, back in the recreation area, the Bears were waiting for them, all grins. Borodov kissed Romanoff's hand. "Well, young lady," he said, "have you decided to take up starship Helmsmanship, now?"

Romanoff's eyes lit with delight. "No, Dr. Borodov," she laughed. "I shall be more than glad to relinquish all starship piloting to the Wilf Brims of the universe."

Brim nodded. "And I," he added gallantly, "shall be quite happy to cede all business transactions to the Anna Romanoffs." He hoped no one would notice how much he had really enjoyed his ride, but it was clear that Ursis had guessed something special had occurred. He and the Bear had been close friends for too many years.

"I take it that the Sherrington performed well during the, er, *trials*?" Ursis asked with a knowing grin.

"Oh . . . the *trials*," Brim said. He smiled. "Actually," he said, "the 224 really is a nice little ship. I'd only flown a few Sherringtons before."

Ursis winked. "In that case," he said, "I shall have my friend report that the flight was a success." He took Romanoff's hand and kissed it. "Miss Romanoff," he said, "it has been much too brief a pleasure. Perhaps some other time, Wilf Ansor will permit us Bears more of a chance to know you."

Romanoff blushed. "Thank you, Nikolai," she said. "I shall look forward to it."

Borodov bowed with all his old-fashioned charm. "And so shall I, Miss Romanoff," he said with a smile.

Clearly surprised by the attention the Bears were lavishing on her, Romanoff opened her mouth for a moment, then reddened, touching her fingertips to her lips again. "I, ah . . ." she stumbled, "thank you both. And you too, Wilf. You have all been so kind." Then she looked resolutely at her timepiece and grimaced. "And now, gentlemen," she said, "I'm afraid that I do have a business engagement I must attend to immediately— and I know the three of you must be off for the terminal." She took Brim's hand. "Wilf, I can never tell you how much I enjoyed my starship ride this evening."

He looked her in the eye. "You already have," he said.

Romanoff frowned. "Wilf Brim," she said, smiling with a lovely blush, "you are absolutely impossible." Then she turned and hurried along the aisle toward an inner exit and presently disappeared into the administrative wing.

"Our Miss Romanoff looked enormously pleased with her ride," Ursis observed.

"Not half so pleased-looking as friend Wilf Ansor," Borodov seconded.

Brim looked at the old Bear and felt his cheeks burn. "There's considerably more truth to that than I'd like to admit," he said.

"And is there something wrong with savoring the company of an attractive woman?" Ursis asked. "Especially one who clearly likes to be with you?"

Brim thought of Margot and closed his eyes somberly. "At this point in my life," he asserted, "that's hard to tell."

"Perhaps, then," Borodov suggested, clearly divining Brim's true concern, "it would be better to let nature take its own course."

"Perhaps it would," Brim answered. "Perhaps it would . . ."

A few metacycles later, he was on his way to Rhodor and the Sherrington Works aboard the *Valeikya Krusnetsky*, another superlative liner of Sodeskayan registry. And once more, someone had upgraded his travel arrangements to first-class.

The Sherrington Works, like most heavy industries on Rhodor itself, was located outside Bromwich, one of the oldest cities on the capital planet. But Sherrington's research facility had relocated some years earlier to a small, up-galaxy Rhodorian planet known as Lys, in orbit around a sixth-order star simply named Tenniel. There, in the hamlet of Woolston, on Hampton Water (a lake in the rural Borealands district), they'd constructed a small development laboratory just prior to the Great War. Until now, however, the facility had managed to produce only a few starships. (One, a rather promising prewar racing machine, had briefly captured the galactic speed record.) However, these were noted more for their originality than the length of their production runs. The company's main work was at Bromwich with repair of starships for the Imperial Admiralty.

Brim arrived at Woolston aboard a Type 224 sent to the Bromwich terminal to fetch him. It was high summer in the Borealands; sunlight and fluffy summer clouds ruled the cool, blue skies as the Sherrington pilot turned onto final and lined up on the lake. When they landed, Mark Valerian was waiting at the gravity pool, looking slimmer than ever in his tweed coat, flannel trousers, and high Rhodorian boots with their pointed toes and thick, elevated heels. "Good to see you, Wilf," he said, shaking Brim's hand as the latter strode off the brow. "How does this compare with Sodeskaya?"

While a company porter in blue livery led his traveling case away, Brim savored the damp, summertime odors of flourishing grasses and forests. "Well," he said, with a grin, "it certainly *is* a lot warmer." He chuckled. "Voot's beard, Mark, I'll bet you don't even have a Becton tube with all that liquid water out there in the lake."

"Don't make that bet," Valerian contended. "In winter,

Hampton Water freezes up just as solid as anything in Sodeskaya. We've got a *number* of Becton tubes that we use, in fact."

"Hmm," Brim ruminated. He had quickly become spoiled by Atalanta's temperate winter. "In that case, I'll be sure to schedule my trips on days just like this."

"Good idea," Valerian agreed. "But any time we catch you 'round *these* laboratories, we'll put you directly to work—as we intend to do as soon as you've had time to freshen up."

"Sounds like a plan to me," Brim declared. "How is the racecraft business these days?"

Valerian frowned. "Good and bad, I suppose," he answered. "The good news is that I'll definitely have a racing machine for you next year—without the new K-P Drive, of course. The bad news is that it won't be the one I'd planned."

Brim raised an eyebrow, but Valerian quickly ushered him through the back door of a limousine skimmer.

"Probably best that I *show* you, Wilf," he promised. "The driver will bring you 'round to the development hangar once you've had a chance to unpack, and I'll meet you there."

Brim nodded affably as he slid into the comfortable seat. There was little he could do about the situation, however things might turn out. Nevertheless, as the car whispered along a tree-shaded, lakeside road, the beginnings of apprehension began to form in the back of his mind. Valerian might be the greatest designer in the Empire—perhaps in the galaxy—but even he was subject to Voot's Immutable Law of Adversity. And when things went awry concerning high-speed starships with prototype StarDrives, doors were opened to all sorts of difficulties, including the worst kinds of bad luck.

Within the metacycle, Brim found himself inside a large building whose curvilinear roof gave more the appearance of a storage shed than a laboratory. The entire rear of the structure —or was it the front?—was composed of huge, sliding door panels that opened directly onto the lakefront. Five small starships, none more than 150 irals in length, were in various stages of construction on the floor, resting on blocks with access panels open, and sizable assemblies missing here and there from their hulls. Cables and hoses connected the ships to outlandish devices that hovered near the floor while technicians studied color patterns that flowed across their surfaces. Here and there, spark showers from collapsium welders cascaded to the floor, and the shriek of hullmetal cutters tore the air. The room was heavy with the scent of scorched metal, fresh sealants, and hot electronic logics. Off in a rear corner of the room beside a large object covered by a tarpaulin, another starship was under construction—much smaller and completely unlike the others. It was to this machine that Valerian was leading him.

"I'm almost certain you'll be flying our M-four next time in Tarrott," the designer confided to Brim as he pointed to the diminutive starship. No more than eighty irals overall, she comprised three separate torpedo-shaped hulls, the bottom two closely joined by streamlined fairings to a smaller, topmost body with a cramped-looking flight bridge faired into its forward end. Hullmetal skin on both lower hulls had been removed, and sturdy mounting rails were being attached inside the ringlike formers that comprised the skeleton.

"Not much chance we could have cobbled up a new M-five in time for the Tarrott race," Valerian said, looking up at the graceful little ship. "But, I don't suppose that matters much anymore now that the Bears have to rethink their control systems." He stroked the ends of his moustache thoughtfully. "At any rate, about a month ago, I assigned a team to start uprating this old bucket of bolts—just in case. And now I'm glad I did. We won't have two entries like most of the other dominions, but at least we'll race. There's not another shipyard in the Empire that's building racers this year, you know." Peering over his horn-rimmed glasses at the little ship, he nodded, as if he had just resolved a controversy. "The M-four isn't a bad little ship, considering her age," he said. "She was remarkably fast for the Drive systems we had before the war—set a galactic speed record just before Anak's first raids." He impulsively kicked aside a small raveling of hullmetal from an otherwise spotless floor. "So I got to thinking what she'd be like with some up-to-date propulsion equipment. Lyon Interstellar, for instance— over in the Avalon Group—built a couple of first-rate Drives for small ships just before Triannic threw in the towel. It made sense that she ought to give those new Gantheissers a run for their money with those on board."

Brim rubbed his chin. It did make sense, all right. With *two* new Drives—and probably half again her original power—the old starship ought to give *anything* a run for the money. *If she could hold together*. He took a deep breath and peered at the two thick fairings—"trousers," Valerian called them—that attached the two lower hulls to the upper. They looked strong enough. But they had been designed more than a decade previously, for Drives that were vastly less powerful than the ones Valerian was talking about. "You don't think they'd tear her apart do you, Mark?" he asked.

"I don't think so," Valerian replied with a frown. "The only worry I've got right now is a possibility of resonance flutter at really high speeds. And a good Helmsman could take care of that by slacking off on the power." He looked Brim in the eye. "Couldn't he?"

Brim shrugged. "I don't see why not, Mark," he said with a grin. "It's a lot like talking to one of those guys from CIGA—so long as I'm standing here safe and sound in the hangar, everything sounds fine." He took a deep breath. "But up there, well . . ." He shrugged.

Valerian laughed wryly. "Yeah," he said. "I understand. SMOP—Small Matter Of Piloting, as they say." He stared for a moment at the stained concrete floor of the laboratory. "Unfortunately," he continued after a moment, "bloody stubborn Prince Onrad has ordered Sherrington to come up with a starship racer that's speedy enough to beat the new Gantheisser 209V-2s—or rather their specifications. And that's what I've done." He shook his head angrily. "Of course, nobody outside the League's actually *seen* a 209V-2 yet, so far as I know." He raised his hands in supplication. "Well, with a pair of Lyon Napier-type Drive crystals—the kind they run in tandem on the latest Fairmile-D attack boats—this little antique has better specs than the ones Gantheisser's been handing out to the media. And believe me, Wilf," he added, prodding Brim's chest emphatically, "until the Sodeskayans get their act together and finish that so-called Wizard, this old M-four is the best I can do." Before the Carescrian could react, Valerian strode across the aisle and grabbed the corner of a tarpaulin covering a shape that was slightly larger than the M-4 itself. "Hey, Paul," he barked to a technician across the floor, "let's have some light over here!" Then he gave the canvas a sharp tug.

Brim nearly gasped as the big cover slid to the floor. "Universe," he whispered. Before him, he recognized the partially completed M-5—a graceful, trihulled synthesis of flowing lines and compound ellipses. Even less than half-finished, it was enough to take his breath away.

"Like her?" Valerian asked.

Brim only nodded, so stunned by the new ship that he feared his voice might betray him. After considerable delay, he managed a weak, "Yeah, Mark. I, ah . . . *like* her."

Valerian put his hands in his pockets. "Even if I could get her ready for Tarrott," he said, "she'd hold only one of those new Napiers—and as heavy as I've built her, she simply wouldn't have a chance." He swept his hand from stem to stern. "This baby's designed for a whole new generation of starship Drives," he said. "When they're ready, she'll be ready; without them, she's nothing much more than a dream."

"*Some* dream," Brim said soberly. "Unfortunately, the League's already got two Mitchell victories."

"Yeah," Valerian said, "I know. If they walk off with it this year, we won't need an M-five."

"That's about the size of it," Brim agreed, turning toward the M-4 again. "How long before I get to take this one up?"

Valerian raised his eyebrows. "Probably you won't want to hold your breath," he said. "I doubt if she'll be ready to fly much before race time."

"*Much before race time?*" Brim asked incredulously. "You mean that I'll have to—"

"—learn to fly it in a simulator? Probably you will. Is that so bad?"

SMOP! Brim shook his head. Valerian was, after all, only a designer. It took a Helmsman to *really* understand. He gulped a deep breath and wrestled his temper under control. "Like you, Mark," he said after a moment, "I'm not all that thrilled with the way things are turning out right now, but by Voot's greasy beard, I'll give it my best shot."

Valerian smiled grimly and extended his hand. "Thanks, friend," he said. "I'm well aware that *my* best shot will be a lot safer than *yours* when race day rolls around."

Brim nodded as he shook Valerian's hand. "I guess that's true," he acknowledged with a chuckle. "But sometimes safety becomes a xaxtdamned small issue." In his mind's eye, he could see Krish Valentin standing tall and handsome in the Tarrott winner's circle. He ground his teeth—if he had anything to do with it, *that* would never happen again. After a few moments of silence, he turned to Valerian and smiled dourly. "Better have someone show me where the simulators are, Mark," he said. "It's high time I got to work."

CHAPTER 6

A Short Ride in a Fast Machine

One week prior to the race, the Carescrian stood in a corner of the Imperial shed at Lake Tegeler watching a Sherrington crew complete the assembly of Valerian's re-Drived M-4. Brim had actually flown the little starship three times before it was hurriedly dismantled, loaded aboard one of the newer cruisers in Greyffin IV's diminished Imperial Fleet, and rushed headlong to Tarrott, where it arrived less than a day before the official deadline for forfeiture by default.

"She'll be ready for you in the mornin', Mr. Brim," a heavy-set Crew Chief in blue coveralls said.

"Very well, Johnson," Brim said, "—and thanks. I know how much work that's been."

"Here's hoping she holds together, now," Johnson said. "We've done everything we can to put 'er to rights."

"I understand that," Brim said with an appreciative smile. He meant it. Johnson's crew had worked sorcery getting the old ship to this stage. Now, it was up to one Wilf Ansor Brim to husband it through the race—and still manage to win somehow. "When would be a good time to show up?"

"How about Dawn plus three?" Johnson asked. "She'll be right ready to fly by then."

"So will I," Brim declared, taking one last look at the handsome old racer. Then he turned on his heel and strode out into the late afternoon sunlight, where a limousine skimmer from the embassy hovered, its chauffeur holding the door.

THE TROPHY / *151*

Inside the passenger compartment, Toby Moulding relaxed in Fleet-blue fatigues and comfortable boots. "I assume she'll be ready in the morning?" he said from a mound of cushions.

"Johnson claims Dawn plus three," Brim replied.

"Then you can count on it," Moulding assured him. "Ted's the best Sherrington has—and they're all pretty good there." He peered into Brim's face. "You don't seem very happy about it, though," he said.

Brim shook his head as the chauffeur picked up the cable and they ponderously started back toward Tarrott. "I wish I were, Toby," he said. "But there's something wrong with that ship. I can feel it in my bones—and don't you laugh. Everybody gets hunches now and then. This one happens to be mine." He folded his arms and stared out the window, biting his lip.

"You don't *have* to fly it, you know," Moulding said at length. "And that doesn't mean that I—or any other member of the High-Speed Starflight team, for that matter—would volunteer to fly her in your place. If you don't think she's flyable, then it's your call." He laughed grimly. "We're here as backup Helmsmen, not potential suicides."

"Thanks," Brim said. "If I stepped aside and somebody else got killed because of it, I'd never forgive myself." He shook his head. "I'm the only one who's flown the M-four since the new Drives were installed. At least I got a glimpse of her little quirks in person."

"I noticed some real corkers in the simulator, myself," Moulding said.

"The simulator didn't get 'em by half," Brim grumped.

"Then what do you plan to do?"

"I don't know right now, Toby," Brim said. "I suppose I'll make up my mind sometime before tomorrow morning."

"Right ho," Moulding agreed, clamping a reassuring hand on Brim's shoulder. "A couple more metacycles either way isn't going to count much difference once you've got your decision nailed down."

Brim nodded. "Meanwhile," he said, "there's the bloody Leaguer's reception tonight. And just living through that ought to be more than enough challenge for the rest of this day."

"Wilf," Moulding laughed, "one *could* get the idea that you don't love the Leaguers—as our friends the CIGAs presume we do."

"Who, me?" Wilf asked, eyes wide in mock surprise. "Dislike the Leaguers? Now where would you get an idea like that?"

"Oh, I don't know," Moulding answered with a careless shrug. "Maybe it has something to do with a prediction of mine."

"What kind of prediction?" Brim asked.

Moulding frowned. "The prediction that you'll be fool enough to risk your neck in that hotted-up M-four just so the bloody Leaguers can't bag the trophy without a fight."

Brim only laughed. "Toby Moulding," he said grimly, "you are a *very* convincing and perceptive predictor indeed."

After his second floodlit procession to the Chancellery, Brim found himself in another reception line with Kabul Anak's innocuous-looking visage near the far end. This time, however, Kirsh Valentin stood in the place of honor at Anak's left hand, clad in dress blacks with a chest full of medals and gold cordons looping down from his right epaulette.

"Aha," Moulding chuckled under his breath, "I can tell right away that this is going to be a *wonderful* evening for you."

"Just *wun*-derful," Brim grumped. "Why, Tarrott is simply *full* of my favorite people"

"Hmm," Moulding said suddenly, nodding toward the front entrance, "now *here* comes someone who doesn't fit your model of Tarrott."

Brim turned just as Anna Romanoff entered the Chancellery on the arm of a tall, handsome civilian.

"See," Moulding said, pointing to the couple as they handed their wraps to a aide-de-camp, "you certainly count her as a friend, don't you?"

"Unfortunately, *only* a friend," Brim admitted absently. He'd never seen her dressed the way she was tonight. She wore a low-cut, white gown, long, white gloves, a stylishly short skirt, and white, spike-heeled shoes that set off a pair of gorgeous legs. All that remained of the formidable businesswoman Brim had come to know was the soft, reddish brown hair, that she still wore more or less gathered into a loose braid at the back of her head. She was everything Brim imagined she might be, and *much* more. He felt a twinge of jealousy when the man took

Romanoff's elbow and guided her to the end of the receiving line, conversing with Anak's aide-de-camp as if such affairs were a commonplace part of his life. "Wonder who she's with?" Brim asked.

"Oh, I know him," Moulding replied. "That's Wyvern J. Theobold—from Civilization Lixor. He's heir to Theobold Interspace, one of the biggest armaments empires in the galaxy."

"Whatever else he's got going for him," Brim commented absentmindedly, "he also has excellent taste in women."

"I say," Moulding observed. "I didn't know you were so taken with our comely ISS Secretary."

Brim felt his face redden. "W-what? *Taken*?" he stammered. "Not at all. I was thinking that she's sort of good-looking. That's all."

"Oh," Moulding said with an unconvinced grin, "of course. Sorry." Clearly, he didn't believe a word.

When they had worked their way to the front of the line, Moulding was announced first even though he was behind Brim in the slow-moving procession. Valentin shook Moulding's hand in a perfunctory manner, mouthed a few words, then quickly passed him off to Anak while he turned to Brim contemptuously.

"Principal Helmsman to the Imperial Starflight Society, Private Citizen Wilf Ansor Brim!" the aide-de-camp announced.

"Brim—my old adversary," the handsome Leaguer brayed. "Welcome again to Tarrott." He grinned with some inner pleasure. "If I remember correctly, the last time we spoke, you promised that you would discuss this year's races—but only at race time." He laughed. "Well, Carescrian, the time has come to talk. I look forward to learning how you plan to compete against our new Gantheissers with Valerian's ancient M-four."

"The race hasn't been run, yet, Valentin," Brim said calmly, trying to conceal the fact that he'd been stung.

Valentin laughed again. "Ah, yes," he said. "That was your friend Moulding's statement last year. Can't you Imperials come up with something more original—or perhaps more meaningful? You *do* remember who won the race, don't you?"

Brim was about to answer when Valentin sneeringly nodded his head toward Admiral Anak. "Save it for the reception, Brim," he said. "I shall make sure we have some time to talk this evening. Your excuses in advance for this year's loss ought to prove quite amusing indeed." Abruptly, he turned to his right while Brim bit his lip in frustration. "Admiral Anak," he said without further ado, "I believe you recall meeting ex-Lieutenant Wilf Brim at last year's race reception?"

Tonight, Anak was dressed in a plain civilian evening suit with only a few medals dangling from his chest, although a portentous black and yellow sash ran diagonally across his ruffled shirt. He nodded at Valentin's words. "Yes, Provost, I remember him quite well," he said without apparent emotion. "Welcome again to Tarrott, Brim," he pronounced in Vertrucht while extending his hand in the Imperial fashion. "I understand that you've returned to wrest the trophy from young Valentin here."

"That is correct, Admiral," Brim answered as Valentin smirkingly turned to his next guest.

Anak glowered. "And you actually *will* attempt high-speed starflight in that overpowered relic of Valerian's?"

"I will, sir," Brim answered, a little startled by the Admiral's abrupt manner.

Anak nodded while for a long moment his eyes focused somewhere distant. "I don't suppose there is any way to deter you from that sort of vainglorious nonsense?" he asked presently.

Brim felt his mind whirl. What was the old Admiral getting at?

"Brim," Anak continued quietly, "listen to this carefully—I have time to say it only once: engineers from both Gantheisser and Gorn-Hoff have calculated that the two Lyon Napiers in your M-four will interact with destructive resonance flutter when you reach approximately eighty-two M LightSpeed. Our covert agents tell me that you have yet to exceed eighty in your tests." He looked the Carescrian squarely in the eye. "In the name of all that is Universal, don't throw your life away." Then, mercurially as he had begun, he turned to the woman on his right, the curvaceous Helmsman who drove her Gantheisser to second place behind Valentin in the previous year's race. "Praefect Groener," he said, as breezily as if he had never seen Brim before in his life, "it is my pleasure to present Mr. Wilf Ansor Brim, Principal Helmsman of the Imperial Starflight Society."

Groener's dress blacks consisted of a tight-fitting black tunic with a military skirt that was short enough to flaunt voluptuously athletic legs and small, high-booted feet. She also smelled slightly of TimeWeed. "Good evening, Mr. Brim," she said in Vertrucht-accented Avalonian. "Kirsh has often described your considerable abilities in Vertrucht. Perhaps later this evening, you might permit me to practice my Avalonian on you?" Beneath a peaked Controller's cap, her blue eyes probed with a half-friendly wariness, as if she expected a rebuff.

Brim silently recalled a futile mission to capture an enemy ship when *he* ended up being captured instead by Kirsh Valentin—and the cold-blooded torture he later endured at the hands of the young Controller. Clamping a firm grip on his emotions, he narrowed his eyes, "I should be honored, Praefect Groener," he said, torn between simple desire for the obviously licentious woman and cold, vindictive hate for her uniform.

"I shall look forward to that, *Wilf*," she said. "And, by the way, my name is *not* Praefect," she laughed intimately. "Inge will do perfectly well later on."

"Thank you, er, Inge," Brim said with an embarrassed bow; then he turned to the next dignitary in the receiving line. Only two more remained to be dealt with, and he passed them quickly. Soon, he was on his own.

A small orchestra was playing intimate dance music by the time he reached the refreshment bar. Locating a seat at the counter, he had just ordered a goblet of meem when he glimpsed Rogan and Margot LaKarn entering the hall with a glittering crowd of latecomers. Clearly, they had been on the town for a considerable time; three or four were having difficulty navigating to the reception line—including Margot herself.

It had been almost a year since Brim had laid eyes on the Princess. Somehow she had become even more beautiful than he remembered. As LaKarn clumsily helped her from her wrap, he revealed a glamorous apricot gown trimmed in hints of antique gold that set her splendid figure off to its absolute optimum. Her strawberry blond hair was short and fashionably disarrayed, as only a woman supremely confident of her own beauty could wear it. Brim took a deep breath to calm his rising excitement. He would have a moment with her alone tonight, somehow. It was only a matter of time.

As he waited at the bar, he sipped his meem and watched

Moulding execute what must have been a most convincing assault on one of the more comely High-Speed Starflight Team members: a tall, fiery redhead in a low-cut green gown who had green eyes to match, a mass of freckles, and breathtaking legs that seemed to go on forever. Brim had noticed her before, a lot of times. Soon, his Imperial friend was standing at the bar, formal cloak over his arm and clearly ready to leave.

"Important mission tonight, old man," he said with an embarrassed wink. "Will you mind terribly if I find my own way home to the embassy?"

Brim laughed. "If you don't, you're a xaxtdamned fool," he said with a look of feigned horror on his face. "You've lined up a *most* alluring target for that mission, old friend."

"Oh, *quite* so," Moulding agreed with a grin that seemed to spread from ear to ear. Then he frowned for a moment. "Wish to bloody blazes we could do something for you, Wilf," he said. "The room's chock-full of eligibles tonight, but it seems as though both the cuties who might interest your egalitarian tastes are here on someone else's arm." Then he put his hand to his mouth. "Sorry, old man," he said. "I didn't mean to . . ."

"It's all right," Brim said, clapping his friend on the shoulder. "Sometimes, I think the whole galaxy knows." He took a deep swallow of meem.

Moulding shut his eyes for a moment. "Your secret's pretty well kept," he said. "But a number of your friends have guessed."

Brim shrugged, then nodded toward the waiting redhead. "I think your mission's going to be in jeopardy soon, friend," he said. "Better get cracking."

"Yes. Right ho!" Moulding said. "Well, I'm off, then." He scowled for a moment. "It would be a shame to sleep alone with all the good hunting here tonight." Then he squeezed Brim's shoulder and disappeared into the crowd. Not long afterward, Brim watched him exit the hall with the redhead on his arm.

"Wilf," a soft voice said, "I thought you might be here tonight. I want you to meet Wyvern Theobold."

Hopping to his feet, Brim turned to face Anna Romanoff, who was even more alluring up close than she had been at a distance. It required all his concentration to avoid simply staring. How did she manage to conceal that splendid bosom with the business clothes she wore? Taking a deep breath, he gripped

Theobold's proffered hand. "Glad to meet you, Wyvern," he lied.

"Glad to meet you," Theobold said. Tall and good-looking, with slate-colored hair and piercing blue-gray eyes, he was dressed in evening clothes that made Brim's rented gear feel even more common than it was. "I've certainly heard about you before," he said. His eyes met Brim's in a way that changed the Carescrian's attitude instantly.

"Anything good?" Brim asked in mock apprehension.

Theobold laughed again. "All of it," he said. "I was *there* in Tandor-Ra the day you virtually saved the city from an attack —led, if I remember correctly, by Kirsh Valentin." He nodded his head. "Your heroism is quite well known in Lixor."

Brim felt his face flush. "I didn't have much choice," he said. "Captain Collingswood ordered me to take the ship out, so I did. Besides," he added, "I was at the helm all the time. The Blue Capes at the guns deserve most of the praise. We had a fine crew on I.F.S. *Truculent*."

"From what Regula Collingswood has to say about it, you deserve a lot more credit than that," Romanoff said. "The Leaguers lost three ships that day."

"Did she also mention that, afterward, *Truculent* had to be scrapped?" Brim asked.

"Yes," Romanoff answered with a little smile. "And she also warned me that you probably still blame yourself for that."

"Hmmm," Theobold mused. "It sounds as if this conversation opens old and painful wounds—besides impugning certain of our more prominent hosts. I must apologize for starting it, but when Anna said that you might be here tonight, I did want to meet you."

"I wasn't all that sure you would be here," Romanoff said.

Brim shrugged, glad for the change of subject. "I wasn't all that sure I'd be here, either," he said. "The M-four and I arrived late last evening. We almost missed the deadline."

A look of concern suddenly clouded Romanoff's face. "Yes," she answered. "That's what I'd heard."

"Is anything wrong?" Brim asked.

Romanoff started to answer, but she was interrupted by the arrival of Kirsh Valentin with Inge Groener on his arm.

"Well, Theobold," Valentin crowed while he took a long and obvious look at Romanoff's low-cut gown, "it seems that you have encountered the Empire's soon-to-be-defeated Helmsman." He drew on a reeking camarge cigarette. "Introduce me to this *gorgeous* little woman you have on your arm," he demanded, turning his back on Groener as if she had ceased to exist.

With a look of amusement, Theobold made the introduction, then stood back while Valentin ostentatiously bowed to kiss Romanoff's gloved hand.

"You must allow me to show you the sights of Tarrott, Miss Romanoff," the Leaguer said, continuing to hold her fingers in his.

"I am honored, Provost Valentin," Romanoff replied. But her brown eyes offered no encouragement whatsoever as she withdrew her hand.

Clearly undeterred, Valentin bowed again. "I shall indeed look forward to our next encounter, madam." Then he turned to the Lixorian. "My compliments, Theobold," he said with a smirk. "Your attraction for gorgeous women is most commendable."

Theobold smiled diplomatically and bowed. "I accept your compliments, Provost," he said, nodding toward Groener, "—and I return them."

Valentin indicated his voluptuous companion with a toss of his head. "Oh, Groener has her attributes," he said, patting her on the posterior with a careless laugh. Then he turned to Brim. "But what attributes do you bring to the race this year, my Carescrian friend?" he asked with a smirk. "Surely you have no higher hopes of winning *this* encounter than you did the last time we dueled. Can you have forgotten what I did to your clapped-out destroyer off Lixor a few years ago?"

Brim started to retaliate, but before he could open his mouth. Theobold spoke in a bitter voice. "Perhaps a number of us remember that incident, Provost," he interrupted, straightening to his full height. "I was in Tandor-Ra during that unprovoked raid you led."

"My dear Theobold," Valentin interjected with an untroubled look, "you must not take wartime events so personally. I was only following orders." He laughed. "And besides, my dear Lixorian, a state of war never did exist between our two domains—only a state of commerce. Or am I mistaken that Theobold Interstellar was one of our main suppliers of collapsium?"

Clearly embarrassed, Theobold glanced nervously at Romanoff while he clinched his fists; then he recovered flawlessly. "As befits the major industry of a peace-loving, neutral domain such as Lixor," he said, "Theobold Interstellar does business with *all* qualified patrons."

"Of course, my dear Theobold," Valentin sneered as he returned his attention to Brim. "And now my unfortunate Imperial friend, are you ready for your next defeat at my hands?"

"What *next* defeat, Valentin?" a familiar female voice demanded suddenly from Brim's left. "I w-wasn't aware that you'd scored a first."

Brim caught his breath as he got to his feet. "Margot," he gasped.

Surprised by the swift barb, Valentin whirled to face his attacker. "Aha . . . Princess LaKarn," he said, recovering with a cruel smirk, "you are quick as ever to defend your onetime sweetheart." He glanced at his perfectly manicured fingernails. "But even Brim admits that Collingswood's old *Truculent* was scrapped after the encounter. No wonder they forced him out of the Fleet."

"*Truculent* died along with *all three* of *your* ships, Valentin," Brim retorted evenly. "Or had you forgotten how it ended?"

"Not at all," Valentin said archly. "But surely you and your delicious Princess recall that your salvation came from the salvos of her cousin's battlecruiser." He took a last drag on his cigarette and snuffed it out in an acrid cloud of smoke. "Had Onrad failed to arrive when he did, you, my intrepid Imperial Helmsman, would be a swarm of subatomics rushing outward through the Universe."

"I s-saw the g-gun camera recordings of that battle, Valentin," Margot said, stumbling slightly over her words. "And Wilf trashed your ships long before Onrad showed up, without any help at all."

Forgetting his clash with Valentin, Brim suddenly noticed that the Princess was steadying herself against the bar. Her eyes were drooping slightly, and she appeared to be . . . drunk. Anna Romanoff—who was staring at her with a horrified frown on her face—turned to Brim for a moment, then made a perplexed look when LaKarn himself strode up and clapped Valentin on the back.

The Baron wore a suit of civilian evening clothes that outdid even Theobold's, especially with the stunning red, green, and white sash he wore diagonally across his shirt front. "Kirsh, old man," he exclaimed. "I see my drunken wife has already found you." He laughed, at the same time placing a lustful arm around Groener's waist and nodding to Theobold. His face was flushed as if he also were suffering from one too many goblets of meem. He glanced at Brim, and abruptly his eyebrows raised in surprise. "Well," he said, "this *is* a reunion, isn't it? I should have known Margot would find you first thing off." He laughed salaciously. "You'll be disappointed this time, though, Brim. Since she's gotten the Habit, she's absolutely lousy in bed."

Brim inadvertently glanced at Romanoff, who had been watching him with an expression of dismay on her face. She looked away immediately as if she were terribly embarrassed, then—without turning her head—she whispered to Theobold. A moment later, the Lixorian made a few lame excuses about busy workdays on the morrow, and they hurried away into the crowd. Brim felt a momentary sense of loss as they left, but when he turned to Margot—who was standing, or rather hanging on, silently at the bar—the sight drove every other thought from his mind. He was at her side in a moment. "Margot," he asked desperately, "what's happened to you? What can I do to help?" Her eyes were glistening with tears.

"You can do nothing," she whispered wretchedly. "I-I'm not drunk—it's TimeWeed, Wilf: the Habit. I love it," she panted, "and I'd *kill* for it."

Clenching his teeth in distress, Brim took her arm in his hand. "Margot," he said urgently. "Don't say that. By the Universe, I'll get you out of this some way."

"No!" she cried with a wild look of alarm and pulled her arm from his grip. "I don't *want* out of it!" She closed her eyes. "I lied to you at the embassy," she whispered. "It's not Rodyard, it's...it's the xaxtdamned H-habit." Then she shut her eyes. "Oh Universe," she groaned, swaying dangerously against the bar. "Don't look at what I've become, Wilf. Remember me the way I *was*." Then she burst into tears.

Brim reached for her again, but he was brushed roughly aside by the squat, masculine matron he'd spied the previous year. In a moment, she had Margot supported upright by some miraculous grip around her waist and was shuffling off toward the exit where a black-uniformed Army officer from the Torond waited with a wrap over his arm. Stunned, the Carescrian heard LaKarn laugh cruelly in the background.

"Well, Brim?" he gloated. "What's the matter? Has she *really* changed all that much? Doesn't she appeal to you anymore?" He sniggered wetly through a goblet of meem Valentin had placed before him. "You didn't even try for a little feel, did you?"

Brim started from his chair, but Valentin stepped in his way, grinning cruelly. "One more step, Brim, and I shall have you ejected from the hall."

"You and who else?" Brim growled, clenching his fists.

Valentin laughed again. "Oh, I shan't even have to touch you, Carescrian," he said with a look of revulsion. "*They* will do it for me." With a nod of his head, he indicated six beefy "civilians" with blond hair and blue eyes who had materialized from the crowd.

Brim narrowed his eyes. "I'll make both of you hurt plenty before they get me, *hab'thall*," he said, using the most insulting malediction he could dredge from his store of gutter Vertrucht. He started for the Leaguer with blood in his eye.

Valentin shrank against the bar while the guards began to close in from all sides. "Wait!" he choked. "Would you really sacrifice your chance to fly in the race, Brim? Remember where you are . . . I shall have you barred from competition *instantly*."

The Carescrian stopped short and bit his lip in anger. He closed his eyes and took a step back. "You cowardly bastard," he whispered under his breath.

Valentin smiled. "Cowardly? We shall see who is cowardly during the race, Brim," he snapped. "Because I shall beat you *there* more thoroughly than you have been beaten before in your worthless life."

At this, LaKarn staggered to his feet and threw an arm around Valentin's neck. "Unless I beat both of you," he said, holding up a boastful index finger. "Then I'll have beaten him even worse." He laughed coarsely. "It'll serve the bastard right for spreading my wife's gorgeous legs so often!"

"All right, Rogan," Valentin said, thrusting his chin forward. "*One* of us will give the Carescrian peasant the thrashing of his life." Then he snickered. "But your drivers will have their hands full beating our new Gantheissers."

"We'll see," LaKarn said, grinning now from ear to ear.

"My new Dampier may send your engineers back to their design boards this year."

With a glance, Valentin reassured himself that Brim was de-
fused and waved away the guards. "Perhaps, my competitive
friend," he suggested to LaKarn, "we should go somewhere and
discuss this—where we can share *special* entertainments."

LaKarn's eyes lit up. "Yes," he said with a look of childish
excitement, "the *special* entertainments."

"See you at the races, Brim," Valentin said airily, steadying
the Baron on his feet, then steering him toward a doorway beside the bar. He turned momentarily to Groener, who had remained standing quietly at the bar. "I shall expect you to be at
the shed *early* tomorrow, Praefect," he said. "There is much
work to be done." Then he followed LaKarn through the doorway and was gone.

Groener made a little bow to his receding back. "I shall be
there, Provost," she said, snapping her heels together uselessly.
"Early. . ." For a moment, her face took on an expression of
hopelessness, then she shook her head and closed her eyes.
When she opened them again, she stared musingly at the Carescrian for a long moment. "Buy you a drink, Mr. Brim?" she
asked, resting against the bar and conspicuously thrusting her
magnificent bust toward him.

Brim looked into her eyes for a moment, then boldly stared
down at the breasts straining at her tunic. "Depends," he said.

"On what?" she asked with a slight frown.

"On what you had in mind for *after* the reception," he said.
"Perhaps I won't even *want* a drink." Suddenly, he felt her hand
on his thigh. It traveled slowly to his crotch. And even though
she *did* smell of TimeWeed, he felt his breathing begin to grow
deeper. "Come to think about it, Inge," he said, feeling his
pulse quicken, "I guess I'm not terribly interested in another
drink—but you do have something I want a lot more than
meem."

"As have *you*," she whispered.

Brim shook his head. "Your embassy or mine?" he asked. "I
seem to have inherited a car."

She looked at him with an honest grin and shook her head in
irony. "Wilf Brim," she laughed, "I have actually been on assignments where I tried to penetrate your xaxtdamned Imperial
Embassy."

"I'm afraid this assignment will get you only as far as a room in the visitor's sleeping wing," he said.

"That will be fine," she laughed, "—and a lot better than I managed on my own." She shook her head ruefully. "I never was cut out for this business of war. I suppose I'm simply more of a Helmsman than a penetrator."

Brim took her arm and helped her to her feet. "Let's go find that car of mine, Inge," he said with a grin. "I'm both a Helmsman *and* a penetrator."

"Ah yes," she laughed happily, "I was *counting* on that."

Uadn'aps was much higher in Dahlem's morning sky than Brim had planned when an embassy car delivered him to the race complex at Lake Tegeler. Three new Leaguer battleships brooded just off the far bank. This morning, however, Brim was more interested in the Leaguer's shed. An empty gravity pad sat in front of its doors. True to her word, Inge Groener must have reported for work early. He only hoped she shared the glow he felt from their lovemaking. The athletic beauty had proven herself both gentle and violent—and always *precisely* at the right times. He shook his head as the car sped along the apron. People like Inge Groener made it difficult to make blanket statements about Leaguers. He wondered how many other nice ones there might be.

Neither Moulding nor the redhead were among the colorful gathering of Imperials taking the morning air. Nearby, the M-4 hovered on its gravity pad looking for all the Universe like a teardrop resting on two fat needles. A small army of technicians still swarmed over her brilliantly polished hullmetal, making last-moment changes to controls and rigging. In spite of himself, Brim's first glimpse of the graceful little ship brought back Admiral Anak's dire query: *I don't suppose there is any way to deter you from that sort of vainglorious nonsense?*

He hurried to the locker room and changed into the latest issue Imperial battle suit—tinted yellow instead of blue to de-emphasize the ISS's many ties to the Imperial Fleet. Then he strode out to meet Valerian on the apron. But Anak's frowning countenance refused to leave his mind's eye: *Engineers from both Gantheisser and Gorn-Hoff have calculated that the two Lyon Napiers in your M-four will interact with destructive reso-*

nance flutter when you reach approximately eighty-two M LightSpeed.

Clad in his usual tweeds, the designer looked up and smiled when Brim was within haling distance. "How does she look to you?" he asked.

Brim forced himself to smile. "She *looks* beautiful," he said truthfully, climbing to the rim of the gravity pad with the breeze full in his face. The morning smelled of high summer—fresh-cut grass and water—blended with the odors of hot metal, fresh sealant, ozone, and heated logics from the ship. "How do *you* feel about her?" he asked.

Valerian shrugged and pursed his lips. "She's solid enough," he said. "I've been with the crew all night and watched just about every fastener slide home and lock." He turned his hands palms up. "I guess she's as ready to go as I can make her. You want to do a walkaround?"

"I'm inclined to take your word, Mark," Brim said. "For this particular bird, you've got to be the greatest Crew Chief in the known Universe."

"Well," Valerian drawled with a grin, "she was all right when I looked her over ten cycles ago—but there's no telling what might have gone wrong since then."

They spent the next metacycle checking drain plugs, access doors, panel tracks, and plumbing mazes before they were finished; each was important—and each was flawless. But the inspection came nowhere near answering the burning question Kabul Anak had planted in Brim's mind the night before. Ultimately, the Carescrian capitulated to his doubts. "How about resonance flutter between those two big Lyon Napiers?" he asked Valerian. "Is the ship really well enough braced for all that power?"

"Resonance flutter," Valerian mused with a nod. "I wondered if there wasn't something bothering you." He scratched his head. "Well, I'll have to admit it's a possibility, all right. Those two big crystals will be putting out some powerful oscillations—especially in the mass component . . ."

"And at exactly the same frequency," Brim finished for him. He shook his head. "How much clearance is there between them?"

Valerian closed his eyes a moment while he pinched the bridge of his nose. "Fifteen point nine three five irals, virtual center to virtual center," he said presently. "It's close, but I *think* it ought to be enough."

Brim made his own mental calculations. "That means I'm safe at least to eighty M LightSpeed, doesn't it?" he asked.

"Probably a little faster even," Valerian assured him. "And, of course, there *may* be no flutter till twice that speed. Voot's beard, you might *never* get any at all." He shook his head in mock confusion. "It mostly has to do with the shape of the side lobes they radiate—and *these* particular beauties ought to be specially safe to work with. Their energy lobes stretch aft—not sideways where they can interact at high time constants. Besides," he added, "the League won it last year for sixty-seven point two M's, so you ought to be able to make a race of it this year for not much more than eighty M's, give or take a few LightSpeeds."

At that moment, a sleek, white Gantheisser GA 209V-2 thundered out of the morning sky, turned gracefully onto final, and descended to the water, skimming the surface in an arrow-straight cascade of spume for nearly a c'lenyt. Brim grinned as it came to a hover above its gravity foot. If Inge Groener's landfall were any indication of her condition, she had a *great* glow going for her. Then his musing was interrupted by a blue-clad messenger rushing from the shed at a dead run, calling his name at the top of her voice.

"They timed Inge Groener from one of our observation ships this morning," she shouted when she reached the gravity pad, "and it looks like the new Gantheisser's a lot faster than any of us thought it would be."

Brim felt a cold finger of dread trace his spine. He glanced for a moment at Valerian, then knelt on one knee and looked down at the messenger. "How many M's?" he asked.

"Seventy-nine point six four."

Brim looked Valerian in the face. "Will this bucket of bolts do better than that?" he asked.

"My calculations say she'll top eighty-eight," Valerian answered.

"And hold together?" Brim demanded.

"I think so—unless you run into resonance flutter, of course."

"Well, eighty-eight M's is a Vootload past the eighty-one you referred to as safe."

"Yeah, it is," Valerian conceded. "But then, nobody knows if that flutter will even happen." He shrugged. "I guess it's pretty well up to you, Wilf."

Brim took a deep breath and nodded. "Yeah," he said, "I guess it is." He looked out over the lake and sniffed the grass and the water. On the far shore, four obviously new destroyers had just joined the Leaguer battleships while Inge Groener taxied her Gantheisser into a gravity pad. Almost eighty M's, he considered with a sick feeling—and she was only the *number two* Leaguer Helmsman. Abruptly, Kirsh Valentin's arrogant face filled his mind's eye, and he smashed his fist against the old racer's hullmetal. "Have them clear the apron, Mark," he said, starting for the ladder. "I'm taking her up!"

Valerian raised an eyebrow, then grinned ebulliently. "That's more like it, Wilf," he said, "—and we'll have extra rescue ships standing by the race course."

"Couldn't ask for anything more than that," Brim called from the ladder, "but I *do* hope we don't have to bother those nice people. They're always so busy during race season anyway." With a quick thumbs-up, he then crawled through a hatch and wriggled into the little ship's single recliner while sirens wailed outside and a cordon of marshals herded straggling spectators from the apron. Sliding open a side Hyperscreen, he was just about to close the master switches when he spied an embassy limousine coasting through the cordon at high speed. Anna Romanoff was at the wheel.

"Wait—don't go!" she called as she braked to a halt beside the gravity pad and leaped to the pavement. Moments later she was on her way up the boarding ladder, slippers, wind-blown skirt, and all. "Wilf," she panted breathlessly, locking her elbows over the hatch coaming and gasping to catch her breath, "I just heard about the Groener woman and her new Gantheisser. You're not going to try and beat that kind of speed in this antique are you?"

"This is the only ship I know of that's faster, Anna," Brim answered. "I have to."

"You *don't* have to, Wilf Brim," she said anxiously, toying with the buttons of her white sweater. "The ISS can't ask anyone to risk his life—no trophy in the Universe is worth that." She frowned indignantly. "I don't care if this is the fastest ship in the whole xaxtdamned *Universe*, even I know that it was never designed to go that fast—and when I called old Bos Gallsworthy, he wasn't even sure it would hold together. He doesn't want you to fly it either, and . . ."

Brim placed his hand gently on hers and peered directly into her troubled brown eyes. Like a typical civilian, she'd forotten the CIGAs, Fluvanna, Beta Jagow, and all the rest. But he hadn't. He *couldn't*. "Anna," he said, "please try to understand. The fact is that I do have to race this ship. There are much bigger issues at stake than the ISS, I'm afraid."

Romanoff looked at him for a moment, then closed her eyes and grimaced. "I was afraid you'd say something patriotic like that," she said, drumming her fingers on the hatch coaming. She took a deep breath and shook her head. "I don't suppose there's anything I can say to stop you, is there?"

"No," Brim said, still holding her hand. "But I'd be a lot more careful up there if I knew that I were going to spend an evening with you when I get back." The bold words surprised even himself.

"What was that?" Romanoff asked.

Brim grinned in spite of a sudden onslaught of shyness. "I said that I'd be a lot more careful up there if I knew that I were planning to spend an evening with you when I get back."

She suddenly looked surprised. "With me?" she asked.

"Your name is Anna Romanoff, isn't it?" Brim asked facetiously.

Romanoff placed her hand over her mouth. "Yes," she said, "it is." Then she shook her head again. "Oh Universe, Wilf. Can't I somehow reason with you?"

"I'm afraid not," Brim said. "But I do want that evening with you when I get back."

She shut her eyes again. "I give up," she whispered in exasperation. "I absolutely give up." Taking a deep breath, she looked him directly in the eye. "All right, Wilf Brim," she whispered, "if you do manage to come back in one piece, by Universe, you can have any evening you want." With that, she pulled her hand from beneath his, shook her head, and started down the ladder without another word.

Grinning like an idiot, Brim watched until her embassy car disappeared along the cableway, heading back to the city. By Voot, he thought as he turned to the master switches again, an evening with Anna Romanoff might just be worth the risks of a high-speed ride in Mark Valerian's old bucket of bolts.

He went through the ship's preflight checklist in short order, then with plasma pressure steady in the green, he turned on the gravity brakes and shunted energy boost to the grav, kicking in power flow, energizer, and antimatter on queue from the auto-sequencer. After four sharp beeps from the interruptor, his big R2600 caught with a limousine-sized belch of gravitrons that shimmered on the apron like midsummer heatflutter. He grinned. If the Napier Drive crystals ran half so well, the remainder of his morning promised to be interesting indeed. Then, gulping down his transition to internal gravity, he released the brakes. As he moved off the gravity pad, he flashed a thumbs-up to Moulding, who had just shown up in the midst of the High-Speed Starflight Society cheering section—with the redhead. The blond aristocrat waved back apathetically, obviously content to stay where he was.

Precisely one click later, the Carescrian discovered one of Valerian's only faults. In his zeal for maximum performance from everything, the designer had set the ship's brakes so delicately that merely *thinking* about the actuator was sufficient to send him crashing into the forward Hyperscreens. Subsequently, his taxi to the takeoff vector was enough to make the greenest student writhe with embarrassment—it must have resembled a Syngallian In'ggo dancer doing a winter mating shuffle. At the strand, he drew to a halt for a moment while a technical crew from Lyon Industries activated his Drives—safely away from the grandstand area—then he set off across the water toward the morning's launch vector.

Centering the ruby takeoff vector in his forward Hyperscreen, he collected what nerves he had left, got clearance from the tower, and completed his checklist. Then running up the grav one last time, he dropped quarter lift enhancers and poured on the energy, gently keeping his steering engine amidships. The bow lifted at first, then fell as the little ship began to rise free from her gravity gradient. Just before transition, he eased back on the controls to overcome a slight heaviness forward and carefully raised the bow again. At a speed of about eighty-three cpm, only the slightest urging on the elevator control was needed for lift-off, while he practically leaned on the steering engine to check an immediate swing to port. The M-4 roared upward.

Even with the nagging fear of impending danger hanging over the flight bridge, Brim felt the rush of exhilaration that comes from flying a true thoroughbred starship—albeit an overpowered one. It was a feeling that he had yet to duplicate in any way. With velocity building rapidly toward LightSpeed and a near vertical climb, he settled back to start the twin Napier StarDrives and another checklist. He'd discovered early in the game that one-man starships made for busy drivers.

As he expected, everything about the Drives was also precisely in order: intercoolers ready, time synchronizers on, mass compensators turning, blast tubes open, overdrivers off, Hyper-Boost on, and reserve energy at maximum.

At 0.95 LightSpeed—while forward vision degenerated to a confusing reddish muzziness—the generators began to run out of energy and he connected the starboard Drive crystal to the power mains. Passing through 0.98 LightSpeed, he keyed in START for about twelve clicks, then hit the plasma primer and ENERGIZE. With a harsh resonance that shook Valerian's little starship like a leaf in a storm, the big Lyon Napier came to life, barking out a satisfying rumble and a cloud of green radiation aft. The port crystal followed suit at 0.99 LightSpeed, and less than a heartbeat later, normal outside vision returned as the Hyperscreens began to translate. Behind him, two pulsing Drive plumes looked for all the world like the wake from a ghostly oceangoing ship.

For the next few cycles, he let the speed build as he headed out for the racecourse. During an actual heat, he'd now be under maximum acceleration, but he was still learning the little M-4, and this morning there appeared to be a hundred spectator starships nosing around the course, from private yachts to full-fledged warships.

When he entered the actual circuit, he took the first turn in a wide arc while he gained the feel of the little ship's stiff controls. Clearly, he chuckled to himself, Valerian's M-4 would never be remembered for her maneuverability.

Lap after lap, he flashed around the course, bettering his speed with each circuit: 72.18M LightSpeed . . . 74.67M . . . 75.91M . . . 78.4M. But with each increase in velocity, the controls grew heavier and harder to operate. Valerian had invested only minimal volume in a steering engine. "She's no attack craft," he was fond of saying. And it made sense at the time. Brim grinned ruefully. At least he could detect no flutter. If there had been anyone to listen, he'd have cheered about *that*, but his only link to the outside was by KA'PPA COMM, and the sole person monitoring his frequency would be a bored Leaguer flight controller.

On the tenth lap, he increased his speed to 79.64M Light-Speed. By this time, the big Drive crystals were howling through the spaceframe like Great Sodeskayan crag wolves, and the controls were growing harder to use by the moment. He made a note about that in the log book, then steeled himself for the long straightaway. Somewhere between his present velocity and the next increase of two and a half M's of LightSpeed, his old ship would either run into flutter problems, or he would push her for eighty-five. Carefully, he gated more energy to the Drive, scanned his instruments, then increased the power again. The second time, he thought he detected a slight wobble in the steady thunder coming from below his feet. Nearly half of the long straightaway remained, so once more, he opened the energy gate. This produced an immediate and definite change in the sound of the Drive, as well as the feel of the controls: almost definitely the onset of flutter. He bit his lip. Now was the time to pull back, at least for any Helmsman with half a brain—or one who didn't have a race he *had* to win. Grimly, he turned the cabin gravity restraints to MAXIMUM, then tightened his chest and shoulder belts. One more increase in the energy. By now the hull was vibrating noticeably and his instruments registered more than 83.5M LightSpeed. He grimaced while he prepared for the next star. At this velocity, he wasn't able to cut the turns so closely.

A moment later, he saw the yacht.

She was a sizable craft—clearly modified from wartime service—and she must have been carrying media people, for she was blazing along where she had no right to be, well inside the restricted lane. Her Drive was throwing up a tremendous wake of gravitron combers—mass waves that Brim's little M-4 violently punched through as if it were smashing a whole succession of brick walls. Few people had any idea at all just how fast 83M LightSpeed was. One had to actually *be there* to know.

Ordinarily, the ship and its wake would have posed no problem, even well inside the restricted lane where they were. Brim, however, was traveling nearly three times her velocity and was under only a minimum of control—his steering engine almost totally useless for anything but wide-radius turns. "Voot's bloody beard—*move!*" he yelled helplessly as the range closed with awesome speed, but even if anyone had heard his voice, it was far too late for help.

No time to pause and consider the multitude of possible alternatives. No thought of saving the ship or himself. A lot of people were on that yacht ahead, and he was about to open it like a rotten fruit! There was only one way out—and if he were wrong, he had to go ahead anyway. Instantaneous decision was 90 percent of being right in all the myriad emergencies he'd survived over the years. To be wrong and follow through on the mistake was better than being right too late.

Desperately, he poured energy to the starboard Drive crystal alone. At the last possible moment, the jolting, bouncing racer yawed sharply to one side, then jogged past the yacht with little more than a c'lenyt between them. But the extra power also increased the M-4's previous vibrations by an order of magnitude. *Resonance flutter!* Instantly, the whole cabin seemed to come apart, a warning klaxon sounded, both forward Hyperscreens disintegrated in a billion whirring crystal shards, and then the whole Universe shattered into one excruciating instant of pain.

It seemed like a thousand Standard years since the accident...

yet Brim had a difficult time remembering anything specific about what had happened afterward. He couldn't even remember his previous evening, although clearly it must have been one *Universe* of a party. A monumental headache was absolutely dissolving his cranium, and he had no desire at all to get out of bed. Who had he been out with? Not Margot—he was sure of that. Inge? He didn't think so.

Anna, perhaps?

He stiffened. She was certainly on his mind. Was *she* in bed with him? He ground his teeth. If it *were* Anna—Great Universe! Why couldn't he remember? Had he been too drunk to make it worth her while? Had he even been able to . . . He felt a surge of panic. Anna—wonderful, fragile Anna—and for the life of him he couldn't remember what she looked like when they . . . His head began to spin with apprehension. Carefully, he started to probe the bed with his hand.

But his arm didn't seem to work. He tried again. Nothing. In fact, he couldn't move anything, not even an eyelid. Abruptly, he stopped worrying about Anna Romanoff—he was thraggling well *paralyzed*! By Voot's greasy beard, what in the Universe had he been drinking?

He tried to calm himself by doing a mental checklist, of sorts. He was breathing, although how long he might keep that up was anybody's guess. And, except for his headache, he didn't hurt anywhere. Mostly, so far as he could ascertain without moving anything, he was sort of numb.

And sleepy, again. To xaxt with the checklist—maybe he was dying! "No!" he yelled aloud. "No!" But try as he might, he couldn't match the wave of incredible lassitude that was overtaking him. After a while, he just stopped fighting . . .

When next he awoke, he could hear voices. And this time, he could open his eyes, too—although he couldn't seem to focus on anything. Nevertheless, somebody *else* certainly could.

"His eyes are open!" Anna Romanoff's soft voice exclaimed in a whisper.

"Hmm, yes," a strangely familiar, masculine voice agreed, though Brim couldn't place it. "And right on schedule. It's nothing less than a miracle."

"He's been through quite a few of those." It was Regula Collingswood. "I wasn't worried."

"We Sodeskayans would be the very *last* to impugn your words, Regula," Ursis chuckled, "but . . ."

"But," Borodov finished for him, "you and Anna were the first two aboard I.F.S. *Renown* when word came through that the M-four's bridge pod had been recovered." He sounded as if he were grinning.

"We were lucky to find that pod at all," Onrad remarked in his distinctive brogue. "Our friend Brim did quite a thorough job of making sure nobody else would fly that contraption of yours, Valerian."

"That luck had Onrad written all over it," Valerian's deep voice commented in a serious tone. "You kept the search alive long after everybody else had given up, Your Highness. All I wanted to do was murder that zukeed flying the media ship."

Onrad laughed. "Well, I am in command of the squadron, after all," he chuckled, "—no trouble there. Besides, you'd have assassinated me if I'd even *looked* as if I were going to give up."

"Lucky for us we had only one M-four," Collingswood said, "or Moulding would have killed himself trying to win for Brim."

"You know, I've got a hunch he can hear us," the mysterious voice interrupted. "What's the scope show, Jennie?"

"I'm getting definite reactions, Doctor Flynn," a female voice interrupted.

That one, Brim was sure he hadn't heard before. But he'd heard of Xerxes O. Flynn! *That* was who owned the other voice. A great feeling of relief flooded through him. Whatever was wrong, he was in the best possible hands. Flynn had been medical officer aboard both I.F.S. *Truculent* and I.F.S. *Defiant.* Clearly, Onrad had signed the esteemed Doctor of Space Medicine aboard his own ship. Flynn was a true master of the healing machine.

"Wilf," Flynn said, "if you can hear any of this, blink your eyes twice."

It took every bit of his concentration, but Brim managed to blink twice.

"Well, I'll be xaxtdamned, " Flynn said. "I guess we'll have to call off the Kerolean taxidermist we sent for." He chuckled. "Poor bastard—he's going to be disappointed. We promised him the ugliest human he'd ever laid eyes on."

"Doctor Flynn!" Romanoff exclaimed.

"I'm getting more reaction, Doctor. . ."

"Hey, Anna," Flynn said breezily. "That's no insult—it's quite an honor. I've seen some *ugly* ones, believe me. What do you think, Wilf? Does that hurt your feelings? Blink a couple of times for us."

Brim managed six blinks in a row. He knew he was going to be all right.

According to Flynn, Brim had been lucky in a number of ways. When he was extracted from the mangled cockpit capsule—using a *carefully* wielded collapsium torch—many bones in his upper torso had been shattered inside an "impregnable" battle suit. By all rights, he deserved to be dead. Only a left shoulder blade and—incredibly—his irreparable spinal column had been spared. His face was nearly flattened when his helmet deformed after impinging directly against a hullmetal bulkhead. Flynn had reconstructed new features only by skillfull interpolation of old Fleet medical records. Additionally, the tremendous concussion had driven bone splinters into the optical portions of both eyes. Repairing those took the most time, working mostly at a molecular level to conserve the incredible clarity that made Brim the finest Helmsman anywhere.

Nevertheless, despite the extent of his injuries, he was now out of danger and well on his way to a complete—if improbable—recovery. Flynn, a fancier of Atalantan rothcats, warned the Carescrian that he now had used up at least ten of his original nine lives.

Perhaps the best part of his recuperation came early, while he was still on board I.F.S. *Resolute*. Onrad brought the news personally. "Well, Wilf," the Prince said quietly one afternoon, "I suppose you've heard that you'll get to race in the Mitchell again, now that LaKarn's driver beat our friends from the League." He chuckled. "Old Rogan said that Dampier of his was fast."

Brim took a deep breath as the machine's warm pseudopods gently manipulated his eyes. "I heard, all right, your Majesty," he said, carefully. "It was the best news I've had since I figured out I was going to live." He meant it.

"Marino's DA.67 is a damned handsome ship," Onrad observed. "Did you get to see it before . . . ?"

"Only in the media, Your Majesty," Brim interjected. "But it looked like a fine ship. And you can bet that old Xnor Marino will be in there next year with an even faster version."

"No doubt," Onrad said. Then he laughed. "You haven't even mentioned second and third places. Aren't you interested —or does it even matter, now that you'll be racing in Valerian's new M-five next year?"

It was Brim's turn to chuckle. "It matters, Your Highness," he said. "I think you know how I feel about Kirsh Valentin."

Onrad laughed. "Well, Brim," he said, "in spite of your efforts to conceal it over the years, I *have* gotten the idea that you don't care for him a great deal." Then he paused for a moment.

"The embassy, however, tells me that you have a much more, ah, should we say, *friendly* relationship with Praefect Groener."

Brim chuckled. "Somehow, Your Highness, I didn't think that was a completely private room they assigned me."

"Actually," Onrad said, "it was. But it isn't often Controllers come to spend the night, so, of course, she *did* attract her share of attention. And the rooms in that particular wing have uncommonly thin walls."

"I'm glad she at least took a third place," Brim said. "I don't suppose we'll ever know for sure if she actually could have beaten Valentin."

Onrad laughed. "He'd have her killed if she did." Then Brim felt the man's hand on his arm. "I'm terribly sorry about what's happened to Margot," he said in a serious tone. "I needed to tell you that. Neither Father nor I know what to do about it, either. She's LaKarn's legal wife, and because of it, she has dual citizenship. Otherwise, we'd demand her back. Unless one grows up smoking it—like most League children do who are destined for Controller training—TimeWeed will affect the brain. Flynn's best guess is that she's got maybe ten years. Then, well . . ." His voice trailed off.

After that, there was very little more to talk about.

Later, at the Imperial Hospital in Atalanta, it was Brim's job to make all the new body parts function as cooperating entities, including his eyes. With Toby Moulding generously supplying transportation, he spent countless metacycles doing physical drills of the most agonizing nature, until he could once again manage his gravcycle. After that, he divided his days between his job at the Fleet base, where he slaved tirelessly, regaining his old knack for Helmsmanship and working out in simulators, learning to fly Valerian's new M-5. Only irregular visits from Claudia Valemont and her husband broke the grueling schedule he set for himself—although he did manage to establish an active correspondence with the busy Anna Romanoff, who answered his messages from nearly every corner of the Empire. He wasn't about to let her off the hook; she'd promised him an evening.

Then, at long last, he was again bound for Rhodor, this time aboard the starliner S.S. *Commerce Enterprise* and luxuriating in first class by order of no less than Emperor Greyffin IV himself. But for all the heady opulence, he was *most* anxious to reach Sherrington's Woolston labs. In his latest correspondence with Valerian, he'd learned that one of the two M-5s ordered by the Society would soon complete her ground trials, and he intended to make her first flight himself. Besides, Dr. Borodov planned to be there this trip, and he hadn't seen the old gentleman for nearly a year.

When he climbed aboard the Sherrington Type 224 at the Bromwich terminal, he knew immediately that something troublesome was afoot. The little ship was already occupied by a quartet of thermal-transfer specialists from Krasni-Peych who had arrived aboard a Sodeskayan liner less than a metacycle prior to *Enterprise*. The Bears—ordered in by Dr. Borodov himself—were all more or less in a somber mood because the PV/12 Drive had lately encountered serious cooling problems. Heat elimination was always a special challenge when large emitter systems were installed in small starships where physical radiator area was at a premium.

A second surprise waited for him at Lys, for it was neither Mark Valerian nor his two friends from Sodeskaya who met him at the little Woolston terminal. When the 224's passenger hatch opened to the predawn coolness outside, it was Anna Romanoff who waited under the Karlsson lamps at the far end of the brow. His spirit soared! She'd written that she was scheduled to complete negotiations at the main Bromwich plant about the same time as his own arrival, but he hadn't expected she would be finished so soon. As he led his traveling bag through the gate, his face was set into a silly, ear-to-ear grin—and there wasn't a thing he could do about it.

"Thought you might need a lift to the labs," she teased with an impish smile, "so I got here a day early." Her beautifully tailored cardigan suit was somehow both formal and casual at the same time. Its coarse weave managed to enhance her delicate charm.

"The labs are fine as long as *you're* going to be there," Brim answered while the Sodeskayans trooped past on their way to a second Sherrington skimmer. "Otherwise," he added, "well, Valerian can come find me wherever *you* happen to be going."

"Hmm," Romanoff murmured. "I don't suppose he would especially appreciate that since he *did* lend me the skimmer. I think he'd like you to fly his new ship today."

"Valerian can wait," Brim said. "Look what happened *last* time I went up in one of his rustbuckets." He laughed and took her arm. "Where's the skimmer, Anna?" he demanded. "We'll spend the day gathering flowers or something—and afterward I'll cash in the evening you promised me a long time ago."

She blushed again. "Mr. Brim," she declared with mock formality, "you are impossible." Then she looked into his eyes and shook her head. "How *do* you feel, Wilf?" she asked bluntly. "The last time I saw you, you were ... well, you know ... inside one of those healing machines."

"I feel damn fortunate to be alive," Brim answered seriously, "and *very* healthy, thank you." He nodded. "I've received a number of new parts and a lot of good care."

"You deserve a *lot* of good care," she said.

"The best kind of care I can think of would be *you* spending the day with me while I avoid Valerian," he said.

"Wilf Brim!" she exclaimed in feigned outrage. "What am I going to do with you?"

"Well, if I *do* have to fly, then you could at least plan to spend the evening with me," he suggested earnestly.

"I think that can be arranged," she murmured with a blush. "There's supposed to be quite a bash after the M-five's first flight."

"You'll go with me?" he asked.

"I'd *love* to," she said.

"In that case," he said, "I'll fly."

CHAPTER 7

Princess Margot
Effer'wyck-LaKarn

Brim and Romanoff arrived at Sherrington's lakeside ramps just as dawn was tinting cotton-puff clouds over Hampton Water. The M-5 already had been drawn to the water's edge and was hovering aboard a gravity pad. Under a light coating of dew she was a velvet study in reflected mauve with rose overtones against the indigo nightward sky.

Here and there, little groups of technicians in dark blue Sherrington coveralls sat under the trees or dangled their feet from the seawall while the aroma of cvceese' from a dozen open vacuum bottles mixed with the fragrances of flowers, trees, and the rich, damp Woolston soil. It was a moment so bewitching that both the Carescrian and his lovely friend climbed wordlessly from their car and tiptoed to the top of the ramp. There they stood, silent, while they drank in the graceful collection of pastel ellipses before them in the morning serenity.

So far as Brim was concerned, Valerian's newest creation was simply the most gorgeous ship in the Universe. Just shy of eighty-five irals in length, she was slim as a needle, with a tiny, ultraraked flight bridge faired into a sharply pointed nose and two prominent, blisterlike housings high on either side of the hull, approximately ten irals abaft the side Hyperscreens. An enormous, faired-in blast tube exited just forward of the tail cone and gave mute testimony to the phenomenal power of the new creation from Sodeskaya, that featured Krasni-Peych's new PV/12 "Wizard" Drive. External surface radiators for crystal coolant passed down each flank and gave the ship a rather stylishly ornamented appearance. Oversized Admiralty NL-4053-C gravity generators rode in long, tapered pods at each side of the hull. They were connected just abaft the beam by streamlined "trousers" that clearly harked back to Valerian's M-4, but these, Brim noted with relief, had nothing to do with her Hyperspace Drive at all. The big 4053 gravs they *did* contain, however, promised astonishing acceleration below Light-Speed, and that was precisely where Mitchell racers spent critical cycles at the beginning and end of each race. Externally, she was a dark blue and carried the number "N218" on red, white, and blue racing stripes applied diagonally across the generator pods. A large "5" appeared on either side of the aft hull.

After staring for a long time, Brim suddenly noticed how cool the morning was and gently slipped his tunic over Romanoff's shoulders.

She jumped slightly at his touch, then smiled with her eyes. "Thank you," she said.

"It took me long enough," Brim replied. "I just sort of got caught up with the beauty of the whole thing."

"So did I, Wilf," she said gently, looking out at the lake and then up at the starship. "It's a moment I shall cherish," she said, glancing at her damp shoes. She looked at him full in the face for a moment. "I don't very often find such beauty in my life."

Brim was about to inquire about that when Valerian strode around the corner of the gravity pad with Borodov at his side, both grinning from ear to ear.

"Aha, Brim! Caught you gawking!" the designer exclaimed, grasping Brim's hand while Borodov received a bear hug from Romanoff. "How does this one look to you, my friend?" he asked.

Brim rubbed his chin and considered for a moment. "She looks *right*, somehow," he answered.

Dressed in his usual tweeds and Rhodorian boots, Valerian grinned and nodded. "If she looks right, then she probably *is* right," he said, "—at least that's how the story goes."

"Well, if the simulators are any indication," Brim asserted, "then she's quite a ship."

"She is . . . ah . . . ready to fly," Valerian said suggestively.

"You're not in any hurry, are you?" Brim asked with a grin.

Valerian adjusted his glasses with a chagrined expression. "I suppose I oughtn't to be," he answered. Then he took a deep breath and grimaced. "Look here," he said, "I'm not going to feel right about the old M-four coming apart like that until I manage to put you aboard a *good* ship." He glanced up at the M-5. "And I think I've got one there."

Brim laughed and winked at Romanoff. "I think he does, too," he said. "Tell you what. If you'll look after my coat for a while, I'll go somewhere and change into a battle suit. Then we'll all find out for sure."

For a moment, Romanoff glanced at Valerian and Borodov. "No offense to either of you gentlemen," she began, "but . . ." Then she turned to look Brim directly in the eye. "You're *certain* you want to fly today, Wilf?" she asked, taking his arm for a moment. "This time, there's no hurry."

"I'm certain," Brim replied, meeting her gaze with what he hoped was a confident look. "If you want to know the truth, I'm always a little anxious the first time I take any ship aloft, even one of his," he said, pointing with a thumb at Valerian. "But that's simply part of being a responsible Helmsman. It sort of comes with the territory. And besides," he added, "I'm not going all the way out into deep space this first ride. I won't do that until later."

Romanoff shrugged doubtfully. "If it's all right with you," she said after a moment, "then I guess it's all right with me, too."

"Nevertheless, Wilf," Borodov added with a playful grin, "I think you need to be aware that the real reason Mark wants this contraption flown immediately is that Anna won't pay for it until you confirm that it's all right." He wore a high-collared beige tunic trimmed in gold piping, baggy white trousers, and soft boots—Sodeskayan summer attire.

Valerian nodded in sham seriousness. "He's right, you know, Brim," he inserted, "—and I just happen to have a spare battle suit your size in the hangar over there. How's that for coincidence?"

"Stick around while I make that party happen," Brim said to Romanoff and strode off for the hangar.

Inside the typically cramped flight bridge, Brim satisfied himself with his initial checklists, then went through the procedures necessary to start one of the two Admiralty 4053s aboard.

It involved seeing if the plasma boost was operative, then energetically alternating high-frequency energy spikes among three impulse points until he got a positive reading on the Bennet gauge. Finally, with both boosters set to maximum, he hit START and ENGAGE at the same time. The interruptor flashed twice, then the generator cut in with a shudder and settled into a smooth rumble as it quickly reached its rated power. The starboard generator followed suit less than two cycles later. After that, it was again time for internal gravity.

Fighting his stomach to a standstill, Brim grinned through the narrow Hyperscreens at Valerian and Romanoff while a group of sleepy mechanics and technicians cheered from the ramp. Then waving away the mooring beams, he called up a burst of power and headed out over the water. This time, he noted, the gravity brakes were set so that humans could operate them, not just engineers. He chuckled to himself—even Mark Valerian could change his ways a little. He taxied around for a bit, checking the various instruments and steering engine while he called for clearance from the tower. Then without too much in the way of preliminaries—she would either fly, or she wouldn't—he simply drove over to the far side of the lake, turned into the wind, and started his takeoff run.

With her generators set on fine pitch, the M-5 fairly leaped from the water and climbed away at high speed while Brim watched the Sherrington labs pass rapidly astern and out of sight. So far, the only criticism he had concerned his view through the forward Hyperscreens, which were very narrow, owing to Valerian's placement of the bridge so far forward on the hull.

Immediately, he took the little ship to five thousand irals or so and confirmed what the simulators on Atalanta had earlier estimated about landings. He tried a dummy one at altitude to establish a good approach speed and to make sure that when she settled, she did not flick on her back or do anything else objectionable. The M-5 stopped flying at precisely the predicted power setting, then paid off at about 130 c'lenyts per metacycle with very little tendency to roll either way. After that, he did a few steep turns to try out the controls.

Finally, having assured himself that everything really important was shipshape, he retraced his path back to the lake, called the tower for an overhead break, then made his descent while he watched trees on one side and Sherrington's hangars on the other gradually rise ahead in the narrow Hyperscreens—keeping half an eye on the altimeters. The M-5 was a slippery little starship, and she took time to decelerate.

In the next few clicks he rocketed across a small island, then cautiously eased back on the controls long after instinct told him to. In the simulators, he'd also learned that there was always a danger of flaring too high, then smashing through the gravity gradient and actually touching the surface. Moments later, he heard the gratifying rush of cascading water only irals beneath the keel. He smiled to himself. Back down in one piece—not bad for the first time.

As he taxied up the ramp and eased to a halt on the gravity pad, the M-5's little flight bridge filled with the sounds of cheering; outside, a considerable throng had joined the morning's brace of mechanics. And two of the loudest were Romanoff and Valerian, both of whom looked as if they were greatly comforted by his appearance back safely on the ground.

In the early afternoon—after busy Sherrington technicians had carried out a number of adjustments he'd noted during his brief morning flight—Brim again took the M-5 aloft. This time, however, he was escorted by a Type 225 carrying Valerian, Ursis, Borodov, and a number of system specialists from both Sherrington and Krasni-Peych. After a second set of maneuvers to prove the morning's control adjustments, he called for deep-space clearance and headed out toward the two-hundred-thousand-c'lenyt limit where Sherrington leased a sizable free zone from the Empire for Hyperspace testing.

"Well, Wilf Ansor," Borodov said from a display, his voice muffled in Brim's helmet, "you are ready to invoke the Wizard, eh?"

"Absolutely, Doctor," Brim answered with a chuckle. Beneath his feet, the gravity generators were thundering away at maximum and his LightSpeed meter read 0.97. "Any last instructions?" he asked.

"You should find no deviations from the simulators except for the temperature problem," Borodov said with a frown. "Unfortunately," he added, "we have not cured that."

"The temperature problems I can handle, Doctor," Brim chuckled, unconsciously tightening his mechanical seat restraints and thumbing the cabin gravity to MAX. "Keep your eye on me just in case this Wiz decides to head out for the next galaxy like the last one did."

"I shall," Borodov answered, "and good luck,"

"Thanks," Brim said, then turned to the control panels. He'd already learned that the plasma choke would be highly sensitive due to the Wizard's prodigious demands for power. In itself, that was a minor problem. As plasma gated through the choke and into a feed tube, it was either consumed by the Drive crystal itself (which directly converted the raw energy into HyperThrust), or it was released to space itself by an automatic wastegate activated when gravitron pressure exceeded certain limits. The problem came in deftly controlling the amount of energy that eventually found its way to the crystal. Too little could easily cause catastrophic failure—most commonly in the form of a meltout at the blast tube. Too much, however, often resulted in a violent explosion, especially when fed to a cold crystal. Either result was guaranteed to be fatal in a ship the size of an M-5.

"Point six four at the Tesla coils," Brim sent, gating more of the ship's energy output to the primary plasma source. The tone of the straining gravity generators shifted slightly, but they held and the LightSpeed meter remained rock solid at 0.97.

"Point six four at the Teslas," Borodov echoed.

With great care, Brim eased the choke open to its first detent. Almost instantly, a whole section of his readouts changed from green to yellow as plasma pressure began to rise at the crystal a lot faster than the simulators had predicted. He opened the wastegate to balance the flow. At the right of his power panel, a D meter began to register available force at the crystal, also rising much more rapidly than he expected. The Wizard was frisky today.

"That's a lot of pressure for a cold crystal," Borodov cautioned, his voice suddenly tense from the display.

"I know," Brim said through his teeth, "I've opened the wastegate, but the pressure's still building from the choke. And I can't get a smaller setting there." Flinching at the thought of an exploding Drive crystal only irals from his back, he opened the wastegate farther, and the pressure at the crystal immediately dropped—below minimums. He had to start all over again.

Slamming MASTER RESET at the Drive controls, he shook his head and sat back in the recliner while he gathered his remaining nerves. Krasni-Peych's new HyperSpeed Drive was proving to be more a demon than a wizard. "We'll need to change out that xaxtdamned plasma choke first thing," he grumped to Borodov.

"I have made note of it, Wilf," Borodov said patiently.

Glowering at the D meter—no longer registering anything —Brim eased the wastegate closed again. Back came the pressure, and this time, a number of indicators in the power section began to glow red as the pressure built. At that point, Brim decided to take command of the situation. If the power controls were not workable, he was reasonably certain that the Drive controls were. It was only a matter of getting the ship started on her Drive. After that, he could make his tests and then turn the damn thing off. This close to home, gravity generators were good enough to get him back to Sherrington's.

Grinding his teeth in apprehension, he jammed the wastegate all the way shut. Moments later, plasma pressure began to build like an oncoming meteor—and suddenly, the D meter was reading in the middle of its safe range. Only the ship's powerful thrust dampers stood in the way of the Drive's awesome thrust. "She wants to fly!" he roared to Borodov.

"So I see," the old Bear said. "Probably that is your best bet—you have much finer controls for the Drive itself."

"That's what I had in mind, Doctor," Brim said. Clearing himself for local traffic, he made a final check of the time synchronizers—everyone had heard nightmares about *those* getting out of tune—switched on the mass stabilization system, then, opening the blast tube aperture, he gently eased pressure on the thrust dampers. A bright blue glow from aft filled the M-5's bridge and the display of Borodov went blank as normal radio waves were left far behind in the Wizard's wake.

Abruptly, the stars went wild ahead, wobbling and shimmering to an angry kaleidoscope that ended in a confusion of multicolored sparks, while on Brim's panel, the LightSpeed indicator began to climb like a rocket. Immediately, he keyed on the Hyperscreen translators, and his view forward cleared.

Nearby stars were mere streaks while those ahead in the distance grew in size even as he watched. A second glance at the LightSpeed meter showed it moving through 73M Light-

Speed, even though the crystal's heat output was easily keeping pace with the little ship's phenomenal acceleration. Brim found himself once more in control, regulating output from the Tesla coil by use of the ship's speed regulators instead of the poorly adjusted plasma choke. In a shallow turn, he craned his head aft, watching the Wizard's distinctive turquoise Drive plume. Then he grinned to himself. *This* would give Kirsh Valentin something to think about!

Abruptly, his KA'PPA display sparked to life with an incoming message: WILF! CAN YOU READ THIS?—BORODOV SENDS.

He grimaced. He'd been so absorbed that he'd forgotten all about the chase ship, which was clearly far behind by the distance indication on the KA'PPA screen. He returned, READ YOU LOUD AND CLEAR. ALL SYSTEMS PERFORMING WELL EXCEPT DRIVE COOLING—BRIM SENDS.

GOOD TO KNOW WE DON'T REQUIRE SERVICES OF DR. FLYNN THIS TIME—VALERIAN SENDS. P.S. HOW ABOUT SOME EASY MANEUVERS AND A RUN FOR HOME? NO WAY ARE WE GOING TO CATCH UP!

DRIVE TEMP JUST BELOW MAXIMUMS. WILL DO A COUPLE OF EASY TURNS, THEN HEAD FOR WOOLSTON. RACE YOU BACK TO THE LABS—BRIM SENDS.

YOU WIN!—VALERIAN SENDS.

After a few of the most rudimentary maneuvers, Brim found himself anxiously piloting with a wary eye evenly divided between traffic and a rising Drive temperature. The M-5 was turning out to be a steady, docile racing machine, while its lusty Krasni-Peych PV/12 clearly promised it would someday live up to its nickname of "Wizard"—once the Sodeskayans managed to overcome its considerable cooling problems.

Just before landfall, he encountered a swarm of media ships again taking turns coming dangerously near for close-up coverage of the Empire's new Mitchell racer. He had nearly aborted his landing sequence to avoid another accident when three Imperial destroyers appeared seemingly from nowhere and sternly warned the civilians off, taking up close escort through reentry and remaining in perfect formation until he started his descent for the lake. The R-class warships absolutely dwarfed Valerian's little M-5 and provided Brim with a startling lesson in perspective. Aboard the light cruiser I.F.S. *Defiant*, he'd considered the destroyers to be runts!

"Thanks for the help," Brim sent as he lined up on the lake. "Those media guys can be downright troublesome."

"Yeah," one of the ships answered. "We saw recordings of what happened the last time one of 'em got interested in your flying."

"Good talking with you again, Brim," another of the ships sent. "That half-pint boat you've got there is a long sight smaller than old *Truculent*, but she looks like she might go a lot faster, too."

Brim grinned. "Who's that?" he asked, his voice sounding muffled inside his helmet.

"Gondor Runwell," the voice answered. "I served aboard I.F.S. *Narcastle* years ago—before the CIGAs sent her to the breakers. A lot of us would like to see you back with the Fleet, mister."

Brim took a deep breath—he couldn't remember the man at all. "Yeah, thanks," he agreed, "so would I sometimes." Shortly thereafter, no time remained for anything but concentration as he brought the little ship in for her second landing.

Long after a thorough debriefing and a much-needed shower, Brim joined Romanoff for a late afternoon stroll along the lakeshore. She had changed into a cool gingham shirt, ivory skirt, and soft, white moccasins. Small pleasure boats still plied the deep blue water, and a cooling breeze was redolent with the fragrance of the lake. Relaxed, Brim set off at an easy pace, but before long, Romanoff began to fall behind, her distinctive, prancing walk turning slowly into what appeared to be a limp. "Are you all right?" he asked, taking her arm.

"I'm *fine*, Wilf," Romanoff answered, continuing along as if nothing out of the ordinary had occurred. "It's so beautiful by the lake this afternoon."

"It is beautiful," Brim agreed. "But . . . are you certain everything is all right with you?"

"Wilf," she said while small beads of perspiration appeared on her forehead, "this afternoon is one of the nicest I can remember in my life—seriously." Then she smiled. "Perhaps we *might* pause and enjoy the view."

Brim stopped while she leaned against a tree. The comely businesswoman was clearly unwilling to discuss whatever was causing her discomfort, and he was glad to respect her wishes.

It was enough that she was there, with him. "I take it you finally paid Valerian," he offered with a chuckle.

"Oh, Wilf," Romanoff laughed as she peered out over the lake, "Dr. Borodov was only joking about that." She blushed and turned to look at him. "Actually," she admitted, "I finished all my contract work yesterday afternoon—and your friend Valerian gets his remuneration on a *very* regular basis."

"I'm glad you decided to stay on," Brim said.

"So am I," she answered quietly. "It's been quite a day for me—and, I imagine, for you, too."

Brim nodded. "It has," he said. "The M-five's turned out to be a pretty special ship. I'd bet that we have yet to find out how special. Valerian's clearly put his soul into the design." He peered through the open doors of the hangar. "Something very basic in me says that she's not just *another* racer."

"What else is she, then?" Romanoff asked, frowning quizzically.

"I don't completely know," he said. "The *beginning* of something, perhaps." He shrugged helplessly.

"A beginning, Wilf?"

"Well," he answered after a few moments of thought, "like the beginning of a whole new line of starships. I can't see them —but I think Mark Valerian can."

"And you flew the first one," Romanoff said dreamily. "That must make you feel pretty special." She smiled. "It makes *me* feel special just being here to watch you."

"You were special to me a long time before you came to Woolston," Brim said quietly.

She looked at him with a soft expression in her eyes. "Thanks," she said, "I'll remember that."

Afterward, they walked back along the lakefront, Brim taking care to make frequent rest stops while they talked. He had never met anyone like Anna Romanoff. Quiet, unassuming, and genuinely beautiful—mostly because it hadn't occurred to her that she was.

Streaks of sunset crimson still tinted Woolston's darkening lavender hills and glens when Brim arrived at Romanoff's guesthouse amid the incomprehensible chanting of a billion unseen night creatures. Nearby, Hampton Water glowed radiant azure while twilight swept the last vestiges of daylight from the horizon, and the air was heavy with spice from a nearby stand of conifers. The earliest stars had just begun to show overhead when snatches of music and laughter started from the direction of the party hangar, a few cycles' walk distant.

While Brim paused for a moment at the doorstep, contemplating the twisted path that had brought him to this particular midsummer night, the door gently opened and Romanoff stepped lightly to the porch. "Waiting for someone, Mr. Brim?" she asked, looking into his face with a mysterious smile. In the shadows, she looked like a lovely dream. As in Tarrott, she had dressed in a low-cut white dress that revealed precisely enough of her upthrust breasts to be provocative and at the same time tasteful. However, Wilf Brim was her escort tonight, not Wyvern Theobold. That meant he could stare at neither her gorgeous bust nor the shapely legs and spike-heeled shoes that a short skirt revealed. What he could—and did—stare at, however, was her glorious hair. She'd let it down from the accustomed loose braid, and it flowed past her shoulders in buoyant waves that framed her face as if she were part of a portrait by some classic master. The strict businesswoman Brim had once met in Atalanta's Grand Koundourities Hotel had undergone a total metamorphosis. He found himself without words.

She took his arm, continuing to look up at him. "You are very quiet this evening," she whispered as mysterious tendrils of perfume caressed his nostrils.

"Merely speechless," Brim muttered at length, starting along the path toward the hangar. "I knew you were beautiful the moment we met, but I . . . I had no idea . . ."

Romanoff squeezed his arm more firmly. "Thank you, Wilf," she said, closing her eyes for a moment. "I wanted to be beautiful tonight."

Brim felt a thrill in the fading light of the lakeside road. "You've got your wish, then," he said, "and so do I." He frowned. "When I saw you in Tarrott, I never dreamed I might someday be here . . . I mean . . . with you on my arm and . . ." He laughed and shook his head. "Wyvern J. Theobold is a hard act to follow."

"Oh is he? Well, for your information, Mr. Wilf Ansor Brim, he doesn't often tell me that I'm beautiful. *Nor* does he pilot starships." She pressed his arm and giggled happily. "But if I had to settle for one or the other, I like to hear that I'm beautiful."

Sherrington's great hangar doors were pushed all the way open, and the M-5 had been rolled into the entrance and decorated with strands of winking holiday lights. Outside on the apron, surplus battle lanterns bobbed overhead in the gentle breeze and a number of gaily decorated tents served as refreshment stands. A string orchestra played from a stage just below the gravity pad while couples swayed to music that Brim barely understood. For the first time in his life, he honestly wished he knew how to dance.

He need not have troubled himself. He and Romanoff never had time for such distractions. From the moment of their arrival, they were introduced to *everyone*: lab technicians, General Managers, even the custodians. Brim had never met so many engineers, scientists, architects, designers, and draftspersons—all of whom had complex questions and comments on the ship or the flight. Throughout it all, Romanoff remained at his side, conversing intelligently when she needed to, smiling quietly when she didn't, quite content to selflessly bask in Brim's reflected glory. Well into the morning metacycles, when the party began to wane, he turned and spoke quietly in her ear. "My feet hurt," he whispered, "how about yours?"

"I can't tell," she confided with a grin, "they went completely numb a couple of metacycles ago."

Brim winced. "I'm awfully sorry," he said. "I had no idea the party would turn out like this."

"Neither did I," she answered, "but I wouldn't have missed a moment of being here with you."

"It's nice of you to say that," Brim asserted, relieved that standing in one place for several metacycles apparently had no ill effects on this beautiful woman. Their afternoon walk had made him very much aware that he would have to look after her comfort. "What *I* wanted, though, was an evening with *you*. All we had tonight was an evening with everyone else."

She smiled. "I've still had a wonderful time of it, Wilf."

"It doesn't have to be over, yet," Brim said, flabbergasted by the boldness of his words. "I'll bet we could find somewhere to have a drink all by ourselves."

Her brown eyes sparkled for a moment, but she shook her head. "I'd love to do something like that," she said, checking her timepiece. "Only . . . well, I'm due out on SS *Sudla* in the morning, and I mean *early morning*. She lifts almost five metacycles from now. I couldn't handle any more meem and still get to the terminal by then."

"It's fate," Brim grumped, shaking his head with a wry grin. "I nearly had to kill myself to get this evening with you in the first place; then I squandered most of it on everyone *else*. The next time I get up my nerve to ask you out, you'll probably be booked up for years."

A sad little smile clouded Romanoff's face for a moment, then she shrugged. "You don't know me very well, Wilf Brim," she said. "The fact is that you didn't have to kill yourself for tonight at all. I'd have gladly gone out with you the day we met." She shook her head. "And the next time we're both in Avalon, if you're interested, you'll find that I'm pretty much available *any*time. I guess I spend a lot of my time making a living. It tends to frighten most men away."

"Doesn't say much for the guys in Avalon these days," Brim declared, again surprising himself. "If I lived there, you'd be mostly busy trying to get rid of me."

At that moment, Anna Romanoff's fragile countenance took on a look of such singular beauty that Brim found himself stunned. "I shall cherish those words," she said in a voice that was almost a whisper.

The short walk along the darkened lakefront to Romanoff's cottage seemed to be finished only moments after it was begun, even though Brim had stopped twice along the way ("to enjoy the lake"). Somehow, his emotions had gone into a turmoil that prevented him from further sensing the mysterious perfumes of the night or the waves lapping beside the road. He walked in silence, afraid to open his mouth, or take her hand. Anna Romanoff had taken on tremendous importance.

At the door, he desperately wanted to wrap her in his arms and . . . no, by Voot, he wanted a lot more than that—he wanted her *in bed*! But for the first time in his life, he was afraid. What if he'd misread her eyes? What if she recoiled from his touch? He couldn't help himself. Shutting his eyes, he touched her arm. "Anna," he said hesitantly, "c-could I have a goodnight . . . ah . . . h-hug?"

Suddenly—impossibly— she was in his embrace: warm and tiny with her arms around his neck. Now he wanted her lips in the worst sort of way, but she wouldn't turn her face to him. And she was shivering slightly, when it wasn't even cold.

They hung together for what seemed like an eternity. Then finally, gently, he released her.

As he moved away, she finally raised her face to him and— Lord of the Universe, how alluring she was! Only now it was probably too late to try again. "Anna," he whispered. In spite of his fears, he took her hands, warm and soft in his. In that moment, he knew. She was also vulnerable. She was *his*! He felt his breathing deepen and his knees grow weak. He wanted her the way he'd wanted the class beauty at the Helmsmen's Academy. Not just for the sex—any woman could give sex. He wanted to make love with her because she was the best. The most beautiful. The most successful. He put his arms around her again, and this time, she yielded completely. Her breathing had become labored as well. "Anna," he repeated urgently, "will you?"

"I-I don't know, Wilf," she whispered after a long moment. "I'm not thinking very rationally."

Suddenly, he went cold sober, as if someone had poured water over him. He had bedded that class beauty as soon as he had gotten the chance, *but only once*. Now, because of that, he was going to walk away from Anna Romanoff, a creature at least an order of magnitude more desirable. He wanted a lot more than a quick romp with this fascinating woman. A *lot* more. Taking a deep breath, he grasped her hand. "I'd better go," he stammered. "I'll message you. All right?"

Romanoff looked relieved and disappointed at the same time. "All right, Wilf," she whispered, opening the door. "I'd love to hear from you."

"Goodnight, Anna."

"Goodnight, Wilf," she said, staring into his eyes for a moment as if she were trying to find something very important there. Then she stepped inside and closed the door.

Alone in his room, Brim got little sleep that night—or the next.

Rudolpho was the largest city on the mostly barren planet Horblein, fifth satellite of Gragoth in the Aakreid Sector. It was also capital of the Torond, a dominion of some sixteen occupied planets whirling within an extensive asteroid belt rich in crystalline Kapal, a critical substance in forging Drive crystals. For an important seat of government, however, the city had grown large much too quickly. It had somehow evaded the mellowing process that with cities, as with many foods, provides the difference between fare for the gourmand and fare for the gourmet. Its architecture was monotonously modern, its streets tediously arranged in a perfect grid, its terrain precisely landscaped, down to the placement of individual trees. Even *people* here lacked any unique personality, appearing to have borrowed from the citizens of Tarrott lock, stock, and uniforms. In the streets, every man, woman, and child wore some sort of uniform, including black-garbed, imitation Controllers called *Grenzen.* "Ugly lot," had been Moulding's only comment as they followed still another intelligence-officer-cum-chauffeur to a waiting limousine. Brim couldn't have agreed more. He'd wondered how Margot managed to stand her life here. Then he'd remembered the smell of TimeWeed and shuddered.

Now, two nights before the race, Brim and Moulding attended the traditional prerace reception in a colossal hall of state constructed on the shore of artificial Lake Garza that served as both Rudolpho's terminal and LaKarn's elaborate new racing complex. The hall, as well as the complex, still displayed signs of damp cement and plaster from the recent construction.

Tonight, Brim was dressed in his *own* suit of evening clothes, the first he'd ever possessed. He'd purchased it used, of course. But that sort of clothing rarely changed style, and it was magnificently cut. Its former owner had clearly been a man of both taste and wealth. More than anything, the suit reflected Brim's mending financial and social status, and he'd been eager to show it off to Anna Romanoff. Unfortunately, she was still en route to the race after an extended business conference halfway across the galaxy and was not due to arrive in Rudolpho until the morning of the race itself.

All things being equal, Brim couldn't decide if Romanoff's absence on this particular night was better for him or not. From the tenor of their correspondence, he had clearly established a special relationship with her. But in only a few cycles, he would have a chance to speak personally with Margot, and he had no idea *what* that would do to his feelings. He'd been peering toward the head of the line where she stood with LaKarn, greeting dignitaries and principals of the race itself. She wore a short, orange-vermillion party dress with matching elbow-length gloves, and as usual, she was gorgeous. Statuesque and seductive as ever, she gave no sign of her addiction as she smiled, occasionally bending forward to better hear the banalities muttered by her awestruck guests, and generally acting as if she were delighted to greet everyone. Brim nodded to himself. He guessed she might be unique in that. Her Royal Highness, Margot, Princess of Effer'wyck really did like people and enjoyed entertaining them.

Then he bit his lip. The Margot he'd known *before* her addiction enjoyed people. With a cold feeling in his chest, he reminded himself that this beautiful woman was no longer his lover. He'd spent considerable time discussing her plight with Xerxes Flynn and learned that the potent TimeWeed would effect drastic, unpredictable changes in her personality.

All the way through the long waiting line, Moulding—who tomorrow would pilot the second M-5—maintained a rapid-fire conversation about the coming race, clearly trying to bolster his partner's spirits as they approached the reception area. Brim truly appreciated his efforts, but with the advent of Anna Romanoff in his life, the effects of his changed relationship to Margot had been considerably blunted. Now, as Moulding preceded him, exchanging greetings with Rogan LaKarn, Brim peered forward and momentarily caught her eye. In one awful instant, their minds met and she conveyed a look of utter torment. The ghastly realization hit him like a body blow, and he understood—as might only a former lover—that she was suffering a kind of anguish he could barely imagine.

At long last, a sleek, black-uniformed protocol officer announced, "Wilf Ansor Brim, Carescrian and Principal Helmsman of the Imperial Starflight Society."

Rogan LaKarn clasped Brim's hand in a firm grip. He was dressed in the ebony uniform of a Grenzen Commodore with double-breasted tunic, black shirt and tie, jodhpurs, and shiny, knee-high riding boots. "Ah, Brim, my good fellow," he said, almost as if he meant it, "welcome to Rudolpho. We are given to understand that you have delusions this year of winning the trophy."

"A few, perhaps," Brim said, glancing sidelong toward Margot who was laughing at something Moulding had just quipped. Then he returned LaKarn's phony smile with one of his own. "I suppose we'll have to run the race before we know whose delusions were appropriate, won't we?"

"True," LaKarn conceded, the smile remaining on his handsome face. "However, if the ISS continues to field space garbage like Valerian's poor old M-four, you may not live to find out." He looked at his fingernails. "This year, we understand that they will risk your neck to prove the Sodeskayan's untried Wizard Drive—with cooling problems, no less," he added as if he were savoring the words. "How generous of you, my Carescrian friend, especially after the treatment you received from your Imperial associates after the war."

Brim laughed grimly, mustering all the good nature left in him. "I can handle the Wizard," he said with a confident nod.

"Yes," LaKarn said, his countenance giving way to a momentary look of speculation, "one is certain that you *hope* you can handle it. However, last time you played with the Imperial snake, you were bitten quite badly." With that, he reverted to his former mood of disdain. "But we shall talk more of that, *soon*, Brim, believe me. For now—well, I am sure you are looking forward to a reunion with your former paramour." He laughed callously. "I know she's anxious to see you." He took Margot's arm and leered at her. "You remember your old lover Wilf Brim, don't you, my dear?"

"You bastard," Brim gasped in anger, but Margot clutched his arm.

"Don't, Wilf," she warned, her eyes distant and glistening. "You can do nothing but make more trouble for me."

"She's right, you know, Brim," LaKarn sniggered. "But as I promised, old boy, we'll talk soon about the race—and a lot of other subjects as well. I'll be in touch." With that, he nodded to the protocol officer, and the next guest in line was announced.

Brim stood speechless before the woman who once had meant more to him than anything in the Universe. "I don't know what to say," he stammered.

"It's all right," she said, "neither do I."

"Y-you seem to be . . . ah . . ."

"Straight?" she finished for him. "Yes," she said, "for the moment."

"But—"

"There are no buts," she said. "Before this evening is over, I shall be the same as I was when you last saw me in Tarrott. The urges come at different times—none predictable, but all irresistible."

"M-margot." Brim began, but already a new guest had been introduced, and the next in line was waiting impatiently behind him. "Will I see you?" he asked desperately.

"Perhaps, Wilf," she said anxiously, "but I can promise nothing." Then, with a look of almost physical pain, she introduced him to the next dignitary in the line: an OverGalite'er of some sort. Brim never really caught his name.

Nor did he see Margot again that evening. Shortly after the last guests meandered through the receiving line, she disappeared for the remainder of the reception.

After opening ceremonies the next morning, Brim, Moulding, and Valerian, all dressed in blue Sherrington coveralls, found themselves balancing on a narrow work platform beneath the number two M-5 while they recalibrated an array of skewed accelerometers in the steering engine. As they worked, a small, wiry man walked up to the gravity pad looking like he owned it. Moulding turned and recognized him immediately. "Hello, it's Drummond from the embassy at Tarrott, if I recall correctly," he declared, peering over his gamma-Zemmerscope. "Aren't you a little far afield here in Rudolpho?"

Drummond laughed, as if his appearance were nothing out of the ordinary. "Oh, we embassy hands get around much more than one might think," he said, stepping over a bundle of glowing, multicolored cables. He was dressed in a splendidly tailored business suit with no trace of embassy green. "Tell me, Gentlemen," he inquired, looking up at the work platform with an impish look in his eyes, "have either of you learned to pronounce '*Arry* yet?"

Brim laughed. "'Arry," he exclaimed.

"Right you are!" Drummond said, pointing a finger at the Carescrian.

Moulding groaned. "Somehow," he replied. "I have lingering doubts that even *you* pronounce it *correctly* most of the time, *Mister* Drummond."

"Gorblimey, Gov'ner," Drummond stage-whispered in overacted horror. "'Ow could you even think such a thing?"

"Just a hunch," Moulding chuckled.

"And here I thought I was believable." Drummond laughed, just as Valerian extricated himself from the hatch with a fistful of glowing wires and a hand-held feedback indicator.

"General Drummond!" the designer exclaimed with a wide grin. "What brings you to our humble shed?"

Drummond laughed. "Mark, my friend, no shed even remotely associated with your starships could be described as humble." Then, abruptly, he sobered. "Actually, I have a message for these two troublemakers you've got working with you."

Moulding raised a blond eyebrow. "For *us*, ... General?" he asked.

"Aye," Drummond replied, "mostly for your friend Brim, Commander," he said, "but you'll likely be involved one way or another." He glanced around the hangar, then looked Brim directly in the eye. "Wilf," he began in an underbreath, "you'll this day be called to a *very* private meeting by your friend Rogan LaKarn and a few of his friends from the League. They're clearly planning to make you some sort of offer concerning the race." He grimaced. "We're interested in learning *precisely* what they want—although we think we know part of that—and what kind of deal they're offering. But most important of all, we want to know who's there to back up the deal."

Brim wondered what branch of the Admiralty Drummond *really* represented. "Very well, General," he said. "I'll learn everything I can: what they want, how much they'll pay, and who's in on the offer. Is that correct?"

"You've got it, Mister," the man said. Then he peered over his glasses thoughtfully. "I know that civilians aren't obligated to help," he continued, "and I'm no prouder than anyone else about the treatment you got from our own dear Admiralty after the war, but . . ."

Brim held up a hand in protest. "That's all past, General," he said, "and no longer very important."

Drummond shook his head for a moment in silence. "Thanks, Brim," he said presently. "It's people like you who give me some hope the old Empire might yet survive, in spite of *many* inexcusable blunders." Then, casting his eyes around as if he were about to divulge some critical state secret, he stepped closer to the gravity pad. "'Ow do you two pronounce 'Arry, again?" he asked in a stage whisper.

"'Arry," Brim repeated with a grin.

"'Arry," Moulding sputtered.

"Good," Drummond pronounced soberly. "Can't be too

careful these days." Then, with a grim little nod, "When you're ready to talk, Brim, call the embassy and ask for me. They'll put you in touch." With that, he turned on his heel and started across the floor, stepping deftly through the clutter of cables and test equipment, as if he'd spent a lot of his life in shipyards. Just as he reached the door, he stopped and looked back toward the M-5. "Oh, Mark," he called. "One thing I almost forgot."

"What's that, General?" Valerian asked.

"After you've been with those two for a while, be sure you check your wallet and timepiece," he called. Then, stepping through the door, he was gone.

Late that afternoon, Drummond's prediction came true. Brim was just climbing from the M-5 after a last practice flight prior to the next morning's race when Moulding handed him a small, white, unmarked envelope.

"Messenger delivered one to both of us while you were up," he said. "Thought you'd want to see it right away. Mine's an invitation to some ghastly sounding bash tonight, with a promise to pick me up at the embassy at Evening plus one."

Brim carefully zipped open his envelope and removed a delicate sheet of expensive-looking plastic stationery. Raising his eyebrows, he unrolled it and began to read:

> Wilf:
> It has been much too long since you so charmingly
> tutored me in Avalonian. With your friend Anna
> Romanoff gratifyingly absent until tomorrow, we might
> get together for another special session this evening. I
> shall have a chauffeured car outside the Imperial shed at
> Evening plus one. Don't be late, dearest—the sooner we
> start, the more penetrating our studies will be.
>
> Inge Groener

Brim scratched his head and laughed wryly. "What ever happened to good old-fashioned privacy?" he grumped.

"Privacy?"

Brim shook his head. "My invitation's not *quite* the same sort as yours, old man," he said. "Kind of personal. But it looks as if they're xaxt-bent on breaking us up for the evening."

"I wonder why," Moulding mused.

Brim pursed his lips. "Friend Toby," he said, "I have a hunch you're about to be entertained in a most extravagant manner." He chuckled. "You'll want to keep your eye on the old timepiece—wherever you might have disposed of your trousers—or you may just miss the whole race."

"Hmm," Moulding said with raised eyebrows. "If I've got to be involved in intrigue, this certainly sounds like the very best kind. But what about you?"

"Probably the only difference between the two of us is that I *may* know the name of the entertainer," Brim answered. He laughed and shook his head. "Crazy, this racing business," he said. "In any other circumstances, we'd be xaxtdamned *fools* to get ourselves tangled in something like this the night before we fly. But our friend Drummond—General Drummond, no less— has got us locked into making *just* that kind of mistake." He shook his head. "I hope he's also prepared to help if we need it."

Precisely at Evening plus one, an unmarked limousine skimmer pulled up at the main entrance to the Imperial shed. "You Brim?" a great, hulking chauffeur demanded through the window. He had light blond hair and the dull, close-set eyes of a bully.

"That's me," Brim answered evenly.

"Get in," the chauffeur ordered insolently.

Brim silently climbed into the back seat. "All right," he said as the man closed his window, "I'm ready."

Without another word, they set off at high speed, clearing the huge racing complex in a matter of cycles, then heading along a major highway toward the shimmering towers of central Rudolpho itself. Before they arrived, however, the skimmer veered through a warren of side streets, skidded into a wide driveway, and drew to an abrupt halt on the capacious front terrace of a huge estate. Brim got out and stood for a moment, staring at the great mansion and taking stock of his situation.

"Inside," the chauffeur suddenly growled from directly beside him. "This is a blaster in your ribs."

Brim flinched as something jabbed his side. It seemed prudent to believe the purported blaster was real. He ground his teeth in irritation. How could he have been so xaxtdamned careless?

"Move," the Leaguer grunted, "and don't get any ideas about trouble, Carescrian. I'd *love* to blow you away."

Brim kept his silence and started across the terrace. He didn't believe the Leaguer had any intention of actually using the blaster. His job was to deliver a *live* Wilf Brim to some sort of meeting, and he had probably only drawn the weapon in muddleheaded arrogance.

Whatever his reasoning, Brim didn't like being on the business end of any (hypothetically) loaded weapon and made up his mind to do something about it forthwith. "Say, *covieel fangovt*," he snorted, the words challenging his captor's birthright in Vertrucht, "does thy mother still sell her scabbed body to Vacca drivers?"

"Brazen *hab'thall*," the chauffeur gasped in rage, grabbing Brim by his left arm and jabbing the blaster roughly into his right shoulder. "You *will* regret that."

More stupidity. Anger was just what Brim hoped for. Biding his time, he continued across the well-lighted terrace, coordinating his steps so they became precisely opposite to those of his captor. Then, at the far end, he pretended to stumble. "Look out!" he whooped, joggling the Leaguer off balance as he was about to tread on his right foot.

"Huh?" came a startled exclamation.

"Too late!" Brim shouted. In the blink of an eye, he dropped beneath the blaster's field of fire, grabbed the Leaguer's forearm and heaved forward. At the same time he smashed backward with his right heel, caught the man just below his right kneecap, and threw him over his right hip.

Howling in bewilderment, the Leaguer spasmodically tossed his blaster into the air, then followed it to the pavement where he landed headfirst with a sickening, hollow thump. He lay still for only a moment, however, then astonishingly shook off his concussion and sprang up to recover the weapon.

Surprised at the man's prodigious endurance, Brim was still too swift. Bringing his own right foot solidly to ground, he snapped his head and kicked forward violently, catching the hulking guard square on the jaw and sending him backward to the pavement in a spray of bloody spittle and shards of teeth.

This time, there was no getting up.

Brim knelt for a moment, retrieved the blaster (a powerful Zspandu-50) from the pavement, then strode directly to the ornate entrance. He aimed with both hands and blew the inlaid doors from their hinges in a shower of glass and splinters. "All right, xaxtdamnit," he shouted fiercely into the ragged, frost-covered frame, "what in Voot's greasy beard is going on in there? I thought I was here to get *laid!*"

Within a few clicks, six surprised and heavily armed guards exploded through the entrance. Triggering the blaster at STUN, Brim dropped the first two in their tracks; the other four expeditiously threw their weapons away and stood with their hands in the air.

"C'mon!" Brim roared at the empty doorway, "who's in charge here? Speak up. I don't have all thraggling night!"

"I-I am in charge," a voice called hesitantly from within. It sounded like LaKarn.

"You get your face out here right now, or I'll drive this limo back to the Imperial shed, and you can forget whatever it was you wanted. Understand?"

Moments later, LaKarn and Kirsh Valentin appeared at the doorway, both in full military dress. The latter stepped forward confidently. "Very well, Brim," he said. "Here we are. Shall we go inside now? There are others who wish to speak to you."

"I should have known you had something to do with this," Brim grumped, striding up the short flight of stairs and tossing the blaster to a confounded guard, who almost dropped it. "Lead on, Valentin. I'm all ears."

Inside a darkly paneled, high-ceilinged room lined with antique bookcases and real books, two men and a woman waited at an ornate table. Brim recognized one of them immediately, Vice Admiral Hoth Orgoth, Commander of the League's newly formed Seventh Battle Squadron. His hard, narrow face had been much in the media lately, supporting the return from exile of Nergol Triannic. "Good Evening, Admiral Orgoth," he said. "I'd been told a League battleship was in the area."

"Good evening, Brim," the Admiral answered, a ghost of a smile on his face. He was dressed in dark-hued civilian clothes —severe, as befitted his high station, but a great deal less portentous than the uniform of a Vice Admiral. "You *do* believe in dramatic entrances, don't you?" he commented.

Brim nodded. "I had a bit of encouragement from your jackass of a chauffeur," he said.

"Somehow, I am not surprised," Orgoth said with a momentary glance of annoyance at LaKarn. "I assume he won't be a bother now?"

"Not for a while, Admiral," Brim assured him.

Orgoth nodded. "In that case, I shall make introductions. The gentleman on my right is OverGalite'er Gorton Ro'arn, Minister of State Security for the League."

Ro'arn—heavyset with hair cut into a short brush—nodded, and then only slightly. It was probably all he could do, considering the great roll of fat he'd grown at the back of his neck. He was also dressed in the black uniform of a League Controller, but flaunted the black and red cordons of high League officialdom draped from his right shoulder. Brim returned the nod. He'd learned during the war that one Leaguer was pretty much like another.

"On my left," Orgoth continued, "is Hanna Notrom, Minister for Public Consensus." He indicated a tiny, middle-aged OverGalite'er, whom Brim suddenly recalled from the first Tarrott race when he encountered Valentin at the Leaguer shed. She had walked with a distinct limp, as if her right foot were injured in some way. Like Ro'arn, she wore black and red cordons on her right shoulder.

Notrom smiled. "So," she said, "you are the famous Wilf Ansor Brim from Carescria. We have watched your career for a number of years now, with much interest."

Brim bowed. "At your service, Madam Notrom."

"You, of course, already know Kirsh Valentin and our kind host Rogan LaKarn," Orgoth continued.

Brim couldn't contain a wry grin. "We've met, Admiral," he said, "—a number of times."

"Won't you have a chair while we talk, Mr. Brim?" Notrom suggested, indicating a place beside her and opposite from Orgoth.

As he sat, Valentin and LaKarn took the remaining seats.

Notrom made a peaked roof with her long, bony fingers while their chairs scraped the elegant parquet floor. Then, when silence returned, she looked directly at Brim. "I shall come to the point quickly," she declared. "You have a race to fly tomorrow, in what appears to be an extremely dangerous ship. Is that correct?"

"I have a race to fly tomorrow," Brim agreed, "but I doubt if our M-fives are any more dangerous than the other racing star-ships here, your Gantheissers included."

"But dangerous, for all that," she persisted.

Brim nodded. "I suppose."

"And last year, you almost died in a cobbled-up ship that should never have left Sherrington's factory," Notrom contin-ued, "—when you *knew* resonance flutter was a distinct possi-bility. We have a recording of your conversation with Valerian just before you took off." She frowned. "You are to be congrat-ulated for such a deduction. Both Gantheisser and Gorn-Hoff engineers *also* came to that conclusion, but only after much calculation."

"Under normal circumstances, the flutter was controllable," Brim asserted, avoiding the whole subject of his "deduction."

"Granted," Notrom allowed, "but the real question has more to do with motivation than with anything else. What we *really* want to know is what motivates you to take such risks in the first place. They benefit a dominion that has historically treated all Carescrians with tremendous callousness. Your 'friends' re-warded your wartime heroism in a most unappreciative man-ner."

The words hit Brim like a meteor. He hadn't expected to hear anything like them. And worse yet, he had no answer. Except for the bilge about his M-5, she was absolutely correct. Historically, a word like *callous* couldn't even begin to describe the appalling treatment meted out by the Empire to its subju-gated citizens of the Carescrian sector. And the scars that had formed over his *own* mental wounds were far from healed.

"Well, Mr. Brim?" Notrom prompted.

Brim shook his head as he desperately tried to come up with some meaningful retort, not just one of the empty slogans the media had blathered during the Great War. He looked around the table at Gorton Ro'arn, the very soul of relentless police brutality; Hanna Notrom, an insane liar known throughout an entire galaxy for her extreme bigotry; Hoth Orgoth, who was deceitfully building a fleet that subverted every extant peace treaty in the galaxy; Kirsh Valentin, cruel, brutal, and utterly without compassion; and finally the high-born Rogan LaKarn, spineless lickspittle to a whole nation of Leaguers—and the misbegotten cretin who had managed to destroy Margot Effer'wyck. He bit his lip as they peered at him expectantly: the very scum of a whole galactic civilization. He should have been able to blow them away with chapter and verse of patriotic dogma. Voot knew that it existed. But he couldn't; he knew the *real* inequities as well as anyone—and so did these people. That was why they'd brought him here! After what seemed at least a metacycle, he took a deep breath and answered simply, "I don't know what motivates me."

"A straightforward answer to a difficult question, Mr. Brim," Notrom said. "My congratulations again."

Brim kept his silence.

"It was also the answer we expected," Notrom went on. "You never were one for lies—official *or* ordinary. Otherwise, you could never have survived the Helmsmen's Academy." She crossed her hands on the table and leaned toward him earnestly, her probing gray eyes drilling into his very being. "What if *we*, the people at this table, could *guarantee* you not only a better life but the rewards you merit and the recognition you deserve? What if we could provide you the rank and privilege that your talents warrant? Wilf Brim," she asked fervently, "would you really want to remain a no-account civilian taking all the risks while others who are more privileged glean the rewards of *your* labor?"

"Think of it, Wilf," Orgoth broke in. "Think of being a commissioned officer once more. Think of being a member of a fleet, an *honored* member, not merely tolerated because of your great talents!"

"Think *security*, Wilf," Notrom continued. "We do not drop our honored starsailors when the combat is over—as Greyffin's Empire dropped *you*. You have seen Tarrott. The uniforms are still there. Honored. Loved. Not vilified. You don't find *our* heroes in the galley of a starliner working as a Slops Mate or begging cvceese' from Gradygroat priests."

"Or running hazardous equipment like a beam axe, or enduring boors like Cravinn Townsend," Orgoth added.

"We can guarantee your dreams, Wilf Brim," Gorton Ro'arn said, finally breaking his silence, "—if you will accomplish only one act: become a citizen of the League immediately. To-night." He snapped his fingers. "Here," he said as one of the guards entered the room carrying a Controller's cape. On its shoulders were the insignia of a Provost—the same rank as Valentin. "You will find that this uniform is a perfect fit. And in its pocket," he added while the guard fished out a thin, golden card, "is a Purser's account with Praefect's pay accrued from the moment of your ignoble discharge at Gimmas-Haefdon." For a moment, his square, glowering countenance took on a look that might even pass for friendly. "Clearly, Brim," he continued, "our new Gantheissers will outperform all other entries tomorrow, including Valerian's M-five. So your acceptance of our offer will have little effect upon the outcome of the race. What do you say?"

Brim found himself dumbfounded. There was no denying that the Leaguers knew *very* well what strings to pull. One by one, they'd offered him most of the dreams of his lifetime. Wealth, privilege, a uniform—even some security for a change. But it wasn't the *right* wealth or the *right* privileges or the *right* uniform. Greyffin's old Empire might be far from perfect— Universe knew he saw the flaws clearly enough—but for better or for worse, it was his genesis, his home. And all the Controller's uniforms in the Universe couldn't make up for the worn Fleet cloak he'd had to surrender. He knew he'd pawn his very soul if that would get it back. He shook his head unconsciously. These Leaguers couldn't buy him because they didn't have the right kind of currency. Only the shoddy old Empire had that, and there was no substitute. He took a deep breath. "It's a generous offer, there is no denying that," he admitted at last, "but I'm afraid it's not for me."

All three principals looked at him in utter disbelief. "You are turning *all this* down?" Orgoth asked incredulously. "How can you do such a thing?"

"A moment, Admiral," Ro'arn said, his face flushed with ill-concealed anger. He looked at Brim and wrung his hands as if his thick fingers were encircling a neck. "What else can we offer, Carescrian? Which of your needs did we overlook? With what we've already offered, we couldn't have missed much."

"I wish nothing more . . ." Brim began, but he was interrupted by Notrom.

"Somehow I thought you might make a basically wrong-headed decision like that, Brim," she said, her voice rising shrilly. "And yet you have seen the corruption from close range. You have seen the stupidity. Brim, you have suffered because of it. In the name of the Universe, what is it about your degenerate Empire that is still acceptable?"

Brim shook his head. While she talked, the answer had came to him, simple, direct, and *true*. He paused for a moment to make sure of the words, then got slowly to his feet and gripped the edge of the table. "Because, Hanna Notrom," he said, "no matter how bad and degenerate Greyffin IV's Empire seems to me—and I know it is bad—at its absolute worst, it is far superior to anything I see in your League."

Clearly holding on to the last shreds of his temper, Orgoth rose and met Brim's stare. "Do you have any idea what you are giving away?" he asked. "Do you think for a moment that your beloved Empire will survive when Nergol Triannic returns to his rightful throne?"

"Enough, Admiral," Ro'arn growled curtly. As he turned to Brim, his thick lips drew back into a cruel smirk. "Clearly," he said, "we have not yet sweetened the offer sufficiently." He laughed. "However," he went on, "our young friend and ally Rogan LaKarn has supplied one further inducement. Rogan," he ordered, "show Mr. Brim the special *inducement* you have for him."

"At your service, General," LaKarn said, striding to a wall switch and dimming the lights. Then, with no further comment, he set out across the floor toward what appeared to be a small stage at Brim's end of the room.

Brim turned to look at the doorway through which he had entered. It was now blocked by two burly guards—both armed with wicked-looking Schneldler blast pikes.

"Don't bother with the door yet," LaKarn called with a great smirk on his face. "We want you to pay close attention here." Then he giggled. "It may just prove to be the one factor that decides you in favor of my friends in the League. Because," he said, opening the curtain, "I'm willing to give *this* away."

Brim turned and gasped in utter horror. There, just inside the open doors, Her Serene Majesty, Princess Margot of the Effer'wyck Dominions and Baroness of the Torond lay nude on a huge pile of cushions, languidly smoking TimeWeed with her once-sparkling eyes empty and half-closed.

"Join the League, Brim, and she's yours *whenever* you want her," LaKarn said. He laughed. "We all *know* how much pleasure you've had together."

Losing the last vestiges of his control, Brim snarled like a wild animal and with a single leap, knocked LaKarn to the floor, manically wringing the man's throat and dashing his head violently against the hardwood tiles until with a mighty wrench, someone yanked him upright. Still beserk with anger, he turned on this new antagonist until he discovered that he was now trying to strangle...General Drummond. Abruptly, a mask covered his face and a cool vapor of some sort instantly calmed his blood rage while other hands gently but firmly pushed him into a chair. As sensibility returned, he glanced around the room. Drummond and eight burly men, all dressed in unmarked military fatigues, were bent over the inert form of Rogan La-Karn who lay crumpled on the floor, his head at an odd angle with blood oozing from his nose and mouth. Both door guards lay sprawled on the floor, either unconscious or dead. Orgoth, Ro'arn, Notrom, and Valentin all sat scowling against the wall, bound and gagged. And Margot remained on the pillows, calmly smoking her TimeWeed as if she were utterly alone.

"Brim, you all right?" Drummond asked, turning from La-Karn. "We've got to get ourselves out of here—right away! We've blanked all communications for about a half-c'lenyt— but they're starting to penetrate it already."

"I'm fine, General," Brim panted, starting for Margot's drugged form. "It's her we've got to get out of here, though."

"Sorry, Brim," Drummond said, holstering a big Wenning .985 autoblaster. "But the Princess stays here."

"No!" Brim demanded. "We can't. Universe—look what they're doing to her..."

Drummond got a sad look on his face. "Unfortunately," he said quietly, "they're not doing *anything* to her. She's doing it to herself. Nobody is required to start smoking TimeWeed."

"B-but," Brim pleaded, pointing to Margot. "We can't just..."

"Son," Drummond said, taking Brim's arm in a grip that suddenly felt like a hullmetal band, "in my business, I see a lot of this. Sure, you love her; she was a magnificent woman once —still looks great, for that matter. But now she's also a smoker, and there's nothing *you* can do for her." He shook his head sadly for a moment. "Nobody *ever* said that life was going to be fair," he continued, "—only that it goes on. Now *move*, before we all end up in prison, and possibly charged with murder. If LaKarn lives, it won't be any fault of yours."

Biting his lip in helpless frustration, Brim followed the General at a dead run, past at least twelve tough-looking commandos-cum-civilians, out of the house, and into a waiting skimmer. Angry sirens were already wailing in the distance as they departed.

He found himself debriefed and back at the embassy long before evening watch ended, but sleep determinedly shunned his lonesome room. After a few cycles of aimless pacing, he pulled on a jacket and took a lift to the roof garden. Flashing his pass to a trio of guards (armed tonight with powerful Trenning NT-53A blast pikes), he wandered out under the stars and slumped into a rustic bench, vowing to resolve once and for all his tattered relationship with the naked blond woman LaKarn had offered. Not too long ago, she had been the very center of his hopes and dreams.

Only where to start? He'd been over the same thing in his head at least a million times before. Pursing his lips, he idly watched a giant starliner thunder out of the heavens, then line up on Lake Garza, her hull reflecting soft yellow radiance from the city below. Lights from a thousand scuttles glimmered along the big ship's massive flanks while enormous flashing beacons at the peak of her KA'PPA tower warned smaller ships away from her wake. He gazed at her huge, glowing form. In many ways, the big ship was a remarkably good presentment of Margot herself. Beautiful almost beyond reason, she had burst into his life with a radiant surge of emotion that carried both of them soaring above the turmoil of a devastating victory and much of the disastrous peace that followed it.

Unfortunately, the metaphor extended all too well into the present, for he could no more have checked her inexorable descent into tragedy than he could have stopped the liner from his perch on the embassy rooftop.

He laughed grimly at the thought, but only for a moment. Once, he'd actually believed in such miracles—she'd taught him how. Tonight, however—years older and a war wiser—he had come to the irrevocable conclusion that *some* things were beyond even the power of love itself.

He absently peered over the wall at the terraced gardens below. Did he still love her? In all honesty, he could no longer claim what he felt was love. During her years of virtual confinement in the Torond, profound changes had come over their relationship. First, there was Rodyard himself. The child's very existence finally brought to an end the few stolen moments he and Margot had once managed to share. Clearly, neither realized how much those all-too-brief rendezvous meant at the time. They were nearly *everything*, now that he thought about it—the promise of excitement and passion that could make long intervals of loneliness almost bearable. And when those promises ceased, the relationship had inexorably begun to wither.

Early on, Brim had perceived the change in himself through his growing attachment to Anna Romanoff. And after some reflection, he'd also come to the conclusion that Margot's addiction had probably began with the selfsame hopelessness—assuming, of course, that she had truly returned his love in the first place. In any case, the TimeWeed had been a last straw. At some point following the Leaguer's debacle of a "meeting," he'd bid a sad farewell to the dream that was Princess Margot Effer'wyck.

He pulled the collars of the jacket tighter around his throat. A chill midnight wind was now blowing in off the lake, and his tired eyelids told him it was time he turned in. He meant to do the best job he possibly could in the coming race—too many people were counting on him to win.

Back in his room, he took Margot's ring and chain from around his neck, then dropped them into the bottom pocket of his duffle bag. He could neither look at them nor throw them away. They were all that remained of a beautiful woman he once held dearer than his own life. The blonde he'd seen smoking TimeWeed was clearly someone he didn't know—and had no desire to meet.

CHAPTER 8

Anna Romanoff

After his previous night's misadventures and wrenching emotion, race day itself was more or less an anticlimax to Brim —even discounting LaKarn's magnificent new lakeside complex with its sweeping grandstands, glittering multitudes, and warships from every known dominion. Going against tradition, LaKarn—*very* noticeable by his unexpected absence—had previously decreed that the prior year's victor would fly first. Consequently, competition for 52006 opened with the takeoff of Dampier's new DA.72, the release of one hundred thousand multicolored balloons, and at least (it seemed) as many loudspeakers braying "Oh Grand and Glorious," the Torond's brassy national anthem.

Primarily a remake of last year's successful entry, the graceful little Dampier put on a rousing performance at the impressive average speed of 82M LightSpeed under the first-rate Helmsmanship of H. G. Esslingen, Captain, StarFleet of the Torond, and made landfall amid wild cheering from the home grandstands.

For Brim, who was watching from the Imperial shed, the heat was especially encouraging. He was certain that the DA.72 would be one of only two *real* competitors. Even with heating problems, his M-5 could fly all day at almost eighty-six. That left only Valentin who might threaten genuine competition for the M-5. And, as he had so often said himself, the actual race alone would determine a winner. From intelligence briefings, he knew that once Gantheisser engineers learned how fast Valerian's new ship could fly, they were forced to radically uprate their new GA 209V before the ship had even completed its initial space trials. It appeared, however, that their efforts had been blessed with success—so far as conventional Drives were concerned. The new Gantheisser GA 209V-3 had an estimated top speed in the range of 85M to 87M LightSpeed.

Fortunately, from an Imperial standpoint, the hard-pressed Gantheisser engineers had achieved this impressive speed by taxing an old design considerably beyond its maximum limits. Sodeskayans at Krasni-Peych predicted that the now-fragile Leaguer Drive could easily fail, especially at high velocities, unless it was handled with extreme care. A clumsy hand on the controls would most assuredly prove disastrous. Nevertheless, because the GA 209V-3 was *also* entirely capable of race-winning velocities, Brim had to take the Leaguer entries quite seriously.

Thanks to Rogan LaKarn, whose condition at the time was still a complete mystery, the League's performance capabilities were soon revealed. Kirsh Valentin, runner-up in the previous year's race, took off next. And not surprisingly, the Torond's boosters in the home grandstands accompanied his departure with the same euphoric Pandemonium they'd bestowed on their own entries less than a metacycle previously.

Brim crossed his arms glumly, wondering how long it had taken for state security forces to free what remained of LaKarn and his masters from last night's debacle. With a great mental effort, he forced the awful picture of Margot Effer'wyck from his mind. In a lot of ways, he hoped he hadn't killed the zukeed who called himself her husband. He very much wanted the pleasure of choking him again someday. Perhaps a number of times!

Abruptly, his grim reverie was interrupted by Ursis and Borodov. "Good morrow, Wilf Ansor," the older Bear said gently. He had dressed for the races in an elegant gray pin-striped suit with wing collars and a black bow tie. "We had thought to leave you in peace because of the recent *difficulties* you have encountered," he started, "but it seemed wiser to inform you that your friend Valentin has encountered mischance on his second lap."

"What happened?" Brim asked as he watched the number

two Gantheisser taxi out onto the water. "It looks like they're sending Inge Groener up for an alternate heat."

Dressed in the Sodeskayan Home Guard uniform of a full Colonel, Ursis peered out over the water through a set of tiny translating binoculars. "That appears to be correct," he affirmed. "Evidently, Valentin overstressed his Drive. Probably he was unnerved by last night's activities. We estimate he manhandled the controls, with predictable results."

Brim felt a dull current of anxiety replace his previous excitement. Was the word out? Had he actually killed LaKarn? Was he not a fugitive from a murder charge? "How did you find out about last night?" he asked.

"In spite of an unfortunate treaty," Ursis explained quietly, "many Sodeskayan intelligence organizations still operate as a unit with their Admiralty counterparts."

"Those units of the Admiralty that we can still trust," Borodov added darkly.

"Be that as it may, Wilf Ansor," Ursis continued, "your secret is safe with us. In fact, we complained concerning your safety when Drummond discussed his plans with us yesterday. What *he* does not know is that we *also* deployed a detachment of special forces—from our own embassy—to back his operation. You were much safer than you knew, my furless colleague," he chuckled, "even when you did such a splendid job on their chauffeur."

"Thank you, friends," Brim said with real feeling. "Do you have any word on LaKarn, himself?"

"We have," Borodov answered. "You and he are both fortunate after last evening's folly," he growled quietly, "although it is not clear that he will ever regain his former state of good health." The Bear looked penetratingly into Brim's eyes. "Healing machines can accomplish wonders, as you well know, Wilf Ansor," he said. "But they cannot work miracles. And you left the Baron much closer to death than even you could have imagined."

Brim shook his head slowly. "Thanks, Doctor," he said after a little while. "That's been a considerable worry."

"All snow melts when necessary, Wilf Ansor," Ursis said. "Considerations among true friends tend to even out over the space of a lifetime."

During the next metacycle, Groener—clearly handling her

tricky controls with special concern—managed to finish the course at an average speed of 83.88M LightSpeed. And that finished the race, so far as Brim was concerned. Unless one of the smaller societies came up with an *extremely* fast machine, the race was nearly his. All he had to do was fly with the same care as had Groener, and the Imperial Starflight Society would gain possession of the Mitchell Trophy!

Toward evening with the night's revelry already underway in the city's lavish nightspots and LaKarn's huge grandstands populated only by handfuls of true racing enthusiasts, Brim completed his pretakeoff checklist at the tail end of a field of last year's also-rans. None had looked particularly threatening; all performed in much the same manner. Now, as he taxied out over Lake Garza toward the start pylons, he didn't particularly care if *everyone* abandoned the grandstands. Anna Romanoff's storm-tardy liner had finally arrived that afternoon, and *she* was watching.

The racecourse defined by LaKarn's SAT (Starflight Association of the Torond) was conventionally triangular in shape and defined by three solitary, type-G stars: Montroyal, Hellig-Olav, and MetaGama. Entry to the circuits portion of the race was close by Montroyal, nearest of the three to Horblein at 375 light-year's distance. From there, a long straightaway of 330.72 light-years stretched to Hellig-Olav, where a sharp turn introduced the shortest leg of 113.48 light-years. Following this, a gentle curve around MetaGama and a second long straightaway of 254.24 light-years returned the course to its entry point. Ten laps plus the round-trip to the start/finish line at Horblein defined a complete race.

Brim got off to an excellent start from the pylons, carried out a climbing turn, and thundered over the grandstands with the K-P generators crooning in his ears. Soon afterward, he passed within visual sight of the flickering 614-G marker satellite, then transitioned from generators to Drive as if he were flying a machine proven over years of successful operation. On his way to the circuits, however, he found it difficult lining up on Montroyal because of the narrow forward Hyperscreens, so he cut to an extreme inside track and took the curve in a vertical bank, close to the star's fiery surface where his field of vision was better in spite of the glare. And except for opening his trajectory somewhat to avoid fouling a timing station midway along the first straightaway, he remained on the inside track, no matter how much more dangerous it was to fly. Turning smoothly around Hellig-Olav, he came out on a perfect line down the course, then bunted past MetaGama and poured on full energy toward the starting point again. When he completed the lap, his computed speed came out to be 90M LightSpeed, an unofficial record!

And his second lap was faster still at 90.27M LightSpeed. With two hairpin turns to negotiate, it was clear that his speed in a straight line must be approaching 100M LightSpeed!

In the middle of the third lap, however, unanticipated trouble struck somewhere aft with a bell-like clang. It was immediately followed by violent shudders that rattled the spaceframe. Multiple indicators turned red at the same time, opening a data dialogue on his Drive-status panel that indicated the crystal housing had unsealed.

Did the bastard Voot never sleep?

Biting his lip, he skewed the ship sideways for a momentary look at his wake. Sure enough, a gleaming ribbon of free electrons marked his path like a thin trail of smoke. He reduced power straight off, and the vibrations disappeared, for the most part. Curiously, his indicated speed seemed unaffected.

Again he skidded the ship sideways and miraculously the free-electron trail had virtually disappeared. It made sense. In combat, he'd had shot-up crystal chambers seal themselves— the hellish reaction inside tended to weld small fissures closed by it own heat. Good luck? Perhaps, he thought as he completed lap four. Unfortunately, nothing, especially good luck, came free. He could indeed continue the race, but at the risk of a complete power loss, with little or no warning. At best, that would leave him careening helplessly off into space at nearly 100M LightSpeed. It might also sent him smashing into one of the pylon stars before anyone could come to his rescue. And no hull in the known Universe could withstand direct collision with a star.

He seriously considered aborting the race during the next laps, but the little M-5 seemed to be running better with each circuit. His average speed had already risen to nearly 90.76M LightSpeed. How could he quit now?

In his days before the Fleet, he'd flown great, lumbering

Carescrian ore barges every day. Most of them had been so badly worn out and poorly maintained that they made his partially crippled M-5 seem as safe as an IGL starliner. He shrugged. It was all a matter of being careful—that was everything. Besides, he could *at least* count on a few click's warning before all the systems failed at once.

Couldn't he . . . ?

Laps eight, nine, and ten passed at the incredible speeds of 92.5M LightSpeed, 93.8M LightSpeed, and 94.1M LightSpeed, respectively. As Brim headed toward Montroyal for the last time, he knew he had flown a good race. In a few cycles, he would not only win the Mitchell Trophy, he was also going to set a record of truly historic proportions.

However, as he skimmed the star and set course for the start/finish pylons at Rudolpho, his Wizard momentarily cut out—completely. It picked up directly, but the brief episode gave him a definite fright. From that point, he flew with his heart in his mouth, keeping his thrust damper nearly wide open —and nearly made it all the way back. Horblein's star, Gragoth, nearly filled his forward Hyperscreens when the Drive began stammering again—this time badly. After only a few moments, he knew for certain that the ship would soon run out of energy. Angrily smashing his fist on the console beside him, he cut power to the crystal.

Not that he'd given up yet by any means, but even with the *best* blessing Lady Fortune could now provide, things were going to be close. Immediately, the Hyperscreens ceased to translate, and a whirling Universe of run-down photons blazed through the clear crystals in the wild kaleidoscopes of color. Grinding his teeth, he disregarded the dizzying phenomenon and concentrated on his readouts. He'd been in tight situations before and so, as long as he didn't panic, odds were that he'd survive. With the Drive off, he could at least count on *some* energy for the gravity generators and steering engine. Enough to get him down in relative safety. The trick now would be trying to stay in the race. He'd already built a considerable lead over the other ships. If he didn't lose too much time in his actual landing, he might *yet* manage to win the trophy—or at least place.

Now, however, he had to remain patient while the Driveless ship bled off HyperVelocity and coasted down through the great

Universal constant of LightSpeed. Biting his lip, he watched the readouts. Timing was everything, now. The LS meter was nearly down to unity. There!

Immediately, vision in the forward Hyperscreens cleared and he activated both gravity generators. Ahead, Horblein's curve had already flattened into a horizon, and a voice began calling into his helmet receivers: "Imperial M-five, Rudolpho tower. Please report. Imperial M-five, Rudolpho Tower. Please report."

"Rudolpho tower, this is Imperial M-five," he answered, peering through his Hyperscreens. "Please hold for position report." Off in the distance, nearly lost against the blue of the planet itself, a ruby pinpoint winked in an odd rhythm. He drew a small tube from the starboard console and aimed its open end at the light. Immediately, a text readout on the closed end displayed: LAYER 32 / LIGHTWARD HEMISPHERE / K-VAIL 1278 BUOY, LEVEL 19.

"Rudolpho Tower, Imperial M-five Alpha is within layer thirty-two, lightward of K-Vail one two seven eight . . . , flight level nineteen."

"Imperial M-five Alpha, we have you now. Are you declaring an emergency?"

"Rudolpho Tower, Imperial M-five will notify you when *and if* an emergency is declared. Request immediate clearance racecourse start/finish."

"I-imperial M-five, Rudolpho Tower clears immediate racecourse start/finish. Wind zero two two at one five."

"Imperial M-five. Thank you." After that, there was little time for anything but judgment and reflexes. Within a few cycles, the lights of Rudolpho were in sight over the nose. Unfortunately, his unplanned approach to the planet denied him the straight-in landing he might have chosen had he been powered and under control all the way. First, he would have to pass over the start/finish pylons going the wrong way, *then* make a sharp turn to reverse his bearings and finish the course in the proper direction.

Again, however, the relatively small size of the M-5's Hyperscreens forced him to fly much lower than he normally would have in other circumstances. He had no margin of safety as he skimmed along just below the tips of the huge, glimmering pylons, following the long beams of his landing lights. In a flash he was past and practically bending the ship around in a vertical bank to reverse his direction, delicately playing the controls while Valerian's spaceframe creaked and groaned from the vicious gravity torquing. He had only managed to come through half his arc when the generators stumbled, struggled raggedly onward for the blink of an eye, then tripped off completely. The tiny cabin went utterly silent—and dark.

Moments later, his M-5 smashed onto the surface of the water in a thundering cascade of inky water, throwing Brim painfully against his emergency seat restraints. Again . . . and again . . . and *again* the ship skipped and cartwheeled across the dark surface of the lake before it came to rest, bobbing low in the water nearly half a c'lenyt from the pylons—and any chance of even placing in the race.

While a hovering rescue vessel took up station above him, Brim suffered every agony of self-condemnation and disgust. Would the Krasni-Peych engineers ever believe he hadn't overstressed the Drive? How could they conclude otherwise with the terrific speeds he had been making? And what would Nik Ursis and Dr. Borodov think of him? He knew how accurate K-P's calculations always were—and he knew for a certainty that if there had been a fault, it must have been his. Poor Anna Romanoff—she had traveled across half a Universe to see him make an utter fool of himself.

So near yet so thraggling *far*!

He was slumped miserably in the cockpit, shaking his head and dreading the probe he knew would follow when an Imperial motor launch drew up alongside in a glare of powerful floodlights. Ursis and Valerian were among the wildly gesticulating crew, waving at him excitedly, full of enthusiasm and smiles. And they were cheering. For the life of him, he couldn't understand why. Pushing open the hatch, he stuck his head out and sourly demanded to know what all the hullabaloo was about.

"About?" Ursis asked with a huge grin on his face. "Since when is winning the Mitchell Trophy not a propitious time for raising hullabaloos?"

"Yeah," Valerian whooped. "Why the long face, Brim? At ninety-one M LightSpeed you beat Groener by more than seven M's. That's not good enough for you or something?" With that, he popped the cork from a magnum that promptly erupted in a stream of bubbling meem and unerringly arced its way to the top of Brim's head.

"Voots's greasy beard!" the disheartened Carescrian groused, ducking inside the hatch again, where he was immediately showered by a second stream of bubbling meem from a similar bottle expertly aimed by Ursis. Moments later, at least three yellow-clad ground-crew handlers began pouring more meem in from atop the fuselage. Then a hirsute paw thrust a fresh bottle through the deluge, foaming from its top.

"Drink, my furless friend!" Ursis boomed. "It is not often one wins *anything* by such a grand margin. 'Glare ice and crag wolves cause stars to shine brilliantly in ice caves,' as *everyone* knows!"

"Ice caves my bloody *ass*!" Brim shouted, angrily waving away the bottle as waves of foaming meem ran everywhere in the little flight bridge. "I thraggling *lost* this one. Didn't you see me pass the xaxtdamned pylons going the wrong way? I never even got to finish!"

Suddenly, Ursis stopped cheering and put a restraining hand on Valerian's chest. "Wait, my friends!" he roared. The spraying meem stopped instantly. "Wilf," the huge Sodeskayan said, narrowing his eyes, "you *do* believe you lost the race, don't you?"

"Xaxtdamned right," Brim spluttered, mopping his face with the great red handkerchief he kept in his battle suit pocket. "The drive unsealed in the middle of the circuits, then gave out completely on the way back. That's why I made landfall from *that* direction—not because I planned it that way. I was trying to get turned around when the generators failed, too. I haven't even crossed the finish line yet!"

"Wilfuska," Ursis cried out with a pained look on his face. "No wonder you look so unhappy. Poor furless human. No wonder you made such a . . . *spectacular* . . . landfall!"

"I don't need your pity," Brim grumped, settling back miserably into a puddle of cold meem that had collected on his seat.

"You can say that again, friend," Valerian said with a lopsided grin.

Brim looked up and scowled. "Don't you make fun of me, too, Mark," he protested. "I feel bad enough about the whole thing all by myself."

"But that's just it," Valerian protested. "You don't need *anyone's* pity because you, friend, are still turned around."

Brim blinked and shook his head. "What do you mean?" he demanded.

"Look for yourself," Ursis said, pointing out from the launch. His huge grin had suddenly returned. "You are *still* turned around—as you were when you flew through the pylons."

Brim stuck his head through the hatch again and peered off toward the pylons. The race complex did seem to be on the wrong side of the lake! He frowned for a moment, then climbed out of the hatch and stood with the ground handlers, balancing atop the M-5's main fuselage. This time, he studied the shoreline and... Voot's beard! If Rudolpho was on *that* side of the lake then... For an instant, he faltered, and was immediately shored up by the handlers. Shaking his head and squaring his shoulders, he took one more look around the lake, then looked down into the launch. "Nik," he said after considerable hesitation.

"Yes?"

"You still got that bottle of bubbling meem with you?"

"It has never been touched, Wilfuska."

Brim grinned. "In that case," he said, shaking off the two handlers "I'll be right there.... *whee!*" With that, he leaped off the M-5 and plunged to the surface, rear end first in a terrific splash of lake water that utterly soaked everyone still in the launch. "Now," he shouted, bobbing to the surface and pulling himself over the gunwale. "Let me at the thraggling meem!"

Later, back at the shed, while riotous crowds of Imperials poured a second deluge of meem all over him and the M-5's flight bridge (as well as themselves), Brim had the distinct pleasure of knowing he'd caused two consecutive nights of profound discord in Rudolpho—*and the second one wasn't even a secret*!

Not long afterward, Moulding took off and cooly annexed second place at a stewardly pace of more than 88M LightSpeed.

The following morning, Brim stood on a dais beneath the winner's flagpole, dressed in a Fleet-blue jumpsuit and listening to an Imperial flag snapping overhead in a stiff breeze off Lake Garza. He had little stomach for ceremonial adulation; his own moment of triumph had come and rapidly gone the previous evening after he skipped his powerless M-5 to a most startling victory followed by celebrations that lasted the rest of the night. All he wanted now was a little peace and quiet, preferably in the *sole* company of Anna Romanoff.

He glanced at Toby Moulding, standing in full uniform on a slightly lower dais beneath the second-place flagpole, and grinned. Always the aristocrat, his tall, handsome partner *looked* the part of a champion, smiling grandly at the media personalities that swarmed like locusts around the base of the flagpoles. Thank the Universe, Brim thought. At least one Imperial ought to look like a winner.

At his right, Groener braced under the Leaguer flag flying from the shortest pole. Wearing a Controller's uniform devoid of any but the most basic insignia, she looked neither right nor left—nor did she smile. For Leaguers, anything except first place equated with absolute defeat.

He endured on the dais for nearly half a metacycle before the media had enough. Then he was glad to steal off and sit on a lakefront bench for nearly a metacycle while Romanoff threw crumbs to a noisy flock of waterfowl. It was the high point of his day. Especially when the breeze occasionally provided him with an enhanced view of her shapely legs.

All too soon, however, an embassy officer ferreted them out. After that, it was a perpetual sequence of parties and receptions until he and Romanoff embarked on separate starliners to opposite ends of the Empire. Shaking his head in irony, he was forced to admit that Hanna Notrom had inadvertently made an important point for herself: he *was* paying an awful price for winning the Mitchell Trophy!

Bedecked with patriotic ornamentation befitting a significant national victory celebration, the cavernous War Memorial Hall in Avalon was literally jammed by Imperial aristocracy—many of whom had never bothered with the Imperial Starflight Society until Wilf Brim brought home its first Mitchell Trophy. Once disdained for his lowly origins, today the Carescrian was an honored associate among some of the Empire's wealthiest and most powerful individuals. He sat dressed in formal evening wear at a special engineering table, directly across the dance floor from Prince Onrad and the Table of Principals. On his left, as his personal guest, was the remarkable Anna Romanoff in a daringly low cut apricot party dress, her huge brown eyes soberly observing the whole affair as if it were some exotic wildlife exhibition. Others at the engineering table included Nik Ursis, Dr. Borodov, Mark Valerian and his wife Cherie, plus a number of scientific luminaries vital not only to the ISS but to the Imperial government itself.

Long after an elegant banquet, the seemingly interminable awards ceremony was at last winding down with a final congratulatory address by Onrad himself. Earlier, Brim had been startled by receiving one or two minor awards himself that had caused Romanoff's eyes to glow with reflected pride. Now he was looking forward to the end of the long celebration—perhaps even escaping the crowd for a few private metacycles with his lovely companion. Universe knew he'd waited patiently for *that* opportunity.

Even at the tail end of the long awards ceremony, lusty applause and cheering greeted the conclusion of Onrad's address. Brim joined in tardily, hoping no one would notice he'd been daydreaming, but Romanoff had clearly caught him. Her eyes were dancing with laughter and her mouth had taken on the mysterious little smile she sometimes wore that both veiled and revealed so much of her complex personality. He was about to suggest that they steal off for the nearest exit when the room suddenly quieted again, and when he turned toward the speaker's table, the Prince was holding his hand up for silence. At the same time, General Zapt appeared behind the podium with a Fleet cloak over his arm. Romanoff met Brim's glance and her eyebrows raised in question.

The Carescrian could only shrug impatiently and roll his eyes. "I have no idea," he whispered, "but enough is enough. Anna, I think we're victims of some horrible conspiracy. . . ." Then with a helpless shrug, he settled back in his chair, arms crossed in a defiant attitude.

"Before I dismiss this celebration," Onrad declared with much gravity, "one final award remains. A special award, personally designated by my father, Greyffin IV. And though it is not even mentioned in your programs, to *my* way of thinking, it is perhaps the most important of all."

He paused dramatically while a rustle of excited whispers swept the room. Clearly, the Prince had caught most of his audience completely off guard.

"This *particular* award," he continued presently, "is not tendered so much for racecourse activities as for *other* services to the Empire—although acquisition of the Mitchell has certainly been part of our consideration." He paused again, this time frowning. "Moreover, in many ways it can not be considered an award at all. Rather, I think, it is the righting of a wrong, or the correction of a particularly unfortunate blunder."

When Onrad paused this time, the rustle of conversation became much more pronounced. "Finally," he continued presently, "this award will *also* have an important secondary effect, because it will serve notice to CIGAs everywhere that we *do* intend to permanently secure the Mitchell Trophy, despite the fact that in *winning*, we now represent an *irritant* to their beloved League rather than the paean to peace that we were when all we could do was lose!" During the laughter that followed, he pursed his lips angrily. "We can expect them to place every possible obstacle in our path," he warned at length, "but we will *prevail*!"

After the applause that followed, Onrad nodded at General Zapt to bring the Fleet cape, which bore the insignia of a Lieutenant Commander, then continued with his booming rhetoric. At the same time, two protocol officers took position at either side of the podium, one holding a pair of regulation white dress gloves on a peaked Fleet officer's cap, the other carrying a small box fashioned from a dark wood.

"Therefore," the Prince boomed, "I summon private citizen Wilf Ansor Brim to the podium once more." In the silence of the huge hall, his deep voice was like a rumble of thunder.

Brim stiffened—he'd half heard it too. "Was that, Wilf Ansor Brim?" he asked under his breath.

"That's what *I* heard," Romanoff replied, a little smile beginning to form on her lips.

"You don't suppose there might be a *couple* of Wilf Brims here?" he asked hopefully.

"I think he means *you*," Romanoff declared, her smile suddenly expanding to a full-fledged grin. "I don't recall seeing more than one Wilf Brim on any of the membership lists."

An orchestra had already struck up the rousing "Summit Noble" when Brim reluctantly got to his feet, cast a momentary glance of mock horror toward Romanoff, then set off across the dance floor. Spontaneously, the huge audience broke into ragged applause, which became a rolling wave of thunder long before he reached the podium.

When the wild acclaim finally subsided, Onrad stepped to the front of the podium and held the Fleet cloak before him as if he were a valet instead of a Crown Prince. "Wilf Ansor Brim," he proclaimed, "by direct mandate of His Majesty Greyffin IV, Grand Galactic Emperor, Prince of the Reggio Star Cluster, and Rightful Protector of the Heavens, I hereby conscript you into the Imperial Fleet with direct promotion to the rank of Lieutenant Commander." As the hall erupted once more into thunderous applause, the Prince motioned with his head. "Wilf," he shouted above the noise, "I'll be proud if I can place this on your shoulders myself."

Stunned, Brim could only nod and turn his back. He felt the weight of a Fleet cloak after nearly five years. Almost instinctively, he turned to the protocol officer on his left, placed the peaked uniform cap on his head (a perfect fit), and struggled into the white gloves. Then he came to attention, turned on his heel to face Onrad, and saluted. "Lieutenant Commander Wilf Brim, reporting for duty as ordered, Your Majesty," he said, desperately fighting emotions that threatened to crack his voice like a schoolboy's.

"Welcome home, Commander," Onrad replied in a voice that carried throughout the great hall. He was clearly struggling with his own emotions while he returned Brim's salute.

Once more, the throng erupted in thunderous applause and cheering, but this time, Brim turned and saluted *them*. At a distance, Anna Romanoff appeared to have buried her nose in a handkerchief—but then, so did both Ursis and Borodov.

Considerably later, Onrad held up both hands for silence, but a lot of time passed until the applause once more faded. "I shan't keep any of you too much longer," he proclaimed at length, "but there are two more presentations to be made before this evening is complete." He motioned to the other protocol officer who stepped forward and opened the wooden box he held. "First," he announced, reaching into the box to retrieve a medal, "there is the matter of a missing Order of the Imperial Comet—which I *personally* pinned on Commander Brim's uniform at Gimmas-Haefdon some years ago." He frowned with mock gravity as he fastened the small pin to Brim's cape. "Next time you lose one of these," he grumped so only Brim could hear, "you'll have to pay for the new one yourself."

"Thank you, Y-your Majesty," Brim stammered.

"Finally," Onrad declared, again to the general audience, "an Emperor's Cross." He reached once again into the wooden box and withdrew an eight-pointed starburst in silver and dark blue enamel with a single word engraved in its center: VALOR. It was attached to an ivory sash embroidered in gold with the words, GREYFFIN IV, GRAND GALACTIC EMPEROR, PRINCE OF THE REGGIO STAR CLUSTER, AND RIGHTFUL PROTECTOR OF THE HEAVENS. Opening the sash, he placed it around Brim's neck. "When you have a chance," he whispered, "notice the serial number. We managed to locate your original decoration." Then he smiled. "But don't *ever* pawn it again; General Zapt will have you killed. It took most of his staff a week to track it down." Then he grinned. "All right, Commander," he said. "I think I've kept you and Anna Romanoff from each other long enough. Report to the Admiralty personnel office during the next day or so and get your admin work straightened out. And when you're ready, it's back to your old job with the ISS."

"Aye, your Majesty," Brim replied, saluting smartly. Then, turning on his heel, he retraced his steps to the engineering table—amid still another round of deafening applause. Strangely, Brim never could remember the concluding moments of the program. After one look into Anna Romanoff's eyes, all he could hear was the pounding of his own heart.

On their way through the vast foyer, Brim and Romanoff found themselves mobbed by a glittering array of well wishers who then urged them to attend more private parties, in addition to the numerous written invitations each had received in advance. Smiling and shaking hands with throngs of eternally prattling celebrity worshipers, it took them nearly three-quarters of a metacycle to reach the luxurious little skimmer Romanoff kept in Avalon for her personal use. It was covered with light snow. Brim had opened the driver's door for her, but she put her hand gently on his arm. "You drive tonight, Wilf," she said, her large brown eyes soft in the glow from the street lights. "It's been a long evening."

"Of course," he replied, following her around the nose of the car to hold the passenger door instead. As she slid inside, her skirt crept a considerable distance above her knees. He tried to appear as if he hadn't noticed, but he was woefully late.

"Like them?" she asked with a provocative little smile, peering critically at herself for a moment before she smoothed the wayward dress back down to her knees.

Brim took a deep breath. "You have beautiful legs," he said, feeling his face flush with embarrassment. "I apologize for gaping the way I did."

"Well, I certainly *hoped* you'd notice," she said, looking him frankly in the eye. Then, with an impudent look, she pulled the door shut.

Brim made his way around to the driver's door with his heart beating considerably faster than it had been moments before. She'd never carried on that way before! But then, he considered while he brushed snow from the windshield, neither had *he*. In recent months, this delicately beautiful woman, all tough and fragile at the same time, had become almost an *obsession* with him. She was never far from his mind. Lately, he'd stopped deluding himself; he was genuinely in love—probably for the very first time in his life. From the beginning, Margot had never realistically been more than a hopeless dream. And his brief, fiery affair with Claudia Valemont was the epitome of wartime romance: all passion and little else. In those days, no one really expected to survive more than a few days at most. He'd blundered into both relationships the way he waged war: totally—and damn the consequences.

Anna Romanoff, on the other hand, was a different story altogether. She was *real*. And although he didn't think he stood much of a chance with her, he *did* expect to live for a few more years. Unfortunately, he reflected, a more or less "normal" relationship was new to him. And because of it, those once-disregarded consequences had become absolutely daunting in significance. What if he'd misconstrued her intentions just now? If he made a pass at the wrong time, a woman like that could rid herself of him with a mere snap of her fingers—and then where would he be? In an utter agony of indecision, he opened the door and took his place behind the controls. "Well, Anna," he asked, staring through the windshield because he hadn't the nerve to face her, "where will it be tonight? We've got more invitations than we can shake a stick at—as usual."

Her answer, when it came, was unexpectedly tinged with a

sense of melancholy. "I don't really know, Wilf," she said after a long moment of consideration. "Every one of them seems like a mandate—especially for a brand-new Lieutenant Commander."

Brim glanced at her wistfully. "If it were up to me," he said, "I'd just as soon stay here in the parking lot with you." He shook his head. "We've logged a lot of time together this past year, you and I—but I'll bet we haven't been alone for more than a half-metacycle."

She nodded, watching through the snow-powdered window while a few stragglers glided toward the exits, their running lights blurred by the softly falling snow. "I wonder if they *all* live frantically like that," she mused absently, then turned to study him. "Did you *really* mean you'd rather sit in a parking lot with me than go to those parties?" she asked presently.

Brim nodded. "Yes," he replied, "I did."

"Even though it's now politically important for you to attend as many of them as you can, *Commander*?"

"Somehow," Brim admitted, "it's been a long time since anything has been so important as being with you, Anna."

For long, silent moments, Romanoff studied his face in the darkness. Then, she seemed to reach some conclusion. "Wilf," she said with no further preface. "I've wanted you ever since that night at Sherrington's—just before I lost my stupid nerve and wouldn't let you kiss me. And I think you wanted *me*, too. But since then, I haven't been able to make you interested again, at all. Not even when I let my skirt slide halfway up my thigh tonight." Abruptly, she slid deeper in her seat and raised her hips. "Well," she said, this time drawing the skirt all the way to her waist, "—if *this* doesn't do it, I guess I'll have to give up." She wore nothing underneath, and in the darkness of the parking lot, her dark tangle of pubic hair stood out in frantic relief to the smooth whiteness of her thighs. The tawny welt of a scar ran the length of her left hip.

Brim felt his breath catch painfully in his throat. "S-sweet thraggling Universe, Anna," he whispered hoarsely as he took her in his arms, "how could I have been such a fool?"

"I was the fool," she said, making a little gasp as his cold hand gently probed between her thighs, "—but I was afraid of losing you and . . ."

Before she could finish, he covered her trembling mouth

with his own in a wet rush of tongues and teeth that left both of them gasping while he struggled to kick his trousers off. Then, impossibly, he found himself sliding onto her seat at the same time she climbed into his lap, her eloquent brown eyes peering into his very being—as they had nearly a year ago at Lys.

"You'll soon enough find that you aren't the first," she whispered with a pensive little smile, "—but for what it's worth, I've never loved anyone before you, either."

Brim was about to open his mouth, but she placed a finger gently across his lips. "Later," she whispered. "Now, nothing matters except *this* . . ." With that, she reached behind her to guide him, then lowered herself until he was enveloped by a Universe of wet, swollen flesh. "Do it, Wilf," she gasped urgently. "Do it *now!*"

She remained in his lap long after their urgent sighs had hushed, making love with her lips and tongue while she straddled his thighs. Ultimately, she took a deep breath, placed her hands on the shoulders of his Fleet cape, and peered intently into his eyes. "Wilf Brim," she said with a troubled look, "I'm afraid that I have become very deeply in love with you lately, and I'm not quite sure how to handle it."

Brim frowned for a moment, then peered into her face. "You mean that?" he asked incredulously. "You're in love with *me*?"

She laughed quietly and looked down at her disheveled clothing. "You don't think I let just *anybody* see me like this, do you?" she asked, unhooking a badly stained skirt to hike it higher on her hips. "Especially the scar. It's part of that limp I never admit to."

"It's a beautiful scar," he whispered, "and whatever *else* it does, it gives you a *wonderfully* sexy walk." Then he shook his head and sighed. "You see, Anna," he said, fondling the firm, pointed breasts that spilled from the top of her strapless dress, "I've been in love with *you*, too. I've known it for quite a while, now."

"*You*?" she gasped, "—in love with *me*?"

"Is that so unreasonable?" he asked.

"I don't know," she said, frowning as if she were having difficulty with her thoughts. "Until this very moment, *I* certainly thought it was." She raised the palms of her hands. "What could I possibly offer a genuine war hero—*and* Principal Helmsman for the ISS. Why, you're known all over the galaxy. People even say you once had a big thing going with Princess Margot Effer'wyck herself. And I'm only a working stiff with a limp, remember? A wealthy one now, perhaps, but a gimpy working stiff, nonetheless." For a moment, the happiness in her face clouded. "Work's about all I ever do anymore. That's why I simply gave up tonight and decided that maybe you'd at least make love once before you went back to your Fleet and forgot about me."

Brim shook his head incredulously. "Forget about you?" he whispered. "Anna, we've *both* been wrong, then, because I've felt pretty much the same way about you. I was afraid you could never care for me because you are so successful and influential."

"Maybe I am *now*, Wilf Brim, but when I started out, I was poor as a street beggar. This limp of mine: when I was a child, I couldn't walk at all. There was nothing wrong with my hip that a healing machine couldn't fix, but at the time there were no credits for that kind of advanced treatment. So my mother hired a local street quack to carve on me. And he didn't do a bad job, considering. I *can* walk—pretty well, too, considering that you thought my limp was sexy. So when I finally did have the credits to get myself fixed properly, I had neither the time nor the inclination—I'd learned to live with it. Wilf, dearest, I've had to fight for everything I have. I'm a *nobody*."

"You're damned special to *me*, Anna Romanoff," Brim exclaimed. "Why, since I met you, I've been afraid that you wouldn't have anything to do with me at all. If you think Margot Effer'wyck is daunting, how about me comparing myself with someone like Wyvern J. Theobold? I mean, Lixor's a whole hell of a lot more impressive than Carescria."

Romanoff took a deep breath and glanced down to watch his hands still gently stroking her breasts. "Probably I shouldn't admit it," she said, "but the impressive Mr. Theobold from Lixor has never gotten very much farther than what you are doing right now. He's sexy, but I don't love him."

"Poor bastard," Brim said devoutly. "He's missed a *great* lay."

"I, on the other hand, have *not*," she giggled with a happy grin. "And those talented hands of yours have put me in the mood for more, Wilf Brim." She kissed him softly on the mouth. "If we really are in love with one another, then there will be a thousand tomorrows when we can rationally work out our relationship. But tonight—this morning, rather—I am much more immediately interested in good old-fashioned sex." Pulling her bodice over her breasts, she raised her hips and, leaning her shoulder on the door, drew up her knee. "Now, lover," she said, "if you would slide yourself back to the driver's seat and pull on your trousers, I know a place where we can continue this wonderfully iniquitous recreation with me lying comfortably on my back, in a bed, instead of pummeling my head on the roof of this skimmer. How does that sound to you?"

Brim only laughed as he slid behind the controls. "Is that answer enough, my beautiful lady?" he asked, indicating his lap. "I'd go anywhere to be iniquitous with you."

"In that case, we'd better hurry," she declared with a happy grin, "because if it's true that War Memorial Hall here is used nearly every day of the week, then I for one am going to be *very* embarrassed when the parking lot begins to fill in the morning while we're still *iniquitizing*, so to speak. It's been a long time since anybody's filled me the way you can, Wilf Brim, and I haven't even *begun* to get enough."

Lieutenant Commander Wilf Ansor Brim, I.F., pulled his Fleet cloak closer around his neck and treaded thoughtfully up the slush-covered marble staircase that fronted Avalon's imposing Admiralty Building. His most recent visit nearly five years earlier had been one of intense personal anguish: a final debriefing after they'd revoked his commission. Now as he glanced at the massive granite building above him, all the old torment seemed to fade into an insignificant past. He was back in uniform and eager to resume the only career that had ever mattered to him: the Fleet.

At the topmost landing, he stopped. From outward appearances, nothing about the old place seemed to have changed *that* much. Behind him in Locorno Square, traffic still careened wildly around the lofty statue of Admiral Gondor Bemus, assaulting his ears with the sounds of a city energetically directing commerce throughout half a galaxy. Overhead, dirty gray clouds still shared the city sky with wheeling squadrons of noisy pidwings. The flocks themselves, he considered, might have become a *trifle* smaller, but individually, the birds were as filthy as ever. The steps bore mute witness.

Mounting the last staircase, he braced himself for changes he knew he would encounter behind the great metal doors. It was a changed world he was about to reenter. Five years ago, the CIGA was only beginning to flex its muscle within a host organization that was still principally composed of warriors— men and women who could prevail against the best the League could field. Now, that situation was almost totally reversed. CIGA advocates had become a major force in nearly every Admiralty program, planned or extant—and they mercilessly rooted out every "throwback" who attempted to resist their efforts to secure peace by disabling the Imperial Fleet.

When he was precisely four paces from the center entrance, two of the four windblown guards snapped to attention while the others yanked open the doors. Brim strode through the entrance without breaking stride. Only old Admiralty hands knew how to do that; invariably, every one else stopped. Laughing at himself, he wished Romanoff were there to share the little victory with him.

Inside, the Great Foyer and Memorial Court were as little changed as the facade, even to the slight tinge of mustiness Brim had always half blamed on his imagination. Familiar murals heroically characterized the same historic victories as always, and the vast oval floor was still crowded by legions of strutting military politicians. At one time, Brim had believed that most of them were actually on their way to something important (indeed, during the war years, some few *might* really have been). Now, he couldn't help laughing under his breath. The place looked embarrassingly like the self-conscious terminal in Tarrott!

Brim's objective, the Central Directorate for Personnel, had moved from what he remembered as an insignificant suite in a sub-basement into a whole wing of the eighth floor. He shrugged as he pushed his way through the crowded corridors, searching for the Records Division to authenticate his updated portfolio. He supposed that Personnel's expansion accurately reflected the Admiralty's new directions: they were now in the business of caring for people rather than projecting an Empire's military muscle. Probably, he reflected, it was a wise direction to follow. The CIGAs had seen to it that a huge portion of that muscle already had been sent to the shipbreakers.

Standing on tiptoe, he finally spied the Records office and pushed his way through the milling throng toward it, arriving only three-quarters of a metacycle later than he'd planned. After this, he waited in line for nearly a metacycle more until he finally reached a counter manned by two bored civilian clerks who moved so slowly that he seriously wondered if they might be closet TimeWeed addicts on some particularly vicious bender. He had just begun to patiently explain his purpose when a full Captain rudely elbowed him aside and literally dragged a youngish-looking Sublieutenant to the counter.

"Dear boy," the captain said to the clerk, "this *particularly* talented young person is to be assigned to my personal staff immediately. Do you understand? I shall wait. . . ."

The man's voice had a somehow familiar ring to Brim who, by now, was so irritated he could chew hullmetal. Grinding his teeth angrily, he grudgingly admitted that returning to the Fleet *did* have its drawbacks. Had something like this happened to him as a civilian, he'd have decked the Captain in the blink of an eye. Now, once more part of a rigidly controlled military hierarchy, he swallowed his pride and waited silently with the rest.

"Captain Amherst," the clerk said presently, with a look of honest apprehension on his face. "Ah, sir, ah, y-your personal staff is already over by *three* persons."

Brim's ears pricked up. Amherst! *That* was where he'd heard the voice before! His eyes narrowed while he craned his neck to see the Captain's face, and . . . he was not mistaken. It was *indeed* Puvis Amherst, the haughty young Lieutenant whose utter callousness and cowardice had made Brim's life utterly miserable while they served together on I.F.S. *Truculent*. Amherst was also son of retired Lord Rear Admiral Quincy Yarell Amherst, which—so far as Brim was concerned—went a long way toward explaining how such a poor excuse for an officer had risen to the exalted rank of captain.

"Well don't *tell* me about the problem," Amherst snapped irritably to the clerk, "—*fix* it!" Then he turned to smile affectionately at the young Sublieutenant "You will *love* it here in the Shipbreaking Directorate, Lieutenant. We are such a close-knit family."

The beautiful young blond man blushed. "Oh, of course, *Captain*," he said.

Brim drummed his fingers on the wall. Amherst! The miserable zukeed was clearly heavier and balder than he'd been aboard old *Truculent*, but he was still recognizable for all that. His cheeks and chin sagged like those of a man who no longer bothered to keep his body fit, and his skin had become office-building sallow. But clearly the Amherst personality had survived intact. Even here in the Records Office he managed to rub everyone the wrong way. Basically, Puvis Amherst was totally indifferent to anyone's needs save his own. And even worse, he clearly believed that he had every *right* to be that way! True to form, he quickly managed to draw both clerks into the fray. And not long afterward, the two lines he had breached began to extend all the way into another corridor. Through it all, however, the man conducted an animated conversation with his effete young friend as if nothing at all were amiss.

Brim wrested his thoughts from the mayhem he would have *liked* to inflict and concentrated on a list of specifications for Valerian's new M-6. Better to keep one's mouth shut than to lose a commission, he thought sourly—especially less than two days after that commission had been handed back from the far side of oblivion. Leaning a shoulder against the office wall, he had begun peering into a holograph of the M-6's proposed Helmsman's console when someone roughly jostled his arm.

"It appears that you actually have wheedled your way back into uniform," Amherst muttered, shaking his arm. "I'd heard Onrad might do something to make that happen."

Brim looked up from the holograph and nodded. "You heard right," he said, "—day before yesterday at the War Memorial Hall."

"Of course," Amherst said, shaking his head disapprovingly, "the ISS celebration. Well, you'd better enjoy the limelight while you can, Carescrian. If the CIGA has anything to say about matters of government—which it *does*, believe me—you'll soon find your silly racing funds cut to nothing." He raised his eyebrows. "The very idea of spending capital for something like that makes my blood boil."

Brim shrugged noncommittally, wondering what Amherst would do with the funds if they were his to allocate. He never put the question into words, however. There was little sense in provoking an argument when what he really wanted was to flatten the man's nose.

After a few moments of embarrassing silence, Amherst gave a sidelong glance at the Sublieutenant, then sneered at Brim. "You don't have much more to say than you used to aboard *Truculent*, do you?"

"I haven't heard anything worth talking about yet, Amherst," Brim returned quietly.

"*Captain* Amherst, to you, Carescrian," the man sneered, "—and *never* forget it!"

Taking the Sublieutenant's arm, he nodded toward Brim. "It's obsolete refuse like this that spoils today's Admiralty," he explained. "As fast as we force them out, some fool like Onrad brings them back again. Very frustrating."

The young officer took a single glance at Brim's glowering countenance and immediately began to study a display of empty forms at the counter.

"You'd better find *this* worth talking about, Brim," Amherst continued presently, glaring at the Carescrian as if he had just committed some particularly detestable outrage. "Imperial entries in races like the Mitchell will soon be things of the past. There are better, more politically desirable uses to which such funds can be put. *And*," he added pointedly, "now is *no* time to compete with the League and win."

In spite of himself, Brim felt his eyebrows rise. "What do you mean by *that*, Amherst?" he demanded.

"*Captain* Amherst!"

"Captain Amherst . . . ."

"That's better, Brim. You never have accepted your rightful place, have you?"

Brim ground his teeth again. "No," he agreed. "I have not —Captain."

By now, the two clerks seemed to have their emergency under control, and indeed, the other line had begun to move again while the clerk in Brim's line appeared to be finishing things up rapidly.

"Eventually you'll catch on, Brim," Amherst sneered breezily. "Otherwise, we'll quickly get rid of you again. And, to answer your question, the *first* thing you'd better learn is that we no longer compete with the League. *At all*. That goes for you, in a personal sense, as well as the obscenity you refer to as the ISS." This time, he glared in overt anger. "Instead of making vainglorious attempts to belittle our colleagues from the League—as *you* recently did in Rudolpho—your efforts should be directed toward promoting peace and cooperation."

"Like what?" Brim asked.

"Like helping to reduce a bloated Imperial Fleet," he said, "—a Fleet that is clearly no longer necessary to the safety of the realm." He put his hands on his hips and looked at Brim as if he were addressing a particularly stupid child. "Can't you understand that the Fleet, by its very existence, acts as a tremendous obstacle to our work?"

Just then, the clerk finished. "Captain Amherst," he called from behind the counter, "we're finished. Soon as you authenticate this, the Sublieutenant will be reassigned *and* your roster will be corrected."

Amherst turned his back on Brim as if he had simply ceased to exist. "There now," he said to the young officer, patting him on the shoulder, "you shall have no more concerns about serving aboard one of those absolutely dreadful military starships."

"Oh, thank you, Captain," the Sublieutenant uttered with a look of admiration on his face. "I simply couldn't have survived . . ."

Smirking jovially, Amherst made his authentication, then, without a single word of thanks, turned and strode from the office, his newly attached Sublieutenant struggling along in his wake. At the door, he stopped and turned once again toward Brim. "We shall watch you closely, Carescrian," he said, glowering. "Others have attempted to subvert the CIGA and have suffered for it." He grinned for a moment. "In some ways," he said, "I should enjoy that. It would give me great pleasure to *personally* remove you and all you stand for from the path of peace." Then, he was gone.

Presently, the clerk looked over his glasses at Brim and shook his head. "No offense meant, Commander," he said, "but are you sure you want to go to all this trouble? If Puvis Amherst hates you the way I think he does, then you are on your way out—right now!"

Brim glowered and checked his new documents in the displays. "Don't count on it, mister," he said, authenticating the records one by one. "As we say in the race business, 'it's not over till it's over.'" Then he looked the man directly in the eye. "And this race hasn't even *started* yet."

After treating himself to an all-too-short interlude with Anna Romanoff—during which both he and the alluring business-woman began to sort out what promised to be a relationship characterized, if nothing else, by frequent separations—Brim returned to Atalanta, resuming his ongoing employment at the Fleet base and preparing for the next trophy race. Throughout the remainder of the year, he and Moulding both sacrificed countless weeks of their own time in travel to Sodeskaya and Rhodor, assisting in development of the M-6 and its control systems.

The rewards, however, were well worth their levy. Long before race week, Sherrington's two new creations had proven themselves as perhaps *the* most naturally flyable starships ever. Painted dark cobalt with diagonal blue, white, and red racing stripes applied to the main hull immediately abaft the feed tubes, M-6s were everything the M-5s had started out to be, plus much, much more.

At ninety-six irals overall, each was slightly longer than its predecessors and followed Valerian's predilection for multiple hulls. Two Admiralty NL-4053-D gravity generators were mounted in teardrop outriggers joined to the needle-slim main hull by Valerian's characteristic "trousers." An uprated Wizard Drive (designated PV/16) rode the keel, cooled by external sur-face radiators nearly twice the area of those on the M-5. For-ward, a redesigned power system reduced the twin blisters covering its critically shaped feed tubes and produced nearly an eighth more energy in the same chamber volume. Its familiar-looking flight bridge was located just aft of the bow behind dramatically raked (and enlarged) Hyperscreen arrays, but in-side, even the controls were different, incorporating innovative concepts from the Admiralty's Living-Factors Design Section that made the new ships an absolute delight to fly.

They were, of course, *incredibly* fast. But just as important, they were reliable as well. Even during early phases of the test program, each of the little starships performed with rock-solid dependability—the result of a conservative approach to *refine-ment* of the M-5's best characteristics instead of attempting a second quantum leap in technology.

As it turned out, however, the ships were ready only in the barest nick of time. During the same period, both Gantheisser and Dampier had wasted little time preparing their own advanced-technology racing craft, no doubt basing their designs on performance parameters obtained from the same sort of espionage that supplied Sherrington designers with their benchmark criteria.

This time, however, the competitors were operating from an extreme disadvantage. Whereas Valerian's M-6's ran on highly *derated* Drive systems—result of hopeless cooling problems on the little racers—designers from the League and the Torond had once more boosted conventional, single-lobe Drive technology far past reasonable limits. And while both manufacturers had produced ships that would be at least *competitive* with the Sherrington entries, their propulsion systems were also fragile in the extreme. It was widely rumored that half the new Gantheisser Drives hammered themselves into junk after only cycles of operation at speed, and top-secret documents from the Admiralty indicated that Praefect Motta Balbo had been killed during a takeoff that ended with a sudden dive into Lake Garza. It was assumed that an energy leak may have entered the flight bridge, and so extra insulation had been installed in the two remaining DA.72/c's. But like the League's new GA 209V-5s, they were largely untried.

Anna Romanoff was a fine-looking woman, with or without benefit of clothes. The previous evening, she had once more proven both to Brim: first wearing a breathtaking white evening gown during the traditional reception hosted by Prince Onrad (at which *both* LaKarns were conspicuously absent), later clad only in perfume at the fashionable town house she maintained near the center of Avalon's historic Beardmore district.

Again today—little more than a metacycle before the ceremonies opening the Mitchell Trophy Race in Avalon—nearly every passing head turned in admiration as she strolled on Brim's arm through charming formal gardens toward the HyperDrome at Alcott-on-Mersin. She was dressed for the occasion in a stylish *costume antique* of the sheerest white crepe, consisting of a low-bosomed gown with a very high waistline —little more than a bust confiner. Its bodice at the widest point was only minimally deep and her narrow skirt draped all the way to the ground. Fitted over the very short bodice, she wore a double-breasted jacket of delicate white lace. A flat, wide-brimmed straw hat trimmed with delicate windflowers was tied about her cheeks with long apple green ribbons, and she wore dainty white lace gloves. Thin, low slippers, also of apple green, completed the outfit. Early that morning, Brim had been absolutely dazzled watching her dress. The conservative businesswoman he'd first encountered three years earlier in Atalanta had again vanished from the face of the Universe—at least for the duration of the races.

Historic Alcott Gardens themselves had been in continuous use since before the dawn of interstellar flight. Located on a high bluff overlooking Irwin's Bay on Lake Mersin, the grounds covered a quarter of a square c'lenyt and were dotted by filigreed pavilions, grandiose floral displays, and cascading fountains, all joined by an intricate network of paved footpaths. On this particular morning, the formal grandeur was greatly enhanced by soft puffs of fair-weather clouds that dwarfed the great starliners thundering out among them from Grand Imperial Terminal, only thirty c'lenyts distant.

Out on the lake, twenty-five capital ships from fifteen-odd dominions hovered as if waiting for a signal to commence warring again. Unfortunately, to Brim's way of thinking, sixteen of them owed allegiance to the League.

Avalon's Imperial HyperDrome was almost as old as starflight itself. Built on a spacious arc of lakefront, it formed a vast stage for the colossal natural arena formed by the bluffs separating the gardens and the lake. Two huge grandstands—set well back from the water and climate-controlled when necessary—divided the extensive apron area into three distinct sectors housing all ten galactic domains that had qualified for this year's contest. Sheds for the Imperial Starship Society, the Nergol Triannic Starflight Society, the Starflight Association of the Torond, and the A'zurnian Starflight Institute—winners of the four previous years' races—were located in the center section. Entries from the less successful domains of Vukote, Beta Jagow, Prendergast, Wooglin, Fluvanna, and Taras occupied the remainder.

Brim seated Romanoff in the Krasni-Peych box with Ursis and Borodov, who were acting as temporary escorts to Moulding's voluptuous redhead. Then he hurried off through the noisy, colorful throng for a lift to the Imperial shed with Valerian in a Sherrington limousine.

Following the traditional parade (in which Brim was paired with Kirsh Valentin!) and interminable speeches by toothsome Imperial officials, the race at last got underway. Earlier, Prince Onrad had decreed that this year, the order of competition would be reversed. Therefore, the contest began when an orchestra struck up the Tarian national anthem, "All Hail the Crinig Tree!" At the same time, blood green flags raced to the top of three flagpoles located on the winner's dais in the center of the HyperDrome. Taras, a first-time contender, fielded two odd-looking starships that earlier had showed *some* promise in practice heats. During the next metacycle and a half, however, they left no doubt in anyone's minds that someone else would carry home the Mitchell Trophy this year.

The entry from Fluvanna—there was only one—fared considerably better, but came nowhere close to the minimum qualifying speeds achieved by many of the other domains. Both racers from the ten-star cluster of Wooglin finished with respectable times, as did those from Beta Jagow and Prendergast; but the day ended on a note of tragedy when a starship from Vukote disintegrated in three terrific explosions before it had achieved more than a c'lenyt of altitude. After protracted conferences between Imperial safety officials and practically the whole Vucotian staff, the latter withdrew from competition and the day ended nearly two metacycles later than anyone had expected.

While most of Avalon immersed itself in parties of one kind or another that night, Brim and Romanoff set off promptly to her town house where they retired almost immediately with vows from both sides that on the eve of such an important event, Brim should sleep all the way through the night, with no interruptions. They broke their vow only once—by urgent and mutual agreement.

Competition resumed the next morning with an outstanding exhibition of sportsmanship when the Beta Jagow Starship society loaned a rare ingot of Relox-31 to desperate Fluvannian technicians. The latter quickly applied most of it to a leaking power chamber in the needlelike Pagona Pc.7 they had entered, and shortly thereafter outstripped their benefactors by two places in the final standings. Afterward, Wooglin's entries bettered both by nearly 7.5M LightSpeed. Early in the afternoon, however, two sleek R'autor M6C-32s piloted by A'zurnians effortlessly swept all previous competitors from the race, boosting the high average speed to nearly 94M LightSpeed, while sending a shock wave through most of the racing community. Brim grimaced when he heard the news. Any possibility of an easy victory had just evaporated, not only for himself but for his adversaries from the League and Torond who would fly next.

As Fleet intelligence had speculated, Rogan LaKarn's uprated DA.72/c's flew with Drive crystals extravagantly overstressed by new power plants installed at the last moment by frantic Dampier engineers. Both Helmsmen gallantly completed the race in their treacherous machines, but the first was seriously burned when the new insulation failed to keep stray energy from the flight bridge, and the second ran at no more than three-quarters power settings after a wildly erratic takeoff. When they were finished, the Torond had managed only a poor second to A'zurn's little R'autors, and as late afternoon into the coolness of early evening, only the League stood between Brim and another Mitchell Trophy.

The setting Triad of Asterious had turned Avalon's nightward horizon into layers of deep mauve and pink as three black League banners shot to the top of the center flagpoles. Valentin raced first, and almost from the beginning his brutish Gantheisser 209V-5 was dogged by trouble. While he was still on the gravity pool, the enormous DB 601ARJ power plant refused to fully energize, and his embarrassed colleagues were forced to plead for an official time-out while squads of technicians sorted out the problem under dozens of bobbing hover-floods. Then, after little more than two laps aloft, both plasma tubes delaminated at the feed end, burning dead spots in the crystal and forcing him from the race. Without sufficient power to make landfall, he had to abandon the badly scorched ship in orbit and return—ignominiously—aboard an Imperial destroyer.

Only cycles after the first reports of Valentin's difficulties swept through the shed area, Brim and Moulding sat on the edge of the Imperial gravity pool, watching through night glasses while a hovering traction machine drew Groener's snow white Gantheisser to the gravity pool, now brilliantly lighted by lofty Karlsson lamps. Soon afterward, two white Majestat-Baron limousine skimmers emerged from a side wing of the shed and sped across the apron, tracing specially installed follower cables. The first deposited Groener at the League's gravity pool where she alighted just below the hovering Gantheisser's boarding ladder among an orderly group of technicians. Even a battle suit couldn't hide her spectacular curves. The second big skimmer drew to a halt directly behind Groener's to disgorge OverGalite'er Gorton Ro'arn and four tough-looking Controllers wearing special Racotzi Police badges on their hats. Groener had a grim look on her face as she glanced sullenly at Ro'arn, and when he raised his hand to attract her attention, she turned away as if she could no longer tolerate the sight of his face. She paused at the boarding ladder for a moment, then ultimately shook her head, issued a few terse commands to the ground crew, and mounted to the hatch with no further communication to anyone.

"A very unhappy-looking lady out there," Toby Moulding commented, handing Brim the night glasses. Both Imperials were already dressed in battle suits and ready to fly.

Brim adjusted the gain and focused in on the Gantheisser's Hyperscreens. "You can say that again," he replied, peering intently through the darkness. Unfortunately, from his angle of view, most of Groener's face was hidden by her instrument panel.

Moments later, the big DB 601ARJ energized in a sparkling globule of heat energy that spilled from the sides of the gravity pool in waves of distorted light. This was followed almost immediately by the thunder of a gravity generator.

"She couldn't be bothering with her checklist!" Moulding observed, raising his voice over the rumble of the Gantheisser's second big generator.

"No," Brim agreed, handing back Moulding's night glasses. "She certainly couldn't—there isn't enough time . . ." At that moment, the brutish starship lurched off its gravity pool and lumbered toward the central access ramp before a surprised Imperial orchestra could belatedly strike up the League's national anthem.

Moulding peered through the night glasses again. "I think she's in some kind of trouble."

"Yeah," Brim agreed with a feeling of absolute helplessness. "And as usual, there's not a xaxtdamned thing anybody can do about it." He watched Groener taxi out over the water and swing her bow toward the starting gates. "If only we cared about individuals as much as we do about cultures," he said, "maybe we wouldn't get into the kind of troubles that end up in wars."

"What?" Moulding asked.

Brim laughed grimly as Groener took the starter's flag and thundered down the takeoff vector, trailing three lofty cascades of spray that shone in the radiance of the bobbing vector markers. "Only a stray thought, Toby," he said, "about not being able to help people because they bring trouble on themselves." He shook his head sadly. "Probably," he said, watching the little starship merge with the evening stars, "it doesn't matter anymore."

Less than a metacycle later, Groener's Gantheisser disintegrated in a terrific explosion. Brim learned of it on his way to the gravity pool. At first, he couldn't believe it. But as his van pulled to a stop, he knew that the League's greed was to blame for the loss of such a good pilot. Above him, the floodlit M-6 loomed gracefully in the bluish green glow of stationary generators. "They'll pay for this, Inge. . . ." Then he pulled himself together. He had a race to win.

CHAPTER 9

Dityasburg

Settling himself in the single Helmsman's seat, Brim opened his helmet and slid the port Hyperscreen aside. A lamp winked from the side of the instrument panel while traces of fresh night breeze swirled into the flight bridge, mixing with odors of hot metal, ozone, and fresh sealant that seemed to permeate every racing machine he'd ever known.

Outside, the last glow of twilight had gone from the nightward horizon, but Karlsson lamps maintained the glare of high noon on the apron. Only essential technicians and a few special guests like Bosporus Gallsworthy and His Majesty Prince Onrad (wearing white coveralls!) remained in the area. It would soon become a very noisy place indeed, as well as dangerous. Brim slid a gloved hand to the COMM panel, bringing its little Universe of winking lights to life with a touch of a finger, then he scanned through crackling channels of electronic blather, setting up links to the tower, the flight controller, the race coordinators, and—by KA'PPA COMM—to a half dozen Imperial starships patrolling the racecourse. The latter had been quietly placed along the racecourse at Onrad's insistence after Brim's encounter with the media yacht.

In quick succession, he touched the console in three locations. Position lamps glowed at the tips of the two gravity pontoons—green to starboard, red to port, following some ancient tradition long vanished into the mists of history. Then a strobe exploded from below as the ventral clearance light came to life.

Finally, whirling beams from an overhead beacon turned the Hyperscreen frames alternating shades of amber, then blue, in time to the gentle whine of a gravitronic phase shifter mounted in his right-hand console.

Glancing momentarily toward Ursis seated below at a console on the rim of the gravity pad, he touched an amber glow on the damper quadrant at his left hand. Six indicators changed from yellow to green and static crackled briefly in his helmet while a flow of plasma enabled the six critical logic circuits of the power system. He scanned the center console again. Colors flowed in orderly codes across the readouts. "Gravs to the power mains, Nik," he announced.

"Connected," Ursis replied. Once again, he was magnificently outfitted in the uniform of a Home Guard Colonel.

Nodding to himself, Brim simultaneously touched glimmering blue circles at either side of the console. A heartbeat later, twin thumps beneath the deck seconded a cascade of information on the power panel. "Looks good," he reported. "Three nine five T-units."

"Three nine five," Ursis announced with a chuckle. "That ought to keep you out of trouble for a while."

"Check," Brim laughed, setting the gravity brakes. He glanced out the Hyperscreens and waved to Moulding who had seated himself atop Ursis's console, drumming his heels idly against the back cover. "Brakes set. Everybody off the pontoons?"

"Pontoons are clear," Ursis said after a pause. "Both Toby and I have checked them with our own eyes."

"Energizing starboard," Brim said, selecting STARBOARD and reaching for the bright sapphire circle marked START. At his touch, the circle changed to red, then strobed in tempo with the interruptor on the starboard outrigger as its gravity generator spun up with a metallic whine. Guided by instinct born of a thousand-odd practice sessions, Brim moved the plasma boost to ON and the feed selector to BOTH. Straightaway, fifty-four hundred standard thrust units thundered into boisterous reality, while ice blue tongues of free ions shot back fifty irals from the open wastegates. The atmosphere glowed with eerie luminescence before the big generator settled to a smooth rumble and green lights on the grav panel indicated steady-state operation. Less than three cycles afterward, the port generator added its deep-throated voice to the rolling thunder while tremendous magnitudes of energy surged through the complex power network, totally under control and perfectly suited to the system's requirements.

Brim was now in the mood to fly. He'd always loved the sound of big spaceborne gravs, even when he was too young to know what they were. With a silly grin on his face, he checked his readouts, reveling in the mighty duet of power on either side of the bridge. "I've got a good start, Nik," he reported.

"So you do," Ursis growled as he peered into his consoles. He was now wearing a huge pair of sound dampers over his furry ears, and Moulding had shut his helmet. Everyone remaining in the area seemed to have retreated to a safe distance except for Onrad and Gallsworthy; they had also donned ear protection and were grinning up at Brim like excited children.

In the corner of his eye, Brim saw three Imperial flags shoot to the tops of the flagpoles—it was time to go racing. He checked for Romanoff's gold earrings (that she'd given him for good luck) and touched the landing light switches. Instantly, three brilliant beams of light materialized from beneath the fuselage—clearly visible, even in the glare of the Karlsson lamps. "I'll be back in about a metacycle," he called to Ursis. "I'm going out to fetch us a trophy."

"Seems like a sensible thing to do," Ursis answered, peering up from his console. "We won't start the victory party without you."

Brim queasily switched to internal gravity, choked back his gorge, then flashed a thumbs-up through the Hyperscreens while he turned the COMM unit to ground control. "Alcott Ground," he announced, "Imperial M-six Alpha requests taxi to drive area."

"Imperial M-six Alpha, Alcott Ground clears for taxi to arming zone one."

"M-six Alpha," Brim acknowledged, waving at the ground crew to cast off his mooring beams. When all six optical cleats were safely retracted into the hull, he delicately maneuvered the M-6 off its gravity pool and firmly applied the brakes. They worked. Next, he taxied across to the Drive-arming area where he eased his ship onto the nearest of three lenslike N-ray emitters and drew the thrust damper back to idle. Immediately, he was surrounded by a squad of Bears in bright green Krasni-

Peych radiation-proof battle suits with huge protective mittens and metallic palm insets.

Brim placed his hands against the Hyperscreens where they could be seen. This signaled the crew that they could now work without fear of "cockpit error" while they accomplished their hazardous task. Immediately, the Sodeskayans set to work, nipping in and out of the glaring landing lights as they swarmed around the ship's belly. Carefully avoiding the deadly gravitron exhaust plumes, they had all five access panels open within moments, and soon the Drive panel begin to glimmer into life, with new color patterns bursting into cascades of information as each new module was energized in its turn. While they worked, he studied the distant grandstands, thinking of the delicate woman there who was just as surely seeking a glimpse of him at the same time. He watched Imperial flags dancing on the HyperDrome flagpoles. When he and Moulding had finished their night's work, the Imperial banner would still wave from the tallest of the three—and very probably the next-tallest as well. Valerian's M-6s were clearly in a class by themselves. Everyone who saw them, even the Leaguers, agreed that they were easily the most graceful starships ever constructed. Now, he was about to demonstrate to the galaxy that they were every bit as functional as they were beautiful, and perhaps a little more.

He smiled to himself. Essentially a hopeless romantic, he recognized the moment as one of great drama and beauty—not because of the fame and power that would come to him for winning, but for the very love of this particular starship, and the majesty of the stars themselves.

Suddenly, the Bears were again grouped under the bow of the starship, and Vaskrozni Kubinka the Crew Chief had removed a mitten to hold his thumb aloft. Brim glanced at the five green Drive hatch indicators—all locked—and then the clock. The crew had set *another* record. Grinning from ear to ear, he returned the gesture, and made a quick scan of his panels while the Bears returned to the radiation shelter at a run.

"Alcott Ground," he said, "M-six Alpha requests taxi to gate."

"M-six Alpha, Alcott Ground clears taxi to gate area one five left, wind two one zero at one six."

"M-six Alpha," Brim acknowledged again. With a final glance toward the grandstands, he moved the thrust damper forward, called up enough power to move the M-6 onto a launch ramp, and taxied out over the water, setting course for the take-off vector.

As he neared the starting gate, he changed communications channels and called the tower: "Imperial M-six Alpha to Alcott Tower at pylon area," he announced. "Request gate clearance."

"Alcott Tower to M-six Alpha. Cleared to enter gate one five left. Takeoff vector zero seven five on green light, wind two one two at one eight."

"M-six Alpha entering gate one five left, wind two one two at one eight, takeoff on green."

"Alcott Tower."

Brim swung the M-6's bow sharply to starboard and taxied into position just short of the start pylons, presently strobing red from each apex. Beyond, two rows of bobbing yellow vector buoys converged into the distance. For a moment, he sat quietly in the darkness, savoring the fragrance of the lake and gathering himself for the flight, while data from his readouts flowed smoothly across his consoles. Then, deliberately, he slid the Hyperscreen closed; it sealed with a distinct hiss as the bridge pressurized. He made a last systems check: flight controls—normal; lift modifiers—on TAKEOFF; flight readouts—normal and set; anticollision and position lights—ON; cabin gravity—FIRM; shoulder restraints—tight; Hyperscreens—SEALED and LOCKED. Everything was ready.

Locking the steering engine at VERTICAL ONLY, he activated the gravity brakes, then signaled the Starter back at the grandstands by opening his thrust dampers. As his powerful generators built up to takeoff output, a cloud of spray and ice particles began to surge skyward behind the ship, and the bridge filled with a growing thunder. Presently, the pylon lights changed from red to amber. At this, Brim fairly stood on the gravity brakes and brought the dampers all the way to their stops. Even in his battle suit, the penetrating howl of the generators—operating now with no restriction whatsoever—became almost intolerable. The little ship plunged and bucked as it battled back the torrent of raw energy, and Brim found himself struggling with the controls to keep her nose pointed between the rows of vector buoys. Only moments before it seemed that he would surely lose control, the lights changed to green and he popped the brakes. Instantly, both pylons disappeared sternward in a cascade of spray as the M-6 sprang forward, hurtling itself along the vector with a chilling liquid suddenness. Brim managed to steer a passable approximation of a straight line only by virtue of sheer agility, plus all the native flying skill he possessed. In the corner of his vision, he checked the power panel —still at a steady three ninety-five T-units—while his eyes scanned up and down, inside and out with one coordinated glance. Airspeed 115 c'lenyts. She was getting ready to fly, her mass rapidly transferring to the thundering gravs while his hands wielded the controls by instinct born of love and experience. With no need for instruments, he sensed the ship getting lighter on her footprint until at about 145 she smoothly changed to a creature of the sky. There was a final moment when the blurred glow of the vector buoys below suddenly quit, ending his dependence on the ground, then he and the ship were in their element, climbing out along the beams of their own landing lights toward the ultimate freedom of the stars.

During its subsequent flight, the superb little ship behaved with utter docility. A perfect combination of hull, propulsion, and control, she snapped through lap after lap at tremendous velocities with stunning regularity, for not only a first-place victory but a new Universal speed record of 94.59M LightSpeed, as well.

Inge Groener's funeral in space was only symbolic; the explosion that took her life also reduced her body, and most of the big Gantheisser she was driving, to subatomic particles that would spend the remainder of eternity traveling outward from the final locus of their existence.

Most of the close-knit racing fraternity attended aboard *Angor Renat*, one of two super-Rengas-class battleships dispatched to escort the League's Mitchell racing team. Brim and Romanoff found themselves amid an unlikely gathering of royalty, the famous, the infamous (depending upon one's political affiliations), and even a few unknowns—although the latter composed a small, privileged minority. In the warship's enormous wardroom, Prince Onrad stood shoulder-to-shoulder with Kabul Anak as OverGalite'er Gorton Ro'arn watched in silence beside General Harry Drummond. Even Ursis and Moulding endured the company of Kirsh Valentin, who remained in stony silence throughout the interminable speeches that preceded the up-galaxy launch of a torpedo filled with Groener's belongings.

To say it was a friendly meeting was to beg the point—but in death, the beautiful Leaguer did bring many of the galaxy's bitterest enemies together for a brief moment that had little to do with politics. When the missile's glow at last faded away among the blazing stars, Brim felt reasonably certain that the ceremony would have pleased her considerably.

After celebrations of the Empire's second Mitchell victory wound to a close, Romanoff was soon abroad on another extended business trip and Brim began to prepare for the following year's defense of the Mitchell Trophy—which was now referred to by members of the ISS as "the hat rack." They were at last tied evenly with the League, two races all. One more victory by either contender would retire the trophy permanently.

Brim had hardly gotten back into the swing of his job in Atalanta when he received an unusual message from Regula Collingswood through the Fleet base's secure communications channels. It was personally delivered to his small office one early evening by COMCOMM herself, a short, pug Captain dressed in an immaculate Fleet uniform with—it was rumored—more seniority than Greyffin IV himself. "Figured I'd better bring this around in person, Commander," she said with a frown. "When I decoded the text, I couldn't help reading it—so I'll be enough of a meddler to wish you and your friend Moulding the best treatment Dame Fortune can provide. You're both going to need it."

"Er . . . thank you, Captain," Brim said with a frown of confusion, "I think . . ."

"You'll understand when you've read it," the Captain said as she turned and started down the hall. "Probably you shouldn't thank me, either," she added as she rounded the corner, "—at least before you've read it. I suspect I've just delivered a whole Universe of trouble."

Concerned by the officer's words, Brim placed his right index finger on the plastic envelope's seal. Instantly, it opened in a puff of smoke. Then, with a growing sense of foreboding, he withdrew a single message sheet and unfolded it:

UN2378523ZXCN

[TOP-SECRET EYES-ONLY PERSONAL
COMCOMM]

FM: ADMIRALTYCOMCOMM@AVALON

TO: COMCOMM@HAELIC:FLEET:COMM

<<KPDK-34583D90S9899-W6D-SD099483-
DJFV389>>

DELIVER TO:
  BRIM@HAELIC:FLEET:FLIGHTOPS
  MOULDING@HAELIC:FLEET:FLIGHTOPS:
INFO:
  GALLSWORTHY@HAELIC:FLEET:FLIGHTOPS

WILF, TOBY:

1. PRINCE ONRAD HIMSELF DIRECTS ME TO
SEND THIS WARNING.

2. PUVIS AMHERST AND HIS CIGAS HAVE TODAY
(MY TIME) FAILED IN ATTEMPT TO REVOKE
YOUR COMMISSIONS ALONG WITH OTHER
OFFICERS (INCLUDING GENERAL HARRY
DRUMMOND) ASSOCIATED WITH THE ISS;
GREYFFIN IV PERSONALLY RESCINDED THESE
ORDERS.

3. APPARENT CIGA MOTIVE: TERMINATE
DEVELOPMENT OF SHERRINGTON M-6 FOLLOW
ON. ALL FLEET FUNDS EARMARKED FOR ISS
USE DISCONTINUED AS OF YESTERDAY.
SODESKAYAN INTELLIGENCE CONFIRMS CIGA IS
UNDER DIRECT CONTROL OF LEAGUE (METHOD:
BLACKMAIL—MANY IMPERIAL FORTUNES MADE
DURING WAR BY PASSING SECRETS TO THE
LEAGUE.)

4. YOU BOTH SHOULD EXPECT REASSIGNMENT
ORDERS TOMORROW (YOUR TIME). CIGA WANTS
ISS TEAM BROKEN UP PERMANENTLY. YOUR
FIRST DESTINATION: AVALON; AFTERWARD,
UNIVERSE KNOWS WHERE.

5. DO NOT, REPEAT, DO NOT DISPUTE THESE
NEW ORDERS. ONRAD WILL INTERCEDE BEFORE
YOU MUST DEPART AVALON.

6. MAY STARS LIGHT ALL THY PATHS.

REGULA COLLINGSWOOD

[END TOP-SECRET EYES-ONLY PERSONAL
COMCOMM]

ADMIRALTYCOMCOMM SENDS

UN2378523ZXCN

He read the note twice more, then touched his thumb to the
top right-hand corner of the form and the message evaporated
into thin air as if it had never existed. Precisely two clicks later,
so did the envelope—at almost the same instant Toby Moulding
appeared in the doorway.

"I say," he started, "those chaps play a rough game, don't
they?" Always the aristocrat, he wore high, black riding boots,
ivory trousers, and a soft, blue coat with a white scarf tied
loosely at his throat.

Brim nodded grimly. "The only rougher game is played by
Leaguers."

Moulding shrugged. "From what Regula sent, I gather there
isn't much difference."

"In a lot of ways, I'd rather deal with the Leaguers," Brim
growled. "They're predictable. You can't tell what traitors are
going to do from one moment to the next."

"Right ho," Moulding agreed, pacing back and forth in the
tiny space in front of the Carescrian's workstation.

Brim shook his head angrily. "What *really* gets to me,
though, isn't so much people like Amherst turning traitors—

every civilization has a component of people like that. It's the *rest* of the Empire that wipes me out. How in the name of Voot can they fall for pro-League stuff so soon after they nearly lost a war to the same people? Why is it that all of a sudden they trust the Leaguers more than the Blue Capes who were only yesterday saving their silly asses from destruction? Can they forget so quickly?"

Moulding put a hand on Brim's arm. "I think you've got *that* answer in your own experience," he said.

"I assume you mean what happened to me after the war," Brim said with a frown.

"Not a very pleasant subject," Moulding conceded, "but it *does* fit, doesn't it? I don't think that people forgot so much as they *changed* the way they remembered. The war was so terrible to them that anything that could stop it—give them a respite, no matter how short-term—seemed beneficial. Even though common logic said that eventually they would have to pay for it with more of the same."

"But, Toby," Brim protested, "neither of us supports the bastards, and we were in the thick of things. In fact, from what I've seen, the CIGAs main support comes pretty much from people who *weren't* involved at all—except when the cities themselves were attacked. What in Voot's name do *they* know about war, anyway? Most of them haven't even seen a Leaguer."

"Ignorance is the word I suspect you are looking for," Moulding reminded him, "—and those largely ignorant people are a majority of the population, aren't they?"

"Yeah," Brim agreed. "I suppose there weren't that many of us out there actually fighting the Leaguers."

"Tells you something, doesn't it?" Moulding answered suggestively.

Their orders—arriving promptly in midafternoon, as predicted—gave them only two days to arrange their affairs for a permanent change of station. Brim had little in the way of belongings. After packing a few belongings and storing his gravcycle in a shed behind Nesterio's Racotzian Cabaret, he messaged Anna Romanoff about the new turn of events and was essentially ready for travel. Moulding, on the other hand, boarded the biweekly mail packet to Avalon with less than a metacycle to spare. Arranging for half a lifetime's possessions would have been difficult had he been given a month or more.

Brim and Moulding arrived in Avalon only a few metacycles after the first communiques announcing that Nergol Triannic had returned to Tarrott and resumed the reins of government, wearing a Controller's uniform. At a single blow, he had abrogated the Treaty of Garak and set up the Congress of Intragalactic Accord as his de facto persona among the other dominions of the galaxy, although embassies and consulates would continue to serve in their historic capacities as "official" League interfaces. Triannic's move was the talk of the city, where it was widely predicted—among people Puvis Amherst had referred to as "obsolete refuse"—that the domains of Fluvanna and Beta Jagow were now living on borrowed time.

The two Blue Capes had no sooner checked into Visiting Officers' Quarters near Avalon's Grand Imperial Terminal than they were ordered directly to the Admiralty, ostensibly for new documents from the Central Directorate for Personnel. At that office, however, they were then directed to the Assignments Office where—after a wait of nearly three metacycles—a senior clerk handed them "Permanent Change of Station" orders.

Outside in the hall, Brim winced as he read his set of flimsy plastic sheets. Instantly, he had become Assistant Stores Officer in a deactivated complex on cold Gimmas-Haefdon, a once-strategic Fleet base that had been largely forgotten in the wake of the Admiralty's present policy of decline. He looked over at Moulding and shook his head. "I'm certainly counting on Onrad to kill *these* orders," he said.

"What exotic location did you draw?" Moulding asked, looking up from his own set of plastics.

"Gimmas," Brim answered. "I understand it's gotten so cold on that planet now that even Sodeskayan Bears refuse to serve there anymore."

Moulding shook his head. "If it's any comfort, old chap," he said, handing Brim his orders, "at least you won't have to worry about poison fluggo darts in the back."

Brim ground his teeth as he read. "Chargé d'Affaires in Hobro!" he exclaimed. "What *else* did you do that I don't know about? Were you fooling around with the Empress or something?"

"Not that I know of," Moulding answered with a grim chuckle. "She is a bit on the chubby side for me, after all."

As he spoke, the clerk rushed out of the Assignments Office waving a sheath of plastic sheets. "Commander Brim," he called peevishly. "Commander Brim!" He now wore a large CIGA badge on the lapel of his pastel jumpsuit—it had not been there a few moments previously.

Brim nodded. "Over here," he said.

"You didn't give me time to finish, Commander," the man said. He made the words an accusation. "I have a *personal* summons for you from Commodore Amherst."

"Amherst's a Commodore now?" Brim chuckled, glancing at Moulding. "All right," he agreed, "I'll see him. Where is he?"

"You mean *you don't know* he's moved to the new CIGA suite?" the clerk asked with raised eyebrows. "Where have you *been*, man?"

"Out of town," Brim snapped. "Now tell me where he is—and be quick about it!"

"Well!" the clerk sniffed in a resentful tone of voice. He pursed his lips. "The CIGA Office is now just off the Great Foyer."

Brim turned to Moulding. "This may take a little time, Toby," he said. "How about if I meet you back at the VOQ? I'll ring you soon as I get back."

"Sounds like a plan, friend," Moulding said. "I wouldn't miss being the first to hear what's up in the CIGA."

"Anything else, boy?" Brim asked the clerk.

"Not from *me*, Commander," the man simpered. "But *your* time is definitely coming. Count on it." He turned on his heel and strutted back into the office without another word.

"Somehow," Moulding said ruefully, "I think we've lost control of our Fleet."

"Whatever gave you an idea like *that*?" Brim asked sarcastically. With that, they started along the hall toward the Great Foyer.

Brim cooled his heels nearly two full metacycles in the ornate CIGA sitting room. Much of that time, he suspected Amherst was alone in his office—if indeed the zukeed hadn't stepped outside for a long stroll. While he waited, he attempted to occupy his mind by scanning CIGA publications on expensive-looking displays the organization had placed throughout the large room, but found he had little stomach for literature that advocated further destruction of the Imperial Fleet. The ones that *really* raised his temperature, though, were travel presentations for the League. Smiling Controllers in the midst of singing children were just a little too much for his stomach.

At length, a squat, brutish woman with a noticeable moustache swaggered into view. She was clad in a flowered dress that added at least a hundredweight to her already massive frame. "Commander Brim?" she demanded, as if it were an accusation.

"That's probably me," Brim said evenly. Except for the woman herself, he was alone in the waiting room.

"This way," she said, jerking her thumb as if she were directing a prisoner. She looked for all the world like a Controller he'd once seen.

Brim waited until she had opened the office door, then strode directly into Amherst's lavishly decorated room before she could formally announce him.

Dressed in a magnificently tailored Imperial Fleet uniform, the Commodore was seated behind a huge, ornate desk. Matching guest chairs were conspicuously lined up along the wall beside the desk, although carpeting directly in front still bore the imprint of their feet. "You Carescrians never did have any sense of manners," he whined, dismissing the woman with a curt motion of his hand.

Retrieving one of the chairs, Brim thumped it down facing away from the desk, straddled its ornate back, and settled into the seat backward. "All right, Amherst," he said, "make it quick."

"*Commodore* Amherst, you mean."

"Listen, zukeed," Brim growled, "so far as I'm concerned, you don't even deserve the title of *citizen*. In public, maybe I'll call you Commodore because the Service Manual calls for it, but in private, you get nothing but *traitor* from me. Understand?"

Amherst turned white with anger. "If our feebleminded Emperor didn't protect your every move, I should have your head for that, Brim. But I will yet remove you from the Fleet. Wait and see."

"Perhaps you will," Brim allowed. "I hear you've managed to pull the ISS's racing funds for next year."

"I certainly have done *that*, thank the Universe," Amherst declared proudly, "—as well as send you back to Gimmas-Haefdon." He laughed boastfully. "I warned you what would happen if you won the Mitchell again. Now is *not* the time to anger our friends from the League. Why, it's only recently that we have managed to reduce our Fleet sufficiently that they are beginning to trust us. And then you idiots come along with your racers and *beat* them." He shook his head angrily. "Brim, I know your kind. You're a war lover, that's what you are."

Brim shook his head. "No, Amherst," he said. "You've got me mixed up with your friends in the League. I personally *hate* war, probably even more than you do. Nobody—except maybe Triannic's ludicrous Controllers—*really* wants me to go off and fight to the death. We *both* hope for a peaceful galaxy. Where we differ is how we should go about achieving it. You seem to be willing to sell out and achieve peace by submission; I believe that peace can only be achieved by *winning* it."

"That is precisely why the Fleet must be purged of your kind," Amherst growled. "Otherwise, the senseless killing will go on forever."

"Luckily, you can't send *everybody* to Gimmas-Haefdon," Brim said with a little grin. "A lot of us won't give in to your kind, Amherst—ever. I've seen you in action, personally. Remember? And I know your secret. Submission—surrender—is acceptable because you can't *face* the price of an honorable peace."

"I *choose* not to pay that price for mere *honor*," Amherst snapped with a red-mottled face, "—nor will I ask the helpless women and children of this Empire to pay it either. Certainly not to satisfy bloodthirsty animals like you, Carescrian!"

Brim laughed sardonically. "You talk about price, fool?" he said. "Do you have any idea what the Leaguers will exact from those women and children as the price of your submission? Their freedom, that's what! And the likes of you will pay with your very *lives*."

Amherst's florid countenance grew even redder. "My *life*?" he demanded angrily. "How dare you impugn the League in such a manner? The Controllers will reward me, because I am a proven ally—a CIGA officer."

"They'll reward you, all right," Brim snarled, "—with a blaster to the head. You'll see soon enough how they operate when your 'peaceful' Nergol Triannic goes after Fluvanna or Beta Jagow. Leaguers want total control of anything they take over—I've seen how they behave, firsthand. Contemptible traitors like you are the first ones they shoot."

"No!" Amherst ranted angrily, "I will *not* permit such fabrication in this office! Shut up. *Shut up!*"

"You can't silence the truth," Brim continued grimly. "Leaguers are absolutely pragmatic in everything they do. Remember when they pulled the wings off those A'zurnian prisoners years ago? They didn't act out of cruelty when they managed that little atrocity. Not at all. Flighted people are simply easier to control if they have no wings. What makes you think they'll treat you any better?"

"I won't listen to any more of this!" Amherst screamed. "No more. Do you hear? The League trusts me. They would *never* harm me. I am their friend!"

"*Friend?*" Brim chortled remorselessly. "Controllers *have* no friends—at least none who are not themselves Controllers. And fools like yourself won't be predictable enough for them, so they'll simply get rid of you. Mark my words, Amherst, you're a dead man if you get your wish."

"No!" Amherst gasped. "No! Nergol Triannic wants only *peace!* He will not attack Fluvanna. You have no sense, Brim. *Y-you* are the fool!"

Brim shook his head and smiled sadly. "Perhaps you're right, Amherst," he acknowledged. "Under the laws of the Empire, every man has the right to make a fool of himself as he sees fit." Watching the CIGA leader's face turn even redder, he knew that he'd exposed the truth. Puvis Amherst dreaded combat so utterly that it obscured even the peril of death. And if that sort of mechanism impelled Puvis Amherst, then similar fears moved his followers.

Brim smiled and shook his head. It was that sort of weakness—the fear of battle itself—that gave him any hope for the future of the Empire, or himself. He relaxed. It was what he'd come for. "Well, Amherst," he said presently, "I haven't got all day. If you've anything else you want to talk about, get busy." He looked at his timepiece. "I've better things to do than sit around and prattle with cheap Leaguer stooges like you."

At this, Amherst's red face faded to white. "You . . . you . . . contemptible *lowlife* scum. How *dare* you."

"I dare a lot," Brim replied lightly. "It's part of my job."

Amherst's eyes narrowed in violent anger while his fingers struggled to twist their opposites from his hands. "I shall have you killed for your lack of respect," he whispered in a low, choked voice.

"Probably a good idea," Brim said carelessly. "Clearly, you don't have the guts to do it yourself."

"Y-you . . . are . . . a . . . d-dead . . . man," Amherst stuttered, clearly at the end of control.

"You may want to think about that for a while," Brim said, rising from his chair and placing it carefully back against the wall. "I'll be a xaxtdamned troublesome corpse for both you *and* your CIGA clowns. Murder is still illegal in this Empire, even for a CIGA—and people will know just who to investigate."

"I could never be convicted," Amherst snarled in a prideful voice. "I have power that you cannot even dream of."

Brim nodded. "You probably do at that," he agreed, "—and pinning a murder charge on someone with your connections very well might not work. Especially since the courts would have to play fair, which you wouldn't." He grinned. "But there are at least *two* other reasons you'll never come after me."

"And what might they be?" Amherst demanded, dripping with sarcasm.

"Names come to mind," Brim said with a grim smile. "Ursis and Borodov. Bears. They don't have to play fair, either. And if anything happens to me, you'll be the first one they go after. Tell me, Amherst, have you ever seen a man die by being disemboweled—like a Sodeskayan crag wolf? Nik Ursis claims it's *very* noisy and takes a long time."

Amherst's countenance suddenly lost its rage. "Disemboweled?" he asked in a diminished voice.

"Disemboweled," Brim assured him. "If *anyone* lays a hand on me, sooner or later you'll become real expert in the matter. Count on it."

"Carescrian *mongrel*," Amherst hissed.

Brim shrugged in dismissal and gathered his orders under his arm. "Better a mongrel than a dupe," he said scornfully on his way to the door. "Goodbye, Amherst," he said, stepping to the reception room. "Next time, don't call me, I'll call you. Understand?"

"I'll get you, Brim," Amherst hissed through his teeth, "if it's the last thing I do."

"Perhaps," Brim said with a sardonic grin, "—and perhaps not. But keep this in mind if you decide to try, my CIGA colleague: one way or another, it probably *will* be the last thing you do."

Not long after Brim and Moulding ensconced themselves at the VOQ's austere bar, a royal courier strode into the room, checked the microdisplay on his wrist, and made directly for them. "Gentlemen," he said dryly, "His Majesty, Prince Onrad, recommended I try the bar first." In a crimson uniform with gleaming knee-high leather riding boots, the ramrod-straight envoy looked like royal prerogative personified. He delved for a moment in a luxurious, crimson-leather briefcase, then produced two sets of Fleet orders in their characteristic blue and gold cover-sheets, made a little bow, and departed without another word. The distinctive uniform's appearance at the bar had attracted no attention whatsoever. Brim guessed that here in Avalon, royal couriers were well known at every military watering place, especially when Onrad was in residence.

True to Collingswood's promise, the new orders countermanded their previous changes of station. But—surprising to Brim—he and Moulding found themselves temporarily attached to the Dityasburg Institute on the Sodeskayan planet of Zhiv'ot as "researchers."

Moulding grinned. "Where did you *think* we might be sent?" he asked. "I can't imagine Avalon's going to be much of a home to the ISS for a while."

"I guess I hadn't given it much thought," Brim said with a grin. "But the Dityasburg Institute, of all places? Somehow Zhiv'ot didn't make it on my guess list at all."

"I don't suppose it *is* all that much warmer than Gimmas-Haefdon, is it?" Moulding commented with a grin. "Bears seem to prefer nippy climates."

"In any case, you won't have to worry about . . . what kind of darts were those, again?" Brim asked.

"Poison fluggo darts," Moulding prompted, rolling his eyes. "At least in Hobro I was in no danger of freezing to death."

"True," Brim agreed, ordering another round of the VOQ's ancient Logish Meem, "and I'll be surprised if we spend too much time in the G.F.S.S. anyway. Onrad's got more on his mind than winning next year's Mitchell Trophy."

Moulding grinned. "You know," he said, "I've had the same frightening thought. Do you suppose we're learning to second-guess the old boy?"

"We'd better," Brim laughed, "—for our own good. I'd say His Highness will probably be part of our lives for a long time to come."

"I'll drink to *that*," Moulding said, raising his goblet.

They both did.

Brim might have settled in quickly at the galaxy-famous Dityasburg Institute. He was instantly fascinated by its voluminous library facilities and radiation-proofed vacuum laboratories—many large enough to house actual starships with operating Drives. As it was, however, he and Moulding had less than a week to sample the sprawling campus before His Majesty, Prince Onrad, arrived aboard the veteran Imperial battlecruiser *Princess Sherraine*. The big starship thundered high over the campus on final into the nearby Dityasburg port facilities, shaking the massive campus buildings to their very foundations. Throughout the remainder of the day, and far into the night, the handsome old warship was joined by a veritable fleet of military and civilian starships from light cruisers to executive transports, while on campus a special dormitory filled quickly with Onrad's guests and their security forces.

The following morning, an extraordinary ISS meeting convened behind heavily guarded doors in one of the Institute's cold, damp lecture halls. It brought together some of the highest-ranking industrial leaders of the Empire, all sitting on harsh, wooden chairs defaced by years of bored students from all over the galaxy.

Brim, Moulding, and Ursis arrived shortly before Regula Collingswood led Prince Onrad and General Harry Drummond through the wide wooden doors. They were followed by a boisterous contingent of Sherrington engineers from Lys. Not long afterward, P. Dvigat Krasni IV, Senior Director of Krasni-Peych, arrived from Gromcow with Chief Comptroller M. Yekhat Poshline, Grand Duke Anastas Aleyi Borodov, and a number of senior propulsion engineers. Within the metacycle, Veronica Pike lead a second Sherrington contingent into the lecture hall, freshly arrived from the administrative and production shops outside Bromwich. A grinning Anna Romanoff walked beside her.

"Anna!" Brim exclaimed as the petite financier bobbed through the massive wooden doorway in a green corduroy dress and white lace scarf.

Eyes sparkling happily, she unabashedly ran the length of the large room, threw her arms around his neck, and hugged him until he thought he would be smothered. "Oh, Wilf," she whispered, her cheek hinting of delicate perfume. "I've been so terribly worried about you. . . ."

Brim tried ineffectually to dismiss the firm breasts pressing into his chest. "I thought you were consulting at Sherrington's this month," he said. "Why didn't you tell me you were coming?"

"Haven't been here long enough," she explained breathlessly. "We came here straight from the port. And I had only fifteen cycles to pack a bag back at Bromwich—fifteen cycles, Wilf! Not only that: I *had* to come—by Imperial orders, no less." She got an awesome look when she said that. "I've never had an Imperial order in my life! Why, I hardly have anything to wear."

"If I have a say in the matter," Brim whispered, "you won't *need* anything to wear—certainly not while you're with me."

Romanoff giggled under her breath. "Somehow, Wilf Brim," she whispered, "I hoped you'd say something like that. It's been a *while*." Then bussing him quickly on the cheek, she followed Pike down the aisle.

"Come sit with me, old chap," Moulding said with a grin. "I realize I'm not quite so attractive as little Miss Romanoff, but I've been told I have a *most* attractive left earlobe. You can study *that* if by chance you find yourself bored."

Brim punched him in the arm as they made their way toward a seat at the rear of the hall. The time for Helmsmen would come later.

Prince Onrad—sipping from a steaming cup of cvceese' and dressed in a heathery brown herringbone blazer, military jodhpurs, and high riding boots—began the meeting at precisely

Morning:2:0; the last delegates finally took their seats approximately fifteen cycles later.

"As an appropriate prologue," Onrad began, "I offer this ancient Sodeskayan fable many of you will already have heard —about two energetic walkers who got thoroughly lost one day in the maze of country roads outside Gromcow. Close to despair, they at last encountered a local peasant and asked how they could best return to their hotel on the inner ring. After much pondering, the local observed, 'If I were you, sirs, I wouldn't start from here.'"

The big room remained silent for a moment, then everyone broke into wholehearted laughter. It was quickly overpowered by pulsing thunder from what could only be a *very* powerful starship rushing by overhead. Onrad paused until the noise died away, peering around the audience with a pleased look on his face. Presently, he replaced his eyeglasses and consulted his notes. "Our situation today," he continued, "*vis-à-vis* next year's race for the Mitchell Trophy, is much like that of the Bearish walkers—like it or not, we *must* start from where we are, and our friends from the Congress of Intragalactic Accord have made that a difficult place indeed."

In the next metacycle, he proceeded to relate the details of how the League-supported CIGA had managed to plunder every government fund earmarked to support the ISS. Afterward, an aide-de-camp in the full scarlet uniform of a Palace Guardsman delivered an intelligence report—courtesy of the Sodeskayan Ministry of Information—concerning Gantheisser's new GA 262-A3 that the League intended to field in Avalon. Clearly, League engineers had achieved a breakthrough of sorts and developed their own extended-technology Drive to counter K-P's new Wizard. And, according to its specifications, this 262 *could* best Sherrington's M-6.

"If everything goes according to their plans," Onrad summed up toward the end of the Morning watch, "Nergol Triannic's Leaguers will not only permanently retire the Trophy to Tarrott next summer, they will *also* discredit the Empire itself—at a time when the loyalty of allied dominions may prove critical to our very survival." He paused for a moment to take a folded message handed to him by one of the huge Sodeskayan guards, then continued without breaking his verbal stride. "We Imperials have *no choice* but to permanently win possession of our 'hat rack,'" he continued. "Even as we speak, the old Leaguer warlords—Triannic's most powerful supporters—are gearing up to resume their war of aggression at the earliest opportunity. Fluvanna and Beta Jagow are ripe for the taking. And there isn't one of you who doesn't understand that power among dominions is reckoned in terms of allies and raw materials."

While heads nodded agreement throughout the room, Onrad replaced the eyeglasses on his nose and glanced quickly at the message. His eyebrows rose for a moment in surprise before he smiled slightly and returned his gaze to the audience. "You already know what I am coming to," he continued, "but I feel constrained to put it into words nonetheless: the Empire—*your* Empire—badly needs new, faster Sherrington racers for next year's race, with even more powerful Drives from Krasni-Peych. And because we have no more government funds, we must procure those ships at no cost to the ISS! Gentlemen," he said, stepping from behind the lectern, "when I return, the meeting will be yours."

As Onrad strode along the exit aisle, Brim peered around the room in rapt fascination. Veronica Pike was suddenly deep in simultaneous conversations with Valerian and Romanoff. Nearby, Dvigat Krasni and M. Yekhat Poshline were conferring in low growls and shaking their heads. Grave looking Bearish and human engineers broke into smaller groups, motioning and nodding to each other with great excitement. Quickly, Pike seemed to reach some sort of judgment. Nodding to Romanoff, she made her way to a seat behind Krasni, where she began a serious converse with the two Sodeskayans. They deliberated apart until Valerian and a Krasni engineer whom Brim knew only as Rimsey rose from a group of engineers and joined them. With that, the room's noisy discourse suddenly faded to an expectant silence.

At last, Onrad returned to the podium. "Well, my friends," he said, "as I promised, the meeting is now yours."

Krasni and Pike turned to each other; then the Sodeskayan industrialist rose slowly to his feet. He wore a sport coat of deep blue yaggloz wool, a roll-neck sweater, heavy gray trousers, and soft Sodeskayan boots. "Your Highness," he began in perfect unaccented Avalonian, "no one in this room questions the importance of winning next year's Mitchell Trophy Race. We have duly conferred, as you requested, and in the brief time span available have agreed that a modified M-six can be built that will both house and *cool* a new Wizard Drive. Unfortunately, it will not be one of the new reflecting models we have under test, but a Wizard nevertheless—of *significantly* increased power output." He glanced for a moment at Romanoff, then nodded. "The cost of such a racing machine—roughly four hundred fifty-three thousand credits—is acceptable if shared between the two firms," he announced.

A very pleased-looking Onrad was about to reply when the Sodeskayan quickly continued. "There *is* more, however, begging Your Majesty's indulgence," he asserted, only a milliclick before he could be accused of interrupting.

"All right, please continue," Onrad said with a quizzical frown.

"Thank you, Your Majesty," Krasni said. "As I indicated a moment ago, we all understand the need for a new racer, and we can build it, sharing the four hundred fifty-three thousand credits between ourselves. *However*, it is our studied opinion that with Nergol Triannic returned to his throne in Tarrott, we —our Empire—now has an even more pressing need of improved warships. The League's fleet has been growing steadily since the Treaty of Garak, while ours has shrunken to a state of weakness unheard of in recent times." He glanced at Pike for a moment, then returned his gaze to the Prince. "Your Highness, the situation has so deteriorated—at least in the eyes of Sodeskayan intelligence organizations—that it is virtually irreparable in terms of conventional starships. The League presently holds an overall two-to-one advantage in nearly every category."

"I am aware of all of this," Onrad interrupted with an impatient edge in his voice. "That is why it is so critical that we win the Mitchell Trophy. We will soon need all the allies we can muster."

Krasni nodded patiently. "Yes, Your Majesty," he said with a little bow, "but there *is* more. And it is now time for my colleague Veronica Pike to continue in my place . . ." With that, he took his seat while Pike rose warily to face the Prince, whose countenance was rapidly turning from impatience to annoyance.

Wearing a bright crimson jacket over her white blouse and slacks, Pike continued with hardly a pause for breath, "Your Majesty," she began, "what we propose is to develop a completely new warship, powered by full-sized, fully reflecting

Wizard Drives and based on a vastly enlarged M-six. We believe that such a ship would represent such a significant leap in technology that a much smaller number of them might temporarily establish a sort of parity with the League when they decide to renew the war. After their first attacks, our friends in the CIGA will be quickly silenced, and with the new starships holding the line, perhaps we shall be able to rebuild our Fleet before everything is lost." She nodded her head as if she were considering her own words. "If I remember correctly, Your Highness," she added, "it was very thin ranks of overworked ships that allowed us to rebuild our Fleet during the previous conflict."

Onrad nodded. "Your point is well made, Veronica," he said. "We do need a new class of warships. I take it you can't build both?"

"Essentially, that is correct, Your Majesty," Pike replied. "Since the war, times have been difficult for industries specializing in Fleet support. Even giants like Krasni-Peych have been severely pinched. Four hundred fifty-three thousand credits is far more than either of us can spend. Both of us have already been forced to secretly liquidate assets for operating capital." She shook her head as she spoke. "And it doesn't take much of a businessman—or businesswoman," she said, grinning at Anna Romanoff, "—to understand what desperate moves *those* are."

At the podium, Onrad shook his head sadly. "I'm sorry," he said, "I didn't know—about either of you."

As the Prince spoke, Brim heard the rear door open and a number of persons shuffle into back seats, but—fascinated by the unfolding drama before him—he neglected to turn around.

"Companies usually don't make all that much commotion about difficult times," Pike replied. "One attempts to appear solid and confident to prospective customers," she added, glancing at Krasni with a grin.

The Sodeskayan touched the tip of his forefinger to his thumb. "Is true," he chuckled. "But in spite of hard times, Veronica and I can, together, raise that sort of capital. It will fund two racers—or the development of one warship, which can then be replicated under normal Fleet procurement processes. And in procurement matters, Your Highness still exerts as much influence as the CIGAs. It is for you, then, to decide which ship it will be."

"No!" an accented voice suddenly interrupted from the rear of the classroom. "We shall have *both*."

Brim whirled around. He recognized that accent. "Zolton Jaiswal," he gasped at the small, muscular man standing solidly in the middle of the aisle, magnificently dressed in a great ebony cloak and velvet hat.

"You know him?" Moulding asked in a whisper.

"Met him once," Brim whispered, breaking into a surprised grin when he caught sight of Pam Hale standing in the background. Clad in a charcoal dress accented by red tartan scarves, she looked as if she had actually *shed* years since he'd last seen her waiting for Jaiswal to give her a lift in his limousine skimmer. Clearly, it had been an *extended* lift.

"I assume, Mr. Jaiswal, that you personally are prepared to ante up the necessary four hundred fifty-three thousand credits?" Onrad asked.

Jaiswal smiled. "Not alone, Your Majesty," he said. "I shall share the honor with an old friend and business acquaintance: the Carescrian magnate, Baxter Calhoun—at one time, Lieutenant Commander Baxter Calhoun, IF. You will no doubt remember that he served most honorably with Ms. Collingswood aboard I.F.S. *Defiant* during the war."

Brim's head spun. Baxter Calhoun again!

"The *two* of you will put up the credits for new M-sixes then?" Onrad demanded in astonishment.

"That is correct, Your Highness," Jaiswal answered, standing straight as a ramrod. "I transferred my half of the credits by KA'PPA moments after I arrived this afternoon. Calhoun's share was in place yesterday. He is much more wealthy than I."

For the first time that Brim could remember, His Highness, Prince Onrad looked positively stunned. "I-I don't know what to say," he stammered.

Jaiswal made a little bow. "A simple thank you will be most welcome, Your Majesty," he said simply. "In spite of a few erroneous rumors to the contrary, both Calhoun and I deeply believe that any *true* Imperial would rather sell his last shirt than admit the Empire could not afford to defend her reputation." He shook his head angrily. "We are not worms to be trampled under the heels of the CIGAs, but true Imperials with a heart for any battle!"

Spontaneously, the room erupted in applause while Onrad rushed up the aisle to clasp the dark little man's hand.

Brim clapped until his hands ached—and long afterward. In the background, Pam Hale was standing with a proud smile, tears streaming down her cheeks.

Less than half a year following the historic Dityasburg Conference, Brim and Moulding—once more permanently stationed at the sprawling Fleet base in Atalanta—traveled to Lys, where they immediately began "flights" in M-6B simulators. The new ship, itself, appeared little changed from its M-6 origins, being lengthened slightly to accommodate both a more powerful Wizard/2 Drive and the radiating surfaces to cool it. Both Helmsmen found the graceful racing machines were serendipitously even better than their predecessors with a lighter, more accurate feel at the controls. And, of course, they were *much* faster. According to the Sodeskayans' best intelligence, speeds in excess of 100M LightSpeed would be needed to win the race, and Valerian had aimed his sights past this mark. Krasni-Peych engineers accordingly managed to wring 21 percent more thrust from their reworked Wizard of 52007 without appreciably increasing its mass.

For Brim, however, much greater excitement resided in a secured laboratory toward the center of Sherrington's design house where a one-twentieth-size model of I.F.S. *Starfury*, Fleet number K 5054, had been placed under a large crystal case. Although she was the name ship for Onrad's "new class of warships," the Prince had never been consulted on what she would be called. When informed of the company's selection, he laughingly commented that it was "just the sort of bloody silly name they would choose." Regardless, *Starfury* was a handsome warship of extremely clean exterior configuration designed for enhanced high-speed atmospheric maneuvering. She was trihulled in the Valerian tradition: a main fuselage complemented on either side by "pontoon" units mounted slightly below the centerline. Housing three Admiralty A876 gravity generators each, these connected amidships through characteristic Sherrington "trousers." A raked, low-set bridge/deckhouse protruded some third of the way back from her sharply tapered bow, and except for blisters housing her main battery, this constituted the only slipstream disturbance anywhere. Inside, control systems had been exhaustively updated according to radical new discoveries in ergonomic science. This was especially true in the bridge area, where traditional offices of Commanding Officer (Captain) and Principal Helmsman had been *combined* at the same console—a move Brim thoroughly applauded.

At HyperLight velocities, the thirty-four-thousand milston starship would be powered by four Krasni-Peych Wizard-C Reflecting HyperDrive units mounted directly on either side of the main-hull keel, each half again as powerful—in *non*reflecting mode—as the experimental Wizard Drive that had wrecked *Ivan Ivanov*. The potent quartet would draw enormous energy from a network fed by eight massive Krasni-Peych K23971 plasma generators.

She would carry twelve specially designed, rapid-firing 406-mmi disruptors—the same awesome weapons mounted as main armament by Imperial battleships—in six unique turrets that were placed to furnish total global protection but permit maximum concentration of firepower forward in attack mode. An additional pair of K23971 plasma generators in the main power network would provide sufficient energy to salvo the main battery every twenty clicks.

Best of all, *Starfury* was already a'building in the main Sherrington yards at Bromwich on Rhodor. Clearly, the new ship had been subject of much secret, long-range planning by Sherrington, because her keel was laid no more than a month following Dityasburg. And unlike I.F.S. *Defiant*, *Starfury* was under construction in a *private* yard. Because of this, Brim expected that she might be finished earlier than generally anticipated, and experience fewer of the problems associated with name-class ships.

Brim flew the M-6B on her maiden flight and proved without a doubt that the little ship would live up to Valerian's promises—as well as his own expectations. Unfortunately, because of chronic funding problems, she was available for testing a great deal closer to the actual race date than either the M-5 or the M-6. Therefore, the Carescrian found himself spending most of his waking metacycles in space, wringing out the new ship in every possible flight regime.

And because of it, he was taken quite by surprise by the course of political events that began to transpire soon after Triannic returned himself to power.

With autumn largely passed in the boreal hemisphere, most of Woolston was under gloomy cloud cover the morning news began to trickle in. Hampton Water had been swept by driving rain since long before dawn, forcing Brim to delay for a break in the showers before taking his morning jog by the lakefront. Endless ranks of breakers drove relentlessly across the dirty gray water while he sprinted around a million puddles with fresh wind stinging his cheeks. Ahead, where ramps from the laboratory hangars crossed Lakefront Trail, a tall figure wrapped in a tightly fastened Fleet cloak waited in the intersection. It was Moulding—and even with his great collars raised, Brim could see that he clearly had something of tremendous import on his mind. He held up his hand as Brim approached.

"Sorry to interrupt your run, old chap," he called out, "but I've got some rather unpleasant news."

"What's wrong?" Brim demanded with a frown, cold wind chilling his sweaty running togs like some baneful warning. "Has something happened to Anna?"

"No," Moulding began, shaking his head. "Another part of your life this time." He pursed his lips. "It seems that our old friend Triannic has finally begun his dirty work in earnest. We've just gotten word through the media that a fleet of Leaguer warships and transports made landfall this morning—Darkness:3:0, our time, I think—in Rudolpho. The bloody bastards met only token resistance there, as you might imagine, and immediately deposed LaKarn's mother."

"Who'd they set up in her place?" Brim probed with a sick feeling in his stomach, "Not Rogan, I hope!"

"It seems that's the story," Moulding said with a grimace. "He's Grand Duke, now. I decided perhaps you might rather get the story here, rather than inside." He frowned. "I suppose I'm butting too far into your life—perhaps you'll forgive me just this once. I know that you and Anna Romanoff have a pretty wonderful thing going, but at one time . . ."

Brim nodded bitterly. "Poor Margot," he whispered, more to the cold wind than to his friend. "She gave everything to prevent this. And now *she's* become part of the enemy."

"More like a prisoner, in my book," Moulding observed.

Brim snorted grimly. "Yeah," he sighed. "When you get right down to it, I suppose she is." He shook his head and stared down at the gray, windswept puddles.

"Anything I can do?" Moulding inquired.

"No," Brim said, managing a smile. "I think I'll run a little more. But thanks for the offer—and the information. It was damned thoughtful of you."

Moulding nodded and started back toward the laboratory. The rain had started again while they talked, and the temperature seemed to be dropping by the cycle.

Brim didn't return for another two metacycles. But when he did, he'd managed to achieve a sort of peace with himself. And a real appreciation for what Anna Romanoff had done for his life.

Two weeks before the Mitchell, Avalon became one great, frantic party. High summer and fair weather had temporarily banished the pall that had settled over the galaxy after Triannic's nearly bloodless coup in the Torond. Brim especially sensed a turn of spirits—since Anna Romanoff had been in residence more or less steadily for the past month and a half. Sleepily relinquishing a warm, still occupied bed in her town house, he had only just stepped to the curb to wait for an early crew car when he heard footfalls close behind him. Whirling instinctively, he found himself facing two hefty figures dressed all in black and wearing face masks. Two more moved into position at his back, cutting him off from the street—and it was clear from the beginning that none of them was much interested in his health, at least his *good* health.

Only audacity and reflexes saved him. He straightaway kicked his closest assailant in the face, smashing the man sideways into his partner and providing himself a momentary opening through which he leaped onto the damp cobblestones, whirling to face them in a fighting crouch. "All right, you bastards," he growled angrily, "come and get me."

At that very moment, a skimmer turned the corner and started up the street, its headlights burning away the early-dawn gloom. Brim heard the vehicle suddenly accelerate while three of his assailants broke into a run. But one—smaller and much slimmer than the others—only froze for a moment as if considering what to do, then pulled a nasty looking dart gun from inside his jacket. Brim dove headlong for the weapon, just as the man aimed it in his direction, but even a Helmsman's reflexes and superb training couldn't beat a trigger finger. In midleap, he heard the weapon fire and felt a stunning pain explode in his neck at almost the same moment as the skimmer slid to a halt. Moments before his face hit the pavement, a huge figure rushed past him in the direction his assailant had fled. And while his vision faded to blackness, the gruff voice of Borodov roared in his ear, "Wilf! For the love of Voot—*speak to me!*" Then, there was nothing. . . .

He regained consciousness with a splitting headache in the Sodeskayan embassy. He knew immediately where he was; Bear beds were *big*. Besides, Ursis and Borodov were both towering over him in full Sodeskayan regalia while Anna Romanoff sat cross-legged at his side in her bathrobe, holding his hand. Opposite, two more Bears stood with very serious countenances. One wore the uniform of a Sodeskayan Guardsman; the other, dressed in a formal business suit, placed a cool, six-fingered hand on Brim's forehead. "How do you feel, Commander?" he asked in that profound demeanor the Universe reserves solely for physicians.

Brim managed what he hoped was a confident wink to Romanoff, then peered up at the Bear. "I have the grandfather of all headaches, Doctor," he replied with a little grin. "But aside from that, nothing else feels wrong."

"A *bad* headache, you say?"

"I shall need a new head if it doesn't go away," Brim replied.

The Sodeskayan grinned. "Aha," he said, raising his furry eyebrows. "Then we shall make you a *true* Sodeskayan, eh?" He looked over at the three opposite him. "Friends," he said, "would this human not make a handsome Bear?"

"Handsome indeed!" Borodov declared. "But Anna, how would you feel about such a thing? A Bear's head on Wilf Brim?"

"If that will make him well, it will be *fine*," Romanoff declared firmly, drawing her bathrobe closer around her neck.

Brim felt her squeeze his hand. "When can I get up, Doctor?" he asked.

The Bear thought for a moment. "Does this mean you wish to forgo a head transplant?" he asked.

"Well," Brim replied, "I suppose my headache isn't *that* bad. But it is passing kind of you to offer."

"In that case, Commander," the doctor said with a smile, "you can get out of bed whenever you feel comfortable doing so." He pursed his lips and began to pack some small instruments into a metal carrier. "The dart did little physical damage," he continued, "but it contained a *very* powerful poison. Had it not been for the fortuitous arrival of Doctors Borodov and Ursis, you would likely now be in a morgue. My colleague from Gromcow immediately recognized the odor of Gamma-Zondal, venom of Sodeskayan crag wolves. He therefore rushed you here to the embassy where I, as luck would have it, possessed the antidote. A normal Avalonian hospital would never have diagnosed your condition in time—which I believe your assailants realized. You are a fortunate man indeed. But then, your friends here have been busy during your period of unconsciousness. They have some interesting words for you while I rejoin my wife for a tour of your beautiful capital."

"Doctor, how can I ever thank you?" Brim called out as the Sodeskayan physician turned and strode through the door, but Ursis gently placed a hand on his lips.

"When you win the race, Wilf," he said with a wink, "you can buy us all a drink at the victory celebration and we'll be even. Is it . . . how do you say . . . a deal?"

Brim shook his head in defeat—it was hard to argue with Bears, especially in their own embassy. "A *done* deal, Nik," he acquiesced, squeezing Romanoff's hand again. Then abruptly, he frowned. "What else did you learn?" he asked.

Ursis frowned back. "Well, for one thing," he declared, "I don't think they originally intended to use the dart gun. It's my guess that they planned to kill you by hand, so to speak, as if your death occurred accidentally during a *chance* robbery instead of a *planned* murder."

"They were Leaguers, of course," Borodov added, "very probably members of the Agnord Legion, an organization that specializes in assassinations." He adjusted his eyeglasses. "You were *fortunate*, my friend," he said. "Our skimmer arrived at a most serendipitous moment. Such persons do not often fail in their sordid missions."

Brim shuddered. He'd heard of the Agnords. "Did they all get away?" he asked.

Ursis pursed his lips. "Three escaped without a trace," Ursis said. "We saw them run for it before we could even brake the skimmer to a halt. Flight is part of their training, you know. But I chased the one who stayed behind to shoot you. I do not personally believe he was an Agnord. He seemed to be more interested in the killing itself."

"I take it he got away, too," Brim said.

"Not completely," Ursis growled. "The filthy zukeed jumped into the Grand Achtite Canal, where he had a boat waiting. But I personally marked his face with my claws—came off with a bit of skin and blood, too." He chuckled grimly. "He'll be recognizable for a while."

"Perhaps," Borodov observed, "General Drummond and his men will discover who he was for us."

"Perhaps he will, Doctor," Ursis grumbled. "But I plan to keep my own vigil, also. I have a feeling that I shall chance upon that particular Leaguer without any help from General Drummond."

Later that evening, after an enforced period of relaxation, Brim and Anna Romanoff were chauffeured to her town house in a huge Sodeskayan Rill limousine skimmer by three armed Sodeskayan Guardsmen. And from that time on, the street was never without at least two skimmers somewhere close to either side of Romanoff's doorway, occupied with both humans *and* Bears.

CHAPTER 10

The Champion

On a stormy evening two nights before the actual competition began, Prince Onrad hosted his prerace divertissement at Cyndor Castle, the most elegant of the royal family's three "country" palaces in the outskirts of Avalon. Brim once more found himself beside Moulding in the reception line, dressed in a formal uniform the elegance of which would have been far beyond the imagination of an impoverished cadet in the Helmsmen's Academy. Shaking his head in amazement, he considered for the ten millionth time how amazingly fortunate he'd been over the years—by anyone's assessment!

The reception itself took place amid perfumes and spice-laden smoke in Cyndor's famous Court of Portals: a lofty, mirrored hall of vaulted ceilings and crystal doorways that opened onto opulent formal gardens, tonight drenched by the chill, steady rain of a passing front. At each corner of the room, string orchestras drenched in the amber light of ten thousand authentic candles blended their harmonies with tongues from all over the galaxy. Now and then, Brim caught sight of Anna Romanoff—dressed in pale lavender—mingling with prospective clients of every living persuasion: humans, Bears, A'zurnians, even less-common creatures like the gentle, feathered Antiirs or three-eyed Orpians who only recently had achieved starflight.

He smiled to himself. Anna Romanoff. What a dramatic change this witty, talented woman had made in his life: giving endlessly, yet demanding nothing, and appreciative of everything —and anything—he did. She'd even ridden with him during a number of wild Atalantan afternoons on his gravcycle, laughing and hugging him with obvious delight as they sped along the twisting little roadways of the island. For the first time in his existence, he felt complete: *loved*—with no strings attached nor limits set. She was perhaps the most elegant, genteel being he had ever encountered, yet she seemed forever thrilled by the *little* things he managed to do, even in bed, where her capacity for innovation appeared to be totally limitless.

"I say, Wilf," Moulding warned during a short break in the line, "you *have* noticed the LaKarns making their way toward us, haven't you? They say he's had some sort of accident. He certainly looks it."

Brim jerked himself back from his musings and glanced to his left, where he immediately locked glances with Margot's sleepy blue eyes. Beside her, Rogan was a withered vestige of his once-formidable self, a ghost whose black uniform hung loosely on a shockingly atrophied frame. On the moment, he knew absolutely that he had damaged the man's spine during his frenzy of rage—a type of internal motor wound that required years of treatment by the most advanced healing machines. "Thanks, Toby," he said in a subdued voice. "I guess I had been daydreaming."

Moulding laughed innocently; he'd never been told the full story of Brim's "meeting" with the Leaguers. "Right ho, I don't blame you in the slightest!" he chuckled, taking the opportunity to straighten his black bow tie. "Your friend Anna is quite the luscious dish tonight, isn't she? I'm afraid I've been just as guilty of gawking as everyone else."

Brim grinned in spite of himself—how she loved her low-cut gowns! Tonight's was even more revealing than usual. "*Luscious* doesn't half describe her, my friend," he said, only scant clicks before the new Starflight Attache from Villibit-3 arrived in a florescent orange gown with both her husbands in tow. After that, the interminable series of handshakes commenced anew, until . . .

"Grand Duke Rogan LaKarn, Absolute Ruler of the Torond and Grand Duchess Margot Effer'wyck-LaKarn," the protocol officer announced in a clear voice.

Abruptly, Margot's chilly hand was in Brim's, and he bent to kiss the perfectly manicured, tapered fingers he had once known as well as his own. "Margot," he said, gazing into blue eyes that again tonight seemed to bear the sorrows of an entire Universe. She was dressed in another apricot gown that perfectly set off her dazzling strawberry blond hair and flawless complexion. "Are you . . . all right?" he asked instinctively. She nodded and made a little smile. "A trifle cold," she said, indicating a flash of lightning that temporarily lit the hall like disruptor fire, "—and you?" she asked.

Brim felt a momentary twinge of anguish as he glimpsed the ruin of her husband at closer range. "Aside from a little rain," Brim answered pensively, "life has been good, Margot."

The Princess nodded and glanced meaningfully out onto the floor where Romanoff was standing with Ursis, staring back with an impassive countenance. "I can see it has, Wilf," she said quietly, "That woman loves you *fiercely*." She shook her head sadly. "When I finally admitted to myself that I must eventually lose, I prayed it might be to someone like her." A tear welled the corner of her eye; she blinked it back. "She hates me—needlessly, of course. I have . . . other . . . loves now. But once . . ." She suddenly turned her face as another flash of lightning lit the hall.

"Enough," the palsied LaKarn grunted beside her. "I can no longer tolerate the sight of this Carescrian assassin. Will you move on, whore, or do you plan to spread your legs for him here in the reception line?" With a clawlike hand, he clumsily slipped Margot's bodice from her right breast. "Here," he crowed, "I shall even help, I've always wanted to watch you two at it."

Brim had never seen her nipple shriveled and colorless as it was now. He heard himself gasp in dismay.

Margot shut her eyes and replaced the bodice with a deft movement of her hand while her face turned a sickly white and her whole carriage appeared to droop. She stood that way for a long moment, blinking back tears of utter humiliation. Then, with a sigh of resignation, she straightened her shoulders and assumed a more customary countenance. "Goodbye, Wilf," she said presently through tight, bloodless lips, "I wish both you and Anna the best of the Universe." Then, without another word, she turned to offer her hand to Moulding while LaKarn doddered along at her side.

During those brief moments, Brim came to realize he had been living under a delusion. He had definitely *not* left behind all emotion for Margot Effer'wyck; the wave of anguish that swept his psyche as he stared helplessly at her lovely back disabused him of that forever. Years of loneliness had erased most of the erotic passion he once felt for the magnificent Princess, but nothing had dimmed his concern. He desperately wanted to help in some way—*any* way—but trapped in the reception line as he was, he could do nothing! Immediately, a new couple replaced the LaKarns, gushing imbecilically about "space racers" and what it felt to be "out there among the stars." In his utter shock, he heard no more than ten words they babbled. If he reacted correctly to them, and to at least the next ten dignitaries that followed, it was clearly done on "autohelm," for he remembered no more of the evening until the royal couple departed—an event that transpired no more than a few cycles after they completed the reception line. At the door, they were surrounded by a whole squad of Controllers from the League—not native Grenzen from the Torond. Clearly, Triannic was keeping his puppet rulers under close supervision, indeed.

By the time the stream of newcomers at last began to wane, Brim had once again relaxed sufficiently to peer around the room and frown. "We've met just about all the important Leaguers who came for the race," he said to Moulding, "but I haven't seen hide nor hair of Valentin. Is he here, do you suppose?"

Moulding rubbed his chin for a moment. "I say," he started. "I *know* I've caught a glimpse of him tonight—he couldn't possibly miss an event like this without drawing a bloody lot of attention to himself. But you're certainly right. He hasn't come *near* the line." He frowned. "I wonder . . ."

"So do I," Brim said grimly, still scanning the guests.

"*There*," Moulding said, nodding his head, "—in that group of Controllers near the turquoise alcove. Isn't that our bloody friend leaning against the door?"

Brim turned slowly, trying not to appear obvious. "I don't know," he said. "It's pretty dim there in the alcove. But . . ." Lightning flared, momentarily illuminating the slim figure of Kirsh Valentin against the streaming door. "Yes. That's him." He narrowed his eyes. "Perhaps I ought to extend some sort of *personal* greetings, now that our 'special duty' on the reception line seems to be at an end."

"Do you think that's wise?" Moulding inquired with a worried look on his face. "It would look rather bad if you started something, you know. Could even give them the race by default—especially if you did in their Principal Helmsman."

Brim nodded sullenly. "Yeah," he said, "I know. But the bastards wouldn't have much of a leg to stand on themselves if Valentin looks like I think he does." He pursed his lips. "Perhaps I'll go pay my respects."

"Right ho," Moulding said, starting the other way. "And I shall go collect Ursis and Borodov—just in case his Leaguer companions decide to be uncooperative."

Brim dodged his way across the crowded room in rapid order; however, Valentin's vigilant "friends" had closed ranks before he was even halfway there. "Excuse me, gentlemen," the Carescrian said, attempting to push his way between two of the high-booted toughs in dress blacks, "but I'd like to speak to my friend Kirsh there."

It was like trying to move a solid rock wall. Nothing budged at all, and the faces of the Controllers remained impassive, as if they understood no Avalonian.

Brim repeated the words in Vertrucht, securing an identical reaction for his linguistic pains: nothing. He was about to apply a sudden elbow to one of the Leaguer's kidneys when, abruptly, a squadron of twelve large Imperial "guests" in civilian evening clothes nonchalantly drifted by to encircle Valentin's Leaguer convoy—and there was no mistaking *their* intent.

Shortly thereafter, Drummond appeared at Brim's side, dressed in magnificent soup-and-fish that must have cost the price of a small starship. He calmly eyed one of the Leaguers, then placed his hands on his hips. "Move aside, whoreson filth," he demanded quietly in lowest gutter Vertrucht, "—I defecate on they father's slopsyard grave."

Blind rage blazed suddenly in the proud Leaguer's eyes. Reflexively, he reached for the little General only a moment before both his forearms were broken by short, deadly chops from Imperials who had moved in silently on either side. It was over so quickly no one behind them on the reception floor could have possibly seen, but Brim distinctly heard bones crack—and it was clear that the remainder of Valentin's guards had too. The wounded Leaguer's face turned a pasty gray and beads of sweat broke out on his forehead as the pain began to register. Instantly, he was supported by his burly Imperial assailants, who slowly turned him, 'round so his startled colleagues could share the view.

"All right, you filth," Drummond whispered, "every mother's son of you saw this bastard attack me. Now clear out quietly and take him with you before I clap everyone in the brig. Understand?"

They understood.

"Except Valentin," he added. "We'll send him around later."

Wide-eyed with fear, the Leaguers quietly made for the door, each escorted by a massive human and followed by a Bear. Only cycles later, a frightened-looking Valentin stood alone within the remaining coterie of Imperials, his cheek stubbornly turned toward the door. Outside in the formal gardens, the storm raged at its height, with rain pounding at the glass and trees bent nearly double. This close to the door, the muffled rumble of thunder could be heard clearly above the noise of the party.

"Wilf, Nik," Drummond called quietly. "I think you two should have the honor of inspecting this *innocent* Leaguer's face."

Brim stepped beside his old antagonist. "Turn around, Kirsh," he ordered coldly. "You know what I'm looking for. If you had nothing to do with my ordeal the other morning, then you go home free—with my apologies. Otherwise . . ."

"O-otherwise . . . what?" Valentin demanded, the whites of his eyes beginning to show again.

"Turn around," Brim repeated after a rumble of thunder that sounded like a distant barrage of disruptors. "We'll talk *after* I see the opposite side of your face."

Valentine cleared his throat nervously. "I don't have to," he sniffled. "If you so much as touch me, I shall complain to the Racing Committee that you . . ."

"Turn, Valentin," Brim persisted. "Nobody's threatening you—yet."

"B-bastard Carescrian," Valentin swore, his lips drawn tight against clenched teeth.

"Turn!" Brim's command was punctuated by a close-in lightning strike followed by its sharp report.

Valentin seemed to shrink into his black uniform, then—with a scowl of purest hate—he slowly revealed the opposite side of his face. Four welts of new, pink flesh extended well into his hairline from his jaw. The leftmost ran through an extensively remade ear.

Brim nodded. "Well, *hab'thall*," he said. "I'll bet *that* hurt, didn't it?"

Valentin only scowled defiantly. "I don't know what you're talking about," he snapped over windblown rain that drummed in sheets against the heavy crystal.

"Oh, I think you know." Brim snarled. "Nik, maybe you ought to see if these welts match your claws."

Ursis's eyes narrowed. "Yes," he agreed in a deep, angry voice," perhaps I shall even reopen them to eliminate any possibility of mistakes." He smiled grimly, his fang gems gleaming in the candlelight. "Hearing you bleat again, Leaguer, would give me great pleasure."

"Flaring a hole in your stinking hide would give *me* great pleasure," Valentin hissed, drawing a sleek blaster from inside his tunic. Brim recognized it as one of the new Maranellos, ultrapowerful, rechargeable hand blasters that could burn holes in hullmetal plate. They were manufactured in Tarrott—and this one was equipped with a slender, crystalline silencer.

Ursis only laughed. "You wouldn't dare use that here, Valentin," he scoffed. "It may be silenced, but its flash would open all sorts of inquiries that neither you nor your filthy League can afford."

Valentin grimaced and slid the little blaster back into his tunic with a sullen look in his eyes.

"Hand that thing over before someone gets hurt, Valentin," Drummond growled. "Otherwise . . ."

Before he could finish his sentence, the Controller whirled and grabbed the handles of the crystal door. Unhappily—for him—his captors were much faster, blocking the heavy panel with their feet. But as the two Imperials instinctively jumped to prevent his escape, they also provided a moment's opening to the *next* exit. Using the door itself as a springboard, Valentin catapulted himself past the two surprised guards and into the noisy crowd, with Brim, Ursis, and the rest of his would-be captors in hot pursuit—everyone moving at no more than a brisk walk, as if nothing out of the ordinary were taking place.

Valentine reached the ornate glass portal only moments before Brim, but the time was sufficient for his purposes. He was through the doorway and onto the rainswept balcony in plenty of time to scramble down an ornate column, then splash into the shadows of the formal gardens beyond with Brim and Drummond close behind.

"Stop, Valentin!" Brim shouted, nearly blinded by the teeming sheets of rain.

Halfway across the garden, the Leaguer slowed to fire a shot over his shoulder. It kicked up a welter of spray and debris through the puddles. Twice again, Valentin stopped to fire, missing both times. But Brim felt the second bolt of cold energy frost his face as he dove for cover.

After he fired his third shot, Valentin veered across a clear space, heading past a sort of maintenance shack, momentarily visible in flashes of lightning behind a stand of windbent crest oaks.

At the same moment, however, Drummond entered the picture, laying down bursts from a rapid-firing blast pike in the dirt around the fleeing Leaguer. "Halt, you bastard!" he yelled as he splashed along the path at full speed.

Whatever other plans the Leaguer might have had at that juncture, he changed them when the ground beneath him erupted in an absolute welter of sharp explosions. Immediately, he jinked left, zigzagged through the whirling debris, and dove headfirst through the open door of the shack.

Running hard behind, Brim straightaway saw a blaster flash three times from the shack's window. He dove to the ground behind a flower display, blood trickling from his cheek where a flying crockery chip had hit.

"Amazing what a few bursts from the old Trenning here can do," Drummond laughed, splashing down beside Brim and patting a great blast pike he held in his hands.

"Sure changed old Valentin's mind about running any farther," Brim answered over a deafening burst of thunder. "Now, all we've got to do is get him out of there." He raised himself carefully and peered over the flower bed. "Valentin!" he shouted above the tumult of the storm, watching the dark figures of security agents move in to surround the shed. "You're trapped, and you xaxtdamned well know it. Throw that blaster out *now* and you'll need face only me."

For long moments, he could only hear the pounding of the rain. "Well, Valentin?" he demanded

Shots from the hut ripped through the teeming flower bed. At almost the same instant, another heavy blast pike began to whump out return fire from somewhere back along the path.

"Cut that firing!" Drummond shouted.

The pike stopped abruptly.

"I'm going in after him," Brim said.

"You sure you want to take that no-good hab'thall on yourself, Wilf?" Drummond asked.

The Carescrian felt himself smile. "I've been sure for *years*, General," he answered. Peering through a space in the flower garden, he studied Valentin's position. Since the Leaguer knew he had little hope of escape, the *real* trick would be taking him alive. Controllers often took their own lives when facing certain capture or humiliation. Brim had seen a lot of this during the war. "I'll need some covering fire around the window," he said.

Just then, another volley of shots spewed from the shed, toppling a statue and blasting a bench into a billion splinters.

"Wonder if you oughtn't wait a little while," Drummond suggested above the downpour. "That Maranello's *got* to be running low on energy soon."

"Not soon enough for me." Brim responded, ducking behind the log as still another volley sent a spray of mud and debris into the air. Suddenly, a shrill tone sounded from the shattered window.

Drummond raised an eyebrow. "Was that what I think it was?" he asked with a grin.

Brim chuckled. "Sure sounded like a power warning to me," he answered.

"If it is," Drummond said, staring through the rain at the stone shed, "your friend Valentin has about five shots left. With all their power, Maranellos won't take cartridges—they've got to be recharged."

Brim nodded agreement. "Time to get him, then," he said, peering through the downpour.

"Now wait a moment, young fella," Drummond cautioned. "He *does* have at least five shots left, you know."

"I think I can handle those," Brim said as a flash of lightning streaked across the sky. "Just give me enough covering fire so I can make it to the door." His words were punctuated by a pealing roll of thunder.

Drummond considered this for a moment, then shrugged in concession. "What about taking one of these blast pikes with you, then," he whispered. "Might come in handy until brother Valentin gets rid of those last five shots."

Brim grinned. "You do have a point, there, General," he said as the rain picked up.

"Sondstrom," Drummond barked through the coursing sheets of rain. "Let's have that extra pike."

"Aye, General," the commando called from a stand of trees. Moments later, she darted across the open path like a wraith— with two Trennings, one of which she silently handed to Brim.

He took the big weapon, switched it to SELF-TEST, and watched for the green READY indication. It lighted almost instantly.

"You're sure you want to go through with this?" Drummond asked.

"I'm sure, General," Brim said, gripping the big weapon at either end. "And I'm also ready," he added, "when you are, sir."

"High covering fire on the window at my signal," Drummond whispered to Sondstrom. "Pass it on and raise your hand."

"Aye, General," the commando said, and crawled to the soldier next to her. Within moments, nine hands were aloft in the driving rain.

"Good luck, Brim," Drummond said.

"Thanks, General," Brim said. "I'll probably need all I can get."

Drummond waved his hand twice and instantly the air was filled with a stunning barrage from ten powerful blast pikes.

Brim fairly exploded across the flower bed, bending low under the blinding hail of covering shots and sprinting toward the shack. Outside the door, he crouched for a moment to catch his breath; then, tensing, he smashed the flimsy door latch assembly with the butt of the Trenning and stepped back while two more shots burst through the door in a cloud of wood splinters. "All right, Valentin," Brim called out, "that's enough. Toss that blaster where I can see it and come out with your hands up—otherwise, I'm coming in for you."

Silence.

Brim nodded his head. He really hadn't expected Valentin to cooperate. Standing the Trenning against the streaming wall, he slipped out of his coat and draped it over the barrel. Then, holding the big weapon by its butt, he poked the decoy into the middle of the doorway.

Two more shots howled out of the dark shed; the second— though noticeably weaker—shredding his coat into flying shards. A moment later, the shrill sound of an alarm came from the hut. Valentin's blaster was finally exhausted.

"That's it, Valentin," Brim growled, "I'm coming in."

After a long silence, he stepped into the doorway and tossed the blast pike into the grass behind him. "All right, you bastard," he growled, "we're even now. Come out here and fight like a man."

A sudden flash of lightning illuminated the interior of the shed, revealing Valentin crouched in a corner with a savage look in his eyes, teeth bared as if he were a cornered animal. Half-blinded by the lightning, Brim discovered his own mistake a moment later when the Leaguer erupted from the doorway like a shot, swinging his inert blaster as if it were a club. While a fearful peal of thunder crashed above them, Brim dodged under the attack, then grabbed Valentin's sleeve and yanked down hard, bending the Leaguer over double and smashing him in the face with his knee.

The blaster went flying into the darkness as Valentin staggered backward into the shack again, with Brim following carefully in his footsteps. But the Leaguer was far from stopped. Backing all the way to the far wall, he pushed off from the rough stones and before Brim could prepare a defense, leaped forward and landed a forward thrust-kick in Brim's groin.

Brim saw the blow coming and chopped downward on Valentin's shin with the outer edge of his right forearm, but could only fractionally limit the blow. The Leaguer's boot slammed into his testicles with terrific force.

In agony, Brim folded at the waist at the same time a brutal punch exploded in his face. He staggered back, trying to catch his breath while multicolored novas exploded in his eyes. Instinctively, he dropped to a crouch; his right knee sagged to the ground in torment. Then, gathering himself in a frantic burst of energy, he stopped another punch by grabbing Valentin's wrist and pushing it over his head, then landing a short but powerful punch, just below the ribs.

The surprised Leaguer bellowed something in Vertrucht, jumped back with a look of agonized disbelief, then yanked his arm free and sprang forward, aiming a double-hand chop against Brim's sides that threatened to shatter his ribs.

Brim met the savage attack by instinct alone, stepping forward and driving both arms downward inside Valentin's, effectively cutting short the attack before viciously landing his own double punch to both sides of Valentin's lower ribs.

Coughing painfully, Valentin pivoted and immediately counterattacked with a murderous roundhouse punch to Brim's left temple that launched him backward through the door and onto the ground in an explosion of agony and smothering rain.

Instantly, Valentin was astride Brim's chest. Powerful hands slipped deep down the sides of his shirt collar, then sharp, bony edges of wrists and forearms closed relentlessly against Brim's carotid arteries, applying deadly, agonizing pressure. "Now . . . you . . . Imperial . . . bastard," he hissed, his voice barely audible with effort, ". . . you . . . will . . . *die*."

Close to insensibility, Brim battled for consciousness. Valentin's face glared malevolently at him while his fingers tightened around Brim's throat. As he gasped for breath, the Leaguer smiled. Brim knew he must break the lock in the next few moments or he would be killed. Desperately, he arched his body and shoved Valentin's hips away from his chest. Growling and panting like an animal, Valentin fought desperately to maintain his position, clawing the Carescrian's flesh, but Brim was better conditioned, and the choke hold weakened significantly. When Brim could shove no farther, he rolled suddenly to the left, grabbed the man's right cuff, and hauled hard across his body, breaking the death lock and rolling the surprised Leaguer off him completely. Before Valentin could recover, Brim grabbed his throat, shoved him backward to the ground, and stomped on his face.

With blood streaming from his nose, Valentin groaned in agony and rolled to his stomach. Slowly, he began to push himself erect, but Brim staggered in from the side, raised his knee for leverage, and delivered a tremendous upward kick to the midsection. His blow lifted the Leaguer more than an iral off the floor before he collapsed in a puddle of his own vomit and lay still, moaning in a low voice.

Moments later, both Drummond and Ursis arrived at the door, both armed with blast pikes. "Wilf," they cried in unison, "are you all right?"

Brim stood over the motionless Valentin, nearly sick to the stomach with pain himself. "Except for a possibly ruined love life, I'm all right," he growled after a long rumble of thunder, "—and unfortunately, so is this Leaguer zukeed."

Valentin retched as he writhed on the stones.

"On your feet, coward," Brim ordered, rubbing his throat. "You're not half so hurt as you ought to be. You'll fly tomorrow—which is a lot better than what you and your bully boys had in store for me the other day."

Valentin only groaned.

"We'll get him back to his people," Drummond said, motioning quietly to men standing outside in the teeming rain. Then he made a little smile. "I think perhaps this evening's activities will send off a pretty significant message for Triannic, too—that CIGAs aren't the only Imperials they'll have to deal with." He shrugged. "Who knows, it might just have bought the whole Empire a little breathing room."

"At the price of two formal uniforms," Ursis observed. "Just look at the two of you!"

Drummond winced, glancing at himself in dismay, then at Brim. "We've done a job, all right," he said, shaking his head.

Brim agreed bleakly. Both knees were out of his trousers, and his coat had been blasted to ribbons. "Yeah," he agreed. "It's going to be tough going back into the reception like this."

Drummond chuckled. "The party *is* getting a tad out of hand, isn't it?"

"Nothing worse than a boring party," Ursis observed, standing back while two of Drummond's commandos half carried, half walked the bent and whimpering Valentin outside. "Wilf," the Bear added with mock sagacity, "you'd better take permanent possession of that trophy tomorrow; otherwise, someone's liable to be injured at these soirees."

Brim chuckled grimly. "I'll do my damndest, Nik," he promised, gladly stepping into the storm again. The odor of vomit had become a palpable entity inside. Suddenly he spied two figures walking rapidly toward him through the driving rain—and the short one was limping perceptibly. "Anna!" he shouted, just as their way was abruptly blocked by three burly commandos materializing out of the shadows.

"Wilf!" Romanoff shouted over the noise of the storm. "Is that you? Are you all right?"

Suddenly, one of the commandos yelped and grabbed his shin. Romanoff dodged past him in an instant, limping along at a surprising clip, with two of the soldiers in hot pursuit.

Brim took off toward her like a shot, shouting. "Wait! She's all right! *Don't!*" He grabbed the little businesswoman by the waist and whirled around to shield her a scant instant before the two angry men slammed into his back with the force of a runaway starship. Down they all went in a bruising, gasping tangle of wet arms and legs, Brim supporting the weight of both men on his elbows and knees in a desperate attempt to keep the three of them from crushing Romanoff. "Anna," he whispered to a panting tangle of wet hair beside his cheek, "are you hurt?"

After a moment of silence, he heard a giggle in his ear. "I'm fine, Wilf," she said breathlessly. "But isn't three at a time sort of kinky for you—especially out here in the palace garden?"

"I say!" Moulding bellowed from somewhere overhead, "you two—off them, now. That's the fellows. Carefully, now..."

His voice was joined by that of Drummond. "At ease, men! Everything's all right!"

Abruptly, the load on Brim's back lifted, and far gentler hands began to pull at him. He shook them off while he knelt and eased Romanoff to her feet. "You sure you're not hurt?" he asked.

She nodded, futilely straightening the soaked and clinging remains of her dress, that now revealed a lot more than they concealed. "It was *you* I worried about," she said. "I got out on the balcony just in time to watch you chase Valentin into the garden—and when I saw the blaster flashes, I ran for Toby." She shook her head. "Rough party you brought me to tonight, Wilf Brim. Just look at your new uniform—and my *dress!*"

Brim grunted; her dusky nipples showed through the wet fabric as if she had nothing on. "Probably I ought to take you home before things *really* get nasty," he urged. "What do you say we call it a night?"

Romanoff melted into the arm he placed gently around her

shoulder. "I'd like that," she said quietly. Then she shook her head. "Mother always warned me to stay away from starsailors —and I wouldn't listen."

"Let's hear it for disobedience," Brim whispered, lifting her to his arms and starting along the path toward her skimmer. Tomorrow promised to be a *long* day.

Brim and Moulding were aloft by late morning and spent most of the day testing their M-6B's for all they were worth. As customary, the race course was triangular in shape, defined by three solitary, type-G stars: Delta-Gahnn, Onita, and Laneer, none with satellites. Course entry was close by Delta-Gahnn, nearest of the three to Avalon at 430 light-years' distance. From there, a long straightaway of 269.2 light-years stretched to Onita, where a sharp turn led to the shortest leg of 149.8 light-years. Following this, a mild angle around Laneer and a second long straightaway of 243.20 light-years returned the course to its entry point.

Starliners from every known dominion traced along the course at HyperSpeed, carrying spectators who paid considerable sums for a chance to see the racers whiz past at close range. But even two hundred-odd spectator ships, with thirty-one military patrol vessels, counted for little more than dust motes when considered within the context of the actual distances involved.

Approaching his first circuit with the Wizard rumbling comfortably at his back, Brim felt the narrow red damper beam warm his hand, then gently urged it farther toward OPEN, keeping the hot spot centered in his palm. Setting a course around Delta-Gahnn at high speed, he edged into the race lane and headed out over the first long leg for distant Onita—only a pinpoint in the forward Hyperscreens but growing rapidly as he picked up speed. Scant cycles later, he took that angle as closely as possible (with the crystal temperature nearing redline), then practically bunted the short leg to Laneer and entered the second long straightaway back to Delta-Gahnn and the race-circuit entrance. IMPERIAL M-SIX B ALPHA TO HYPERDROME, he KA'PPAed. REQUEST TIMING, THIS RUN.

His display directly manifested a message: HYPERDROME TO IMPERIAL M-SIX B ALPHA, TIMING IS AFFIRMATIVE.

M-SIX B ALPHA, Brim KA'PPAed. While he bent the little

ship around the distant emerald star, a small display began to blink above the left Hyperscreen—first orange as he tweaked the damper toward OPEN again, then green as he passed through the timing beam and started along the circuit.

Charging into an approach tangent at about a quarter million c'lenyts distance, he trailed the gravity brakes a little, juggled the damper closed for the interval of a heartbeat, then rolled a half-turn and hit the steering engine hard to port. Instantly, the tail hung out, twitching while he tested gravity flow into the star. When he sensed the ship was precisely aligned, he willed the damper open and rode around the curve, tensing himself for the one perfect instant when he was lined up on the next lap, while the artificial cabin gravity struggled to shield him from colossal centrifugal forces that could mash his frail body to a reddish blob in his recliner. Scanning between his instruments and the Hyperscreens, he tensed, searching for his first glimpse of Laneer moving out from occlusion behind the small blue orb that was Onita. ... Now! He eased the damper forward and smoothly unwound the steering, feeling the M-6B spring forward into the straightaway as if it were something alive. Behind him, the new Wizard/2 thundered deafeningly through a bulkhead, its prodigious growl nearly unbearable even in his battle suit.

After this, he simply continued in a flattened curve some two hundred thousand c'lenyts out from snowy white Laneer, then blasted off down the second straightaway while the crystal-head temperature again worked its way toward redline. Cycles later, with Delta-Gahnn a large emerald ball some 450,000 c'lenyts off to port, he skidded the M-6B into another extravagant high-speed curve until the green timing light returned to yellow and the average velocity meter read—his eyes widened with surprise—average speed, 98.21M LightSpeed: a new galactic record!

When he finally hauled back on the damper beam, the Wizard/2 spun down with a sound that approached a sigh of relief. Brim nodded to himself. His Leaguer competition would need one *xaxt* of a ship to win this year! Steering a gentle curve back to Avalon, he wondered if the Gantheisser engineers had been able to come up with it.

Less than a metacycle later, as he taxied in to the shed area, he lifted the visor of his helmet and slid open the windward Hyperscreen. Cool spray and fragrant lake air instantly filled the bridge, refreshing his face and soothing the gas-dried membranes of his eyes and nose. A storm front during the afternoon appeared to have rejuvenated the whole Universe. All the great bluffs around Avalon's ancient HyperDrome were now awash in delicate mauves and pinks while an early-evening sky glowed in palest peach, dabbed here and there by scudding lavender remnants of the storm. Across the choppy water, a sizable crowd had gathered near the ramp, jumping and waving as he approached. Clearly, news concerning his last circuit had spread rapidly through the racing community. He could hear cheering when he turned upwind and headed for the ramp. In spite of himself, he grinned with genuine exhilaration. He had a galactic speed record in his pocket, and even though it wasn't official, he had an undeniable sense of confidence that he, along with Valerian's magnificent M-6B, could handle anything the Leaguers might field.

Brim steered his sleek little starship up the seaweed-encrusted ramp, then drew to a hovering stop over on Sherrington's portable gravity pad as technicians wearing huge reflective mittens raced to secure the optical moorings. He fought back waves of nausea as he switched to planetary gravity, then powered off a final set of systems and opened the hatch, climbing out onto the ship's light blue hullmetal amid wild cheering and whistles. Moments later, two technicians carefully placed a boarding ladder near his feet, and he climbed down to what seemed like a thousand hands, all either waiting to be shaken or to clap him on the back. Significantly, no one seemed the least interested in the large bruises under both eyes; race drivers had a *rough* reputation. It was a long time before he could work his way through the crowd of well wishers to where Romanoff stood in white sweater and slacks atop the seawall, her lovely face wearing the same mysterious smile she'd had for him the first night they'd made love. Then he found himself smothered in warm, wet kisses that were—in their own way—better than any speed record he could imagine.

Later, at supper in the shed refectory, Brim and Romanoff had just taken their seats with Nik Ursis, Mark Valerian, and Praznik Krasni, when K-P's senior propulsion fellow, Alexyi

Ivanovich Pogreb, strode into the dining room wearing scorched K-P coveralls and a deep Bearish frown. Looking neither right nor left, he marched directly to the Senior Director. "Praznik Dvigat," he began in a concerned voice. "I believe ve have serious troubles. I thought it vould be best if I notified everyone at same time."

Dressed in a loose Sodeskayan tunic with brass buttons, baggy trousers, and soft boots, Krasni stood and matched Dvigat's frown. "The new Wizard, Alexyi Ivanovich?" he asked. "We have troubles with the Wizard Two?"

"Is true, Praznik Dvigat," Pogreb asserted, broodingly raising his eyes to the heavens. "I myself inspected plasma tubes on Commander Brim's M-6B."

"And you found?" Krasni prompted.

"Crystal particles, vould you believe?" the Bear reported. "Lining both tubes, Praznik Dvigat. Ve still have not overcome our heating problems, Devil take it." He turned to Brim. "No offense, Commander," he said, "but during last high-speed run, the crystals actually began to disintegrate, depositing—rather *sublimating* by reverse feedback—collections of atoms from the Drive crystals themselves. The process may well have been slowly going on for days."

Krasni remained silent for a moment, then sipped his meem and looked contemplatively into the goblet. "I assume, Alexyi Ivanovich," he said, "that Commander Brim's Drive is ruined."

Pogreb nodded. "Same for Commander Mouldink's. Both have sustained much crystal erosions at tube junction and will have to be changed out before either ship is safe to fly."

Valerian shut his eyes and squeezed the bridge of his nose. "That practically means taking both ships apart," he said flatly.

"Would that circumstances were that easy," Krasni groaned. "Unfortunately, those are the only Wizard Two crystals in existence. We *can't* change them out."

"What?" Ursis yelled. "You only grew two of them?"

"No, Nikolai Yanuarievich," Krasni explained. "We actually grew five of them when we started the program. Two were destroyed in system testing at the Gromcow labs, two were installed in the M-6B's, and . . ."

"And the spare?" Valerian interrupted tensely.

Krasni shook his head. "The spare, friend Valerian, was accidentally destroyed as it was moved in the shed yesterday. A force line parted on the portable lift, and before the driver could recover, it had been cracked in half."

Brim slumped in his seat. "Just thraggling wonderful," he groaned. "Now what?"

"Unless you have some other ideas." Krasni replied, "I'm afraid we're simply out of the race."

"Not necessarily, Praznik Dvigat," Pogreb said. "Perhaps there are more crystals for the M-6B's than we think."

"If there are, I know nothing about them," Krasni snapped with annoyance.

"Is true we have no Wizard Two crystals, sir," Pogreb said. "But is *also* a fact that three Wizard-C *prototype* crystals are in the propulsion laboratory on nearby Melia, the science planet —complete with control systems. They were delivered on the same ship that brought the M-6B's from Lys."

"Wizard-C's, Pogreb?" Krasni demanded. "Those are *re-flecting* Drives, remember?"

"Aye, sir," Pogreb agreed, "—and almost a perfect fit for an M-6B, even with the reflector in place. A little machining here and there—most at the starboard mounting flange, and . . ."

"*Pogreb!*" Krasni interrupted, "those prototypes have only been run a few times. What makes you think that they'd stand up in a race?"

"Begging the General Manager's pardon." Pogreb replied, "but they have only been run a few times in *reflecting* mode. In standard mode, each has run full-out for nearly three metacycles—and with a power output within two percent of the Wizard Two." He grinned. "Not only that, Praznik Dvigat," Pogreb added, "—they should be somewhat easier to cool!"

Krasni turned to Brim. "Would you be willing to fly something like that?" he asked.

Brim glanced over at Romanoff. "I've got to do it," he whispered.

"I know that, Wilf," she replied.

"I'm game, Dr. Krasni," Brim said presently. "Do you think you can have the switch done in time?"

Krasni paused, looking off into some other dimension for a moment. Then he passed the question on to Pogreb. "Can we?" he asked.

"Is already starting the process, Praznik Dvigat," Pogreb

said, nodding his head. "Crystals should arrive from Melia within a metacycle."

"I rather imagined that would be the case, Alexyi Ivanovich," Krasni said with a little smile.

"Ah, but is badly needink help from you, Mark Valerian," Pogreb added.

"You've got it," Valerian said, rising from the table and struggling into his tweed coat.

Brim pushed his chair back with intentions of following, but Valerian and Pogreb were already on their way. "Finish your supper, Wilf," Valerian called over his shoulder. "You've been at it all afternoon. I'll call as soon as there's something you can do."

Brim sank back in his chair. "I think it's going to be a long night," he mused, bleakly, dallying with the contents of his plate.

"Not for you, Wilf Ansor," Ursis asserted.

"How come?" Brim demanded with a raised eyebrow.

"*Because*, my furless friend," the Bear replied, "if they *do* fix the Wizard in time for the race, it is your job to *fly*—and be sufficiently rested to fly *well*. If, on the other hand, the Wizard is inoperable, then your help won't matter anyway." He winked at Romanoff. "Additionally," he said with a twinkle in his eye, "your fellow humans all appear to enjoy the sight of Miss Romanoff. Perhaps the productivity of the Sherrington team will be higher without such a beautiful female to stare at, eh?"

Romanoff blushed, but it was clear she was delighted by the compliment. Generally, unless one was being pursued actively by an angry Bear (almost always a fatal situation) it was difficult to be provoked by one.

After supper, the three hurried down to the Imperial shed area where every available technician and engineer had been called out to work on the M-6B's. In the repair yard outside, an orderly contingent of Bears had so far unpacked two gleaming Drive crystals with strange silver housings from wooden crates marked "KPOCHbl-II3TY." They were now connecting banks of test equipment to one of them through what looked like a c'lenyt of glowing cables. Inside the shed itself, Sherrington engineers and technicians were at work on Brim's machine, busily removing sections of the racer's skin; others had already lifted the massive crystal cover from its Drive chamber.

"How's it look?" Brim asked when Valerian had come to rest for a moment nearby.

The designer pursed his lips and frowned. "I think it's going to be close, Wilf," he admitted. "But then, we Sherrington people won't be the ones who actually pull off the necessary miracle—this is mostly a Krasni-Peych show. All I can do is help when I'm needed and keep out of the way when I'm not." He frowned for a moment, looking over Brim's shoulder. "I say, there, Jaech," he yelled at a young engineer standing atop the Drive compartment with a glowing coil over his shoulder, "let me help you with that assembly!" Then he grinned again at Brim. "Come back in the morning, Wilf," he said as he started across the floor. "We'll know a lot more at that time." Before he started up the ladder, he turned, his face broken by a little grin. "And don't forget to bring your flying togs!" he added.

The following morning, Brim awoke long before dawn and dressed in his fatigues without waking Romanoff. The latest report from the HyperDrome indicated that both technical teams had worked straight through the night and were nearly ready to test their handiwork. Results of those first tests would be a good indication of how he might spend his afternoon, watching or flying.

As his driver turned toward the Imperial shed, Brim could see that the whole area was bathed in the harsh glare of Karlsson lamps burning at their highest intensity. Clearly, work *had* gone on all night, and the very fact that nobody had given up yet was a highly encouraging sign so far as he was concerned. Inside the shed, Moulding's M-6B was reduced to a skeleton amidships while his own could be seen huddling atop a gravity pad in one of the Drive-arming circles. At a distance, it appeared to be mostly in one piece—at least compared to its sister ship.

"You want the shed or the Drive circle, Commander?" the driver asked.

"Better make it the Drive circle," Brim replied, "I might as well get the news firsthand." Less than five cycles later, he flashed his badge at a manned security gate and strode onto the giant lenslike system of N-ray emitters. Above him, the M-6B loomed on its gravity pad, gleaming dark blue in the bright artificial light and literally covered by technicians. Hundreds of cables glowing in a rainbow of hues led from openings in her hull to an armada of vans laden with diagnostic equipment.

Twelve additional cables, each thicker than a man's arm, ran to massive connectors abaft the ship's trousers. Brim recognized these as superconducting power transmission lines, now glowing dull red from the enormous energy required to electrosaturate the new Drive crystal before it was powered the first time. Unprepared crystals often shattered at the first application of Drive energy, and this particular prototype was clearly getting special but time-consuming care. Brim shook his head—the M-6B would never be ready to fly before late afternoon at the earliest. If for some reason this year's heats were quickly concluded, the Empire could lose the trophy by default.

Shortly thereafter, as he stared out at the frantic work going on around the starship, he saw Valerian and Pogreb—both dressed in the same clothes they had worn the previous evening at supper—step out of the blockhouse and hurry to one of the larger consoles that was mounted on a heavy flatbed skimmer. He scurried across the lens in short order. "How do things look?" he asked anxiously.

Both engineers jumped. "Oh—Wilf," Valerian exclaimed with a frown, "we were just about to call you."

"And?" Brim asked.

"Well," Pogreb began.

Brim tensed. "*Well*," he prompted.

Valerian grimaced. "We just finished connecting the new control systems, Wilf," he reported. "With a little luck, we'll have her all buttoned up in little more than a metacycle," he said. "And—praise the Universe for small miracles—we might even finish Moulding's in time, too."

This time, it was Brim who grimaced. "There's an implied *but* here somewhere," he said with the beginnings of real concern forming in his mind. "I wonder why haven't I heard either of you use the word *fly*?"

"The electrosaturation process," Pogreb explained, "is taking nearly ten more metacycles before it finishes."

Brim understood the issue immediately. "And since by that time, the racing program will be well underway," he said with a frown, "there'll be no opportunity for flight tests. Right?"

Valerian nodded. "That's about it. Wilf," he said. "If either you or Moulding is going to race, you'll have to fly an experimental starship that has just been hurriedly bolted together, along with a newly saturated, *prototype* Drive crystal—and then immediately run it flat out. How does that sound to you?"

"Wonderful," Brim grumped, shaking his head and rolling his eyes skyward, "just thraggling *wonderful*."

"Will you do it?" Valerian asked.

"Will I do what?"

"Fly it."

"Of course I'll fly it," Brim said. "One of these days, Mark, you've got to go to Carescria and check out the ore barges I used to fly." He shook his head. "We'd have been overjoyed there just to get halfway reliable crystals. Then we could spend more time wondering if the hulls would stay together." He looked Valerian in the eye. "Lots of times, they didn't."

Valerian mumbled something unintelligible, then shook his head. "Do you suppose Moulding will fly, too?" he asked.

Brim smiled. "Probably you'll want to ask him yourself," he said. "But I'll bet he's just as suicidal as I am—especially when it comes to this race."

"For Voot's sake, just don't push your thrust damper into the reflector zone." Valerian warned. "... whatever you do. *That* might definitely qualify as suicidal from what I've heard. The system's never been tested at all in this spaceframe."

"I'll watch it," Brim promised grimly. "I've got a race to win."

"That," Valerian said, "is what worries me the most. . . ."

Exactly ten metacycles later, Brim was suited up and ready to go; his M-6B had somehow been cobbled together again with its new reflecting Drive. But the only change he could see on the flight bridge was a new thrust-damper assembly, equipped with a row of indicators on a small panel marked REFLECTING. All were dark except a glowing, jewellike lamp above the words SCAN ON. The damper itself had an elongated throw, but the clearly hurried application of metalized tape prevented damper beams from advancing farther than halfway forward.

Outside, Bears were now decoupling the last electrosaturation cables from the Drive chamber. With Moulding's ship still largely unassembled on a neighboring Drive-arming lens, they were only *just* in time. As usual, the heats had been ordered in the reverse of last year's finishing sequence, and the last A'zurnian entry had just landed in towering cascades of spray between the glaring marker buoys.

Only the Imperial heats now remained to be run. . . .

Because the League had failed to complete the previous contest with *either* racer, this year they had been among the very first to compete. Both of their angular new Gantheisser GA 262-A3s ran the course with astonishingly high velocities: 99.56M LightSpeed turned in by Kirsh Valentin (who had shown up that morning with a clearly painful limp) and 95.82M LightSpeed by Groener's replacement, one Provost Wogan Arn. The blinding speeds had certainly placed a damper over the remaining activities of the day—as well as answering any lingering questions about Gantheisser engineers and their ability to come up with a starship that could compete with an M-6B.

Highest speed for the two Dampier entries from Tarrott had been a disappointing 96.79M LightSpeed. Clearly, puppet states were permitted to compete with their League masters only up to a point. And that did *not* include winning!

Now, with the second little A'zurnian R'autor taxiing back to the sheds (after turning in a credible speed of 97.45M LightSpeed), Brim opened his face plate and leaned out of the open Hyperscreen while he watched Krasni-Peych engineers seal the last access covers. Word of Imperial difficulties had spread rapidly. Behind the barriers, a huge crowd was now gathered in the glare of the Karlsson lamps, watching to see if Krasni-Peych and Sherrington could bring off their overnight miracle. Many were taking pictures—just in case. There was even a contingent of Leaguers with two bulky orange and yellow cameras, overdoing things, as usual. Even at a distance, he could see the cameras were equipped with awkward electronic lens systems that Brim usually associated with long-distance image recording.

"Is ready as we can make her," Pogreb called from the edge of the gravity pad. He was now wearing a clean set of coveralls, but the worried look on his face persisted.

Brim grinned—the Bear would be a terrible cre'el player. Everyone would know what kind of assets he'd been dealt just from watching his face. "You figure she'll fly, then?" he asked.

Pogreb rolled his eyes heavenward, holding up a tutorial index finger. "Best way to keep one's word not is not to give it," he called with a smile. "Is promising only that she is ready as we can make her."

"That's good enough for me," Brim said undauntedly.

"Not for me," Pogreb said. "But I add these words, brave Wilf Ansor: were there room for this Bear to accompany you on your flight, I should go with a minimum of hesitation."

"For that, my Sodeskayan friend, I owe you many *large* drinks when I get back," Brim replied with a grin.

"Is going to be fine victory celebration," Pogreb said, ambling off toward the other M-6B. "Perhaps ve may even get Commander Moulding in the air, too—then *beeg* dronk for everybodys!"

Moments later, Ursis's voice crackled in his headset. "Last chance to back down, my furless friend," he warned. "If we're going to compete this year, we've got to tow you to the gravity pool immediately. Then, *voof*—off you go."

"I'm ready, Nik," Brim said quietly, looking down at the Bear, who was dressed in Krasni-Peych coveralls and standing near a stout optical bollard mounted at the front of the gravity pad. His headphones were connected to the M-6B by its last set of external cables.

Ursis looked up and waved, then signaled to the driver of a traction engine, who backed carefully to within a few irals of the bollard and switched on a heavy mooring beam. It blazed up for a moment when the driver shifted into forward to tension the load, then settled into a steady green.

Outside the gates, onlookers were already dispersing, most toward the Imperial gravity pool to get a last shot of the M-6B as ground crews prepped it for the race. Everyone, that is, except the party of Leaguers who were hotfooting it in the opposite direction toward a big Majestat-Baron idling just beyond the crowd-control ropes. As soon as they were aboard, the arrogant limousine wobbled to a temporary follower cable (one of many installed for this year's race by CIGA behest); then it took off like a starship for a media parking apron where Brim could see the ugly fins of a Gorn-Hoff 810.C reconnaissance ship painted in civilian colors.

Brim frowned as his own gravity pad moved smoothly toward the Starter's pool. The zukeed Leaguers were certainly sure of themselves this year, hurrying off with the latest race images even before it was all over. Probably, he conjectured, the recordings were destined for late-workday delivery to one of the many dominions Triannic had his eye on. That way, they'd physically beat the other media services by nearly half a day—and, depending on local rotational speeds, perhaps gain as much as a Standard day in actual viewer coverage. He laughed grimly. If he had anything to do with it, the hasty bastards were in for an unpleasant surprise, indeed. . . .

Presently, Ursis's voice growled in his headset again; the Bear was now riding at the rear of the tractor, still connected by voice wires to the M-6B. "You can relax for a few moments, Wilf Ansor," he said. "It seems the Leaguers have requested a break while they inspect the racecourse—just to make certain that everything is legal when you race."

Brim frowned. "What in xaxt is *that* all about?" he asked.

Ursis shrugged his huge shoulders. "Aside from the grandfather of all insults to the Empire, the whole thing remains a mystery to me," he replied. "It seems to have been imposed by a committee of CIGAs over protests by nearly everyone else." He shook his head. "They are certainly galactic-class experts at raising a stir."

Brim relaxed in his seat as the tractor pulled him toward the Imperial gravity pool. Through the open port Hyperscreen, he caught a look at a Majestat-Baron drawing up beside the civilian Gorn-Hoff. It looked like the same limousine the Leaguer media people had been riding. He drew a small pair of night glasses from his emergency case and focused them on the limousine. He'd been right! Here came the big orange and yellow cameras: weird-looking devices without question. He peered in fascination while a pair of white-suited civilian technicians opened the hatch on a sizable pod mounted just abaft the Gorn-Hoff's forward cooling radiators, and—as he watched—lowered one of the orange cameras inside. Brim smacked his fist on the instrument panel. He'd been wrong—the zukeeds had actually brought a special inspection ship, and the crew had simply been killing time with its recording system! When the hatch was again closed, he could see that it was shaped with a custom blister to accommodate their awkward lens system. They'd planned the xaxtdamned inspection all the time! He shook his head in anger as the second camera was carried out of sight around the nose. What could the Leaguers possibly hope to gain by this?

Just then, his tractor stopped at the gravity pad, and he had no more time for Leaguers *or* their psychological games. Putting his night glasses away, he watched carefully as tractor beams from the gravity pool flashed to the ship's mooring points and gently drew his M-6B from the pad onto the pool—a ticklish operation at best. It took fifteen cycles of tension, shouts, occasional profanity (in a surprising number of tongues), and more than a little muscle (mostly Sodeskayan) before the graceful little ship was hovering in a proper position, gently testing her new moorings in light wind sprung up from the lake. Brim had just finished verifying her attitude when he caught the big Gorn-Hoff thundering along the lake on her take-off run. "What do we know about that ship?" he asked into his microphone.

"Big Leaguer cheeses," Ursis replied from the pool console after a rapid-fire consultation with a number of technicians standing nearby on the wall. "It carries officials who will conduct the 'inspection,'" he grumbled. "When we see that Gorn-Hoff return, it will be time for you to fly."

In fact, it took the Leaguer "officials" nearly a metacycle to complete their probe—and even then the race didn't resume. CIGA representatives had rubbed the collective ISS nose in their shutdown by halting the race completely until the Leaguer ship had made landfall and was parked. Brim watched the Gorn-Hoff touch down and taxi to the strand, grinding his teeth with impatience. As it moved up a ramp and under the Karlsson lamps, he frowned. Somehow, the ship didn't look the same; something subtle had changed, but he couldn't tell precisely *what*. Even the two strange "camera" pods were still in place on its flanks. He pulled out his night glasses and studied the Leaguer ship as it turned to face him and came to rest on a gravity pool. The pods . . . That was it! Their hatches no longer had the characteristic "camera" blisters in place; they were completely smooth from tip to tail.

"Five cycles," Ursis warned suddenly. "The Leaguers have at last declared the course acceptable."

"Thraggling decent of them," Brim growled, starting the prerun-up checkout. With that, he put the Leaguers from his mind. Finally, he had a race to run! After he switched to internal gravity, he devoted his whole concentration to preparing the little ship for her most important—and unequivocally final—

flight. There was always the chance that the Drive would blow before she even completed the heat—if, of course, she didn't fall apart at HypoSpeed first. But barring disastrous circumstances of this sort, she would most probably end her days either in Avalon's Science Museum (if she won) or piled ignominiously on a scrap heap (if she didn't).

. During the next cycles, Brim set up the COMM panels, activated position lamps and beacons, then connected both generators to the power main—at a full 510 T-units on the panel. After this, he set his gravity brakes and started the gravs; each fired almost immediately without so much as a stutter. "I'm ready to race, Nik," he reported. "How does she seem from where you sit?"

Below, wearing huge ear protectors, Ursis rubbed his chin and rose from his console to peer carefully at the ship. "Doesn't appear to be anything *large* falling off," he declared.

"Oh, *wun*-der-ful," Brim laughed. "Nik, I simply can't tell you the confidence that gives me."

"Think nothing of it, Wilfuska," the Bear said with a huge grin. "The fact is that I see nothing small falling off, either." He consulted his consoles. "She looks fine, my friend. May Lady Fortune speed you on your way."

"See you after I nail down the old hat rack," Brim said. With that, he called Ground Control and taxied out to the Drive-arming area. In a matter of cycles, Vaskrozni Kubinka's team had prepared the Wizard/3, and he was once more in touch with the tower.

"Alcott Ground," he said, "Imperial M-six B Alpha request taxi to gate."

"Imperial M-six B Alpha Alcott Ground clears taxi to gate area one five left, wind two one zero at one six." Somehow the litany never changed.

"Imperial M-six B Alpha," Brim acknowledged again. He checked for Romanoff's earrings—which would never go to a museum as long as Wilf Brim was alive—then powered the M-6B around to a launch ramp and headed to the takeoff vector, savoring the last delicious whiffs of fresh lake air he might ever take.

"Imperial M-six B Alpha to Alcott Tower at pylon area," he announced. "Request gate clearance."

"Alcott Tower to Imperial M-six Alpha. You are cleared to

enter gate three one right. Takeoff vector zero seven five on green light, wind zero one nine at one nine."

"Imperial M-six B Alpha entering gate one five left, wind two one zero at one six, takeoff on green."

"Alcott Tower."

Brim taxied into position between the start pylons, staring at the two bobbing rows of yellow vector buoys that stretched into the distance—and his future. Taking a final breath of fresh air, he deliberately snapped shut his helmet, closed and locked the side Hyperscreens, and made a last systems check: flight controls, lift modifiers, flight readouts, lights, cabin gravity, shoulder restraints. Setting his jaw, he locked the steering engine and activated the gravity brakes, then opened his thrust dampers. Again, the thundering gravity generators built up a surging cloud of spray and ice particles behind the ship. Presently, the pylons changed from red to amber while Brim battled the controls and kept the ship's nose pointed between the rows of vector buoys. After what seemed to be half a lifetime, the lights changed to green and he released the brakes, with the pylons themselves disappearing aft in a great rush of spray. Moments later, the vector buoys passed below and astern as he cranked the M-6B into a nearly vertical climb on his way out of the atmosphere.

At about half LightSpeed, he began his Drive Checklist: intercoolers at minus thirty-one hundred, time synchronizers counting in perfect congruence with the ship's clock, mass compensators running at speed, blast tubes—he touched a red panel near the Drive readouts, then paused while whining motors cracked the iris—OPEN, overdrivers READY, HyperBoost drivers ON, and reserve energy at 451,000. Everything *seemed* ready to go, but until he actually gated operating-level power to the big crystal, his personal future beyond the next five or so cycles was anybody's guess.

At 0.95 LightSpeed, forward vision through the still-inert Hyperscreens degenerated into a streaked, reddish muddle that worsened at 0.96 and became altogether unintelligible as the gravity generators exceeded their force curves. Heart in his mouth, Brim connected the Drive crystal to power, then pushed the plasma primer twice, keyed in START for a few clicks, and —without daring to breathe—hit ENERGIZE.

With a throaty rumble that shook his little M-6B from stem

to stern, the new crystal bellowed to life like some ancient god waking angry from an agelong slumber. The Hyperscreens synchronized less than a click afterward, and the whole Universe took on the look of a light-streaked tunnel through which he was passing with steadily increasing velocity. Aft, a familiar sapphire Drive plume stretched toward the receding pinpoint of light that had been Avalon a few clicks previously. Once more, he was coursing through deep space with the honor of a whole empire riding beside him, this time in a largely untried ship that would have to fly faster than it had ever flown before.

Covering the distance between Avalon and the race circuit at better than 104.29M LightSpeed, he completed the first lap at a very credible average speed of 98.81 LightSpeed, but even though it was the fastest lap he'd ever flown before, it wasn't enough to win the race. The next lap slid astern at 99.5M LightSpeed. Much better, *and*, it didn't look as if the new crystal was about to reduce him to cosmic dust, either—though he was still a long way from moving his damper all the way to the tape.

He charged into lap four at nearly 100M LightSpeed and arrived at Onita in a little under two cycles, then skidded into the sharp curve with such tremendous velocity that he found his vision distorted—it almost seemed some sort of object had been climbing toward his ship from the blue star looming overhead. The bunt over Laneer took significantly less than a cycle, and he returned around greenish Delta-Gahnn 1.2 cycles later for an average speed just under his 102M goal.

Starting lap five, he sent even more energy to the crystal and thundered down on Onita at 102.8M LightSpeed indicated. Skidding into the sharp turn again, he peered ahead through the Hyperscreens trying for a more optimum line to Laneer when . . . this time he was *not* mistaken. Something was approaching from starboard, as if it had been waiting for him. And it was clearly traveling at very high speed. Space junk? The thing was still too distant to make out more than a vague shape. Nevertheless, there was no excuse for its presence anywhere near the course; the lanes were swept every few cycles by squadrons of fast launches. He resolved to complain to the race committee as soon as he landed. Then he wrenched attention back to flying, bunted around Laneer, and sped off for Delta-Gahnn: this time his average velocity of only 99.1M LightSpeed illustrated how much concentration counted in a race.

As he blasted into lap six, he poured on the energy, determined to make up lost time. Completing the first leg in under two cycles, he threw himself into the sharp turn, only to find the "space junk" suddenly positioned off his starboard bow. It was close enough now that it looked like . . . one of the camera pods on the Gorn-Hoff! He could clearly see the blister on its cover.

Then it came to him!

This was no mere camera pod! It was *actively* searching for his particular M-6B: a diabolically intelligent HyperMine—the favored instrument of would-be assassins who were too cowardly to confront their victims face to face. Preset to cruise at speeds only slightly faster than their targets, the infamous devices traded range for speed, too quick to elude. They were *also* too small for most patrol ships to detect. Clearly, this one had already locked on to his M-6B and was moving in for the kill.

The bastard Leaguers had done their job well, too! As he came out of the curve and headed for Laneer, the little missile still had considerable mass to consume and his M-6 was already traveling at the top edge of its velocity envelope. "Inspection," indeed. What a fool he'd been. He watched in fascination while the device approached. He had nowhere to hide, nor any way to estimate at what distance its proximity fuse would set it off. But it was already so close he knew he'd never complete the sixty-odd clicks of the turn before . . . The reflecting Drive! That could stop the xaxtdamed mine.

He glanced down at the damper assembly, almost afraid to look. If it *were* hooked up—and working—he could outrun anything in the known Universe, including a HyperMine. But there was no sure way to tell if the Bears had even bothered to connect the reflector controls, in spite of the SCAN indicator, whatever *that* was. Of course if they had—and he switched it on—it might also blow him in to subatomic particles. However, since the HyperMine was going to finish him off in the next few moments, it really didn't seem like so much of a risk. Taking a deep breath, he peeled off the strip of metallic tape, glanced quickly through the Hyperscreens, and eased the damper beam forward.

As the tiny beam passed SCAN, the OUTER REVERSE indicator

suddenly lit and the ship lurched slightly. Simultaneously, the REFLECTING indicator came on too, followed by blinking illumination of the EXTRA lamp. The Drive's velvet growl deepened. Brim glanced out of the Hyperscreens just in time to see the HyperMine begin to lose ground, then attempt to correct with a speed increase. In a moment, it had begun to narrow the distance again, its tiny Drive plume blazing brighter than before.

He nudged the damper again . . . with the same results! This time, however, the missile made up distance with a greatly diminished relative velocity, its Drive plume blazing out now like a tiny star. Again he nudged the damper. This time, the Hyper-Mine slowly began to fall behind until he had to skid the ship to track it, still less than two thousand irals distant.

At this point, he had it. Skidding the ship once more, he took a bearing on the diminishing missile, then straightened course, aimed the Drive's exhaust blindly, and slid the damper forward to its detent. The M-6B shot forward with an acceleration that caught Brim totally by surprise. At the same instant, he found himself engulfed in a tremendous fireball—blasted forward again as if slapped by some colossal hand. Moments later, he had left the roiling flare far behind in a burst of phenomenal acceleration. But *now* Laneer was dead ahead—and expanding in the Hyperscreens like an oncoming meteor! Instinctively pulling back on the thrust damper, he listened to Valerian's tough little spaceframe creak and squeal over the shrill warning of the DRIVE OVERHEAT alarm. Swerving in desperation, he rolled the ship on its back and skimmed inverted through the star's chromosphere, close enough to the boiling photosphere below that he could make out individual granulation cells, each more than twice the diameter of Avalon herself. Then—miraculously—he was once again flying through open space, the Wizard howling behind him like all the evil spirits of the Universe. Only now the ship was trailing both a seemingly endless Drive plume and a lengthy prominence of flamelike structures—gasses, Brim guessed numbly, disturbed by the Wizard's high-energy exhaust.

An instant later, he blinked in surprise. He'd come out on the far side of the star! He was still in the race—and *alive*, of all things! Reining in the ravening Wizard before it carried him clear out of the Universe—or melted from its own hellfires—he aimed the ship on a straightaway to Delta-Gahnn, then skidded around the entrance turn, and finished the lap at an average speed of more than 121.31M LightSpeed!

At that instant, his KA'PPA screen came alive: ALCOTT TOWER TO IMPERIAL M-SIX-B ALPHA. ALCOTT TOWER TO IMPERIAL M-SIX-B ALPHA. DO YOU READ ME? The characters were broken and indistinct on the little display. Brim guessed that the explosion had damaged his HyperLight COMM system—perhaps melted its external antenna array.

I READ YOU, ALCOTT TOWER, he KA'PPAed back as he rushed headlong past Onita on his seventh lap. AM SAFE AND UNDER CONTROL. WILL EXPLAIN EXPLOSION LATER. A moment afterward, he shot out of the curve and battled his way past the glittering cloud of radiation that marked his latest escape from the League. Then he was past Laneer and sprinting once more for Delta-Gahnn. He finished that lap at better than 103.56M LightSpeed—and the eighth and the ninth as well.

It was on his tenth and final lap that Brim spotted the second space mine. He'd assumed there would be one for some time now; if the Leaguers had troubled themselves concerning him, it only made sense that they'd have similar plans for his partner. The device was still distant and only beginning the great climbing spiral that would bring it to Moulding's M-6B on *his* sixth lap, but he could already make out its distinctive spindle shape, interrupted by a camera blister. Now, however, by the chance survival of his own ship, the diabolical weapon would wait for an Imperial warship to take it back to Avalon where it might be used for evidence, should the ISS decide to prefer charges. Be that as it may, the Leaguer's maliciousness would soon be irrelevant—especially since he would clearly finish the race at least 1.24M LightSpeed faster than Valentin, with no second chances available.

Twenty cycles later, he brought the M-6B streaking in low over the glare of Avalon City, sped through the night sky along Lake Mersin (trailing a sonic shock wave that, according to irate city officials, leveled thirty c'lenyts of ornamental trees), and thundered *inverted* between the pylons at better than forty-five hundred c'lenyts per metacycle—winning the Mitchell Trophy once and for all by a margin of better than 2.24M LightSpeed. Then, banking around the grandstands in a slow curve, he brought the little Sherrington racer down flawlessly.

Moulding did not fly in the race—there was no need for

such a risk. The Mitchell Trophy had already become a true Imperial hat rack.

Early the next morning, Brim gently untangled himself from Anna Romanoff and stole quietly to the salon, where he watched to see how the public media had interpreted General Drummond's brief explanation of the night's events:

> . . . Turning to the latest Mitchell Trophy news: popular race figure and Carescrian, Lt. Commander Wilf Brim, I.F., broke all existing speed records at the HyperDrome last night to permanently secure the Mitchell Trophy here in Avalon at an average speed of 101.8M LightSpeed. His Sherrington M-6 B racer, however, was extensively charred during a near disaster in the final heat.
>
> According to HyperDrome spokesperson, General Harry Drummond, Brim's spirited Helmsmanship averted a freak tragedy when he avoided what is generally believed to be an ancient space mine, relic of the forty-second-century War for the Glaring Eye. ISS officials removed the record breaking M-6 B to a repair facility immediately after brief victory ceremonies, while Imperial Fleet vessels conducted a thorough search of the area to insure no more of the dangerous artifacts were encountered.
>
> The ship itself is presently undergoing restoration prior to its installation in Avalon's Science Museum, where it will be on display during the metacycles of . . .

Brim shook his head in bemusement. Since the end of the war, he'd been everything from down-and-out civilian to "popular race figure," *and* a Lieutenant Commander. He'd even found love, in the literal sense of the word. The experiences had turned him into a very different man than the one he was when he'd entered the Fleet as a raw Sublieutenant some fourteen years previously. For one thing, he walked a *lot* more confidently these days. Shrugging happily, he watched Romanoff pad through the archway dressed in a lacy negligee, her long brown hair bobbing in glorious tangles about her shoulders. She put her arm around him possessively, then leaned over to deposit a kiss to the tip of his nose. "Seems a shame we're letting the Leaguer bastards off scot-free," she grumped, staring sleepily at the display. "They ought to get what they *really* deserve."

"I think they already *have*." Brim chuckled, pulling her into his lap. "Drummond had the right idea last night, you know. They came for the Trophy and left empty-handed."

Romanoff nodded. "I understand, Wilf," she conceded. "But they *did* try to blow you away, you know—and it just makes me furious to see them get off so easily."

"I can't think of much else we could do for punishment," Brim answered with a shrug. "They really *did* want that old hat rack of ours." He gently unfastened the ties of her negligee. "Probably there wouldn't be a great deal of use in having them disqualified, either—especially since we've won what *we* wanted. Unless," he added with a wide-eyed frown, "we fancied having the whole race voided."

Romanoff smiled and laid her head back on his shoulder. "I hate politics," she said, wriggling completely out of the sheer lingerie. "If this were a business situation, I'd simply ruin the bastards—put 'em out of business for good."

"In my line of work," Brim said, "We call that *war*."

"Yeah," Romanoff agreed grimly, "and it looks like they've *already* declared war on *you*, lover."

"They did that a long time ago, Anna," he said with a dour laugh. "I'm actually getting used to it."

The businesswoman shook her head and sighed. "*Wilf*." she said abruptly, her breathing suddenly labored. "I'm not *at all* getting used to what you're doing down there, and . . ."

"You don't like it?"

"I didn't say *that*," she declared urgently. "It's just that, well, S.S. *Dowd Enterprise* leaves in the middle of the afternoon, and if you have the same thing on your mind that I have on mine, then we ought to get busy right away. I won't see you for most of a month."

Early that evening under a lowering sky, Brim stood alone on the nearly deserted apron of the HyperDrome, watching two last pallets of Fleet-owned test equipment disappear into a white government van. Behind him—where only last night thousands cheered while he received his victor's laurel—wind rattled through deserted sheds and grandstands, whistling sharply at the three colossal flagpoles and sending their empty halyards clanging against the bare metal columns. A rogue gust tossed a gaggle of empty cvceese' cups hollowly across the pavement while on Lake Mersin, lumbering gray rollers advanced in white-capped succession like endless ranks of soldiers in dismal uniforms. He turned up the heat in his Fleet cape—spring could turn cold quickly on Avalon.

Out some distance from the far shore, a brooding Gorn-Hoff cruiser was arrogantly churning downwind toward the takeoff vector, its roiling footprint shouldering aside the big rollers in lofty, windblown clouds of spume. The Torond's new black and red banner streamed forward from its KA'PPA tower. Brim followed the cruiser's progress with a dour frown and decidedly mixed emotions. Margot Effer'wyck-LaKarn rode aboard that sleek warship, trapped as much by addiction to the loathsome drug TimeWeed as by the ship's powerful disruptors themselves. He rubbed his chin as the Gorn-Hoff put her helm down and momentarily fell off broadside to the weather before coming all the way around with her rakish bows hard into the mounting gale. His passion for the magnificent blond may well have perished, but he had far from purged himself of the potent emotional bonds that remained.

For a moment, the big cruiser seemed to hesitate, as if gathering itself for the prodigious journey across half a galaxy, then settled slightly by the stern as a mighty plume of vapor suddenly shot aft and skyward. Presently, the deep thunder from her powerful gravity generators blasted the air and rumbled in echo from the great bluffs surrounding the HyperDrome.

Brim ground his teeth in a rush of pure, uncontrollable emotion: yes, he *did* love Anna Romanoff—with a warmth and devotion that *still* surprised him. She was the sole reality amid the cynicism and conflict of a most unpleasant Universe. Nevertheless, he *also* understood that within the very depths of his soul a second bond held strong—his feelings for Margot Effer'wyck. The apparent dichotomy was not something that tormented him; both realities simply existed, and he found he could live with them. He *had* to. . . . "

As the Gorn-Hoff began to move forward and gather speed, he took a deep breath and steadied himself against an irresistible assault of pure melancholy. War clouds were gathering all over the galaxy, and this time, Margot was on the *other* side. He might well never see her face again. Then he shook his head. In comparison to the forces that were presently building in the Universe, his own feelings were of small consequence indeed. With the Torond in Triannic's hands, half the Empire's supply of Drive crystal seeds was gone—while the other half in Fluvanna was anything but secure.

Faster and faster the cruiser accelerated, throwing lofty cascades of spray to either side and shaking the air with the rumbling tumult of her laboring generators. At considerable distance down the lake, the cascades abruptly ceased and Brim could see light appear beneath her hull as she smartly rotated skyward and began to climb. For the next few moments, she appeared to hang motionless in the air, ascending almost imperceptibly until at an altitude of about a thousand irals she banked sharply to port and soared into the clouds. The rolling thunder of her passage echoed from the bluff for nearly a cycle before it lost itself in the cold, lonely wind. . . .

Epilogue

Brim found the KA'PPA message on his desk one afternoon just after he brought a heavy cruiser safely to landfall with only half her gravs functional—all on the *same* side. The blue and gold envelope marked PERSONAL—EYES ONLY attracted him, so he tore it open even before he called up his normal messages. . . .

PERSONNEL ACTION MEMORANDUM
IMPERIAL FLEET
IFPC42746T-12C GROUP 198BA 189/55008
2398XCV-99-D0349CDC/573248 PERSONAL COPY
UNCLASSIFIED

FROM:
BU FLEET PERSONNEL;
ADMIRALTY, AVALON

TO:
W. A. BRIM, LT. CMDR, I.F.
ATALANTA, HADOR-HAELIC

SUBJECT: DUTY ASSIGNMENT

(1) YOU ARE DETACHED PRESENT DUTY AS OF
189/55008.

(2) PROCEED MOST EXPEDITIOUS TRANSPORT
SHERRINGTON YARDS, BROMWICH, RHODOR,
REPORT I.F.S. STARFURY (K 5054) AS
COMMANDING OFFICER.
(3) SUBMIT TRAVEL EXPENSE VOUCHERS DIRECT
ADMIRALTY C/O H. DRUMMOND, REAR
ADMIRAL, I.F.

FOR THE EMPEROR:
ZORN E. BALGEE, CAPTAIN, I.F.

Captain of the *Starfury*!

At first, he thought the yellow plastic sheet must be some
kind of joke, but there was really nothing humorous or even
clever in the wording. It looked like every other Personnel
hardcopy he'd ever seen. Read like them, too—totally imper-
sonal and worded for easy interpretation by the most backward
of simians.

Was it real? He fretted about it until mid-evening, then
marched into the message center and fired off a KA'PPA to the
Bureau of Fleet Personnel in Avalon:

FROM:
W. A. BRIM, LT. CMDR, I.F.
ATALANTA, HADOR-HAELIC

TO:
BU FLEET PERSONNEL;
ADMIRALTY, AVALON

SUBJECT: DUTY ASSIGNMENT

REQUEST RETRANSMIT DUTY ASSIGNMENT
ORDERS
IFPC42746T-12C GROUP 198BA 189/55008
2398XCV-99-D0349CDC/573248. BELIEVE
PERSONAL COPY
ARRIVED GARBLED OR INCOMPLETE.

WILF ANSOR BRIM, LT. CMDR, I.F.

Less than a metacycle later, he picked up a second blue and gold envelope. With trembling fingers, he ripped it open and withdrew another yellow scrap of plastic:

PERSONNEL ACTION MEMORANDUM
IMPERIAL FLEET
IFPC42746T-12C GROUP 198BA 189/55008
2398XCV-99-D0349CDC/573248 PERSONAL COPY 2
UNCLASSIFIED

FROM:
BU FLEET PERSONNEL;
ADMIRALTY, AVALON

TO:
W. A. BRIM, LT. CMDR, I.F.
ATALANTA, HADOR-HAELIC

SUBJECT: DUTY ASSIGNMENT

(1) YOU ARE DETACHED PRESENT DUTY AS OF
189/55008.
(2) PROCEED MOST EXPEDITIOUS TRANSPORT
SHERRINGTON YARDS, BROMWICH, RHODOR.
REPORT I.F.S. STARFURY (K 5054) AS
COMMANDING OFFICER.
(3) SUBMIT TRAVEL EXPENSE VOUCHERS DIRECT
ADMIRALTY C/O H. DRUMMOND, REAR
ADMIRAL, I.F.

FOR THE EMPEROR:
ZORN E. BALGEE, CAPTAIN, I.F.

The news traveled rapidly. Next morning, his message queue was inundated with messages of congratulations, including an ecstatic one from Anna Romanoff, still a day out from Atalanta aboard S.S. *Gertjens Enterprise*. He also heard from Nik Ursis and Dr. Borodov, from Regula Collingswood and Erat Plutron, from Baxter Calhoun, from Lieutenant Commander Glendora Wellington, from Aram of Nahshon, and from an old shipmate named Utrillo Barbousse—though the latter message came through a little used communications channel with no address of origin attached.

Later that day, Romanoff rushed into his office direct from Atalanta's sprawling civilian terminal. Dressed in pink coveralls and high heeled boots, she carried two fragile goblets and a large bottle of sparkling Logish Meem. So far as Brim was concerned, she was the greatest sight in the known Universe— even without meem.

"So congratulations are in order, eh?" she asked, handing him the bottle and setting the goblets carefully on the desk. "Regula KA'PPAed me as soon as she heard about it. Now, I want to hear firsthand."

Brim felt his face redden. "No big deal, Anna," he said bashfully, struggling to quietly uncork the old-fashioned bottle under a large red handkerchief. "New ship—new job. That's all." Moments later, the stopper came free with a hardy pop.

Romanoff brushed back a lock of her hair and perched on the corner of his desk. "I *did* read correctly about a position as the *commanding officer*, didn't I?" she asked with a knowing grin.

Brim nodded, carefully filling each goblet so the foaming meem wouldn't run all over his desk.

"I guess I wasn't surprised," she said, "—you were the *only* possible choice for Sherrington's new *Starfury*."

"Me?" Brim asked.

"Universe!" Romanoff groaned, rolling her eyes toward the ceiling. "Even I know all about *that*. Not only do you have more experience with *Starfury* prototypes than anybody else in the Fleet, but you have *also* earned yourself something of a reputation as a Helmsman in the last few years." Then she frowned. "Besides that, Wilf Brim," she said with a serious look in her eyes, "Onrad's said on a number of occasions that you've come a long way in the last few years. You're ready for a shot at command."

"I wonder," he said, sipping his meem spontaneously, "am I really?"

She peered at him thoughtfully. "I suppose that depends," she said, looking him directly in the eye. "Is *Starfury* what you want?"

Brim stared down at his goblet for a moment. "As a ship?"

"As a *Skipper*," she said.

"I think I've wanted to be her skipper so badly, I couldn't admit it to myself for fear somebody else got it. . . ."

For a moment she got a faraway look in her eye. "You *have* come a long way," she whispered, "—even in the few years I've known you, lover."

"What was that?" Brim asked.

"Nothing," she said with a little smile. "Sometimes, love makes me mumble. That's all." She poured more bubbly into their goblets.

Brim grinned as the fine old meem started to his head. "How in xaxt did you get this stuff into this office building?"

Romanoff grinned. "Oh, that wasn't much trouble," she said. "I called old Bosporus Gallsworthy from the front desk and simply told him what I was going to do."

"I'll bet he had a few choice comments about *that*." Brim commented with a grin.

"Not really," Romanoff said. "Since you don't work for him anymore, he claimed there wasn't much he could do."

"You mean that's all there was to it?" Brim asked.

"Except that we should get rid of it as quickly as possible. Otherwise, he'd be down to help."

Brim's eyes widened. "Gallsworthy's coming here *now*?"

"No." Romanoff said with a grin. "I told him we could handle it ourselves."

"In that case," Brim chuckled, "fill this goblet again. We've got a lot of meem to put away."

All too soon, Romanoff was on her way, leaving a tantalizing scent of perfume in her wake with the promise of a *special* celebration the moment he got back to his apartment. Afterward, Brim sipped slowly at a hot mug of cvceese' and stared at the scrap of yellow plastic that was still tucked into a corner of his desk. He *did* want *Starfury*. After years of challenge and excitement on the race circuit, his job as Diagnostic Helmsman seemed routine now—although he quickly reminded himself how glad he had once been to secure it.

He browsed a few volumes of technical data concerning the new ship, then called it a day. Before switching off his workstation, however, he downloaded several crew psychology volumes from the base library. In his new job, he would be responsible for a *lot* more than good Helmsmanship—and he meant to start with all the background he could get.

Little more than six months following the last Mitchell Trophy Race, *Starfury* coasted off the stocks with Brim at her partially finished helm. That evening, he found himself promoted to full Commander. Afterward—for the remainder of what seemed to be an interminable ordeal of administrative bilge—he spent most of his waking metacycles managing her fitting out, as Regula Collingswood had gleefully predicted he would. At long last, however, K 5054 was ready for space. Finished in pale blue hullmetal, she was so fast and powerfully armed that Wogord's famous yearly publication *All the Galaxy's Starships* termed her a "pocket battlecruiser."

The morning of her first flight, Brim was in the left-hand seat, commanding mostly Sherrington technicians—with a few old hands to assist. Bosporus Gallsworthy, once the greatest Helmsman in the Fleet, backed him up at the right console. Dean Nikolai Yanuarievich Ursis, Master of the prestigious Dityasburg Institute managed the systems console. P. Dvigat Krasni IV, Senior Director of Krasni-Peych, presided over the Drive chambers while Mark Valerian and Veronica Pike rode at the structures and navigation consoles respectively. *And*—unknown even to the Emperor—Crown Prince Onrad occupied a huge weapons-control station behind the helms.

History would never record that totally ridiculous crew—in the first place, nobody would have ever deemed it credible. But as they taxied out onto cold, gray Glammarian Bight, each understood that everyone aboard was riding much more than a starship. I.F.S. *Starfury* was a *commitment*.

Later, amid steady, velvet thunder from four Wizard-C Reflecting Drive units, Brim checked hundreds of colored patterns flowing across his readout panels, trimmed the autohelm slightly, and then relaxed with a feeling of real satisfaction. A few minor systems problems had surfaced so far—some still flashed angrily on warning panels here and there. But all in all, *Starfury* was nearly flawless. Outside her dimly lighted bridge, speeding stars streaked the Hyperscreens in a familiar "spaceman's tunnel" while five recently commissioned K-class destroyers struggled to maintain formation—after requesting a *third* reduction of speed. Following a day of intense concentration, he had a few moments to himself before he again busied himself reversing course for their scheduled return to Bromwich.

He took one last check of the readouts, then sank back into the deep cushions of his recliner with a grim smile. The future promised little in the way of his present tranquility. Ominous shadows of war once again darkened the galaxy in every quarter. Nergol Triannic busily augmented his already impossible demands against neighboring dominions like Fluvanna and Beta Jagow, bringing the delicate fabric of galactic civilization a little nearer to disaster with each new exaction. The Torond—rotten from within by Leaguer fifth columns—had already fallen with hardly a shot fired in its own defense. And in the Empire herself, League apologists like Commodore Puvis Amherst functioned with little or no oppostion, shrilly contesting every effort to preserve what few squadrons remained of the Imperial Fleet.

Starfury was potentially the most deadly warship ever launched. But alone, she could have little effect against whole fleets of powerful—albeit old-fashioned—enemies. *Squadrons* of *Starfuries* were needed to restore the Imperial Fleet—and soon. Yet even with the most up-to-date shipyards, building programs of such magnitude required time.

Brim pursed his lips as the great warship gracefully steered herself clear of a huge planetary system that materialized ahead. Could Nergol Triannic be stopped this time—or was it too late for anything or *anyone* to save Greyffin's Empire? He had a premonition that this and a number of similar questions would be satisfied sooner than anyone suspected.